BOOKS BY MARK HARRIS PUBLISHED BY
THE UNIVERSITY OF NEBRASKA PRESS

Bang the Drum Slowly
It Looked Like For Ever
The Self-Made Brain Surgeon & Other Stories
Something About a Soldier
The Southpaw
Speed
The Tale Maker
A Ticket for a Seamstitch
Trumpet to the World

THE SOUTHPAW

By HENRY W. WIGGEN

Punctuation freely inserted and
spelling greatly improved
By MARK HARRIS

University of Nebraska Press
Lincoln and London

First Bison Book printing: 1984
Most recent printing indicated by the first digit below:
8   9   10

Library of Congress Cataloging in Publication Data
Harris, Mark, 1922–
   The southpaw.
   I. Title.
PS3515.A757S6 1984   813'.54   83-19821
ISBN 0-8032-7220-0 (pbk.)

Reprinted by arrangement with the author

DEDICATION

HOLLY says that many a man will write a book and then dedicate it to somebody. I said okay. I said I would dedicate it to the 100,000,000 boobs and flatheads that swallowed down whole the lies of Krazy Kress in his column of last September 30, 1952. The main reason I wrote this book was for their benefit in the first place, so they would have my side of the story, which is the true side, and not Krazy's, which is more or less of a lie from start to finish.

But Holly said no. She said you cannot dedicate a book simply to "100,000,000 boobs and flatheads." She said it would be best to pick out somebody that never believed Krazy to begin with, somebody that knows me for what I am no matter what. "Think of somebody that would never throw you a curve come thick or thin," she said.

So I lit on Donald and Britta Wetzel. Donald is a writer, 1 of the best, and Britta is an up and coming painter. They have 1 kid, name of David Richard Wetzel. This book is dedicated to the 3 of them.

Certain things in this book been copied out of still other books. These are as follows:

7 paragraphs from "Sam Yale—Mammoth," by Sam Yale (actually wrote by Krazy Kress), printed by All-American Boys' Shelf, Inc., 1943.

1 paragraph from "My 66 Years in the Big Leagues" by Connie Mack, printed by the John C. Winston Company, 1950.

Krazy Kresses whole column from "The Star-Press," April 15, 1952, and Krazy Kresses whole column from the same paper, date of September 30, 1952, both columns hogwash.

1 paragraph from an article called "Durocher on Durocher Et Al.," by Gilbert Millstein, which was run in the New York "Times" Magazine section on July 22, 1951.

SPECIAL WARNING TO ALL READERS!!!

RIGHT up till the time this book went in the mail there was practically a running feud amongst a number of people over the filthy and vulgar language. Pop argued hard that the least I could do was blank in the filthiest and the vulgarest.

"I can swallow the "damns" and the "hells" and even worse," said he, "but as for the "f---s" they are simply too much for my eyes to bear. I wish you would blank them in, Hank."

"I suppose I could blank them in at that," I said, "but I cannot see where the gain is."

"It will protect the women and the children," said Pop.

Then Aaron whipped out this book called "Tom Jones" by an Englishman with the following underlined in ink in Chapter 10 of Book 4: "D--n un, what a sly b--ch 'tis." "Read it out loud," said Aaron to Pop.

Pop read out loud as follows: "Damn un, what a sly bitch 'tis."

"Ho ho," said Aaron, "you have blanked out the blanks in your mind."

"But at least it is not there for the eye to see," said Pop.

"How are the women and the children of England protected?" said Aaron to Pop.

"I do not know," said Pop, "but they are protected nonetheless."

"Would not England be better off for forcing their eyes to face up to the words?" said Aaron.

"To hell with England," said I. "I am sick and tired of the wrangling, and the book must go in the mail. I will blank the word in and put an end to the whole rhubarb."

I suppose the women and the children will fill it in to suit themself, though. That's up to them. I blanked it in, for Pop's sake, and whoever blanks it out again learned the word from somebody else, not me.

(signed) HENRY W. WIGGEN

OFFICIAL ROSTER

New York Mammoth Baseball Club, Inc.

1952

Lester T. Moors, Jr.
Patricia Moors

Manager

SCHNELL, Herman H. "Dutch." Born February 23, 1893, St. Louis, Mo. Residence: St. Louis.

Coaches

BARNARD, Egbert. "Egg." Born October 2, 1896, Philadelphia, Pa. Residence: Philadelphia.

JAROS, Joseph Thomas. "Joe." Born March 31, 1895, Moline, Ill. Residence: Oak Park, Ill.

STRAP, Clinton Blakesley. "Clint." Born April 1, 1906, Mason City, Wash. Residence: Scranton, Pa. Capt., U. S. Army, 1942-1946.

Outfielders

BURNS, Allen Bruce. "Scotty." Born February 26, 1919, Glasgow, Scotland. 5'10", 175 pounds, bats R, throws R. Residence: Portland, Me.

CARUCCI, Pasquale Joseph. Born August 10, 1923, Port Chester, N. Y. Cpl., U. S. Army, 1941-1945. 5'10½", 180 pounds, bats L, throws R. Residence: San Francisco, Cal.

CARUCCI, Vincent Frank. Born July 17, 1925, San Francisco, Cal. Pvt., U. S. Army, 1944. 5'10", 175 pounds, bats L, throws R. Residence: San Francisco.

JUDKINS, Lawrence Paul. "Lucky." Born July 1, 1926, Durant, Okla. Cpl., U. S. Army, 1945-1946. 6'½", 185 pounds, bats L, throws L. Residence: Tulsa, Okla.

TROTTER, Calvin Phineas. "Sunny Jim." Born October 23, 1918,

Durham, N. H. Seaman First Class, U. S. Navy, 1941-1944. 5'10", 185 pounds, bats R-L, throws L. Residence: Durham, N. H.

WILKS, Brendan Knight. "Swanee." Born June 11, 1917, Laurel, Miss. 5'11", 195 pounds, bats R, throws R. Residence: Amarillo, Tex.

Infielders

GOLDMAN, Sidney Jerome. "Sid." Born May 7, 1928, Bronx, N. Y. Pvt., U. S. Army, 1946-1947. 6'1½", 210 pounds, bats L, throws L. Residence: Manhattan, N. Y.

GONZALEZ, George. Born February 11, 1926, Pinar del Rio, Cuba. 5'9½", 175 pounds, bats R, throws R. Residence: Havana, Cuba.

JONES, Robert Stanley. "Ugly." Born September 6, 1921, Batesville, Ark. Sgt., U. S. Marines, 1942-1945. 5'11½", 185 pounds, bats L, throws R. Residence: Little Rock, Ark.

PARK, Ellsworth Eugene. "Gene." Born December 1, 1920, Springfield, Ill. 5'11", 185 pounds, bats R, throws R. Residence: Glendale, Cal.

ROGUSKI, John Llewellyn. "Coker." Born April 2, 1930, Fairmont, W. Va. 5'10", 180 pounds, bats R-L, throws R. Residence: Fairmont.

SIMPSON, Perry Garvey. Born May 27, 1931, Savannah, Ga. 5'10½", 175 pounds, bats R, throws R. Residence: Detroit, Mich.

SMITH, Earle Banning. "Canada." Born October 14, 1929, Winnipeg, Canada. 5'11", 180 pounds, bats R, throws R. Residence: Winnipeg.

Catchers

PEARSON, Bruce William, Jr. Born June 4, 1926, Bainbridge, Ga. Pvt., U. S. Army, 1943-1945. 5'11", 185 pounds, bats R, throws R. Residence: Bainbridge.

TRAPHAGEN, Berwyn Phillips. "Red." Born December 9, 1919, Oakland, Cal. U. S. Medical Experimentation Corps, 1943-1946. 6'1", 195 pounds, bats R, throws R. Residence: Carmel, Cal.

WILLIAMS, Harold Hill. "Hal." Born August 26, 1920, Terre Haute, Ind. Sgt., U. S. Marines, 1942-1945. 6'½", 200 pounds, bats R, throws R. Residence: Chicago, Ill.

Pitchers

BURKE, Lindon Theodore. Born March 12, 1930, Lusk, Wyo. 5'11", 190 pounds, throws R, bats R. Residence: Lusk.

BYRD, Paul Richard. "Horse." Born November 19, 1921, Culpeper, Va. Pvt., U. S. Army, 1943-1946. 6'1", 225 pounds, throws R, bats R. Residence: Washington, D. C.

CARROLL, Donald King. "Don." Born August 27, 1919, Trenton, N. J. 6', 230 pounds, throws R, bats L. Residence: Albuquerque, N. M.

JOHNSON, Edwin Corliss. "Knuckles." Born February 19, 1919, Wapakoneta, Ohio. 5'10½", 210 pounds, throws R, bats L. Residence: Wapakoneta.

MACY, Herbert. "Herb." Born October 1, 1928, Athens, Ga. 6'1", 180 pounds, throws R, bats R. Residence: Long Beach, Cal.

STERLING, John Adams. "Jack." Born March 16, 1925, East St. Louis, Ill. U. S. Navy, 1942-1946. 5'9½", 165 pounds, throws R, bats R. Residence: Newport News, Va.

WIGGEN, Henry Whittier. "Hank." Born July 4, 1931, Perkinsville, N. Y. 6'3", 195 pounds, throws L, bats L. Residence: Perkinsville.

WILLOWBROOK, Gilbert Lillis. "Gil." Born May 15, 1929, Boston, Mass. 6', 190 pounds, throws R, bats R. Residence: Phoenix, Arizona.

YALE, Samuel Delbert. "Sad Sam." Born March 13, 1918, Houston, Texas. 6'2½", 210 pounds, throws L, bats L. Residence: West Palm Beach, Fla.

Physicians: Ernest I. Loftus, M.D., Hyman R. Solomon, M.D.
Trainer: Frank T. McKinney.

Roster compiled by Bradley R. Lord, secretary.

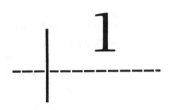

1

FIRST off I must tell you something about myself, Henry Wiggen, and where I was born and my folks.

Probably you never been to Perkinsville. How you get there you get an Albany train out of Grand Central Station. About half-way to Albany the conductor comes down the isle mumbling "Perkinsville." Then the train slows and you got to be quick because most of them don't exactly *stop* at Perkinsville. They just slow to a creep, and if you're an old man or woman or if you got a broke leg or something of the sort I don't know how you get off. Generally there will be no trouble. You just throw your bags clear and you swing down off on the cement platform and you fall away the way the train is going, and then you go back for your bags. Now you are in Perkinsville.

The last time I come by train through Perkinsville it was a rainy night and the platform was slick and I damn near skidded when I hit the cement. You have saw an outfielder start after a fly ball on wet grass and how he skids before his spikes take hold. That was how I skidded on the wet platform. But nothing come of it. It was midnight or after, and it was quiet on the square, and I cut across past the Embassy Theater and down past Borelli's barber shop where I remember a long time ago they had a big picture of Sad Sam Yale hanging over the coat-hooks. But they have since took down the picture of Sam and put up 1 of me. Now my picture is took down, too, and the space is bare.

Next to Borelli's is Fred Levine's cigar store where you can get most any magazine, in particular magazines like "The Baseball

Digest" and "Ace Diamond Tales" and such newspapers as "The
Sporting News" and 1,000 other things. Then after Fred Levine's
is Mugs O'Brien's gymnasium, just opposite the statue of Horace
Cleves, and on the corner is the Perkinsville Pharmacy.

The way you get out home from Perkinsville is a question. If
you own a car like me (a 50 Moors Special) or any other car for
all of that, you just drive out the hard-top road 2.7 miles from the
square to where you will see a sign saying "Observatory" with an
arrow pointing west. This Observatory (star-gazing) is exactly 1
mile west of the highway. It has a big telescope, 1 of the biggest.
The Government wanted to use the Observatory during the war,
but Aaron turned them down. Aaron rules the whole works under
orders from his group of scientists and it can be used only to look
at the stars and moon and such. I have saw Mars and Saturn and
all the rest through it, and they all look the same except Saturn. I
have also saw the moon. Sometimes there will be a squad of pro-
fessors come down to look at some particular situation in the sky.

Aaron Webster kills me. I was very young when the argument
with the Government took place, but I remember there was a good
deal of discussion in the papers, not only in Perkinsville but everywhere, Aaron holding fast and finally winning out, and you have
got to admire him for that. He is over 80 years old, his face all
wrinkled up but otherwise in excellent shape, a gangly man, built
like Carl Hubbell, though lighter of course, weighing about 140,
mostly bone. If you ever stop at the Observatory he will come right
up to you, squinting and looking at you, and tell you his name and
pop right out with questions and answers, what do you think of this
and that and your politics. It used to be I never liked him much.
But you got to get to know him and he will grow on you.

It is partly on account of Aaron that I am lefthanded in the first
place. Pop wanted me to be righthanded. Not that Pop had anything against lefthanders because he himself is lefthanded and
pitched for a long time for the Perkinsville Scarlets. But Pop
wanted me to be righthanded because when you come to think
of it a lefthanded baseball player has got 2 strikes on him from
the beginning. First off, as everybody knows, a lefthander has got
only 5 positions he can play. He can pitch or play first base or 1

of the outfield spots. But he can't be a catcher or a second baseman or a third baseman or a shortstop, not usually. If you are righthanded you can play anywhere. Then too, even a lefthanded pitcher is considered a sort of a risky proposition because many of them are wild and most hitters are righthanded, and a lefthanded pitcher is supposed to be at a disadvantage against a righthanded batter. So Pop wanted me to start off right in life, and he done what he thought was best at the time, and nobody blamed him.

But nothing he could do could change me, and finally what he done he took me to Aaron, for Pop has the greatest faith in whatever Aaron says, and Aaron said there wasn't nothing wrong with being lefthanded and some of the best people were lefthanded and all.

I guess I could not of been more than 4 at the time, and Pop done what Aaron said and it all turned out for the best.

Yet you should not get the idea that Pop is simply some sort of a wooden dummy that Aaron can twist around his little finger, for Pop has a mind of his own as you will see between here and the end of this chapter. This chapter is Pop's, for it seems the least I can do is give him number 1 like the club give Swanee Wilks the number 1 shirt last spring, Swanee the oldest of all the boys. I am putting the club roster up in front of this book. Take a look at it once in awhile and keep things straight in your mind.

Pop is everything you could ask for, and more, born and raised in Perkinsville. When he was a sophomore at Perkinsville High he was the first-string pitcher, though I will admit that is no special trick even in a place which takes their baseball so serious as Perkinsville. He finished up and would of graduated but got sick and tired of school in his senior year and took off in May, right after the Tozerbury game which is always the wind-up for Perkinsville High, and went to Cedar Rapids in the Mississippi Valley League, winning 12 and losing 5 on what was left of the year. He says he always wished he had stood for graduation, though I myself graduated from Perkinsville High and can't see any special benefit in it. Graduation night was probably 1 of the most boring things I ever been through. I wore a cap and a gown and felt unusually foolish and wouldn't of bothered to go a-tall except it give

Pop a terrific thrill. Aaron said it was rubbage and I agree. Aaron belongs to the Board of Education of Perkinsville and once in a fit of disgust voted to abolish the whole entire system. He got ruled down. He usually always does.

Pop played 2 years with Cedar Rapids, weighing about 180, standing 6 feet in his socks and just about full growed. The second year he won 19 and lost 7, mighty good pitching in any class of ball.

The exact story on what happened after the second year is still not clear in my mind and probably never will, though after last summer I can actually see where a man might do what Pop done. It is partly on account of last summer that I am writing this book for the benefit of the 100,000,000 boobs and flatheads that swallow down everything they read in the papers, in particular the writing of Krazy Kress in "The Star-Press." That fat horse's tail! All I know is that Pop simply up and quit after the second summer at Cedar Rapids. He done this in despite of the fact that his wife that he married the previous winter was expecting a baby, which was me, and in despite of the fact that Pop had all the makings of a great. He could of been an immortal. He was fast and had good control and an assortment of curves of all speeds and a smart head for baseball. More then anything he loved the game, and when you love the game of baseball you eat it and sleep it and are bound to succeed if you got the stuff to go with it.

Pop was none of your average ballplayer. He was the stuff which greatness is made of. They will tell you in Borelli's barber shop in Perkinsville that Pop was the greatest that ever come out of the area, not even barring Slim Doran that won 18 and lost 11 in the 1 good year he had with Newark before his arm give out from a cold he caught in Montreal.

Pop could of went up with Boston the following year, and you would think he would of jumped at the chance. But he didn't, and I do not know why, and over all the years I have pumped him time and again for the answer but never got a good 1. All I know is that he built on land he bought from Aaron, located right next to Aaron's house about 1 mile up from the Observatory, and he got the job driving the school bus, which he still does, also working as caretaker at the Observatory, and he pitched semi-pro ball for a long time for the Perkinsville Scarlets, right up till last summer. They play the touring teams such as the House of David and the Cuban clubs and the Columbus Clowns. They used to play only Sundays until night ball come in, and now they play Wednesday nights as well.

Concerning my mother I can tell you practically nothing, for she died when I was 2. Pop don't talk much about her. About the only thing she means to me is I think of her whenever I write my middle name, which is Whittier, because she was a fan of a poet by that name. Holly says Whittier was quite famous.

When professional baseball lost Pop it lost a great southpaw. Yet you might say that between Pop and my mother in their short time together come a greater southpaw yet, which was me. I believe that some day I will be counted amongst the immortals and have my statue in the Hall of Fame at Cooperstown. Connie Mack says Lefty Grove was the greatest, and maybe so, and some say Mathewson and some say Walter Johnson, some say Bobby Feller and some say Satchel Paige. Yet you will see some writers that say that on my best days I am better and faster than any, and I believe them. You got to believe. Pop says you got to believe in yourself and know every time you pitch that ball that it is the best pitch ever throwed.

Another thing Pop says is, "Hank, never feel sorry for yourself. You will have good days and bad days. Keep thinking, keep learning, keep throwing, and you will have twice as many good days as bad." Pop himself has followed his own rule. He never feels sorry for himself. He is really a pretty happy fellow. He is crazy about kids and gets a big bang out of driving the bus, and he likes to work for Aaron, for he admires Aaron. Such spare time as he has got you can usually find him hanging in Borelli's. He keeps busy. If he ain't monkeying with the school bus he is under the hood of his old 32 Moors. He is in love with that crazy car. Myself I own a 50 Moors Special. Right at this moment it happens to be sitting out in the yard, its Evva-life battery deader then hell.

It been sitting there since after the Series last October, and it can sit there 80 years more for all of me.

1 other person I had better mention fairly quick is Holly Webster, Aaron's niece, now Mrs. Henry W. Wiggen by marriage. However, there was a number of stormy brawls before it come to pass.

So Pop is actually moved out of the house now, and over with Aaron, and Holly is moved in over here. I kid Aaron and tell him I have got the best of the swap by far. We kid back and forth a hell of a lot.

That's it. Those are the folks and also the end of the chapter. Holly says try and write up 1 thing and 1 thing only in every chapter and don't be wandering all over the lot, and then, when the subject is covered, break it off and begin another.

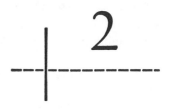

2

THE earliest thing I remember was Sundays in summer, going out in the morning with Pop to look at the sky. If it looked like a good day he would twirl his arm around a few times, and he would say, "Son, I am going to pitch 3-hit baseball today," or if there was a little nip in the air he would say he would pitch a 7-hitter. Pop was a good hot-weather pitcher. He was great in any weather, but better in hot, and we would go back in the house for breakfast. Then he would lay down until lunch. He would eat only very light. Pop says a hungry ballplayer makes the best 1.

After lunch he would change to his suit. It was gray, and the stockings were gray with scarlet stripes, and the letters across his shirt were scarlet, but small, because it is hard to say all the letters in Perkinsville on a shirt, and there was a white "P" on his cap. The rest of the cap was scarlet. Then he would say, "Hank, my glove," and that was me. I always carried Pop's glove, and I was proud to do it. Sometimes he would let me oil it. It had that leathery oily smell which is 1 of the best smells I know. Then he would get his shoes, and sometimes he would let me carry them, though not always. His shoes had a steel toeplate on the left 1 because that was the foot he dug around with on the mound when he was pitching, to make the mound just right. When you are pitching everything has got to be just right. The spikes on the shoes were bright and silver, not all run down like you see on seedy ballplayers that don't care how they keep themself up. Every year Pop bought new shoes, which is what any self-respecting ballplayer will do. You have noticed how these straggley semi-pro clubs wear run-down shoes. But not Pop. Nor me. I have saw players that wore shoes 3 and 4 years, and they never amounted to much.

Then we would pile in the 32 Moors and start for the park. I would sit high in the seat when we went rolling in town so as everybody could see me with Pop. Everybody in Perkinsville knowed him.

Pop would say, "Now, Hank, the first thing I do when I come near the park is look up and see which way the flags is blowing. Keep studying the flags all through the day, for you have got to know what the wind is up to." If the wind is blowing towards the right field fence you want to take care not to give anything too good to a lefthanded hitter, and so forth and so on.

Or Pop would say, "Look at the sky and see how many clouds is in it," for there is much to the weather. If it's cloudy and hard to see you will throw your fast ball more then your curve, and the other way around.

We would pile out in the lot behind the park, and Pop would walk in his stockings in through the private gate that was only for players and relations. As a kid it always give me a great thrill to go in any park through the player gate. It made me feel important—made me feel like I was *somebody*. These thrills wear away with the passing of time. I would go up in the seats right next to the rail, and Pop would lean with 1 hand on the rail and rub off the bottom of his stockings and make sure there was no stones nor pebbles in them, and then he would put on his shoes and lace them with a double bow. Then Slim Doran would come over and toss a ball to Pop, and the 2 of them would toss it back and forth easy between them. Slim was up with Newark for a time and had a good year and would of rose to the majors but for a cold he caught in his arm in Montreal. Slim was a righthander. There was always a wad of tobacco in his mouth. Pop never chewed, nor never smoked nor drank. Slim was used mostly in relief. They would lob it back and forth, and then when Pop was ready to warm he would yell to Tom Swallow, the Perkinsville catcher, and he would start throwing serious, and here is where the beauty come in.

I have seen many a pitcher, but there's few that throw as beautiful as Pop. He would bring his arm around twice and then lean back on 1 leg with his right leg way up in the air, and he would let that left hand come back until it almost touched the ground behind, and he looked like he was standing on 1 leg and 1 arm and the other 2 was in the air, and then that arm would come around and that other leg would settle down toward the earth, and right in about there there was the least part of a second when his uniform was all tight on him, stretched out tight across his whole body, and then he would let fly, and that little white ball would start on its way down the line toward Tom Swallow, and Pop's uniform would get all a-rumple again, and, just like it was some kind of a magic machine, the split-second when the uniform would rumple up there would be the smack of the ball in Tom's mitt, and you realized that ball had went 60 feet 6 inches in less then a second, and you knowed that you seen not only Pop but also a mighty and powerful machine, and what he done looked so easy you thought you could do it yourself because he done it so effortless, and it was beautiful and amazing, and it made you proud.

He would do it time and again, maybe 20 times, and he would be all a-sweat, and his arm would loosen, and by 15 of 2 he was warm and ready to go. Then he would go to the batting cage and swipe out a few. The Scarlets always hire a high-school lad to throw batting practice. Pop could hit, too, but he didn't put no effort in it. A pitcher is supposed to pitch, not hit.

By this time the park would be full (or as full as it would get, for there was times when we drawed some fairly sprinkley crowds) and I would be nervous for Pop. I was always nervous until after he went out to the hill and throwed that first pitch through and there was the first thump of that fast 1 in Tom Swallow's mitt.

I would generally get terribly nervous when Pop got in a jam. Maybe he would relax too hard and whoever the other team was they would bunch a couple hits and Pop would be in a tight spot. I would shout "Bear down, Pop!" I would yell "Strike this bum out, Pop!" and the people around me would laugh. I was just a little kid. Sometimes Pop smiled, and some of the other players, and he would pitch out of the jam and toss down his glove near the baseline and stroll to the bench. He would pull on his jacket and take a swig of water out of the bucket and spit it out in a straight silver stream.

Maybe once or twice in a summer he would lose. I remember 1 time he got lumped up pretty bad by a team that called themself the Westchester Rockets. Teams give themselves names that make them sound fierce, such as Lions and Tigers and Indians. These Rockets had an old-time ballplayer name of John Zack that been up with Pittsburgh, and he started the trouble with a home run out into Lincoln Avenue. I didn't think nothing of it, for many a second-rate ballplayer will lay hold of 1 once in awhile. Then he will go around in life talking about the time he homered off a great pitcher that he couldn't hit another 1 off in 70,000 years. Pop was so surprised that an old broke-down ballplayer like Zack had tagged a home run against him that he lost control and walked 2 men and then went to work on the third but couldn't seem to find the plate. I seen Jack Hand come up off the bench, and I knowed that Pop had struck a bad day.

Then Jack lifted him and Pop went down to the bench and slipped on his jacket and took a swig of water and sat down. The people give him a hand and he touched his hat and probably coached at first or something of the sort the rest of the afternoon. The Scarlets never carried more then 12 or 13 men at 1 time.

As for me, everything busted loose, and I cried for 2 innings. I was ashamed, but I was very small. Yet even ballplayers will cry. I seen them. I might of cried the whole game through, but then I looked up and Mr. Horace Cleves was by my side. He was a very old man at the time in a wheel chair with an electric motor that it used to be the most marvelous thing to see him get around in. I never seen him except in that chair unless you count the statue on the square where he is standing with his hand inside his coat. There is a joke in Perkinsville that he has got his hand in there wiping off the pigeon dung. Many a battle Aaron Webster had with Mr. Cleves, and I suppose I will never forget standing on the square with Aaron when the funeral went by, and Aaron muttering that Mr. Cleves had at last met a foe that he could not swindle.

"Boy," said Mr. Cleves, "why are you crying?"

I don't know if those was his exact words. When I put down words that I say somebody said they needn't be the exact words, just what you might call the meaning. You must keep that in mind as you plow on through this book. Many a time in the Mammoth clubhouse the writers will say to the skipper, "Dutch, what do you think about so-and-so or this and that?" and Dutch will say, "I think that so-and-so or this and that is a load of crap." The next day I will look, and they have wrote, "Mammoth manager Dutch Schnell expressed the opinion that so-and-so or this and that will probably never come to pass" and a lot more fancy words which I guess what they amount to is the same load of crap Dutch was referring to in the first place.

"On account of Pop getting knocked out of the box," I said. "Why do you think?"

"That ain't no reason to cry," said Mr. Cleves. He had a blanket around his legs, and he dug under it and come up with a purse, and he opened it. My eyes was blurry, but I could see a big stack of money there, and he tore off a dollar and give it to me and rumpled his hand in my hair.

That was the first dollar I ever made in a ball park. Pop got 25 per Sunday from the Scarlets in the early days, 50 and 75 and as much as 100 in later years.

Another thing I remember from way back was the picture of Sad Sam Yale that hung over my bed. It was not as big as the picture that hung in Borelli's barber shop, but it was pretty big, and you could see why they called him Sad Sam. He had a sad face. He had just come to the Mammoths at the time, nothing but a raw youngster with a powerful amount of baseball in his bones and a sad, sad face, and they called him Sad Sam because of that. Most writers rate him the equal of Grove or Johnson or Mathewson, and even now, at 34, though much of his stuff is gone, on a good hot day with a break or 2 he can make most hitters wish that they never showed up at the park.

You may not believe it, but I used to *talk* to that picture. Practically every night when I went to bed I looked up at Sam and I said, "Well, Sam, I am 19 years old and we are off to spring training." I thought 19 was awful old. The bed become a car to me, and I shoved over behind the wheel and opened the door and left

Sam in, and I would say, "You got your glove and shoes and all?"

He would say, "How is that great left arm of yours, Henry old boy?"

"Never better," I would say. "How many games do you think we ought to win between us this coming year?"

He would say, "Well, 25 for me and 20 for you," and then he would laugh and I would laugh and we would argue about who was the best pitcher in baseball, me or him, and laugh and joke and zoom along at 60, and all the people along the way would look at us and say, "There goes Henry Wiggen and Sad Sam Yale off to spring training. Notice how friendly they look. They are probably great friends, them 2."

Somewhere in about that point I drifted off to sleep. But I must of begun that trip with Sam 1,000 times at least over the years. This is the first time I ever told a soul.

Another crazy thing I done as a kid was I pitched about 5,000 games of baseball against the back of the house with a rubber ball. I had a regular system. I throwed the ball from out where the clothesline begins, and if I hit the house in 1 certain spot and caught the ball it was a strike. If I missed that spot it was a ball, and if I missed the ball but recovered in 1 bounce it was a single, 2 bounces a double, 3 a home run. All over 3 was a triple, triples being rarer in baseball then home runs, and I kept a score with pebbles, putting some in 1 pocket and then moving them to the other when runs was scored against me. I used to cheat a hell of a lot, though.

It was all very real to me. Out behind the house was Moors Stadium in New York City, thousands of people and a good deal of cheering. Sometimes the ball would hit the clothesline, and there was no way to explain that, and I did not try.

Or sometimes it would bounce crazy off the side of the house and roll in Aaron Webster's yard, in amongst the flower beds, and I could not explain what flowers was doing in the middle of Moors Stadium. Or sometimes Pop would poke his head through the window and shout advice, "Follow through a little more when you throw so as to get more power," and I would pretend that Pop was Dutch Schnell shouting from the dugout.

Or sometimes it was Ladies Day, by which I mean that Holly would be over in Aaron's yard and watching. Holly is Aaron's niece that when she was a little kid used to live partly in Baltimore with her own folks and partly with Aaron, there being a running family squabble between her mother and her father for many years. When she was 18 she come and lived with Aaron for good, hating and detesting her own folks and giving them no end of trouble until they turned her loose.

As a kid I couldn't stand her, though Aaron was forever trying to make us friends. She wanted to, for she was a sweet and gentle little kid, and I suppose I wanted to, too, but I fought against it because of some idea I must of had that your *real* ballplayer steered clear of girls. This makes me laugh when I think of it now. Aaron would come out in the yard and look up at the sky and just *happen* to notice the moon, and he would say something about the moon. Or he would find a rock in the ground and pick it up and show it to me and her and tell us something about it, how old it was or how it come to have its shape. Or he would have a leaf in his hand, and he would show us the leaf, and it looked like any other leaf I ever seen, or a piece of bark from a tree, or a bug he caught in the ground, or a baby bird that fell down from the nest.

Or he would have a book such as "Moby Dick" concerning the white whale, and we begun to read it together, Holly and me, and we never come to the whale so I give it up. And there was "Huckleberry Finn" that begun "You do not know about me without you have read a book by the name of "The Adventures of Tom Sawyer"," and I told Aaron that was a dirty trick to start a book that you no more opened then the writer was telling you to read still another as well. He just laughed, though probably I flung the book at him. I was a terrible kid for flinging things at people. I once knocked Holly unconscious with a sour apple.

No, there was only 1 thing I was fond of, not moons nor rocks nor leafs nor trees nor bugs nor books nor baby birds, nor least of all Holly Webster. Only baseball. And the older I growed the greater my interest become.

I give up the game behind the house and begun to play catch with Pop with a regulation ball and gloves, and after that I would pitch to Pop and he would catch me with a lefthanded catcher's mitt made on order through a connection of Mr. Gregory N. Oswald, baseball coach at Perkinsville High, and a grand fellow. I should say a word of thanks here to Mr. Oswald, my coach for 3 years at Perkinsville High. Though there was much that he learned me that I later realized was strictly crap I know that he also drilled in me many good habits.

But as time went on both books and girls come under my notice. These will be covered in chapter 3. Chapter 2 is already longer then I originally figured it for.

THE way I first knowed for sure I was growing was I was out behind the house 1 day, throwing the rubber ball, and the clothesline kept rubbing me along the top of my head.

Later on my eyes was so high they was *over* the clothesline, and I kept seeing it all the time, and it spoiled the game for me because there was no way to explain it.

Then too all kinds of things begun to happen that scared me at the beginning until after I read about them in these various books of Aaron's. Aaron has 2 rooms full of books, 1 of them the big living room, the other being the sun porch at the west end. The *other* sun porch used to be Holly's bedroom.

1 of the things that happened was I kissed Holly Webster 1 day. I thought nothing of it until about a week later I told some kids on the William B. Saddleman playground what I done, and they said she would get a baby, and I told Pop, saying I had kissed her not knowing she would get a baby, and Pop told Aaron, and Aaron invited me in 1 night. He said he did not believe Holly would get a baby.

Then he showed me these books, and he give me 1 that he believed I could whip, and I took it home and read it through. It turned out you didn't get a baby from kissing, but from intercourse (fornication), and a load was lifted from my mind. The book was quite helpful in many other ways as well. I was about 10 at the time, and my mind settled down a good bit, and I just went on growing and not worrying. It said in the book that when we was at the age of fornication there would be new worries crop up. As it turned out, when I come to it it all went off rather pleasant.

As near as I can figure out that was the first book I ever read clear through. This does not count Pop's scrapbook, covering his years at Perkinsville High plus the 2 at Cedar Rapids in the Mississippi Valley League plus 20 with the Scarlets, all yellow by now and tore in many places that I must of read once a week at the very least between the age of 6 and 13.

There was other ways I could tell I was growing. First off, Pop said I was because I had developed a good deal of speed. In a few years I was ready for the regulation distance, and we went out in the field across the road and measured it off—60 feet 6 inches—and after I got used to it it seemed like that distance was a part of nature. It was natural. If Pop would move 3 feet back or 3 forward I would know it. Sometimes he done it a-purpose to see if I would notice, and I would, and I would stand there with the ball in my glove looking down at him and not saying a word, just waiting for him to get back in the right spot. He would. Then he would say, "That is right, Hank. Never throw that ball until all the conditions is exactly how they should be," and I would be proud that I done it, and I knowed I was growing by the way the ball begun to zoom in there, not on a lob nor as if it was about to peter out, but with plenty of smoke, and it would whack in Pop's mitt and send up a little puff of dust, and Pop would shoot it back to me and crouch down again and hold the mitt for a target, and I would wind and pump and rear and let fly, and down she come. Wham!

Then we would set up an imaginary team and I would pitch to it. We would work on the different batters like they was right up there, according to whether they was lefthanded or righthanded or big men or little and which way the wind was blowing and what inning it was and what was the score. Pop would crouch and give me the sign, what kind of a pitch and where. Sometimes I would disagree and step off the mound and come down a bit and make Pop come for a conference. Pop learned me to always make the catcher do most of the walking so as to save energy. "What is wrong?" he would say. "I want you should follow them signs."

"There is a man on third with only 1 out," I would say, "and I ain't going to throw high and give the hitter a chance to fly to the outfield and leave the runner score after the catch."

"I am the boss," Pop would say.

But I would stick fast, and after a bit his face would crease up in a smile, because I had done the right thing and he was just testing me. Pop always told me you are libel to find yourself pitching to a lunkheaded catcher, and if that happens you have got to set him straight. No need to be made to look like a fool just because your catcher happens to be 1. Pop played dumb many a time and put on the stupid act so I would learn to play it smart. I was not only growing in the body but getting more brains as well.

Then there was just a general way I knowed I was growing, nothing you could put your finger on, but just a general thing. 1 day you are not allowed to do something, and the next day you are doing it, and nobody told you you could, but you do, and nobody stops you or says you are too little. It might be just driving a car. Pop was tinkering with the school bus 1 day, and he said what he needed he needed his welding cap that he left over at the Observatory, and I said I would get it, and I jumped in the old Moors and buzzed down, 1 mile there and 1 back. Somewhere along the way I passed over from being a mere child and become a man. At least I thought so then. Looking back now, however, I see that there was still a good deal to be learned about life.

I begun to be pretty itchy in school. It struck me as all a waste of time, and nothing took, or at least if it took it done so in such a way I never noticed. Now, as I read back over what I have wrote so far I can see where grammar might of come in handy. It is definitely on the weak side, and the punctuation no doubt smells. When in doubt I punctuate. 1 thing that beats me, though, is when somebody says something that somebody else said. Where in the world do you put the quotation marks? For instance, suppose Perry Simpson was to say to me, "I seen Dutch and Dutch said, "Perry, you made that play very good on that slow roller in the second inning last night"." I do not recall Perry ever saying any such thing. I am only trying to discuss the punctuation of it. Christ!

Anyhow, school pretty much sizzled past—history and geography and algebra and geometry and civics and French. French floored me, though there was 1 thing I could rip off like I was born and raised in Paris itself. J'habite dans une ferme a cinquante kilometres de Marseille. (I live on a farm 50 kilometers out of Marseille.) I quit French after 1 year and elected Spanish. That floored me, too, though I afterwards wished that some of it took for I might of been able to know George Gonzalez better. As it is he is always a mystery to me and to all the Mammoths, all except Red Traphagen. Red learned it at Harvard plus which he also spent some time in Spain in the war there. If I was to tell you all the things that went against my grain in school it would take a book. I would start in in the fall, and the first thing that would happen would be that the World Series come up. It is impossible to sit in school when the World Series is going on, and I would lam out of there and sneak down to Borelli's and sit towards the back on the shoe-shine chair not far from the radio. If anybody connected with school would be passing they could look in the window and never see me. Just about game time Pop would show up. There was several years running when the Mammoths was in the Series, and it was about this time that Borelli got his hands on the big picture of Sad Sam Yale that hung up over the coat-hooks. Pop would lay in 1 of the empty chairs with his head back on the shaving cushion, and the whole shop would be full of people listening to the game. Pop would figure out the strategy as the game moved along. If somebody was to be give an intentional base on balls Pop knowed it before the announcer ever did. Sometimes there would be a pause in the game and the announcer would dip back in history and mention some event, and Pop would bolt up in his chair if the information come in wrong, and sure enough a little while later the announcer would announce that he had pulled a boner and was sorry and so forth and Pop would lay back down. Sometimes some of the men in the shop would argue over a date or a rule or something of the sort, and if they couldn't settle it they shouted over at Pop, and he would tell them, and they looked on Pop as the final word.

Soon the Series would be over and school would be staring me in the face again and the whole long year would stretch ahead.

October, after the Series, was like death to me. The ground

would begin to get hard. The leaves would float down from the trees and pile up all over, red and yellow and rotten, and the wind would whip in off the fields, and then about December there would be the first snow. You would get up in the morning and look out the window and the snow would be laying in the fields, all white like a corpse.

Then just when it looked like winter was fading there would be a fresh snow piled on top of the 1 before. There was nothing to do. Such time as it was light I was supposed to be in school. For my part it could of stood dark all day and nobody the loser, and I begun to take off for town more and more, spending the day in the Embassy Theater or talking baseball in Borelli's or hanging in Mugs O'Brien's gymnasium or in the Legion hall or sitting in the back of Fred Levine's cigar store and reading the literature there.

I also took to reading books. I had begun to think there wasn't any books worth spending time on, for I had went all through Aaron's, looking for things to kill time until spring, but there wasn't a 1. I come across a book called "Giants in the Earth" which I thought at first might have to do with baseball, but it turned out to be a dud. There was others such as books with the word "Yankee" in the title, and "Reds" and "Senators" and such, but when I took them off the shelf they turned out to be something else, and I begun to give up.

Then 1 day I was roaming down in Perkinsville. There was a girl there that I begun to take up with. I had a date to meet her in the Rexall, but when I got there she was not there, and afterwards some of the girls she hung with come with their schoolbooks and I asked them where she was, and they giggled amongst themselves but was too idiotic to give a straight answer, so I slammed out and started walking around. I swung over towards the library, know-ing she sometimes went there to look up things for school, and I hunted for her there, looking behind all the shelves and waiting outside the ladies room, but she didn't show up, and I was about to leave when my eye caught a book on a table called "How to Play First Base," which is a part of a series of 9 books, "How to Play Second Base," "How to Play Shortstop," and so on and so on, each of them wrote by a famous player. There was a grayheaded lady name of Mrs. Thompson at the desk, and I asked her if she had a book called "How to Pitch," and she looked it up and said she did and give me a wide smile and took me down to where it was. My eyes just about jumped out of their socket. There was not only this book, "How to Pitch," by Michael J. Mulrooney, once an immortal and now the manager of the Queen City Cowboys, where I played for 2 years before going up with the Mammoths, but the whole shelf was full of books about baseball. Mrs. Thompson asked me if that was what I wanted, and I said it was, and she went away, and I sunk down on my knees by that shelf and tore them out of there. I forget all that was there, but there was the 1 by Sad Sam Yale called "Sam Yale—Mammoth," and I read it clean through crouched there on my knees. I suppose every boy has read that book at some time or another so there is no sense going too deep in it here. You will remember that in the front there is a picture of Sam from the shoulders up, looking right out at you, and then on the page beside it is a little bit of writing, telling about him and what is yet to come. I studied the picture, noticing every little detail of how his nose was shaped and his eyes and his mouth. I looked real close and seen a little bit of hair sticking out around the sides of his cap. The writing said:

My name is Samuel (Sad Sam) Yale. I was born in Houston, Texas, on March 13, 1918. I had the good fortune of becoming a member of the world-famed New York Mammoths five years ago. I pitched my first game for the Mammoths on Opening Day, April, 1938, shutting out Boston, 4-0. In the five years since that memorable occasion I have pitched and won 112 games, while losing only 63, and have been acclaimed by baseball experts as one of the game's outstanding pitchers.

This book is written in the hope that every American boy now playing the great game of baseball in his home town, wherever that may be, will take inspiration from my straightforward story. Some of my readers, in the not-too-distant future, will be wearing the uniform of one of the big-league clubs. His success or failure in reaching that goal, and in remaining there once he has reached it, depends on him and him alone.

I have three simple rules which I live by:

1. Take the game seriously, playing it for all you are worth every inning of the way.

2. Live a clean life, shunning tobacco and liquor in all forms.

3. Follow the instructions of your high-school coach, for he is a man of wisdom gained through experience.

Most important, have faith in yourself, for the road lies before you, and success will be yours. By the grace of God you will succeed.

I studied the words over and over again, and the picture, and I knowed that moment and ever more that some day I would be a Mammoth and all my dreams come true. I took the book and an armful of others and started out the door, and then I felt a hand on my shoulder and I turned around and it was Miss Thompson the grayheaded lady. "You have not checked out your books," she said. "Can I have your card?"

"I do not have any card," I said.

She steered me to her desk and pushed out a bunch of papers for me to fill in and sign, and I done so, and then she said, "Your card must first be put through the process before you can have any books," and I beefed but she held fast and grabbed the books and give them to some kid with glasses to put them back on the shelf.

I turned away and started out the door, and then I glanced around and seen that she was looking another way, and I circled around with my head hid and went to the shelf and found the book by Sad Sam Yale and crouched down in a corner and opened my shirt and stuck the book in and buttoned it. I edged back out the way I come, and I went through the door in a rush and fairly flowed down the street with the book in my shirt.

That night I read it through again. I didn't even tell Pop I had stole it, and when I was through reading it I took the blade out of the razor that Pop had used in Cedar Rapids in the Mississippi Valley League and sliced the picture of Sad Sam out of the book, and the inspiration he had wrote, and I folded them and stuck them in my wallet with a picture of Pop in his Scarlets uniform that I clipped 1 time from the Perkinsville "Clarion" and a picture of a girl name of Thedabara Brown that she had took at the beach in the summer and a picture card of Sad Sam Yale that come with bubble gum. I put the book in a secret place in the closet.

Many a book I borrowed that winter from the library after my card was put through the process. I returned them all, all except "Sam Yale—Mammoth," and I read them all, too, laying on my bed with my feet stretched over the foot, munching on candy bars and milk. I cannot remember all the names. I learned a good deal about pitching and strategy and the ways of big-time players and managers, and after I finished a batch of books I would read through Sam's again.

There was also some books of baseball stories, such as those by Sherman and Heyliger and Tunis and Lardner, although Lardner did not seem to me to amount to much, half his stories containing women in them and the other half less about baseball then what was going on in the hotels and trains. He never seemed to care how the games come out. He wouldn't tell you much about the stars but only about bums and punks and second-raters that never had the stuff to begin with. Heyliger and Sherman and some of the others give you a good baseball story that you couldn't lay it down.

There was 1 fellow name of Homer B. Lester that wrote a whole series of 16 books about a pitcher called Sid Yule, which was just another way of saying Sam Yale. There was "Sid Yule, Kidnaped," and "Sid Yule, No-Hit Pitcher" and "Sid Yule in the World Series" and 13 more, and all the books had 24 chapters and run 240 pages and you couldn't skip a 1. There was always a picture in front and 1 on page 80 and 1 on page 160 and 1 right at the end, but I would try not to look at the pictures until I come to them, otherwise I would know what was coming.

I guess I knowed, though, pictures or not, for 1 book got to be pretty much like the next after awhile. In the beginning there would be some plot being hatched against Sid, and it sounded pretty tight and you knowed he was in danger, and you itched to warn him. Usually it was gamblers, or traitors on his own club. Chapter 2 was always a discussion of what went on in previous books, so I always skipped it. Then Sid would come in the picture, unawares that anything was being hatched to do him in, and he would walk right in that trap. He might get a telephone call saying a kid was sick in a hospital, and he would rush over to cheer that kid up and sign a baseball and then some of these gamblers would creep up behind and smash him over the head and cart him off to some dark place in a rough part of town. Then he would come to, and be dizzy, and he would unloose the ropes and fight his way out against 4 or 5 of these chaps.

In the background of your mind you would remember that there was a big game going on this very day, and his club was losing, and he would grab a cab and off they would go at 60 or 70, and Sid would dash in there just in time to pull the fat out of the fire. You never knowed for sure if he would make it because Chapter 23 would bob up, telling you all about what would happen in the next book and where you could buy it or send for it by mail, but then you got back in the story, and he always won out, and there was a moral at the end, such as "Friendship Pays" or "Live Clean and Win."

I read the whole 16 that winter, and then spring come, and things begun to happen so fast and so frequent that I laid off books and never read 1 again until last summer when I went in a good bit for quarter murders.

Such corny crap as that is all behind me now. I ain't even interested in Sad Sam Yale no more. You spend a long period with a fellow and he stops being a hero all of a sudden. Sam ain't all he is cracked up to be. But I didn't know it then. I wasn't but a kid.

IT WAS in May of my junior year at Perkinsville
High that I was signed on as batting practice pitcher for the Perkinsville Scarlets, and it was also about then that me and Thedabara
Brown begun to go together. She was 16 and as pretty as many a
girl that passes for a movie star. She later married Mort Finnegan
that was the catcher for Perkinsville High and not bad a-tall but
used to drop third strikes an awful lot. He was afterwards killed
in the war against Korea and she married a catcher for Sacramento
in the Pacific Coast League.

I had not yet had the experience of fornication at the time, although I read a good bit about it in Aaron's books. When I brung
the subject up she did not know what I was talking about, saying
she never heard it referred to before in such a vulgar way, and she
chased me out of the house and told me never come back.

But I come back the very next night, and her old man was sitting
and waiting. He asked me where did I learn my manners and did
I think his daughter was a whore, and I said no, and he said he
had a mind to punch me in the nose right then and there. Then
he rose and seen that I was larger then him, so he sat back down
again but invited me to make myself scarce. He went on to say a
number of nasty things about young men of my type and ballplayers in particular.

Finally I left. I was shaking all over and quite uneasy, for I was
scared of old man Brown. I pretty much duck out of a fight whenever I can. Every time I ever been in a fight I usually always just
covered up and left this other chap, whoever he was, whale away

36

at my wrists and elbows and the spaces between. Pretty soon some-body would break it up. Just to *see* 2 guys fighting makes me weak. When I was a senior at Perkinsville High we had this military training where the class would split up in 2 groups and fight over Callahan Hill in the lot on Callahan Avenue with bayonets with boxing gloves on the end. We must of fought this fight 100 times and I was always the first 1 killed. Not killed really, but I would just lay down and die, too weak to fight, crouching around until somebody stabbed me with the boxing glove. The fellows used to call this my Coward Crouch. Actually the trouble was it give me loose bowels and how in the hell can you go on fighting with loose bowels? We had this soldier name of Sten Stennerson over from the National Guard that would yell at me, "Wiggen, on account of you we are always losing Callahan Hill," and finally they sent me to the psychiatrist at the Vets Hospital in Tozerbury. But nothing come of it.

Then about a year later I come up for the draft and went for the examination and seen this same fellow again and he give me a deferment. I was turned down again this past October for the same reason, and to tell you the truth if they never get me that's okay, too. I mention this for the benefit of the same 100,000,000 boobs and flatheads that read Krazy Kresses column of last September 30th. This used to bother Pop a lot, but Aaron said to Pop, "Why should it bother you? Is it not better for a fellow to go down in his Coward Crouch and live to fight another day?" and Pop said he supposed it was.

I know that it always worried Pop. Yet I cannot help it, and the older I grow the worse it gets until sometimes I think that if they do not stop the wars I am libel to wind up with loose bowels 24 hours a day. I suppose this is a weakness, but everybody has their weakness. About 2 weeks ago a fellow wrote me a letter saying it struck him as very peculiar that a man with so much guts on the ball field is afraid of the war. But throwing a baseball and throwing a hand grenade is 2 different things, and I am at my best with 1 and scared to my toes of the other. Actually when you really stop and think about it it probably wouldn't be too stupid of an idea if the Koreans and Chinese and Russians and Americans and all the rest come

down all at once with a bad case of loose bowels and went somewheres back of the lines and settled down on the John and done
some thinking about what fools they were making of theirselves.
Where in hell is it getting everybody?

I shouldn't of gotten off on the beaten track here, for this chapter was supposed to be about Thedabara. Yet when the war comes
up I can't hardly get it off my mind half the time, especially in the
winter. All winter long pick up a newspaper and what do you see?
War and football, mostly war, until you're never sure any more
how much your nerves can take.

Anyways, I seen her on the street a number of times and never
thought a thing of it. She was going at the time with a third baseman that played around in the factory leagues. This was before she
went with Mort Finnegan. She was with him 1 Sunday in Patriots
Park where I was tossing batting practice, and she waved to me but
I did not wave back. Pop always told me to act big-time whether it
was semi-pro or Legion or anything else, and I did not wave nor
would not even wave to Holly or Aaron when they come.

But I kept thinking about her all through the game, sitting on
the bench, and afterwards I caught hold of her by the exit and
swung her around and asked her whether she was free that night
or if she planned to waste her time on that imitation of a third
baseman. "If you must know," said she, "he has got a 42 Moors."
I laughed. I said I had a 46 and not some old heap of a car that
been drove through the war. This was a lie, but Mort Finnegan
had a 46 and used to loan it to me all the time. She said she figured
she could ditch this other fellow and meet me on the square at 8
by the statue of Mr. Cleves. He was long since dead by now.

I went in and picked up my pay, which was 5 dollars. I thought
it was good money at the time. Then me and Pop piled in the 32
and headed for home, Pop pumping me full of advice like he always done after a ball game when everything was fresh in his mind,
but most of it sailed past me for my mind was on other things,
particularly on 1 thing, which was fornication.

We ate fairly light, and then I believe me and Pop set some sort
of a record doing dishes. We used to do dishes for 2 in 8 minutes
and once done them in 4, and then I decked out in clothes that I

must of thought was pretty sharp. Pop said he believed I had a girl in Perkinsville. Then I bolted out and no sooner got past the door then I met Holly Webster coming up the walk. She become permanent at Aaron's about that time, having went for awhile to college at New Rochelle but in 6 months was in hot water 6 times and finally pooped out and as far as I know was never missed. She was developing a practically sureproof method of cornering me for a lift every time I left the house, Aaron owning no car and never libel to. He gets pretty worked up on the subject. "How did the game go?" she said.

"Pop won," I said, and she asked me was I headed for the square, and I said I was, and she asked me would I run her down, and I said I would. I dropped her at the square and then continued out to Mort Finnegan's and borrowed his 46. Mort always thought high of me and would do practically anything, and it is quite unbelievable when you think about it—him loaning me his 46 to take Thedabara out in and then Mort later actually marrying her. Even to this day it is hard for me to believe Mort was killed in the war.

I parked on the square. It was only a little after 7, and I went down in front of the Embassy Theater and lolled around some, standing at the curb with 1 foot up on somebody's bumper that was parked there. I studied the pictures on the theater, noticing how the men was dressed, and when I got tired of that I ambled across to the Legion hall. It is supposed to be for members only and their ladies, but Mayor Real said I could come any time day or night, for I had pitched for the Legion team from Perkinsville that won the State 2 years running and the National once. You will see his banners on telephone poles, saying "For Mayor, a REAL Man." This passes for great comedy in Perkinsville.

If you will read in Connie Mack's book called "My 66 Years in the Big Leagues" you will see where chapter 18 is about the Legion. It says:

My baseball career has brought me into intimate contact and relationship with many national movements for civic and social betterment. One of the most important of these movements, in my

estimation, is the American Legion. . . . Our American Legion-
naires and the members of all our veterans' associations have helped
to make our national game an exemplification of the true American
spirit. . . . The American Legion . . . is engaged in a program for
molding the future of our American youth by utilizing baseball as
a powerful factor in the social, moral, and economic development
of the younger generation. Inaugurating a campaign for good citi-
zenship, the Legion has organized more than 500,000 boys into
baseball clubs. In 1949 it had 15,912 American Legion Junior
Baseball teams competing for the Junior World Series.

Then he goes on to tell where 255 young fellows have come
up through the Legion to the big leagues, including more then a
few immortals. Legion hall is really a great place where you can
relax and hear music or play the slots or poker or shoot a little pool
or drink some beer and take your mind off things. Mostly I just sat
around talking. Sometimes they had some campaign going and
there was something to sign, and you would hear plenty of jokes,
mainly about fornication and different unusual cases of it which I
never thought was particularly funny.

Around 10 of 8 or so I lazied back across the square and stood
by the statue of Mr. Cleves waiting. I could hardly stand. I was
vibrating a good deal around the knees. I begun to suspect there
was a large difference between fornication as it was wrote up in
the books and as it goes off in the flesh. It is like baseball. There
is a chapter in Sam Yale's book called "Nervousness and How to
Overcome It," and I believe I read that chapter 20 or 30 times. Yet
it took me years and years to overcome being nervous at the start
of a ball game.

It was 8, and then it inched around to 15 after on the big clock
in front of the Arcade Department Store, and I looked high and
low and all around the square, and every girl I seen looked like
Thedabara, and then, about 20 after, she come along with a white
dress with flowers sewed in all over, quite short, and her legs was
all brown and better shaped then many a movie star, and white
shoes with high heels that clicked along on the sidewalk. She come
across towards the statue where I was standing, and she said, "I am

sorry to be late," and I said, or begun to say, "That is all right," but the words got stuck in my throat.

She wore a little gold chain around her neck, and on the end of it was a medal showing a mother and a baby, and the medal bounced down between her breasts, flopping now 1 way and now another, and without hardly thinking I stuck out my hand and grabbed hold of the medal, and the back of my hand rested against her skin, and the skin was warm and smooth, and my eyes closed and she took my hand and lifted it up and away. "I only wished to see the medal," I said.

"Touching is not seeing," she said. "Where is your car?" I pointed to it and she took my arm and we went across and got in and hardly went more then a block or 2 when she said, "This is Mort Finnegan's car."

"Jesus," I said. "They turn them off the line about 1,000,000 a week. 2 cars of the same make and model are naturally bound to look alike."

"You are a liar," she said. "But drive on. I hate and detest Mort Finnegan. I never met such a dirty mind as his."

We drove out past Patriots Park, which is where I played my first professional ball and got the first money I ever got for doing the 1 single thing I would rather do then anything else in this world. I told her how it all come to pass, how Pop telephoned Jack Hand 1 morning and said "Jack, this rascal of a boy of mine is a comer," and Jack said "Leave me see him throw a few," and Jack called Tom Swallow and told us to all be at the park at 11.

Me and Pop drove down, and Pop kept chattering in my ear, discussing everything under the sun and building me up in my mind, knowing I was nervous. "Tom Swallow was at the park when we got there," I said. He was dressed in his Texaco overalls, for Tom runs the Texaco station on the square. "What have you got?" he said. "You name it and I will throw it," said I, and he dusted off the plate with his handkerchief and took the sponge out of his mitt and stuck it in his pocket. Pop and Jack Hand was standing behind me, and Pop said, "Tom will put that sponge back in," and Jack said, "Seeing is believing for doing is proving." I throwed about 6 warm-up pitches down the line, and Jack said I had a nice motion. I throwed slow and easy, and I felt in my mind like the sight of Pop out there on that same pitching hill. Pretty soon I was loose, and I give Tom the sign that I was ready.

"What was your signs?" she said.

"Not really signs," I said. "In a regular game it is usually the catcher that gives the signs. I just signaled to Tom that I was ready to go. He crouched in the business position and I took the full wind-up and reared and let fly, and it cut the corner and whammed in his mitt. It was as fast a pitch as I had ever throwed up to that time, and Tom held up his hand and took the sponge out of his pocket and put it in his mitt. A catcher will use a sponge in his mitt to save his hand."

"I know," she said. Thedabara knowed a good deal about baseball and followed it close. We was soon some 10 miles out of Perkinsville, and I stopped under a grove of trees by the side of the road and flicked on the radio and turned it low.

"Well," I said, "Pop said to Jack I told you so, and Tom crouched down again and held his mitt up for a target, and I burned it through again. I throwed about 8 fast ones and then about 5 curves, and Jack said that was enough. He said he would sign me on as batting practice pitcher and fire this other kid and maybe later I would work in in relief and maybe after that as a starter."

"Leave him throw the screw," said Pop.

"Just what is a screw?" she said, and I explained to her that what it is is a curve in reverse that me and Pop worked on out of the chapter in Sam Yale's book called "Enemy Poison—the Screwball" plus what knowledge Pop had of it. It is the pitch that made Mathewson an immortal back in the olden time, although it was called a fadeaway then, and it is the pitch that made Hubbell an immortal, and Sad Sam Yale, and it is the pitch that almost never fails me and will make me an immortal. I throwed 2, and Jack Hand whistled between his teeth and we called it a day.

We was both interested mainly in baseball and automobiles, and we talked about that. Her favorite big-time ballplayers was Sad Sam Yale and Swanee Wilks, and she had wrote them letters and sent them her picture and got 1 back from Swanee, signed, and her favorite car was Moors. You don't meet somebody like that every day in the week that has got so much the same slant on life as you, and I pulled her over to me and kissed her, and she pulled away, and I went after her and crowded her in the corner and her head bumped the light switch and the light went on, and I turned it off, and I held her in my arms and kissed her 8 or 10 times, the sweat running down me and down her as well. I could feel where she was wet all up and down her legs and nothing between her and her dress to sop it up, which come as a surprise to me and got me in the worst dither ever.

But as to fornication she would have none of it. She said that nice girls never fornicated until after they was married, which was a blow to me, for the book said nothing of the sort. The book said it was a natural thing, like eating or sleeping.

So we took off about 10 more miles down the road to a place called Washington Irving Inn. It was now 9 at least, and I had not ate since supper and not much then, and I had steak and fried potatoes and 2 glasses of milk, and she had beer, about 3 glasses, and the music played, and we danced real close and my mind begun to shift back on fornication. We got out of there soon after. It cost me 4 dollars.

We drove back towards Perkinsville and come to Patriots Park again, and we got out and went in the park by the player gate and sat in the stands and looked down on the field. The stands are cement with wooden benches fastened in. It is a pretty good semi-pro park, although nothing like Moors Stadium of course where the seats are of rainproof plastic with backs to them and a place to rest your arms, and the moon shone down on the field. It was quiet and peaceful there, and we did not talk much for we had just about talked ourselves out over cars and baseball.

We held each other close. She shivered a little. Then there was a certain amount of struggling, and the next thing she was laying on the cold bench with her dress climbed way up on her and crying and breathing heavy and strangling me and saying 1 minute "Hank! Hank! Yes!" and the next minute "No! No!" and I said "For the love of Pete which is it, yes or no?" and then her mother and baby come loose from around her throat and dropped to the cement, and it made a loud noise because the park was so quiet, and she stuck her arm out, trying to get it, and we rolled off the bench and down in a heap. She laid there and cried and I did not know what to do, and after awhile she come to a bit and said she was freezing cold. "No wonder," said I, "for you are sitting with your bare ass on the cold cement," and she slapped my face and said she never met such a dirty mind as mine.

We was both about played out by now, and I was real ashamed of what I done, and I said I did not deserve her, and I would take her home. She said I better. She said I was a no good character. But she said she would need about 2 more beers to get over the strain of what I had put her through, and we went to a little place just off the square, and she had 3 or 4 beers and never said a word the whole time except now and then she laid me out, telling me what a rotten egg I was. My 5 dollars run out, and I took her home, and she asked me when she would see me again. I said I guessed I did not deserve to ever see her again. But I asked her if I could give her 1 final kiss, just a friendly kiss between old friends, and she slid over under the wheel and for a minute I thought the whole wrestling match was about to begin over again, and when she got out she said she would see me at the ball game Wednesday night. That was the first year of night ball in Perkinsville. It meant a good deal in a cash way to Pop.

I swung around and rolled back through town. I had the most unusual pains in and around my groin, and I was so weak I could hardly drive. I parked the car on the square and stretched out my legs a little. It felt much better that way. I was about to back out and take off when I seen Holly Webster coming up the sidewalk. I waited until she was smack in front of the car, and then I honked at her. She jumped about a mile, and I laughed, and she shook her fist at me and come over towards the car. I remember that she had her arms full of phonograph records. Sunday nights she goes down to these people name of Pecunio's house and listens to records. That is my idea of nothing to do. "Are you going back?" she said.

"First I have got to take this car to its proper owner," I said. "Then I am going home if I do not die. I am either going to die or not, and the next few minutes will tell."

She climbed in. "I will sit here. If you die I will take the bus," she said. "Why do you look so beat up?"

"From rolling on and off the cement grandstand," I said.

"What was the purpose of that?" she said.

"I was with a girl," I said.

She laughed.

"It ain't no laughing matter," I said.

"No," said she, "it is not," and she stopped laughing.

"You would not laugh if it was you," I said.

"I am not laughing," she said. "I understand it perfectly."

"How could you understand it?" I said.

"I have did the same thing," said she.

"In Patriots Park?" I said.

"No, not in that particular park," and she laughed again.

She kept up a running stream of comment, calling me by the name she tagged me with, which is Henry the Navigator, which is what she calls me to this day. "You are Henry the Navigator," she said. "The world is a big sea," and I snapped back, telling her to talk sense or not a-tall.

After a bit I started the motor and glided out of the square towards Mort's, and I took him his key and me and Holly drove on home in the 32. And she kept right on chattering, and I said whether she knowed it or not I was dying of a ruptured groin. She said that millions of people died of the same thing every year. She said a chicken sandwich and hot chocolate with marshmallow was good for a ruptured groin in case I was interested and wished to drop by home with her. I said I might think about it.

We went past the Observatory. Aaron's office was all lit up, and I honked like mad. He hates it when people honk. I don't know why in hell I would do it, but I done it a lot. That's exactly the kind of a rattleheaded kid I was, and then I parked in the drive in front of the house, off to 1 side so as Pop could get the bus out the first thing in the morning, and then I said I would take her up on that chicken and chocolate for I had not ate since the steak and potatoes at the Washington Irving Inn.

"I am just about dead," I said. "My mind is beginning to go blank, and all the memories of my life are jamming up in my head," which was what they done in the books of Homer B. Lester when Sid Yule was in a fix. I begun to thrash around in circles, saying I was Henry the Navigator, saying "Here we are in Portugal," which is where he operated out of, putting on this idiotic act. Don't ask me why. But I remember it, and I am ashamed of it. The thing of it is I was just so nervous I probably *was* half out of my mind. This was all building up a long time over the months between me and Holly.

I laid on her bed till the pain simmered down a bit. She said she would phone for the doctor. I said no. She said if I was about to die I ought to have a physician to help, and I said I was too far gone and what I needed was a priest to give me the last rights like in the movies. "In that case," said she, "there ain't even no use trying chicken and chocolate," and I said we might at least try it as a last desperate chance.

Then she brung it, and I wolfed it down, and she sat there and watched me, and I give her back the plates and cup and told her she had give me the exact thing I needed, and I said, "You are pretty," and she said if she was it was none of her doing, but she seemed pleased all the same, and she said if I was noticing things of that sort I must be past the crisis and about ready to go home, and I fell back on the bed and begun to groan again, saying a new crisis set in, and she laughed and sat down beside me and stroked my head, and every time she touched my head the rupture acted up again in my groin, and I reached for her and grabbed her wrist, and she pulled away, and I said it was a sorry note when someone rushed off from a man about to die in my condition, and she said she was not leaving me to die but was merely turning out the lights, which was what she done.

The rupture was spreading throughout my body. I was pumping all over, in my groin and in my stomach and in my head, and it was like I had a dozen hearts and each was beating all at once in a dozen different locations, and I bust into a sweat and my throat was dry as dust and my hands like ice.

After a long time she come back through the dark and sat beside me, and I held her hand in mine and drawed her closer, a little at a time, expecting any minute she would yank loose and draw off. Yet she never did. "You will get a baby," I said.

"No I will not," she said, and I took her at her word.

Then all the beating stopped, and the various hearts in their various places all drifted back to the 1 single slot where they belonged, and the cold got warm and the shivering stopped and my sweating body dried, and I was peaceful. I begun to hear the sounds of the night, crickets chirping and traffic on the highway far in the distance, and I seen stars in the window.

I slept, and when I woke it was beginning to get light, and Holly was asleep. I took her in my arms and woke her, and she did not seem to mind, for she smiled and I give her 1 back, and she laid with her hair spread out on the pillow like a crown behind her head, all golden and brown in the dawn. I said, "I am Henry the Navigator," and she launched into a speech herself, saying she was queen of the ship and mistress of the sea and lover to Henry, meaning me.

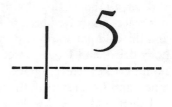

CHAPTER 4 shoots out a little bit ahead of things, however. I should of told you first about April 13, 1948, when me and Pop went to the Opener at Moors Stadium, that being the first time I ever seen a big-league ball game and the *last* time I ever paid my way in. Pop hired his regular sub to drive the bus, a wimpy fellow name of Mr. Hilbert from East Perkinsville that ain't happy unless he is holding down 5 or 6 jobs at once. Myself, I never worked a day in my life except 2 months in the winter following graduation pumping gas at Tom Swallow's Texaco station and never hope to.

We got up that morning when it was still dark out, and cool, and we rustled up a quick breakfast and grabbed a couple oranges for my pocket. It did not seem possible that on this very day I would see Sam Yale in action. Nothing seemed real or true. It was like a dream, and when we left the house there was a mist hanging down, making things more like a dream then ever, and the road was bare of traffic and Pop lost no time in getting down to Perkinsville. We swooped in the depot and piled out and went inside and bought our tickets and a Perkinsville "Clarion" and a New York "News," both filled with a lot of dope concerning the openers. Brooklyn and Washington opened the day before down in Washington, and there was a picture of the President throwing out the first ball. There was a big picture of Sad Sam on the front of the "News," and over it it said READY TO HURL. It was the eleventh straight time Sam Yale hurled the opener for New York. He was posing with a ball in his hand and that mighty left arm stretched out before him. Pop said he looked old. He was then just turned 30.

The train come in on the dot of 6, and then she pulled away through Perkinsville and we sat with our feet stretched out on the seat in front, all green and soft, and we read the papers and then swapped them and read the other, and the conductor come past and punched our ticket and said where was we going so early in the morning, and we told him, and it turned out that he was from St. Louis and often seen Dutch Schnell's house. Dutch owns a big house way out on Delmar Boulevard. He asked me if I was a ball-player, and I said if he was still around in a couple years I might get him a pass or 2 for the Mammoths. He said that was very generous of me.

We come down through Westchester County, 1 of the richest counties in the world though rather slummy in along the railroad. The sun come out bright, and we fairly flowed through them towns. There was people standing on the stations, but we went down the middle track and never stopped. I hate these trains that as soon as they work up a little speed they stop at a station.

We got off at 125th Street and lazied over west. Pop asked a man how to get to Moors Stadium, and the man reeled off a set of directions that I couldn't hardly understand.

"How about if we wish to walk?" Pop said.

"You cannot walk," said the man.

"Why not?" said Pop. "I want my boy to see the town a little."

"You simply cannot," said the man. "What are you? A radio show?"

"No," said Pop, "we just wish to walk," and the man said we was crazy, but he told us how, and we started out. There begun to be less and less white people and more and more colored, and soon we come to a part of town where there was no white people a-tall, and the worst run-down houses I ever seen. Pop said that people lived in the houses.

Then we come to the Stadium. Everybody has saw pictures, but seeing it in a picture is nothing. It made me feel like a pebble in the sea, and we stood still and looked up at it, and Pop said, "I could of played ball in that park," and I said, "Pop, I will play

there sometime and it will be the same thing," and we stood looking upwards like 2 boobs from the country. There was men on
top, raising the flags, and people waiting on line for the gates to
open, and then there was a whole lot of excitement and some kids
busted loose from the crowd, shouting "Sad Sam!" and a few ballplayers got out of a cab togged out like 1,000,000, and I seen him
and tore over and charged through them kids and stood smack in
front of Sad Sam Yale. He looked up at me, right in my eyes. I
was froze to the spot and could not think of a thing to say until
afterwards, and the kids clung to him and shoved papers out for
him to sign, and he signed a few, keeping on the move, and some
of the specials come and cleared the way, and he went up the steps
and in the clubhouse, disappearing from sight. I begun to shiver
from excitement, and all the plans I ever had seemed small and far
away, and I knowed I had a long way to go, for somehow, being
there right on the spot, things seemed bigger then they seemed
when I was home, and it seemed impossible, something I could not
carry through no more then I could climb up the walls of the
Stadium or go through all that brick and stone and steel just by
sheer will.

When the gates opened Pop bought the tickets. You had to keep
moving to keep from being trampled on, and we headed for seats
behind the plate, romping through that place as fast as we could
go. I jumped over things and now and then collided with someone. After we got settled we begun to study the park. It was vast
and huge, and it was like the sea opened up and left a great dry
place in the earth. After you been playing ball in a park the size
of Perkinsville and then you see this 1 it is like being blind and
then getting eyes, and for a good while I could not believe that
such a place was really in the world, and Pop laughed and said,
"She is a big 1, she is a big 1, she is a big 1," several times over
like a busted record. "She is the park to end all parks," he said,
and I hadn't no argument there. There was not a worn spot in the
grass, and around the infield the sod was brown and smooth like
some kind of polished wood.

By game time there was about 30,000 there, although it looked
just about empty for they can seat 80,000 if need be. The bleachers

was full. There is a big clock behind the bleachers which is the famous clock that more people can see at 1 time then any other clock in the world. Sometimes you will see a man sitting on the big hand and riding around, polishing up the numbers. We bought scorecards and pencils and checked the cards against the boards, and everything checked.

The Mammoths at this particular time was rather a different club from a few years later. It was an old club that the newspapers sometimes called The Nine Old Men, many of them past 30. It won its last pennant in 45, whipping Chicago in the Series in 6 games, Sam Yale winning 2, which I remember hearing in Borelli's. But it was not about to win any more pennants and everybody knowed it.

The players begun to straggle on the field, coming up through the dugout, and my heart missed a beat every time a new face come on the scene. Little pepper games started up here and there, 1 fellow hitting slow and easy to 3 or 4 ranged out in front of him, just loosening themself up. Every time they worked around to a position where I could see their number I would check it against the card, and slowly the field filled up with Mammoths and the Boston players, and Egg Barnard, 1 of the Mammoth coaches, begun to loft flies to the outfield with a big long fungo bat.

It is a beautiful sight to see a good outfielder gather in a fly ball, moving over as graceful as you please while from 250 or 300 feet away someone has tossed the ball up in front of himself and laid into it and sent it upward and upward in a high arc until the ball is just a white speck against the blue sky, and then it hits its highest point and begins to drop, and you look down and there is a player loping over, moving fast or slow, depending on how he sizes up the situation, and he moves under the ball and it zooms down in his glove. It looks so easy when a good ballplayer does it. It is not easy. Ask any kid that has ever tried to play ball whether it is easy, and he will tell you. But when a big-league ballplayer does it it looks easy because he is so graceful, and he gathers it in and then runs a few steps on his momentum and digs his spikes in the ground and wheels and fires that ball back where it come from, and it hops along, white against the green grass. I watched them shag flies awhile, and then batting practice, and soon afterwards Pop poked me and he said, "Here he comes, Hank," and about 30,000 people seen him just an instant after Pop, and he come up the dugout steps with his jacket on and his glove on his hand, and a cheer went up and some of the people stood and clapped, and he turned and talked to another player for a few seconds, and then he moved on those long legs down to the warm-up rubber.

A batboy run up and took his jacket, and Red Traphagen moved over behind the warm-up plate, and Sad Sam took the ball the batboy give him and studied it awhile, and then he studied the rubber under his foot and scuffed it up some. Near him there was kids hanging over the rail and waving scorecards, and a little girl leaped the rail and run towards him and the whole park begun to laugh, and some men in park uniforms come charging out from the stands, and the little girl run up to Sad Sam and he just stood there with his arms folded, waiting for them to take her away. The men of the park closed in on her and hauled her off, and the people begun to boo. He begun to warm, unwinding and throwing down the line to Red, throwing very slow at first, and gradually faster and faster. Dutch Schnell went over and talked to him a minute and then moved off, and I watched every move that Sad Sam made. He stopped once and took his hat off and wiped his forehead, and I seen for the first time that he was ever so slightly bald on top. That surprised me some. About 2 rows behind me a fellow yelled, "Do not worry, Sam, for you pitch with your arm and not with your hair," and a number of people laughed.

During the infield drill I kept a close eye on Gonzalez. This was his first year, and I wondered if he would show up nervous, but he did not seem to be. He is a little fellow, very fast on his feet from Cuba. Clint Strap, 1 of the Mammoth coaches, was belting the ball around the infield. Each time he come to George he would make him go a different way, first to his right and then to his left, but it made no difference to George for he would gobble her up and all in the same motion fire across to Monk Boyd who was then the Mammoth first-baseman.

Then the field cleared and the players went down through the dugout to the clubhouses and about 15 men in overalls come out with hoses and rollers and smoothed the infield over again. Then the band played "East Side, West Side" in honor of the mayor of New York who come down and took a seat in a box behind first. There was a lot of cheering, and some booing as well, and the mayor waved his hand and pretended he did not hear the booing.

Soon the players come out again in fresh shirts. The Mammoths lined up in front of the dugout. I was so nervous you would of thought I was in the game myself. Then they broke for their positions and the crowd give them a great hand. The Mammoths that started that day was as follows:

At third base George Gonzalez, playing his first big-league game. At shortstop Ugly Jones, just beginning to hit his heights. At second base Bryce Chapin, now in carnival work in California. At first base Monk Boyd, now with Washington. The outfield was as follows: Trotter, Wilks and Burns, all still Mammoths but all due to be cut loose before long. Scotty Burns is definitely for sale since Dutch has turned Canada Smith back into an outfielder. Red Traphagen was behind the bat, then and now generally considered 1 of the great receivers in the game today, and Sam Yale was on the hill.

Amongst the men on the Mammoth bench that day was the following: Vincent and Pasquale Carucci, outfielders. Lucky Judkins, also an outfielder, was then the property of Cleveland. Gene Park, then playing second base for Chicago, was bought the following year by the Mammoths, was then drafted by the Reserves and then quickly released by the Reserves in the case that caused so much scandal that you probably read about in the papers. Some writers claim to this day that Old Man Moors wangled Gene free, and now and again you will see a reference in the papers to "Twice Bought" Gene Park. Not yet even a part of the Mammoth system was the following: Sid Goldman, Coker Roguski, Perry Simpson, Canada Smith and yours truly Henry W. Wiggen.

There was an announcement by the loud speaker, "Ladies and gentlemen, our national anthem," and the band struck the tune and some lady that I could not see begun to sing, and a mighty powerful pair of lungs she had. It is really beautiful, for as the last words die away a roar goes up from the people, and for a minute there is no sound but the echo of the singing, and no movement or motion except maybe a bird or the flags waving or the drummer on his drums, and then the music dies and the people spring to life and the chief umpire calls loud and long "Puh-*lay* ball" and the game is on. I stood there, and I looked down on the Mammoths, and I said to myself, "2 years, 3 years, I will be standing there with my cap over my breast as Sad Sam Yale is standing there now," and I choked up, for between the music and the thoughts I was on the edge of tears. I seen Sam with his hat over his breast and the top of his head bald in the sun, and then the music stopped and the roar went up, and Sad Sam walked very slow out towards the hill. Over in front of the mayor the photographers was bent down on 1 knee, and the bulbs was flashing all over, and the mayor wound up and throwed the ball out on the field towards Sam. He scooped it up and went to the mound and stood looking down at the ball in his hand. He studied it some, and he seen that it was scuffed, and he throwed it to the umpire for he will not use a ball that don't suit him no matter if the mayor or the President or the King of England or anyone else has smudged it up. The umpire slapped a new ball in Red Traphagen's mitt, and Red whipped it down to Sam, and Sam looked all about him to see that everyone was in the exact position they ought to be. Then his eye caught something over near the box that the mayor was in, and he pointed, and the mayor himself come out of the box onto the grass and picked up a flash bulb that 1 of the photographers dropped. He put it in his pocket and went back in and took his seat, and there was a big laugh all around.

Then Sam got his sign and wound and throwed, a fast curve about knee-high that Black, the Boston batter, drilled out into center for a single. We was sitting right behind the plate, and I seen Black start to swing and then hold it and then swing after all, so it was pure luck that he connected a-tall, and Pop turned to me and said, "He was the most surprised person in the park," meaning Black, for Pop had saw what I saw. Behind us some fellow begun to moan, "Old Sad Sam is all washed up," and he begun to sing a song, "Oh the old gray mare she ain't what she used to be, ain't what she used to be, ain't what she used to be," and I turned in my seat and shouted at him, "You have got your brains in your shoes."

"Who says so?" said he.

"I said so," I said.

"Okay," said he. "I was just wondering."

Granby moved Black along to second with the sacrifice.

With a 1-1 count on him Fielding cut under a letter-high fast ball and fouled it behind the plate. Red Traphagen come racing back. It did not look like he had a chance, but if you know Red you know that he is the type of a ballplayer that makes his play and stops to think about his chances afterward, and off come the mask, and the cap with it, and Red come roaring towards the fence, moving plenty fast, even with all that gear, and his red hair was flying in the wind, and he hauled it down about 2 feet from the fence. That was 2 down but Casey Sharpe at bat and trouble in the wind, for he is a dangerous man every day of the week. He fouled a couple off, and then Sam struck him out with the screw, and 3 was down and I turned to the moaning fellow and I said, "Who is so washed up? How many times did you ever strike out Casey Sharpe?"

We bought red-hots and soda, and the Mammoths went down 1-2-3 in their half of the first. Fred Nance was working for Boston, a right-hander that then had plenty of speed but now relies a good deal more on curves and brains. It was no score for 5 innings. The fellow behind said he wished somebody would score, for he was running out of zeros on his card, and me and Pop got a laugh out of that.

I did not keep score in the regular way, but I kept a careful track of what Sam throwed to each batter. You could see his brain at work. He mixed his pitches plenty, keeping Boston guessing, now speed, now a curve, now a change-up, now a screw, now high, now low, never the same thing twice except when you *least* expected it.

Nance batted first for Boston in the sixth. He got a good hand, for people usually always give the pitcher a hand, knowing how hard he works, and Nance slapped a single into right and the crowd begun to whoop it up a bit. Behind me this fellow shouted, "Say, son, I will bet you a bag of peanuts Boston scores," and I said I would bet him 10 against his 1, and he took me up, and Sam whiffed Black on the same curve he had throwed the very first pitch of the game—the exact pitch that Black least expected—and Pop looked at me and winked. Granby popped out, and the pressure was off, or so it seemed, but Fielding walked on a curve that looked good to me and looked the same to Dutch and Sam, and Dutch roared up out of the dugout and give the ump an earful.

Then the game took up again, Casey Sharpe batting. How careful they worked him! They throwed him a wide curve that he went after and missed. Then Sam throwed him a screw that he give it the go-by, and finally he laced a 2-2 fast ball that was good but not *too* good on a line into center, and Swanee Wilks took it without moving more then 5 feet. Probably no outfielder in baseball knows better how to play hitters then Swanee. He been around a long time. I seen the peanut boy and I shouted, and he tossed me a bag and held out his hand for the money, and I said, "That genius back there has got your money," and the fellow tossed it to him.

In the last of that inning, with 2 on, Ugly Jones looped 1 in the lower tier in right, and 3 was in and the game looked just about on ice.

But Sam got in trouble in the ninth. Dopey Davidson singled, and the crowd that was milling towards the exits slowed down a little, and Felsheimer singled and Dutch Schnell come up out of the dugout and him and Sam and Red and Ugly had a little conference out on the mound, and then Dutch signaled down to the bullpen and a young fellow name of Gordon Wood come slowly across the green, and Sad Sam went slower yet down in the dugout. He got a mighty hand, nobody probably clapping any louder then me. This gives me a laugh now—me standing there and pounding my hands to a pulp over Sam Yale. Another thing that hands me a laugh when I think about it is me sending 2 bucks through the mail about a month afterwards for a collection towards Sam Yale Day when he was give a Buick by the fans. In fact, this never fails to hand me a laugh—a couple thousand clucks making 60 a week throwing their chips on the pile for a fellow like Sam making 60 a day Sundays and holidays averaged out over the whole year, 4 months vacation a year against 2 weeks for the cluck, 4 hours a day against 8 for the cluck.

Wood warmed up some more with Red, and this stupid fellow said, "There is a kid with a style that will go places."

Where has Wood went? I can find no trace of him in the books. However, for that 1 inning at least he had what it took, though it struck me whilst he pitched that he had nothing to speak of—a little speed, a little curve, fair control—and I turned and said to Pop, "Why, Pop, pitch for pitch I am the equal of him."

"I can see that," said Pop. "I been thinking the same. But we will give it a little time yet. We must not rush these things. We will give you a couple years yet for flesh to grow on your bones and experience to gather in your head. You are still but 16," which I was, 17 that July.

Then we drifted away with the crowds and out of the park and down to Grand Central by subway—the wrong 1 the first time— and home on the train, and dinner on the train, the first time I ever ate dinner on a train. That was a great day for me, when I first seen Moors Stadium and Sam and Dutch and Swanee and George Gonzalez and Scotty Burns and Sunny Jim Trotter, and we talked it over all the way home, and that night I laid in bed and went over it time and again in my mind, play by play and inning by inning.

In the morning I woke up, and it was like I dreamed a dream so fine that you want to go back and dream it again, and I looked out the window and seen things laying there just like always, and I pounded the window sill until the glass shook, and I said "Thunder, thunder, thunder," and I knowed that some day I would get up in the morning and it would not be this view a-tall. It would be the big towns, New York and Brooklyn, Cleveland and Chicago, Boston and Washington, Pittsburgh and St. Louis, big towns and big parks, and there would be 30,000 people and my name on 30,000 scorecards and the music and the singing and the cheering, and I would touch my hat when they cheered, and I would wind and rear and fire and they would see, and they would know an immortal when they seen 1, and I dived back on the bed and pounded the pillow, and I shouted again, "Thunder, thunder, thunder and THUNDER," and I felt better and went downstairs to breakfast.

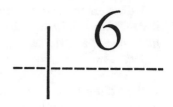

6

2 SUNDAYS after I graduated from Perkinsville High Pop had a very bad day against the Columbus Clowns that he had beat many times in the past. The Clowns usually play 2 games a year in Perkinsville, coming in May for a Wednesday night and then going up to Boston for a couple with the Standards, and then back to Perkinsville for Sunday afternoon. They had whipped us the Wednesday night before, lumping up Slim Doran plenty.

The day was hot, the kind of a day Pop likes, and there was a good crowd, maybe somewheres between 1,500 and 2,000, for the Clowns was always popular. They had a trick pepper game they played with a hollow bat 3 times the size of the regulation, and folks always got a good laugh out of that. They had 1 fellow that put on an exhibition of juggling, slick enough if you like juggling, though I always thought that kind of thing a little out of place in a ball park. When he got through a clown come on the scene holding up his pants with 1 hand and his fingers to his nose with the other to show what he thought of the juggler. Then he grabbed a couple bats and tried to juggle them, but he could not, and the crowd laughed, and me and Pop just about busted our sides over this fool though we had saw him year after year.

But when the umpire calls "Play Ball!" all laughter stops for Pop. Now he becomes dead serious, for when he is pitching he is a different man. Pitching he is king of the roost. At home we may be all sitting around, me and Pop and Holly and Aaron, Aaron blathering away and Pop sitting there and looking from person to person, and you can see that the talk is far above his head. He is like some joker in a foreign country where no safe and sane language is spoke. They could be ordering him to hang for all he would ever know of it. After awhile he might go up to bed. Or me and Pop will be walking along the road and come upon Aaron Webster, and Aaron will talk, and Pop will stand there and nod and shake his head and go down the line with Aaron. Yet I can see that he ain't got the faintest notion what the score is, and I will say later, "Well, what is it all about? What did Aaron say?" and Pop will shake his head and say, "Beats me."

But dress Pop in his uniform and give him a glove and a ball and set him down on the hill in Patriots Park and he is somebody else again. He is the master. There is nothing from the beginning to the end of a ball game that Pop does not know why and who and how and what and when and where.

But that particular day he was not quite in form. In the first inning he throwed several curves that did not break. 1 of them got past Tom Swallow and rolled clear to the fence, and Jack Hand looked at me, and he said, "Sonny, I have watched your daddy many a year and never seen him do that before." In the fourth the Clowns got to him for 2 runs, and in the fifth, after 1 was out, somebody singled, and Jack Hand said to me, "Sonny, why do you not go back and throw a few?" and I said "Why?" and he looked at me very stern. "Sonny," said he, "you had best learn to take orders if you wish to get anywheres in this game called "baseball". Now do like I say," and I got up off the bench, and Slim Doran come along with me, Slim taking along a catcher's mitt. We went back behind the fence and out of sight.

I was pretty well warmed, for I had throwed practice, so I throwed very easy to Slim. We could not see the ball game, but we could hear it and we knowed what was happening. You can tell by the sounds of the bat against the ball, and by the sounds of the players and the people, and the next thing that happened there was the batboy scooting around the fence. "Mr. Hand wants you," he said, and I went. There was a big conference around the mound, the whole infield and Pop and Tom and Jack Hand, and there was runners on second and third, sitting down on the bags. Pop watched me as I come across the grass, and he give me the ball and whacked me on the rump, and the batboy give him his jacket, and I give the batboy mine. Pop did not say a word. He just trudged in towards the bench. I asked Tom how many was out, and he said 2, and we talked about signs, and he reminded me that there was men on second and third, and I said yes I seen them.

I got set to pitch. I looked over my shoulder at the man on third, and he was close so I put him out of my mind, and I pitched, and the batter teed and swung, but he had not expected anything so fast, and he met it late and popped it down the first-base line and the inning was done.

I do not remember the sixth or the seventh. A kind of a fog settled down over me. It was like a dream, and I heard all the sounds that you will hear in any ball park of a Sunday afternoon, and men come up to hit against me, 7 I guess, for 1 man singled. As for the rest they come up and went down, and I seen Pop on the bench and it seemed like he was somewheres where he ought not to been, and I looked for myself and could not find myself though I ought to been sitting on the bench and was not, and then the fog begun to lift, and things that was wrapped in the clouds come out in the open. I remember the last 2 innings, for I begun to enjoy myself. I was loose and fast and every pitch broke the way I wanted them to break, and all the pages of Sad Sam's book come into view, and all the words I ever heard from Pop on the subject of baseball, and all the talking and all the thinking and all the dreaming—everything—everything poured out of me that I stored up during all the years.

2 was out in the ninth when Bobo Adams pinch-hit. Bobo is boss and part owner of the Clowns, a man of 45 and grayheaded, and the crowd give him a hand. In his time he was a great ballplayer with Philadelphia, hitting 51 home runs in 1935. I guess it was curiosity made him bat, for the Clowns did not need the runs. He hits lefthanded.

Tom give me the sign for the fast 1, 1 finger. In semi-pro work there is nothing fancy about the signs, 1 finger for a fast ball and 2 for a curve. It is not complicated like in the big-time where the other team will steal your sign if they can. I throwed the fast 1, and it nipped the corner, and Bobo stepped out of the box and got a new grip on his bat and then looked at me, and I shouted down the line, "Too fast for you, old man?"

"I seen faster," he said.

"Not awake," I said. "Only in your dreams." 4 innings of semi-pro baseball and I was now telling Bobo Adams what he seen and what he did not!

"You are a fresh kid," he said, which was putting it mild.

Tom called for the curve, and I throwed it, and it broke very fast, knee-high and outside, and Bobo swang and then halfway checked himself when he seen it break, but too late, and the ball glanced off his bat and looped back foul and out of play towards the visiting bench on the third-base side.

Then I throwed half-speed, close. I have good command of a half-speed fast ball that looks like it might just be a curve, and Bobo stood waiting for the curve to break. But of course it never broke, for it was never meant to, and when he swung he met the ball up close to the handle and blooped another little foul.

Then I fanned him with the screw, and almost before he finished his swing I was ambling over towards our bench. I had made a fool of Bobo.

We scored in the ninth, but not enough, and Pop pumped my hand for the job I done, and the batboy brung me my street shoes and I snatched them and told him to go on about his business and not be getting in everybody's hair, and me and Pop went in Jack Hand's office under the stands and picked up our pay. Jack called me back and said I had took the wrong envelope, and he give me another containing 2 fivers instead of the usual 1.

Outside the park we seen Bobo Adams standing by the bus that the Clowns traveled in. Semi-pro ballplayers travel mostly by bus. If they play in a park like Patriots Park where there is no club-house set-up they might travel miles and miles without ever shower-ing. The condition of the air must get pretty rare at times, al-though I suppose a semi-pro ballplayer is used to it. Bobo flagged us down, and he went around by Pop's side of the car and stuck his hand in the window and shook hands with Pop, for they knowed each other from way back. "Good boy you have got there," said Bobo, but he did not look at me. "He has got a good variety."

"He will go places," said Pop.

"But green," said Bobo. He still did not look at me.

"He will get over it," said Pop.

"He better," said Bobo, and then they talked a couple minutes about some common friends they had, and they shook hands again, and Pop talked about Bobo all the way home, dwelling on different times he had struck him out and made him look silly.

When we got home we showered together and sung some of the old songs Pop learned when he was with Cedar Rapids in the Mississippi Valley League. We felt pretty good, and I guess we had a right to feel good.

I pitched every Wednesday night the rest of that summer—the summer of 49—every night but 1, starting 11 games, finishing 9, winning 8, losing 1, getting no decision twice. Jack Hand fired Slim Doran and picked up a kid that worked at half the price and was used in relief when needed. It was a great education for me in rough and ready baseball. It was the only bush-league ball I ever played, jumping from Perkinsville straight to AA.

There was a considerable hoot and holler over me in Perkinsville, and a lot of articles wrote in the "Clarion" by Bill Duffy, and the word spread near and far that here was a great young southpaw working for the Scarlets. Several times the Wednesday night attendance went up to where the only seats left was standing room only. This was partly on account of a rumor begun by Bill Duffy in his column, saying that several big-league clubs had offered me a contract. Sometimes I do not know what gets in Bill. Anyway, the attendance busted all records. They paid me 40 per game.

The 1 game I missed all summer was on account of a crazy incident that was partly Holly's fault and partly my own. It was a Tuesday in September, and it was hot, and me and her went for a swim in Silver Creek which is off the Observatory road and down in a valley where nobody goes. We discovered it years and years ago and went there often, and still do. It is the most peaceful place you will find anywheres. You can hardly hear the cars, and you cannot see buildings or people, and Silver Creek comes roaring down through the hills and gets to this spot and flattens out, and the water is clear and pure, and cold, and deep enough to swim though truth to tell we went there not so much to swim as for the sunshine and the quiet, and she would lay there and read to me out of a book of poems. There was Shakespeare and Marble and Champion and Johnson and Dunn and Milton something and Browning and Yates, and I am not ashamed to say that I took to it pretty well, for I would lay there with my head in her lap, and she would read to me with 1 hand whilst rubbing my temples with the other. Some of them poets have really got a knack of making words into music, for it soothed me and made the air smell sweet, and it made ripples run up and down my spine.

Maybe she would read as long as 2 hours, and then we would strip and go for a swim, and then we would come back and sit in the sun to dry, and she would read some of them over again, and they sounded better the second try then they done the first. Holly says just because you have read a poem once does not mean that you have got the full charge, and I agree, for the more she read them the better I got to like them, and I even got so that I felt like I could whip out a poem or 2 on my own hook, and I done so, and she read them and said they was minor league but showed promise. She said if I stuck at it I might amount to something some day. She says any lunkhead can play baseball but he has got to be something special to write a poem.

That Tuesday we laid there in the sun, and she read to me from 1 that I liked. It opens like this:

> Come live with me and be my love
> And we will all the pleasures prove.
> That valleys, groves, hills and fields,
> Woods or steepy mountain yields.

> And we will sit upon the rocks
> Seeing the shepherds feed their flocks
> By shallow rivers to whose falls
> Melodious birds sing madrigals.

We had the valleys and the groves and the hills and the fields and the rocks and the shallow river and the birds. The only thing that was missing was the madrigals (songs) and the shepherds, but for the biggest part the poem held up fine. You would of thought the writer was on the spot, and it brought out all the love that was in me for Holly, for I loved her and believe she loved me, though what she seen in me I cannot say, for a stupider, thickheaded, stubborner smart-aleck never lived, and she read it all through and said Rawley had wrote an answer to it, and she started through the book, looking for the answer. "Here is the answer," said I, and I kissed her, and we laid there in the sun in 1 another's arms, and the sun was warm on our skin, and we done no more reading that day.

Soon afterwards I felt something bite me on the left elbow. We looked at it and there was a little red mark, and Holly said we should go home and put something on it, but by the time we got home I could not feel a thing, and I forgot about it.

But when I woke up in the morning the elbow was swole to the size of a grapefruit, and I rushed down to the hospital and they let out the infection and tied the arm up in a sling.

I could not pitch that night. Pop pitched and won. But I went down to the park nonetheless with my arm in the sling, and a bunch of kids crowded round and asked me what happened. "Nothing," I said, "but this will teach you the price of fornicating in the out of doors."

I knowed at the time I shouldn't of said it, but I was such a big shot then, or thought I was, my head about 17 times bigger then it had any right to be, and the next thing I knowed my remark was all over town. I got a call in the morning from Bill Duffy, and he said he was give orders to get an apology. I told him go ahead and write 1 out, and he wrote a dandy. Bill Duffy is a great writer and a great friend of mine. He can recite "Casey at the Bat" from beginning to end when sober, and it is longer then most of the poems in Holly's book.

THE Mammoths finished fifth in 49, out of the money altogether. They started off fast enough, and they led the league through May, but Boston took over in June, and Cleveland and Brooklyn crowded past in July, and they lost 7 in a row in August and dropped to fifth, just behind Pittsburgh, and they settled there and could not go up nor down.

It was the first time in many a year that the Mammoths wound up in the second division. Yet it was expected. It was an old club that had saw good days in its time, but old men cannot stand the wear and tear of baseball day in and day out and night after night. They will miss the close ones. They will be throwed out at first base by a step where 2 years before they would of beat the play, or a fly ball that in the past they would of gathered in now drops between them for a base hit, or the power that a few seasons ago would send a ball into the stands for a home run is gone, and the ball drops short and is just another long out. That is how pennants are won, by a step here and a few feet there and just that little extra power when it counts.

In the winter the Mammoths cut loose 6 ballplayers. It was sad. Pop said you cannot let sentiment interfere, so I did not, but it was sad nonetheless to see those great names cut adrift, for they was my heroes for many a year.

There was talk that Dutch Schnell was through as skipper, but in the fall it was announced that he was signed on for 3 years more, and he made a statement saying he would win more pennants before he bowed out for good, and he begun to rebuild, and

65

before long he was on his way to that pennant he had spoke of. The Mammoths bought Hams Carroll that winter, and picked up Sid Goldman for a song. Also, their farms begun to produce in a big way. The Mammoth farms are spread all over, from AA in Queen City down to these rickety leagues that play only weekends and maybe 1 night during the week. Plus this there are a dozen full-time scouts beating the bushes all over America and down in the Latin Leagues as well, including contacts in colleges and semi-pro ball in all the 48, plus the Legion tournaments plus private individuals that pass on information to the club. The Mammoths leave no stone unturned in their hunt for the ivory. Herb Macy and Gil Willowbrook and Piss Sterling become a part of the system that winter as well as Canada Smith and Coker Roguski and Perry Simpson and me. This is the cream that was sifted in the long run from the dozens and dozens of punks that put their name to a Mammoth contract. Mr. Moors spared no expense. He turned his pockets upside down and bought the best. If you have got the cash you can win pennants so long as you are willing to spend it. Them that has gets, according to the old saying.

(I should mention something here about the name of "Piss" Sterling, for I know that many fans will wonder how come. I see where his nickname is listed on the official roster as "Jack," but I never in my life heard a soul call him that and I doubt that he would turn around if they did. He has got terrible kidney trouble that acts up in tight situations. 2 and 3 times a game he will rush back to the John, and in a tight game, or down the stretch like last summer, he might make that little trip just about every inning. He has also got sinus trouble. But we call him Piss, and a better fellow never lived.)

That winter I worked like a fool. I suppose I had the idea I was keeping in condition, though I since realize that when you are a kid you are *always* in condition, never stiff, never above your weight, never sore anywheres from top to toe. But I read in "Sam Yale—Mammoth" in the chapter called "Keeping In Condition" where hiking was good for the legs. A pitcher's legs are as important as their arm, so I hiked a good bit, me and Holly, up through the hills. 1 time I pulled her on a sled clear to Berrywick Mountain, 5 miles.

Also I played handball in Mugs O'Brien's gymnasium, and I rowed the rowing machine. Mugs said he never seen anyone so faithful about keeping in condition. I topped 6 feet that winter, just 1 inch under Pop, and was 170 even on the scales.

I also played basketball at the Young Men's Hebrew Association of Perkinsville with the club that finished first in the city leagues. I was supposed to join it to be eligible but I did not have the money and Albert Goldenberg, a Jew, put up the money and got me a card. I do not think much of basketball. Actually I consider it pretty nearly as dreary as football. Do you call that a game where your best bet is to put 5 men on the floor that their chief quality is that they are overgrowed? Where do your brains come in, and your speed and your lightning strategy, your planning and your figuring and your careful decisions? Compared to baseball what they call these contact games are about on a level with a subway jam. I do not wish to aggravate people that like these particular sports, but when you stop and think about it it is really tragic that so much energy is wasted in such a great deal of pushing and shoving and trampling and getting up and falling down or else some 7-foot ox standing and dropping a ball through a hoop.

Besides this I pumped gas at Tom Swallow's Texaco station on the square. This was for the money pure and simple and had nothing to do with conditioning. I worked for Tom from after the World Series through Wednesday, December 14, 1949, when I quit him flat. It was the most boring period of my life.

All this time Pop kept saying sit tight and 1 day soon a scout would appear. Around Thanksgiving a man come from Chicago. He had reports on me from a number of people that seen me pitch, and he showed us the reports and they all had good things to say, and he offered me 1,000 to sign. Pop said 5,000 or nothing, and the man said he had no orders to pay anything like that, and Pop directed him back to Perkinsville, telling him there was a train every few hours. I did not say a word. Pop said leave it all to him.

About a week afterwards a man come from Cincinnati. He said he had signed up 25 young ballplayers between October and De-

cember. "How much are you paying a young fellow to sign?" said
Pop, and the man said he was not paying a cent except fare to
spring training, and Pop said if Cincinnati had such splendid habits
of saving money they might just as well save their breath besides
because I was not signing up free like somebody's slave. The man
hemmed and hummed and said he might pay 500 as a starter. Pop
said he did not care where he started so long as he ended up at
5,000.

"There are boys all over the land that would give their right
eye to put their autograph on a Cincinnati contract," the man said.

"I am pleased to hear these remarks," Pop said. "I am sure you
can win many pennants on sheer enthusiasm."

They could not get together, and then finally it was December 14
when the telephone rung early in the morning, and it was Jocko
Conrad down at the railroad, and he said could I meet him there,
and Pop said no but I could give him a few moments here at home.
Jocko is an immortal that played with the Mammoths from 1919
to 1931 and had a lifetime average of .323. I was nervous, and I
shook, and then he pulled up in front of the house in a big red
1950 Moors Special. He climbed out with a brown envelope in
his hand. He was a little fat around the middle. If you did not
know who he was you would of took him for some ordinary business man and not an immortal in the Hall of Fame. He rung the
bell and Pop left him in. "I am Jocko Conrad," Jocko said.

"We was expecting you," Pop said. "We are also expecting a
man from Cleveland." (A lie, though Pop carried it off. All the
time Jocko was there Pop give him the impression he was practically
run ragged entertaining scouts.)

"I am glad to meet you," said I to Jocko. "What can I do for
you?"

"Leave us put it the other way around. It is me that has come to
do something for you," he said. He took some papers out of his
envelope and begun to fire questions at me, my age and my height
and weight and married state and the condition of my teeth and
general health and was I ever arrested or inside an institution, and
at last he popped the question. "Young man," said he, "how
would you like to belong to the Mammoth organization?"

"I might not mind," I said.

"Do you not like to play ball?" he said, studying me real close.

"Sure I do," I said. "I love baseball. It is a great game."

"We are looking for boys that really want to be in the organization," said he.

"I would just as soon play in Perkinsville," I said.

He did not act like he heard me. He dug down through his papers and come up with a letter from Bobo Adams. "I have a letter from Bobo Adams," he said.

"I struck Bobo out on 4 pitches," I said.

"Bobo says you are a good boy," said Jocko.

"Anybody will tell you the same," I said.

We must of talked above an hour. He had letters on me from Jack Hand of the Scarlets and Mr. Gregory N. Oswald of Perkinsville High as well as Bobo, plus a raft of clippings from the Perkinsville "Clarion". The sum and total of it was he asked me would I sign a contract agreeing to sign a *new* contract if I produced the goods at Aqua Clara in the spring and was kept by the Mammoth system. I said I would like to help him out by signing such a contract but that I could get *cash* from the Perkinsville Scarlets and never be put to the trouble of traveling. "Well," said Jocko, "suppose I was to throw in a little bonus for signing?"

"That might help," said I.

"1,000," he said.

Pop snorted.

"2,000," said Jocko.

I begun to think fast. I thought and thought, and while I done so my eyes roamed about, and Jocko said, "Maybe 2,750," and my eyes kept wandering and went clear out the window and lit on the 50 Moors sitting in the sun. The figure 4,000 jumped in my mind.

"4,000 and your 50 Moors," I said.

"Done!" he said, and he screwed open his pen and filled in the contracts and handed them to Pop, for I was a minor and under 21 and could not sign, and Pop looked them over and signed them and I signed underneath. "By golly," said Jocko, "that was quick work and we will never be sorry. You will get your check in the mail. Could I use your telephone?" and we said yes, and he went over and telephoned Detroit, which is where the head office of the Mammoths is, reversing the charges and telling them to send me a check, and he said he needed a new car for he had give away another.

He gathered up his various papers and put them in his envelope. He put on his overcoat, huffing and puffing, and that reminded him to tell me to keep in condition through the rest of the winter and be in Aqua Clara no later then March 1. I said I was in good condition and doing a lot of walking in the woods and playing basketball at the Hebrew Association. "No basketball," he said. "That is in your contract when you get the time to read it. It is too dangerous. We do not mind if you walk in the woods. But we do not want you getting your teeth knocked out on the basketball floor," and I said if it was in my contract I would do what it said.

Pop went off in the school bus, but me and Jocko got in the 50 Moors, me behind the wheel. I reached down by habit for the gear, but there was none, for all you got to do is give her the gas and off she goes, changing gears by herself, yet plenty of pickup. The only time you think about gears is to put her in reverse, and then you press a button and she is set to go ahead backwards. We swung out towards town, and I worked up some speed, and Jocko said to me, "Without looking at the speedometer how fast are we going?" and I said I judged 60, and he said look, and I looked, and we was doing 75 and yet it was like we was barely moving a-tall. I hit 85 by the time we got to Perkinsville and waited with Jocko until the train come. He already had his ticket bought. I said I guess he *expected* to give the car away, and he said he did, and he laughed.

Afterwards it begun to dawn on me what happened—that I was a Mammoth at last, or at least a small cog in the system—and I went over to the "Clarion" like I always promised Bill Duffy I would if it come to pass, and I told him all that happened, and he wrote it down, and they made some pictures of me reading the contract, and Bill give me a top-notch write-up with a lot of pictures dug out of the file as well as some new ones they took, plus a picture of Pop and an article about him, and some quotations by

Jack Hand and Mayor Real and Mr. Gregory N. Oswald. I just about shoved basketball off the sporting section.

When I come out of the "Clarion" there was a number of kids standing around the car and gawking in the windows. The windows work off the dash, no need to crank them by hand like your old-fashion cars. I chased the kids away, asking them didn't they ever see an up-to-date car before.

The horn has 3 places you can press. Dead center it will play "Take me out to the ball game." But if you are bowling along the highway and some car is creeping along like a snail press down the left side of the horn and it plays "Lazy bones, lying in the sun." The third part plays "I love you as I never loved before," and the longer you hold your hand on the more it plays, over and over, "I love you as I never loved before since first we met upon the village green."

I pressed the switch and geared her in reverse, stopped for a little gas at Tom Swallow's and then done 80 all the way home.

When I got home I parked her in the shade. I went upstairs and sat by the window and looked down on her, and after awhile the shade from the tree shifted, and I went down and inched her over in the shade again. I begun to think I had swindled Old Man Moors. She is red with whitewall tires with treads that do not bog down in mud nor snow and will not skid on ice nor ever blow out.

That night in front of Holly's I blowed the horn all 3 different ways, and she come out to look her over. She has a light up front that you can spot on anything you want, and I shone it on her as she come down the walk, like a spotlight at a floor show, and I played the music, and she opened the door and the lights went on inside so you do not need to be fracturing your shins climbing in and out in the dark, and Holly got in beside me, and she said, "Henry the Navigator has now got the flagship of the fleet."

"I guess you was never in a boat like this before," said I.

"Way anchor," she said, and I asked her if she had ever rode 100 miles per hour, and she said no, and I informed her she was now about to do it, and she opened the door and begun to climb out. I laughed and coaxed her back in, and I backed her around and floated out on the highway, and I asked her if she had ever rode so smooth before, and she said no, and we rode along towards Perkinsville. I played the radio. It all works off the wheel, no need to be reaching down to the dash all the time. We got New York and Albany. Bing Crosby was on in both places, singing "White Christmas," and we circled around Perkinsville and then come home again. She was in a mood. She invited me in, and then when I got there she read to me out of a number of gloomy books.

About the middle of February I begun to get my things together. I oiled my glove and put new laces in my shoes and hung my Perkinsville suit in the sun to air. It looked funny seeing a baseball suit hanging on the line in the middle of winter. I bought a ticket to Aqua Clara. You pay your own fare and bring your own gear unless they keep you in the organization, which if they do they give you back your fare and you naturally get uniforms from whatever club they assign you to.

The days drug along, and finally I could not stand it no longer and decided to get moving all in a hurry. I was all jittery and excited and moving my bowels about 12 times a day. Vincent Carucci is the same way. Get him excited and half his free time he spends in the can. Many the long hour me and Vincent kept each other company in the clubhouse can last summer.

I went over the night before and said goodby to Holly, and then I come home and me and Pop gassed about 3 hours, and on the following morning, February 20, I got up at 5. Pop wanted to get up, too, but I made him stay put.

Everything I done that morning I thought how it would be the last time for awhile, brushing my teeth for the last time with my foot on the pipe like I always done and working the spigots of the sink for the last time and looking in the mirror whilst I shaved and seeing for the last time the nick I put in 1 side with the handle of a bat when I was a kid because I sometimes stood in front of the mirror posing for photographers in my imagination, and I dressed in the suit I bought at the Arcade in Perkinsville and thought was so sharp at the time, and overcoat and hat and scarf and shoes, all new, and I grabbed my bags and shot downstairs, ducking under the beam at the bottom step that when I was a kid I leaped for and sometimes just managed to graze with the tip of my fingers, and out I slammed.

Then I just about fell over. Who is standing by my 50 Moors but Aaron Webster! "Good morning, Henry," said he. "Off at last?"

"Oh no," said I. "I always carry 2 suitcases around with me at half past 5 in the morning for the sake of balance."

This was purely sarcastic, but he went right along with it. "Balance," said he. "I do hope you keep your balance in the time ahead."

"I will try," I said. I had only the skimpiest notion what he was saying at the time. "Holy Christ," said I, "it is freezing out here." It was about 5 degrees above and my teeth was beginning to chatter. How he stood it I do not know, standing there with nothing on but this raggedy green jacket about 25 years old that he always wears. I used to practically vomit looking at that jacket. Aaron never lets the weather bother him. If I am in that much shape at 80 I will consider the job well done.

"Yes, it is cool," said Aaron, "but I am planning no long discussion. I just come to give you a little gift." He dug down in his pocket. "Besides, it is 1 of my observations on life that old people cannot tell young people the score. We cannot pass along our knowledge. Young people must learn for themself. I am just hoping, Henry, that no matter if you fail or succeed in what you are about to try that you will keep your sense of humor. I also hope that you will keep your ways. You have always looked at things in a good way, finding the good things good and the boring things a bore. It would do no good for me to tell you that the bright world of glitter and glamor that you are heading towards is nothing but Graduation Night at Perkinsville High plus Tom Swallow's Texaco Station. It is all a lot of hardware tinsel to cover the fact of the bore."

"It is 25 of," I said. "The train is at 6."

"A great bore and a great fraud," he said. "Yet I wish you success, for that is what you want. I only hope you will bear in mind that success is never a matter of how many people slap you on the back on your winning days. You must also be on the lookout for the few good friends who will come around on afternoons that you been knocked out of the box."

"I certainly will," I said. Time was inching by and he had yet to hand over the gift. I suppose I may of been short with him, and I am sorry for that. But it was not until more then 2 years afterwards, riding the lobby in Chicago 1 evening, that it all flashed in my mind, and I said upstairs to Perry Simpson later that night, "Does it not strike you as queer that at half past 5 in the cold morning it was not Bill Duffy nor Mayor Real nor Mugs O'Brien nor Jack Hand nor Mr. Gregory N. Oswald that give me my send-off, but Aaron Webster in his raggedy green jacket?" And Perry said it struck him as queer sure enough.

"I brung you a little something," he said, and he give me a package all wrapped up, and I thanked him, and then he wished me luck about 9 times whilst I got the car started, and 1 minute later I was off and rolling. I done 75 clear to Perkinsville, parking the car in the slot in the depot that Gordon Heffel said was mine as long as I was gone. Gordon is the station master, a great Mammoth fan and a great personal friend of both me and Pop.

ON THE train between Perkinsville and New York I was dead from hunger and the diner shut tight. I would of give 10 dollars for breakfast right about then. Everybody was asleep all up and down the isles, slumped over in queer positions, and the man I was next to was grumbling away and adding up a lot of figures out loud until finally he woke and asked me where we was, and I told him we was about 30 minutes out of Perkinsville. "Where the hell is that?" he said.

"I guess you never heard of the Perkinsville Scarlets," I said.

"Sure I did," he said. "I suppose you are 1 of their players."

"I used to be," I said.

"I could of guessed it," he said. "You *look* like a ballplayer."

"I am a pitcher," said I.

We talked for a long time, and I suppose I told him my whole life history the way I been writing it here, though quickened up a good bit, right down to that very morning, and he asked me what was in the package Aaron give me. I clean forgot about it, and I reached up and took it out of my coat pocket.

In the package there was a money belt. It was made of waterproof leather with a zipper down the middle, and inside the zipper there was 5 bills of 10 dollars each, all green and crisp. He said I ought to put the belt on, and we went back in the washroom. There was a gang of men there, standing at the sinks in their undershirt, and this fellow give me a big build-up and told them I was going down to Aqua Clara to play for the Mammoths. Some of the men turned and looked at me, and 1 of them glanced me up and down and asked me if I did not think I was too undergrowed to get anywheres in baseball. We all got a good laugh out of that, for I was about twice as big as him and still growing. I could of stuck him in my pocket. Then this other fellow showed the belt around, and they felt the material and said it was the best, and I pulled up my shirt and strapped it around my middle, and they all admired it, and a number of them asked me if I was really and truly signed to a Mammoth contract. I did very little talking. This other fellow chattered away, telling them my life history like I told it to him. We had breakfast, and pretty soon we was under the tunnel and in Grand Central, and we said goodby, and he said he would look for my name in the papers, and I said no need to look too close, for it would be up in the headlines. Then he went 1 way and I went another and I have not saw that wretched bum since.

I shuttled across to the west side and down to Penn Station. I had a layover of about 2 hours, and I checked my bags and went across Seventh into the building where the Mammoths have got their New York office. The office had a glass door with a lot of names wrote on it that I never heard of before, and I went in and seen a girl typewriter, and she smiled at me, and I said, "My name is Henry Wiggen," and she said, "Yes, Mr. Wiggen. What can I do for you?"

"Nothing," I said. "I just come to see what the office looked like." I looked around. There was a big collection of pictures on the wall, a few baseball players but mostly a lot of men all dressed up sitting around the conference table, and there was a date wrote under each. The typewriter got up and disappeared out a back door, and soon she come back with a man, and he said, "Can I be of some help, Mr. Higgens?"

"Wiggen," I said.

"Can I be of some help?" he said.

"I was just looking," I said. "I am Henry Wiggen." He give the typewriter a look of puzzlement, and she give him 1 back, and I figured they did not catch the name, and I told them again, and the man asked me what my business was, and I said I was a baseball player. "It is funny I do not strike no bell in your head," I said, "for you have just signed me on. I am on my way down to Aqua Clara."

"Oh yes," he said. "Of course, there are a great many young men."

"But there is only 1 of me," I said.

"That is undoubtably true," he said, and he give the typewriter another look, and she begun to giggle. The man did not giggle. But he stood there like he was about to bust out laughing, and I said to them, "I would like to know what the joke is all about if you 2 clucks would have the common ordinary decency to tell me."

"There is no joke," said the man.

"Then why in hell are you laughing?" I said. "Does your underwear itch?"

"My underwear does not itch," he said. "Nothing itches, and I ain't laughing," and now the girl begun to giggle louder and the man got all red in the face. "The reason I am laughing," said the man, "is this," and he went over to the wall where there was 3 green cabinets, and he begun to slide some drawers out as far as they would go, and he run his hand up and down the papers in the drawer. "Records," he said. "Every 1 of these papers is a record on some kid that thinks he is another Joe DiMaggio or another Honus Wagner. They are just names. Your name is somewhere amongst them. How do we know who you are except just a name? You are but another name."

A cold chill went through me. It was like somebody opened me up and slid a long icicle in and sewed me over, and I did not say another word, but I turned and went out of there and down the elevator and in the street.

I got my bags and got on the train, and soon she started, getting away without hardly so much as a lurch, and then we was in the sunshine and out of New York. I craned my head around and looked backwards at the city, and the buildings was all silver and misty in the sun. I watched a long time, and then the city begun to sink behind, and I knowed there would be a time when you could go in that city and go up in any of them buildings and collar any 10 people you meet and ask them, "Who is Henry Wiggen?" and 9 times in 10 they would know, even though now I was nobody, and the farther we went the nearer I was coming to the dream I dreamed all my life from the first time I seen Pop pitch a baseball. We was barely in Jersey, and yet I was excited, and all around there was houses and people, and I felt sorry for the people, for they was not going anywheres. They was stuck. And I was on the move and off towards the bright life, and I felt like life never been life a-tall, but just some sort of time of waiting, and now it was beginning, and all the past was dropping back at 70 miles an hour and maybe more, all washed away out of my sight and out of my remembrance.

I ate 2 steaks in the diner and a heap of fried potatoes and pie and 2 bottles of milk through a straw, and I give the waiter the last dollar bill from the open part of my wallet where I kept the small stuff, and I told him who I was and where I was going, and he claimed he was a pitcher himself in his college days.

I changed trains in Washington, and it begun to grow dark in Virginia, the whole country spreckled with lights, and it was about now that my money begun to run out except for what I had in my belt. I guess I did not figure it right when I started, or else I spent it too much in 1 place. I had forgot that meals was so high on the trains, and then on top of that I was tipping just about everybody I set eyes on. A fellow in the washroom said you got to tip them, for that is the way they make their living, and I said I did not mind tipping so long as I had the money, and he said he did not like tipping noways but did not see how to get out of it.

Still and all it sometimes went too far. That night they grabbed a hold of my shoes and shined them up. I never asked them to, and besides they had a high polish on them to begin with. Then just about every time we stopped for a few minutes I would slip my coat on and go down on the platform for a breath of fresh air, and they would come along with a whiz broom and brush me off with 1 hand and hold out their hand with the other, and I would plunk down 50 cents. When my money begun to run out I would plunk down only a quarter. Pretty soon I was down to giving out dimes, and then they stopped brushing me off altogether.

I loaned my last 5 dollars out of my wallet to the girl in the bunk below. I was just about dropping off to sleep when she stuck her hand in through the curtain and shook me awake and asked me did I have a match. I told her I did not smoke. I said she could probably get a match from the porter for no more then 50 cents or a dollar. She said she did not wish to bother him. I said he was getting paid for the bother, and I was not, and I buckled up the curtain again and started back to sleep. She went and got a match somewheres and about 15 minutes later she woke me again, saying she was hungry, and I told her she come to the wrong place. "All I want is a sandwich," she said, "but I seem to have run out of money."

I said I would loan her a little if she would make herself scarce and let me get some sleep, and I give her 5, which was all I had except a couple dollar bills and some change and what was in the belt, and she wrote down my name and address, saying she would send the money, and by morning she was gone. The porter said she got off in North Carolina.

These porters are mostly good fellows, though liars. They are full of a lot of chatter about how many different colleges they been to and how many degrees they have got. To hear them tell it we have got more educated people riding around in sleeping-car washrooms then there is at Harvard and Yale lumped together. In the morning the porter brung me my shined-up shoes that didn't need it in the first place, and he give me a big line of cackle, hoping I had a good night in the sack and what a beautiful day it was, and I give him a quarter.

It seemed like overnight winter had faded out of the picture, and spring had come, and spring always sets my heart a-beating. The snow was gone off the ground and we was somewhere in North Carolina, and there was buds on the trees and barefoot kids outside the window, and brooks and streams was bubbling along, not all froze over like back home this time of the year. You could fairly smell it. In the diner I sat by the window and looked out at the spring that had come so sudden, overnight, and I could smell it even over the smell of the food, which is saying a good deal because I have got a good nose for food, and I could hear sounds like the sound of people cheering and the chatter of the infield and the voice of the umpire and the thump of the ball in the glove.

But I did not let even the spring get in the way of breakfast, and I ate up and paid for it with the last of my dollar bills, and the waiter said to me, "It looks like winter is over," and I give him 50 cents.

I went back through the cars to my place, and I sat there and looked out the window, and the more I looked the greener it become, and the more like true spring, and it must of been somewhere in the middle of the morning when I seen the first baseball of the year. It was in a town, and I guess a big 1, for we slowed some, and it was off in a sandlot close by to a schoolhouse, and there was an old rickety backstop full of holes, and there was a kid with a bat in his hands, and another kid throwing, and the thrower throwed and the batter swung and the ball went up in an arc behind where second base would be when the kids laid out their diamond later in the year. There was a lad behind second, and you could see by the way he run that the earth was soft, and you knowed he would not catch the ball because his mind was on his running, and he dropped it like I knowed he would, and then the train whooshed on and out of sight.

That was the first time I ever seen kids playing ball from a train. I have saw many since, and you always think when you see them that maybe right there before your eyes is some immortal of tomorrow, for 1 of the beautiful things about the game is that the immortals rise up from nowhere, and you think about it every time you see kids on a sandlot.

I kept a sharp eye out, but I did not see any more sandlots that morning, and about 11 I begun to make plans for lunch. I went back in the washroom and unloosened my shirt and unstrapped the money belt and took it out and stuck my shirt back in my pants.

There was an old fellow sitting there on a leather seat with a cigar in his mouth, and he watched me the whole time. "I guess you ain't the type that believes in taking chances," he said.

"It ain't that," I said. "It was give to me as a present by a friend back home. As long as I had it I figured I might as well use it as not."

"I do not blame you," he said. "The world is full of thieves." He set fire to his cigar and puffed a big blue cloud and sat back like he had said something real smart. "Everybody and their brother is crooked," he said. He looked me through and through like he was waiting for me to give him an argument.

"You are cockeyed," I said.

"I have been told the same thing before," he said.

"Then it is a wonder you are not yet wise to yourself," I said.

"Yes," said he, "I suppose it is a wonder." He puffed 2 or 3 more times on his cigar. It smelled like the St. Louis stockyards in August, and I told him so, and he took it out of his mouth and looked at it and let it die. "No doubt you are the ballplayer," said he.

"How did you know?" I said.

"I sit here and keep my ears clean," he said. "Since yesterday afternoon you have told about 2 dozen people that you are a ballplayer on this train. That is how I know. But you are not a top-flight ballplayer yet."

"I will be," I said.

"When you are a top-flight grade-A ballplayer you will not go around telling everybody," he said.

"You remind me of someone I know," I said, thinking of Aaron Webster, for he reminded me of Aaron, sitting there like everything there was to know in the world he was telling it to you now. I paid him no more mind. I went over to the sink and took off my coat and hung it up, and I hung the belt over the coat and washed my hands and face, and he sat there with the dead cigar in his hand, and he watched me. I could feel him watching me, and I said, "What in hell are you studying me for?"

"I am just wondering why you have got a money belt if you do not know no better then to hang it on a hook and then bury your eyes in soap and water," he said.

"Why not put the cigar back in your mouth?" I said. "I can stand the smell better then the gab," and he lit up and stuck it back in. Then I finished washing and dried off and unzipped the zipper of the belt and reached in. There was no money there.

My jaw dropped halfway to my stomach and everything begun to reel around, and it seemed like the train had suddenly took off from the tracks and started upwards to where the air was thin and you could not breathe. Things revolved and took on unusual shapes like in them mirrors in the amusement park in Queen City, and when they settled down again the old fellow was looking up at me, and I screamed at him, "Put out that damn cigar!" and he went over and run water on it, and it sizzled and went out. "Somebody has stole my money," I said. "There was 5 bills here of 10 each."

He was very calm. I guess it is easy to be calm when it is somebody else's money. "When did you last have it?" he said.

"Between Perkinsville and New York," I said, and I knowed right away who it was that took it.

"That is a big area," he said. "There is about 10,000,000 thieves all concentrated in along there. Have you got any more money?"

"I have got some change," I said. "I suppose I could send a wire home." The old fellow got up and put a penny in the machine and brung me a cup of water, and I drank it and soon begun to feel better. "What about my meals?" I said.

"You will only miss 2 meals," he said, "for we will be in Aqua Clara this evening."

"2 meals!" said I. "Maybe a skinny old gent like you can live all day on cigars made out of low-grade manure, but I cannot."

"Have you not ever gone without 2 meals?" said he.

"No," said I, "and I do not plan to begin."

"Well," said he, "come along with me and I will fix you up," and I said I could not dream of eating off a stranger, but he argued some, and I give in pretty quick I guess, and he bought me lunch and then again supper, and he give me an envelope with his name and address wrote on it for me to send him back the money in.

But I lost it and never mailed it, and I suppose he thinks I am a thief like the rest. The last I seen of him he was sitting by the window smoking his cigar when I got off the train that night at Aqua Clara.

9

THE camp was like a dream. It was night, and I could not see it too well, yet I could feel how big it was, and how it stretched away towards the beach. The moon shone down, and I could see the flat land beyond the barrackses where we was all to sleep, and the next morning I could see that the flat land was all baseball diamonds, 1 after the other as far as the naked eye could reach.

I walked clear through Aqua Clara when I got off the train. It was quiet, and I did not see many people on the street, and finally I come to the camp according to the instructions in the letter. It was an air field for the Army during World War 2, and then the Mammoths bought it from the Army, but it still had the fence around it the way they do to keep the spies out and the soldiers in, and there was signs directing you to the main gate, and I followed the signs, and there was a guard at the gate. "What is your business?" he said. He shone a flashlight in my eyes.

"I am Henry Wiggen," I said.

"Are you a ballplayer?" he said. "Leave me see your letter."

I took out my letter and showed it to him, and he checked me off on a list and told me I was in Barracks Number 10, Bed 5. "Ain't anybody showed up yet?" I said.

"No," he said. "There is 1 n----r. He is in the same barrackses as you."

I wondered who he was. I knowed before I ever seen him that the odds was that he was a good ballplayer. The reason is that 9 times in 10 your good ballplayer is your early ballplayer. It is true. I will sit in any clubhouse and watch, and I will tell you who are the strength of your club, for I will notice who comes early and stays late, and who hustles out and watches the other club drill and sizes them up, and I said to the man, "I do not know that fellow but I will bet you he is a pretty fair country ballplayer."

"Maybe so," he said, and he shone the light down the lane between the barrackses and flashed it on Number 10. "There is a light on your left as you go in," he said. "Good luck."

"Good night," I said, and off I went and in through the door of Number 10 and found the light and switched it on. There was about 30 beds, all made up for sleeping, all of them empty but Number 7, and I made a good deal of noise with my bags so as to wake him, and he woke and sat up in bed. He was all naked. He always slept naked, for it left his skin breathe. Yet when he was in the money he begun to wear pajamas. That was later, though, and now he was naked, and he give me a big smile and I give him 1 back, and he give me his name, which was Perry Simpson, and I give him mine, and I sat down on the edge of the bed marked 5 and pulled off my shoes and begun to strip down, and he watched me, and he said, "A southpaw."

"That is right," I said.

"Well then," said he, "you ain't in competition with me, for I am a second baseman."

"That is a lucky thing for you," I said. I undressed, and then I went down and switched off the light, and we talked a long time, and it turned out that Perry was straight from high school in Colorado where he busted all records, batting .675 the year before and running the 100-yard dash on the track team. He come away from school with more medals then he could use, and about 2 weeks after graduation was signed by Jocko Conrad, the same as me. He told me his whole life history, and then I told him mine. I was about halfway through mine when I heard him breathing deep, for he had fell asleep. But I did not care, for I was tired anyways, and it is no matter, for between then and now we told each other our life history back and forth many times over.

In the morning, when I woke, he was sitting on his bed and looking at me. The sun was shining in on him, and he was all brown and red and fresh from sleep, and his teeth was white when he smiled. He was sitting in his underwear, and I asked him if he was hungry, and he said he was, and I said I would take a shower and then we would go for breakfast, and I went down to the end of the barrackses and showered and come back and dressed. But he did not dress. I said, "If you are going to breakfast in your underwear you are not going with me."

"I do not think I will go to breakfast," he said.

"Are you sick?" I said.

"Maybe you will bring me some breakfast," he said, "for I cannot go on account of the regulations," and he give me a thermos that he kept under his bed amongst his gear, and some money, and I asked him could he loan me a dollar until I could lay my hands on some cash, and he give me 1 and I left the camp and went down about 4 blocks to a place called Aunt Jennie's Old Southern Fried Food Heaven which I remember the name because I took a menu and kept track on the back of what I owed Perry, and I ate 1 dollar's worth and with the other ordered the same for him and wrapped it up in napkins, and Aunt Jennie herself filled up the thermos.

After the camp got under way there was a regular cafeteria. It was run by the Mammoths in the building that was a mess hall during the war. They sold food there so cheap that it is a wonder old man Moors did not go broke. After about 10 days, when many of the rookies was cut loose, we all ate there as free as air, and Perry as well, but up until the time the camp got started he did not go out and eat on account of the regulations. Personally I think them regulations are pretty damn scurvy.

He ate all the hash I brung him. Then we went down to the latrine and set there awhile. By now the sun was out bright and strong, and we got in our suits. I put on my Perkinsville suit, and he wore an old uniform that he wore in the factory leagues in and around Denver. It was a little tight, for he had growed some over the winter. He had an old ball amongst his belongings, and we went out of the barrackses and over to 1 of the diamonds and begun to throw back and forth real easy.

There was nobody there but 1 fellow all bundled up in a rubber shirt. He was jogging along by the fence, and I did not get to see his face, and he did not look at us. He done about 3 turns around the field, and then he slowed down to a walk, and he walked very slow, like he was thinking deep, and then he come up behind me, but I did not know it, and he stood there watching us throw. I do not know what finally made me turn around, but I did, and it was none other then Sad Sam Yale.

"Sad Sam!" I shouted.

He just stood there. His face was wet, like he was fresh out of a shower, and he was breathing fairly heavy and all wrapped up in his rubber shirt with a towel around his head, and I could not think what to say, and I said, "Sam, you are fatter then in your pictures."

"God damn you," he said. "That ain't hardly exactly news."

"Sam," said I, "I am Henry Wiggen. I am a pitcher. I am proud to meet you," and I went over to him and took off my glove and stuck out my hand, and he took it, and he smiled a little with 1 corner of his mouth. "Perry," said I, "come here and meet Sad Sam Yale," and Perry strolled over very slow.

"I am pleased to meet you," Perry said.

Sam said to me, "If you ever get anywheres in this game remember that a good pitcher can kill himself in the winter time. I put on 15 pounds this winter and killed my damn self and maybe took 3 years off my playing days as well. I am an old man rushed in my grave by women and liquor. Give them the wide go-around and keep in the out of doors all winter."

"I know," said I, "for I read it in your book."

"Some day I have got to read that book," said Sam, "for I have got to find out where I done wrong."

"You have not done wrong," I said. "You are an immortal. You are a great pitcher, and if I am half as immortal as you I will consider that I done good."

"I have got to get back to the running," he said.

"A week of good hard running and you will be down to weight," I said.

That was not the exactly right thing to say. "God damn you!" he said, but he smiled a little and started off on a trot again, and me and Perry throwed some more. Soon I was loose. I felt like the middle of summer, and Perry said the same. "But we have got

to take it gradual at first," he said, and soon we stopped throwing
and went back to the barrackses. We showered, and we sung in
the shower. He said I had a good voice, and I said I must of got
it from Pop, and he said he bet Pop was a wonderful sort of a
fellow, and I said he was, and I told him all about Pop and all
about Holly and Aaron Webster.

I went down for lunch at the same place and brung back 2 whole
lunches all wrapped in napkins. I kept a close track of all the
money I owed Perry, and I paid him back later on. When I got
back there was 3 new fellows in the barrackses, just off the train.
Of these, 2 was later my close personal friends, Canada Smith and
Coker Roguski, and no finer men ever lived. I do not know who
the other was. He was missing half the teeth in his mouth. He
said the Mammoths was to buy him a whole new mouthful if he
made the grade, for it was all wrote up in his temporary contract.
He was a righthanded pitcher, and I seen him work in a camp
game a week later. I have saw better pitchers on the squad of
Perkinsville High, but I do believe that with a few years of experience this fellow might of become a fair Class C ballplayer.
These 3 unpacked their bags, and I said, "Leave us all go out and
throw a few," and Canada and Coker and Perry was all for it, and
this other fellow said, "I must stay here and get my gear in order,
and tomorrow I will start in to work. Tomorrow is time."

Well, there you have it! Tomorrow is always time enough for
your second-rater. Probably he is still fussing with his gear somewheres for all anybody knows. But what about Canada and Coker
and Perry and me that got out there and went to work right off
the bat? Where are we? Are we holed up somewheres in Class C?

We got out in the sun and loosened ourself playing 4-way catch.
Canada and Coker are infielders, and very stylish ballplayers. Coker
is a switch-hitter besides. He was born a righthanded hitter, but
he drilled and drilled, learning to hit both ways, and it paid him
off in the long run. The 3 of them made up the infield when we
was at Queen City in the 4-State Mountain League together that
year and then again the year after plus Squarehead Flynn at first
base. Squarehead is still there and will never rise higher. But a
better infield the Mountain League never saw nor ever will.

When we got back in the barrackses the place had filled up a good bit, for by now the lads was piling in on every train. Some come by car, many in a brand new Moors, and some by thumb, and some had rode halfway across the country by bus. There was a young catcher there that started out at Christmas. He would get to 1 city and work a week and then haul ass by bus as far as his money went and work another week and then light out again. He said he washed dishes in 9 cities betwixt Idaho and Aqua Clara.

In a few days most of the beds was taken, and the place was full of noise and chatter. It was the same in the other barrackses along the line. The newspapers said there was 600 of us.

On the Monday afterwards things begun in earnest. About 6 A.M. in the morning an announcement come over the loud speaker. There was a speaker set up in all the barrackses, and whenever there was something to say they done it from the main office in Number 1. "Hit the deck," it said. "Everybody up and at them. Everybody on diamonds 3-4-5-6-7 in shoes and shorts in 5 minutes." Then there was a big line-up down in the latrine, and then a great hustle and commotion to get over to the field, and we all lined up, me and Coker and Perry and Canada there amongst the first. For about 20 minutes we done exercises according to the loud speaker. It was cool when we got there, but we was all in a sweat by the time we was done. We done all kinds of exercises, giving every part of the body a thorough workout, and then we went back and got under the showers, and we sung, and me and Coker and Canada and Perry done a quartet, for we was all good singers. That was the first of the quartet, down there in the early morning in Aqua Clara.

Naturally there was some that never quite made it for the exercises. They stood in the sack, thinking they was putting 1 over on somebody. Here was this fellow without hardly any teeth laying there in the sack when we come back, and here was this dishwasher from Idaho, still in the sack, and many another all up and down the line.

Yet I noticed they got up when the call come for breakfast. Oh, they was the first on line. You can be sure of that. But they was not there ahead of me, for when the doors opened in I went. About the third morning when I went for my tray I felt a big push behind me, and it was none other then this fellow that had most of his teeth gone, and I swang about and asked him who he thought he was pushing around so early in the morning, and he said, "I am not pushing anybody but some green punk that calls himself a ballplayer."

"Who is a green punk?" said I.

"Henry Wiggen," said he.

"Time will tell," said I. "Time will weed out the punks from the ivory," and I turned back and begun to load my tray when the next thing I knowed this poor miserable character took me by the shoulder and spun me around and begun whaling away with both hands. What got in him I will never know. I sometimes think maybe when I said "ivory" he thought I was poking fun at his missing teeth. Or maybe it was just that everybody was on edge, and their nerves raw. Anyways, I covered up my face with both hands and went down in what Aaron called my old Coward Crouch and rained off what blows I could while Coker and Canada grabbed the boy and sat him down hard on the floor. It made me so nervous I could barely eat breakfast.

While I was eating a man come along and sat down opposite. He was not a ballplayer, for he was too old, and I did not know who he was at the time, and he said to me, "What was all the ruckus about?"

"There was no ruckus a-tall," I said, "but just some pitiful moron that is losing his nerve."

This fellow every little bit he would tug at his coffee, but for the most part he studied me and watched me eat. He was very red of face. You would of thought he just tumbled out of a Turkish bath. He had blue eyes and he laughed a lot, and it was Mike Mulrooney, manager of Queen City which is the Mammoth AA farm, the best they got. Old Man Moors is forever dickering for a AAA city but never gets 1. He did not look a-tall like his picture in the books.

"Why?" said he.

"Because I guess he just does not have the stuff," said I.

"Do you?" said he.

"Yes," said I. "It so happens that of all the ballplayers in this camp there is damn few worth much and still damn fewer yet that has got as much baseball in their whole body as I have got in my little finger."

He asked me what my name was, and I told him. He was very friendly towards me, and by the time breakfast was over I told him my past history, and then I said he would have to excuse me as I had to go back and get ready for the 9 o'clock drill.

"But it is just barely 8:15," he said.

"That is right," said I, "and I will be on that field by 8:30. I am a hustler. It is your hustler that wins ball games," and I, got up and left him and was on the field by 8:30, like I said.

Things begun to be less crowded soon after. In the beginning there was 600 or so. Mornings some of the Mammoths come over and give instructions in various specialties, infielders working with infielders, pitchers with pitchers, and so forth. I was hoping I could get a few pointers from Sad Sam Yale, but he was spending his time running and taking off the blubber. You could see him all the day, plodding around the field, first running and then walking. But after awhile announcements begun to come over the loud speaker calling 5 names at a time down to the Number 1 barracksses where the front office was, and these were the duds and the lemons that the coaches and the scouts reported on as being no damn good a-tall, not even for some Class D club. Most of them was never under contract to begin with. They was told to go away pronto and never come back. Some of them been told the same thing the year before, and some of them for 3 years running. Yet they would come back nonetheless, for they did not seem to know that they could never make the grade. The worse a ballplayer is the less able he is to size himself up. There was a catcher from Indiana let loose, and he bawled like a baby and claimed he would kill himself rather then face the folks back home, and the club put Mike Mulrooney on him, and Mike give that kid a good talking to and cheered him up for the time. Mike is a wonder at lifting your spirits. But the kid later killed himself by jumping off a bridge in Albuquerque, New Mexico, a Class C city in the West Texas New Mexico League.

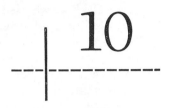

10

BY THE end of the second week there was only about 100 of us left in camp, these being the Mammoths themselves plus what would be the Queen City squad.

Of those cut loose there was not 1 that did not get a fair shake. No matter what you done it got wrote down on the charts or in film. Dutch is a great 1 for charts. They had a record on every pitch I throwed and every move I made, and a record of what I told Mike Mulrooney that morning at breakfast, and they knowed just who showed up for exercises and who stood in bed and who run off to town every night and chased the women and drank in the dives and played the dogs, and who stood in the barrackses and hit the sack. 1 afternoon there was a squad game amongst the Mammoths, and we was give the afternoon off, and I went over and watched the game, me and Perry and Coker and Canada, and the club knowed just who had the interest to go and who did not, and what kind of shape you was in, and the state of your eyes and your ears and your teeth. They knowed everything, and you never guessed it until the time they called you up to the office and told you your final fate.

That morning after I first met Mike Mulrooney at breakfast they brung a moving picture camera on the field and took pictures of the various pitchers. It was a long business, taking up a lot of time, and between times they ordered us up to an old airplane hanger and we seen a movie. Personally I thought it was a bore, and Perry said the same.

It opened with a man and a woman getting out of a new Moors.

The man was Lester T. Moors, Jr., himself, and his daughter Patricia. The boys whistled. He give a little talk, saying we would now see the history of America right before our eyes.

Then we seen this old-fashion sailboat, and people climbing a rock and cooking a turkey and fighting off the Indians, and later George Washington riding a big white horse whilst behind him come Americans in tatters and rags. Off in the distance we seen the British in red coats, for it was all in technicolor. The British looked tough, and myself I would of run like a bastard, but not Washington. He romped right up to them, and then the firing begun and the British went down like flies clutching their breast. Then shots of the war at New Orleans and Andrew Jackson on a white horse that looked like the same horse Washington had rode, and I said so to Perry and he laughed.

Between the various wars there was pictures of the map. First we was practically no bigger than Hungry or some such minor country, and then we took in all the territory out west. Then along come Abe Lincoln on an old-fashion train, writing down the Gettysburg address and then fading into smoke curling upwards from factories and the wheels all a-spinning and things coming off the factory lines that Perry said was like the Ford plant where he used to work in his summer vacations.

Soon come another war, and off went the marines, and they whipped them, the Spaniards I think. Who knows? And then another factory and more trains whizzing by, and cars on the highway—all Moors cars and shiny new Moors factories of course—and airplanes and the war in France and cannons, bombs and music.

Then there was some shots of Russia, and a more bedraggled lot of people you never seen. There was 1 poor old woman with a handkerchief around her head, walking along the road and praying with her hands folded on her breast. Then up behind her come a soldier on a white horse, and it still looked like the *same damn white horse* that Washington and Jackson had rode, and I said so to Perry, and he laughed again, and he come up behind this lady and whipped out his sword and walloped her over the head for no reason whatever.

When we come out it was raining. The newspaper in Aqua Clara claims that it never rains, and it hardly ever does. That was the only time but 1 that it rained to speak about in the 3 springs I was there. Every time it rains the City of Aqua Clara pays 1,000 dollars to the Mammoths.

The only other time it rained was 1 day after about 3 weeks, and that is a day I will never forget. There was less then 100 rookies still in camp. More then 300 been sent home and most of the rest was assigned to farm clubs. The rest of us was put down in 2, 3 and 4 barrackses. Mornings we worked out, and in the afternoon we broke up in teams and played amongst ourselves. I pitched 24 and ⅓ innings altogether and done better then any other pitcher in camp. Perry and Canada and Coker all showed up well, and we was riding high.

Then Mike Mulrooney called off about 20 names, and he took us over to the farthest diamond where the Mammoths always worked. When we got there it was raining a little bit, just a drizzly spray, and Mike told me to warm, and I done so with a kid name of Porkpie. Dutch Schnell come over behind me and watched me, and then Mike come and him and Dutch talked about the weather, wondering if it was too wet to play, and I turned around to Dutch and I said, "If you are not afraid of a little dampness you are in for an opportunity of getting a glimpse of your new 20-game winner."

"Well," said he, "that settles it, for I am willing to be swallowed in the sea if I will get a 20-game winner out of the deal." Some of the Mammoths beefed about playing in the rain, but Dutch called "Play ball!" and I noticed that 1 word from him put the lid on all complaints.

Bub Castetter was throwing against us. Bub was cut loose just this past year to make room for me. Somebody is always getting the ax for my sake—the batting-practice kid at Perkinsville, then Slim Doran, then a fellow name of Duckworth at Queen City, and finally Bub in May of 52. I suppose that right now there is somewheres a kid in short pants that will someday crowd me out. Perry Simpson led off for us and drilled a single into center, and he no sooner got on base then he stole second. However, we could not push him around. Canada and Coker both connected but flied to Pasquale Carucci in right, and Squarehead Flynn struck out to end the inning.

I went out to the hill. I cannot tell you how nervous I was. I scuffed my shoes on the mound and built myself the right kind of a toehold. Joe Jaros was coaching over behind third, and he yelled at me, "Let us go there, punk, for we wish to pile up about 8 or 10 runs before it rains down hard," and I did not give him so much as a look.

I got the sign from Porkpie, and I throwed high and hard to George Gonzalez, and it cut across his letters, and it was a strike. He stepped back out of the box and looked down at the Mammoth bench like he was saying, "Where did this kid get this speed?" and then he stepped back in and I throwed him another, and he swang and fanned the air, late, and he stepped back out again to think matters over, and the rooks on the bench begun to whoop things up, and they shouted out at George, saying, "What is the matter, Cuban? Have you never seen that kind of speed down there below the border?" and a number of things along that line. Then I struck him out with the screw.

It was not the best screw I ever throwed. In fact it was not too good of a 1 a-tall, for the ball was a little wet, and I asked for another, and Dutch said go ahead and pitch with the 1 I had. "Do you think this club is made of baseballs?" he said.

Porkpie give in and throwed the damp ball back to me. I tossed it back at the ump. "If you do not mind if a few boys get their skull broke it is no matter to me," I said, and the ump looked at Dutch, and Dutch said give me a new 1.

Lucky Judkins was batting second in the order for the Mammoths. As it happened, the new ball was a little bit wet and Porkpie did not have no more sense then to call for a curve, and the curve never broke, and Lucky spanked a single into right. Things was a little quieter down on our bench. Vincent Carucci come up. He bats left. There was some dimwitted kid in right for us, and he shifted over close to the line, and I waved him towards center about 10 feet, for I knowed that few hitters pulled any pitch of mine down the line. The kid in right did not do like I said. I got

2 strikes on Vincent with the fast ball, and then I wasted 1, and then he lined 1 into right that if the kid been playing where he should of he would of had it without hardly moving. He got 1 hand on the drive but could not hold it, and it went for a single and George moved to third and Sid Goldman come up.

Sid is from New York. He is a power hitter, though weak in the field, yet still and all the best first baseman in baseball except for Jim Klosky. We thought about walking him but then changed our mind, and he swang hard on the first 1 and missed. He cut a little upwards on the ball, and I noticed that and decided to throw high, and he swang again and missed again, and me and Porkpie talked it over. "Now we must waste 1," I said, "and maybe he will bite. Then we will fool him with the fast 1 again," and Porkpie said that was a good idea. I throwed just above the shoulders, very fast, and Sid give it the go-by. Things was going according to plan.

I got set to pitch. I checked my runners, and they was close, and I reared all the way back, almost to the ground behind me, and I let fly, and it was burning fast, right where I wanted it, and Sid swang, and he connected, and the sound sent my heart tumbling 65 miles an hour down in my shoes. The ball sailed upwards and upwards and out of the park across the street and clear over some damn house that was sitting there.

Now, I do not consider it no honor to be the pitcher that somebody hits the longest ball in history off of. But I might as well tell it straight. Besides, you probably read it in the papers since after the game the writers went down on the field and paced off the distance from home plate to where the ball fell in the back yard of the house across the street. There was big write-ups coast to coast, for that ball went 591 feet, breaking a record that stood for 31 years since Babe Ruth hit 1 in Tampa, Florida, off the Giants in 1919, good for 587 feet.

Well, these writers get in my hair. Did they consider that the wind was with it all the way? Did they consider that the pitch was so fast that it was no wonder Sid hit it so far? Did they consider that the ball was a good deal livelier then the 1 that was in play back in 1919? Did they mention in the papers that I almost struck

him out on the previous pitch? Did they mention that I had fanned
George Gonzalez? Did they mention that there was men on base
and I never took a full wind-up? No, they never considered none
of these things plus a few more I could mention. They consider
what they *feel like* considering. They send only the juiciest angle
back to their paper and leave out the rest.

But after it happened I was not thinking of this. All I was thinking was that this was it. I was through. Hail and farewell, punk,
there is always a job for you pumping gas for Tom Swallow. Mike
Mulrooney come down to the hill, and he said, "Well, Hank, maybe
this is just not your day. Why do you not go back and get under a
nice warm shower?"

Somebody tossed me my jacket and I slung it over my shoulder,
and I walked back across to the barrackses, across all the diamonds,
and it was 1,000 miles and I never looked back.

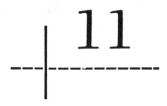

11

NOBODY can possibly imagine my misery that afternoon. All the people of my life swum before my eyes. I could see Pop, and he was sad, and I could see Holly and Aaron, and I laid on my bed and did not take my uniform off nor take a shower, but I covered up my head with my jacket, and I laid there a long time.

Soon the boys come trooping in. Lindon Burke had went in to relieve me, and he pitched the rest of the game. It only went six innings because the rain come down, and the Mammoths beat the rooks by 5-2. Lindon went up with the club that summer and is still with them as you know. Sad Sam pitched the last inning for the Mammoths. It was his first time out that spring and he set the side down 1-2-3.

My head was hid under the jacket, and I could hear them talking. Perry had got 2 hits and Coker 1, and the 2 runs we got Canada drove in with a triple, so it was a good day for them though misery for me, and they was talking and laughing. Then Perry seen me on the bed with my head hid, and he said, "Boys, leave us be a little quiet for Wiggen is asleep," and they tiptoed around, and they talked about me, and they said it was too bad I had not showed up better. It was like I was in a coffin and the people was walking around and whispering and saying, "It is too bad he has passed to the great beyond so young."

Then the loud speaker said dinner. There was a big rush of feet, and they all left, and I uncovered my head, and Perry was standing there looking down at me, and he said, "Dinner, Hank."

"I do not want none," said I.

"What is that?" said he. "Say it again, for I must not of heard right," and he picked up a towel and scrounged in his ear like he was cleaning it out. "Henry Wiggen does not want dinner," said he. "Then I guess they are giving away money free and the seas has dried up and they have elected me to the White House." Then he sat beside me and put his hand on my shoulder, saying things that you would say to a man when he is just about dead, and you tell him he will be up on his feet by tomorrow when already you have bought him a coffin and hired a preacher to speak at his grave.

"Get out of here," said I, and I pushed his hand from off my shoulder, and he went off to dinner and I laid there on the bed.

Soon in come a kid about 8 years old. He had a baseball in 1 hand and a note in the other. The note said:

Dear Mr. Wiggen,
This is the baseball that Mr. Goldman hit 591 feet off you this afternoon. Will you please put your signature on it if you know how to write, or your mark if you do not.
FAITHFUL FAN

"Who give you this?" said I to the boy.
"A man at the hotel," he said.
I took the ball and made an X on it and give it back to the boy. I do not know to this day who wrote it, probably Sam Yale or Swanee Wilks or 1 of their stooges—Knuckles Johnson or Goose Williams. Knuckles is a righthanded knuckleball pitcher. The knuckles of his hand stick far out. It looks awful when you look at it much. Goose is the second-string catcher. If you ever goose him he will howl blue murder. The boys have tried for years to get an umpire to goose him when he goes down in his crouch behind the plate, but they never will.

I stuck the note in my gear, and I have it yet. Soon the boys come trooping back from supper, and just about then my name come over the loud speaker ordering me down for a conference at the Mammoths office in the Hotel Silver Palms.

"What is the hurry?" said I. "They are going to do no more then tell me to clear out." I begun to undress and shower. Perry brung me a pie and a quart of milk and come down to the shower and give me hunks while I was under, and now and then a swig of milk.

"Leave us sing," he said, but I did not feel like singing. Besides, it never really sounds good except when you are all in the shower. I did not have the spirits to sing, and I dried and dressed, and every few minutes the speaker would speak, saying "Henry Wiggen. Where is Henry Wiggen?" and I shouted back at it, saying, "What in the hell is all the rush to fire me?"

"The fewer the better," said Coker, "for if you eat a meal or sleep in a bed it is costing old man Moors plenty because he is now down to his last 25,000,000 in the bank." This give us all a laugh, for it was about this time that Moors was setting up about 1 new factory a week in case of a new war. Old man Moors was hardly even finding much time to give to the club, most of the business handled by Patricia now, though he was down in Aqua Clara 2 weeks this past spring. Dutch says he would as soon he stood in Detroit.

"They ain't going to fire you," said Canada. I guess I knowed it too but got some kind of a kick out of feeling sorry for myself.

In come Mike Mulrooney. He was all dressed up. I had never saw him so dressed before, and I hardly recognized him, but you can never forget him once you hear him laugh. He laughs a great, rich laugh, and he shakes all over and his face gets redder then it was before. I had read a good deal about him in the books before I ever met him, and some of the writers called him "Laughing Mike." Yet there was never a 1 that did not have the highest respect for him as a ballplayer, and then when he was too old he went to Queen City and managed the club there, the Queen City Cowboys. He was laughing now, saying "Damn it, where is Henry Wiggen? Henry, have you not heard them calling you for the last hour on the speaker, and old man Moors in a fit of temper?" and he hustled me in my clothes and took me by the arm, and out we went. "He is waiting at the hotel," said Mike.

He come to town to see Ugly Jones, and he figured he might see a few more at the same time between planes. Ugly is the Mammoth shortstop, and every year he is a holdout. He was asking

17,000 and Mr. Moors said in the newspaper that Ugly could rot in Arkansas before he would get that sum, and finally they agreed to talk it over in Aqua Clara, and they had both flowed in that afternoon. Ugly got his name because he is so Ugly. He is married to a moving picture actor by the name of Linda Lee Harper, and a beauty she is, for I seen her in several pictures and later a number of times in the flesh.

"It seems to me," said I, "that you have not got to call in the boss himself just to can a man," and Mike laughed and told me not to worry about that.

Old Man Moors had a whole sweet to himself in the hotel. Mike went in, never even knocking, and I practically fell over from the smell of perfume. The first person I seen was Dutch, and I said, "Dutch, that is a mighty strong perfume you are wearing tonight," and Mike laughed and laughed. Nobody else laughed, though I thought it was rather a comical remark myself.

The top of the club was there, Mr. Moors and Dutch, and Egg Barnard and Joe Jaros, both Mammoth coaches, and Jocko Conrad the head of the scouts, and Bradley Lord the club secretary. They had a number of tables shoved together, and they all sat around them. They was all covered with papers and beer, and every little bit the bellboy would come in with a telephone, and then Mr. Moors would talk in it awhile, and then come back to us. Between them all they just come through a long session with Ugly, and he signed for 15,000 about an hour before.

Then I knowed what the smell of perfume was from, for in walked Patricia Moors. She is vice-president of the club. Her name is on the contract. She is the daughter of Lester T. Moors, Jr., about 30 years old and 1 of the most beautiful women ever seen, bar none. She come in through the door behind where they was all sitting and took a place at the table, and I looked at her, and her at me, and nobody said nothing, and then Mike introduced me to all the people, and I shook hands all around, and when I shook her hand it was all smooth and covered with rings, and her bracelets jangled on her wrist like a metal tag all a-clink on a running dog, and she drawed her hand out from mine very slow, rubbing it along my palm, or so it seemed at the time.

"This is 1 of the boys I want," said Mike to Mr. Moors.

"How would you like to play at Queen City?" said Dutch to me. Queen City is AA in the Four-State Mountain League.

"We will start you at 225," said Mr. Moors, "for we have had good reports on you all up and down the line."

The price sounded low. "Many of the AA boys I been talking to are getting lots better then that," I said.

"Ho ho," said Mr. Moors. "I see where we have got another problem on our hands. Are you 1 of them ballplayers that plays only for the money or are you 1 of those kind of young men that we wish to have in our system that is in there for the love of the game?"

"Well," said I, "anybody will tell you that I love the game, but Pop says never sell myself short. I am worth more then 225."

"He loves the game," said Mike. "I know that he loves the game."

"Who is Pop?" said Patricia.

"My pop," said I. "He was with Cedar Rapids in the Mississippi Valley League."

"Here is the thing," said Dutch. "You must not get the idea that you are doing us any favor in Q. C. You are going to Q. C. as a favor to yourself. A season or 2 under Mike Mulrooney will make a ballplayer of you."

"We are building," said Mr. Moors. "It is next year and the year after that we are aiming at. You are not yet ready. You are still not a ballplayer a-tall."

"I would not put it just that way," said Mike. "He is a very fine young ballplayer, but he has got his faults."

"Pop says I am just about the finished product," I said.

"Maybe Pop is not the final word in these matters," said Mr. Moors. "You have got to start considering Mr. Mulrooney in place of your pop, for he is in charge of you from now on."

"Leave us look at a few pictures," said Patricia. Bradley Lord jumped up out of his chair and run around the room turning off the lights. Then he run over to the movie camera and switched it on. Bradley is a frog. You know how a frog does. When he is sitting on the ground you give him a little touch on the behind and up he leaps and starts to run. If Mr. Moors or Patricia Moors is to say a word up he jumps and begins to do what was said. Naturally they don't go over and touch him on the behind, but it adds up to the same thing. 1 time in the Mammoth clubhouse I was sitting with Red when in come Bradley Lord, and he walked past, and Red said to him, "You are a frog. Did you ever think to yourself what a frog you were?" Bradley Lord said he never considered himself as a frog. "Yet at least," said Red, "a frog will sometime not jump when he is touched on the behind, for at least sometime a frog has got the sense to lay down and die and not be a frog no longer." He switched on the machine and throwed the beam against the wall, and it showed my name and the date, and there was pictures of me throwing. "Put her in slow motion," said Mr. Moors, and Bradley Lord done so. "Now, Dutch," said Mr. Moors, "tell this boy what is wrong with him."

"Watch yourself very careful," said Dutch to me. "Watch your left hand when you throw," and I watched, and he said, "See how your hand is all out in the open. The batter can see which way your fingers is wrapped around the ball. He knows what is coming. Sid Goldman says he seen your hand this afternoon, and that is how he knowed what was coming. He knowed it was not a curve."

I watched the pictures very close, and I think I seen what he said I seen. Yet I am not sure. For you must remember that I do not pitch in slow motion.

"That is terrible," said Mr. Moors.

"Very bad," said Bradley Lord. He turned off the camera and turned on the lights.

"Then there is another thing," said Dutch. "You cannot get by in the big-time on fast balls alone. In the camp games according to your charts you throwed all in all in 24 and $\frac{1}{3}$ innings a total of 366 pitches. More then 325 was fast balls. What is the exact count on the chart, Mike?"

"I do not believe in these charts," said Mike. "286."

"That is why we are sending you to Q. C.," said Mr. Moors. "Mr. Mulrooney will get you over your bad habits."

"Yet the salary is rather small," I said, "though I suppose I have got no choice in the matter." I was under contract, and once you are under contract you cannot get out of it.

"You have got to start at the bottom and rise," said Mr. Moors. "It is all a risk with us. Any minute you might get took by the goddam government draft or break a leg or fall off a train. Speaking of that, how do you stand in the draft? Perhaps you have a punctured ear drum or water on the knee."

"No," said I, "I am in the best possible shape."

Mike studied my chart. "Turned down," he said.

"Excellent," said Mr. Moors. "Why?"

"Fighting roils my bowels," said I. "I am a coward at heart."

"That is most excellent," said Mr. Moors.

"Do you belong to 1 of these crazy churches or something?" said Bradley Lord.

"No," said I. "I belong to no churches, crazy or otherwise. I do not even know for sure what I believe. Aaron Webster says when I find out what I believe I should do it but meanwhile sit tight."

"Who is Aaron Webster?" said Patricia.

"Goddam it," said Mr. Moors, "have I got to sit here all night and listen to this palaver? I am due back in Detroit in the morning. Give me the contract," said he. Bradley Lord give him the contract out of my envelope, and he shoved it across to me. The figures was all wrote in by typewriter. "Sign it," said he, "for I have got to see some other boys tonight. Do you realize that I have not yet had no dinner?"

I had not realized that, but I realized that *Henry Wiggen* had not had no dinner. I run my eye up and down the contract. I seen a reference to meals, saying we was to get 3 dollars cash every morning. I had ate nothing but a pie and a quart of milk since lunch that Perry give me whilst I was taking a shower. Then I thought of all the money I owed to Perry.

"Well," said Mr. Moors, "are you going to sign it or not?" I looked all around me. They was all looking at me, and I would look at 1, and he would turn away his head, all except Mike Mulrooney, and he said, "I think you are worth more. But it is not my pie to slice."

"Damn it," said Mr. Moors, pounding on the table, "I have not had my dinner and all this fuss and bickering is giving me the indigestion. I do not think I should of give Ugly Jones so much to begin with and I do not like to be robbed blind by every ballplayer that gets their foot in the door."

"I will sign," said I, "for 250 per month plus 50 dollars in cash right here and now on the spot, for I owe a good bit to Perry Simpson, besides which I have not had my dinner neither and have got a bigger belly then Mr. Moors." Mike Mulrooney laughed, and pretty soon they all begun to laugh. Mr. Moors whipped 50 out of his pocket and handed it over, and they scratched out 225 and put down 250, and I signed, and Bradley Lord signed as witness, and they said they would send it up to Pop to sign, too, for I was under the age.

Then I went downstairs and ate in the Hotel Silver Palms Grill, and then I went back to the barrackses and give Perry his money in full and told the boys what happened, and then I went to sleep.

About midnight Coker Roguski woke me up. They all been over for a conference—Perry and Coker and Canada and Lindon Burke—and they was all assigned to Queen City along with me. Lindon was recalled that summer, too soon I think, and I do not think he will ever really hit the heights within him. Lindon needs to be mothered like a baby, and there was never nobody but Mike willing to give him the time. "We should have a good celebration," said Lindon. "Leave us all go get a beer."

"I do not want the beer," I said, "but I could go for a bite as I ate my dinner too fast in the excitement." Then we all went back to the Hotel Silver Palms Grill, all except Perry Simpson.

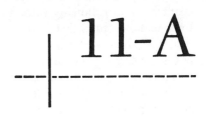

11-A

IT IS now 3 A.M. in the morning, and I am disgusted. It is a very cold winter night out, and I have got a fire in the fireplace.

I begun this book last October, and it is now January, and I doubt that I am halfway through. I will give 1 word of advice to any sap with the itch to write a book—do not begin it in the first place.

I got 12 chapters wrote on this blasted thing and it was not easy. My hand does not grip a pencil so good, for it is rather large, and I went and bought a couple big fat pencils called an Eagle number 4 from Fred Levine that does not make my hand so tired. Fred is still rather cool to me.

After I got through the 12 chapters I bumped into Aaron yesterday morning, and he said, "Well, Henry, I do not see much of you any more. Ain't you afraid of putting on weight staying indoors like that?"

"I have wrote 12 chapters," I said, "and lost 12 pounds at the least."

"I admire your get up and go," he said.

"Get up and go hell," said I. "It is the sit down and stay that gets books wrote," and he got a great laugh out of that.

Well, like a fool I stood there gassing with him, and the next thing I knowed I promised him that if him and Pop dropped over tonight—that is, *last* night—I would read the works out loud. Then I went back and polished up number 12 a bit, and in the evening me and Holly slung sandwiches and coffee together, and about 7

Pop and Aaron come. I begun to read out loud, starting with chapter 1 and following through in order, though here and there I skipped over parts that seemed too personal to mention. I did not read the pages concerning me and Thedabara that night, nor the pages concerning me and Holly. Holly knows it's there, though, and says okay, and Thedabara will never know the difference because I doubt that she ever looked at a book since Perkinsville High and ain't likely to take up the habit now. I left out the swear words, too, for Pop's sake. He gets all red when you swear around him around women.

Every so often they would laugh, and then again they would sit so still it was like if it would of been a book it would of been 1 of those that you can't lay it down. Sometimes when they laughed they would laugh in the wrong spot, though.

After number 6 Holly called the halt for food, and we all drifted in the kitchen, and afterwards I begun to read out loud again, burping most of the way through 7, and when I got through with number 12 I said that was all I done to date.

Nobody said a word. They all just sat there, and I said, "Do not be bashful. Say anything you want, pulling no punches," for to my mind it was all very good. I damn near broke my hand doing it. Finally Holly was the first to speak, and she said, "The first 11 chapters is just about right, but number 12 is too long."

Now, if that was not a dirty crack! Of all the chapters number 12 was the 1 I was proudest of, for it run 73 pages on both sides of the paper, and I done it in less then a week. If that is not some kind of a record I will be mighty surprised.

"Yes," said Aaron, "I think number 12 is too long."

"Have you ever wrote a book?" said I to him.

"No," said he.

"Well then," said I, "why are you so quick to run down what another writer did?"

"That is not the proper attitude on your part, Henry," he said, "for we are gathered here for the purpose of being helpful. I agree with Holly that number 12 is too long. But we must take it apart and see *why* it is too long and how we might cut it down and aim it to the point."

"Well then," said I, "half of it is wrote on yellow paper and half on white. Leave us throw out all the yellow," and I took all the yellow and tore it in 2. However, I tore it so as to be able to paste it up again, for I will be damned if I will write 73 pages front and back and take a week doing it and bust my hand besides and then just heave it out.

"No," said he, "that is not the way to go about it."

"Very well," said I, "then we might just as well forget the whole thing and skip number 12 and start in on number 13."

"In my opinion," said Aaron, "all that is wrong with the chapter is that it has got too much material that does not belong. It is up to us to try to decide what is good and what is too much."

And then it all begun, and the sum and total was this:

First off, I had wrote 9 pages front and back covering the time from when we broke camp at Aqua Clara to the time we arrived in Queen City in the Four-State Mountain League AA. I give an excellent picture of all the cities we went through, all the games, and the view that you got coming down off the slope of the mountains into Q. C., and then I told a good bit about the type of a place Q. C. is and the Blue Castle Hotel, which was the headquarters of the club when we was at home. "That is too much space to give to things of such little importance," said Aaron.

"That is a lot of rubbage," said I. "If you have got the sense to think back on chapter 11 you will remember that it run 9 pages front and back between the time Sid Goldman hit the home run, about 3 o'clock, until midnight. That is 9 pages covering 9 hours, while this is 9 pages covering 3 *weeks,* so it seems to me that you are the slightest bit cockeyed in your calculations."

"But the things that happened in number 11," said he, "was important things concerning important people such as the remarks of Mr. Moors. I actually think that the whole exhibition trip could be knocked off in 1 page." Well, I finally agreed.

Then I done 9 pages front and back about Mike Mulrooney, telling about his family which I met in Q. C. and his whole life history. Part of it I copied out of a book called "Forty-One Diamond Immortals," but mostly it was my own writing. I give him a great build-up, for he is 1 of the grandest men that ever lived. That is just what nobody liked. Holly said, "About 1 dozen times you said Mike Mulrooney is 1 of the grandest men that ever lived. That is not saying anything."

"The hell it ain't," said I, "for if you knowed Mike you would say the same."

"I do not say that Mike is not all you say," said she, "but you must tell us why."

"Because he *is,*" said I. "Because he does not wish to run the whole show but just live an easy going life and not worry you ragged about setting the whole world on fire. Because if you make a mistake he will not eat you out in front of all the rest nor give you the icy glare every time he runs into you in the hotel. He will stand by you and not go about talking behind your back. He will treat you all the same, no matter if you are on the way up or the way down, for he takes the attitude that if you are not the greatest ballplayer in the world still and all you are a human being. He is not a frog," said I, "that goes about kissing the ass of every writer and every club official and everybody else that he thinks can do him any good. Mike says if they do not like the way he runs his club in Q. C. he will go back to his ranch in Last Chance, Colorado, but he will never stoop down to where his head is lower then his shoulders for the purpose of getting a brown nose."

"Excellent, excellent," said Holly, and up she jumped. "You have told us more about Mr. Mulrooney right there then you done in the 9 pages of Chapter 12 concerned with him."

"Rats," I said.

Then Pop throwed in. "Here is what they mean," said he. "It is like a baseball game. If you was to pitch a ball game and win it by a score of 1-0 would you tell me how it went inning by inning, every foul ball and every little detail along the way? No, the main thing is how was the run scored and what particular scrapes you was in."

"Very well," said I, "out goes the 9 pages on Mike."

"Then there is the description of all the cities of the league," said Aaron.

I done 16 pages front and back on the different towns of the Four-State Mountain League, and I thought I done a fine job, and Aaron said, "Yes, you done a fine job. Yet it is like your pa says.

It is not to the point. You do not need to tell us about the cities, for we know all about them. I have never seen a 1 of them, yet I know what they are like. They are like Perkinsville. They are all the same."

"They are all different," said I. "In some you have got the mountains, and in others you have not, and in 1 place you will have a fine and modern ball park while elsewhere it will be an old park."

"But they are talking about building a new 1," said he.

"Why yes," said I. "Naturally."

"And in every town you was in you walked about on the main street," said he, "and then you got tired and went back and laid in the hotel. You and Coker and Canada and Perry."

"Yes," said I. "You guessed it."

"You said to 1 another, "This is a dull town and there is nothing to do until game time," and you laid on your bed in your shorts, and you talked about everything, baseball mostly, and you told each other over and over again your whole life history."

"Why, yes," said I.

"In Salt Lake you went and seen the big tabernacle, for that was where everyone told you to go. In Denver you went and seen the capitol with the big gold dome on top, and you also took a trip through the mint, for that was where everybody told you you must go in Denver. In all the cities you admired such places as these, though as a matter of fact you thought they was rather a bore. So after awhile you went over and laid in the park, and you fed the squirrels and birds and looked at the girls, and after awhile even *that* become a bore. There was the railroad station and the hotel, and each was the same as the next and it got so you could not hardly tell them 1 from the other."

"Yes," said I, "that is about the way it was. Yet they was all different."

"No," said he. "No, they were not. For they was all about like Perkinsville. There was a Legion club in Wichita, and you hung at the Legion club, and they made a big fuss over you. Maybe they even give you a dinner."

"They did not," said I. "It was the Chamber of Commerce of Queen City that give me the dinner."

"They sung songs to you," said he. "They sung For He Is a

Jolly Good Fellow, For He Is a Jolly Good Fellow, and they give
you a wrist watch."

"They give me a traveling bag," I said.

"With your name in silver," said he.

"With my name in silver," I said.

"They are all the same," said he. "There is no need to have so
many pages concerning the cities."

I give in. Out they went.

There was a long letter waiting at the hotel when I hit Q. C.
the second summer from Thedabara Brown, broke in Sacramento
and wishing she could see me in Q. C. I copied it down, 5 pages
front and back, and nobody could see the sense in putting it in.
"There will be nothing left," I said. "You are blasting away my
chapter until there is nothing left but air. It was 2 whole summers.
You cannot skip over 2 whole summers in a couple pages."

"I am after the high spot," said Aaron. "Never mind the mail
of little Miss Brown. What was the very biggest thing about the
2 summers at Q. C.?"

"I guess," said I, "the big thing is that I shook off my greenness
and got myself ready for the big-time."

"Ah," said Aaron, "now we are getting somewheres."

"If so," said I, "we are getting there in reverse gear. It took
up 4 days of my time to write the 39 pages that you have just
throwed out like it was so much wrapping off a load of fish. It
took me 1 whole afternoon alone to put my hands on the letter
from Thedabara Brown and then copy it down, plus a whole morning copying out the material on Mike Mulrooney from "Forty-One
Diamond Immortals," holding the book in 1 hand and writing it
all down with the other. That is how you do everything—backwards and in reverse." I would not of stood for it, but we had
another break for coffee and sandwiches, and Pop said he thought
they was right in connection with Chapter 12.

"You take that business with Lindon Burke," said he. "That is
too much on that."

I had give 12 pages to Lindon. He is a fine fellow. In July of
the first summer Mike got a telegram from New York, asking for
Lindon right away. The Mammoths was flagging at the time, and
Dutch was of the opinion that they needed a righthander for relief,

maybe for a starter, though it was my opinion then and still is that the Mammoths have always had *too goddam many* righthanders. Nonetheless we was all glad for Lindon. We had a big celebration before he went. We was in Denver, and we beat Denver that night, and Lindon's train was not until morning, and we stood him a dinner at Boggio's. We all made speeches. I wrote down what I could remember of each 1, for each and every 1 was a dandy. Then I copied down the menu, for I swiped 1. It was signed by everybody who was there that night. The last speech of all was that of Mike Mulrooney, and after he finished he give Lindon the present we bought, consisting of a silver bracelet with his name. Then we all started in to sing, "Stand up, stand up, stand up and show us your ugly face," and he stood up and begun to speak. But he could not speak, for he was bawling, and the tears was racing down his cheek. Then Mike got back up, and he was laughing, and he said, "Lindon need not make no speech. Instead of that, he must win the first game he gets to pitch up there in the big-time, for after all he is a pitcher and not an after-dinner speaker." Lindon shook his head, meaning he would do it, and sure enough he done it, beating Washington the first full game he pitched, and that night we got a wire saying "I done it, and I am thinking of all you boys," signed Lindon Burke.

"Very well," said I to Pop, "I will trim that down."

"You could also chop out the amusement park," said he.

I done 8 pages concerning 1 afternoon me and Perry and Coker and Canada went to Mountaineer Park in Q. C. For a dime you could throw 3 baseballs at wooden bottles stood up on a barrel, and if you knocked them all off you got a prize. "If I cannot knock them bottles off," said I to the boys, "I will turn in my suit and go home and pump gas," and I got up close, and I throwed, and I will be damned but I could not knock them off.

Then Perry give the man a dime. He did not get up close but went off to the side a bit, and he bent down like he was fielding a ground ball, and then, still in the bending position, he flipped in with that little snap throw a good second baseman knows how to make, and he clubbed the bottle dead center, and off they all went. The man give him a prize, consisting of a raggedy doll.

Then I said to the man, "Give me 3 more, and here is your

dime," and I took the balls, and I said, "How far is it from that barrel to this here counter?" meaning the place you was to throw from.

"About 6 feet," said the man.

"Well then," said I, "I will pace off 54 more and make it an even 60," and back I went. There was people passing back and forth up and down the midway, and I said, "Out of the way, folks, unless you wish to be beaned," and the people lined up to see what was going on. I throwed from the 60 feet, which is the regular pitching distance, and I tagged the center bottle on the nose, and off they all went, and Canada collected my raggedy doll and I come down and flipped the man a dozen dimes or more and went back to the 60 feet. About 2 throws in 3 I turned the trick. There was quite a big crowd gathered around, and the bigger the crowd the hotter I am, and Perry and Canada and Coker gathered up my prizes. I must of spent 4 dollars in dimes, and we had about 50 dolls and wind-up toys and candy canes and balloons and circus masks and glass jugs and a little red fire engine and a bowl of goldfish, and I give it all away to the kids except a couple candy canes that I ate myself. It warmed me good. That night I shut out Omaha.

"Why," said I to Pop, "it was a good time and ought to be in."

"Son," said he, "as long as you are doing it you might as well do it in a straight line. Aaron and Holly have read many books and know how they ought to be wrote."

"They do not know center field from the water fountain," I said. "They make me dizzy. What is the sense of writing a chapter for them to tell me chuck it out the door?"

"Now," said Aaron, "we was saying that the big thing about the 2 summers in Q. C. was that you shook off your greenness and was getting ready to go up to the big-time." He never forgets what he was saying. He will meet you and pick up the conversation he was snarled up in 3 weeks before, after you had forgot all about it.

"Right," said I.

"Just what is left?" said he.

I shuffled through the pages, and there was nothing left but 14 pages front and back regarding Coker and Canada and Perry. We was the closest of buddies in Q. C. If someone was to come looking for 1 all they need do is find the other 3. We was either in Perry and my room or Coker and Canada's, or else the coffee shop, or else we was somewheres out on the town, whatever town it may be, walking along and seeing the sights.

The only other place we could be was at the park, and we always went there together, and we had our lockers 1 next to the other, and we would dress and then go out on the field together. If it was not my day to work I might take a turn at first base during the infield drill, for Squarehead Flynn would leave me do so. He is a prince of a fellow but still with Q. C. He will be there till he is old and gray.

When I worked it was a pleasure to have that infield behind me. Ground balls was sure outs. Then, too, Coker and Perry was a grease of lightning on double plays, and Canada down at third had no little hand in double plays himself. They set a record for the Mountain League in that department the first summer, and they busted their own record the summer after.

After the ball games, in the clubhouse, the 4 of us sung together in the shower. I wrote out all the songs we sung, such as "I Love You As I Never Loved Before," "Some Enchanted Evening," "Going to Wash That Man Right Out of My Hair," "The Good Old Summertime," "Sweet Adeline," "Down by the Old Mill Stream," "Meet Me In St. Louis," "Goodnight, Irene," "White Christmas," "God Bless America," "A Bicycle Built for 2," "Old Black Joe," "My Old Kentucky Home," and some songs that Coker sung back in the coal mines of West Virginia, and it took up 7 pages front and back. That was a good deal of work.

Nonetheless Aaron said it had no place in the book. "For God's sake," said I, "they was the best infield the Mountain League ever seen and if it was up to you they would be slid over without hardly a mention."

"Just exactly what is a double play?" said Holly.

I leaned forwards and put my head down on my arms.

"Go ahead and tell her, Hank," said Pop, and I lifted up my head and begun to explain.

"The most usual type is when you have a man on first," I said.

"Then the batter hits a ground ball to the infield, and the infielder scoops it up and tosses to second. That gives you a force on 1 man. Then the second baseman or the shortstop, whichever took the throw, he rifles it down to first base. If it gets to first base ahead of the runner you have worked the play. You have got 2 men out on the 1 pitch."

"That does not sound hard," said Aaron.

"It is a beautiful play when done right," said I. "It is harder then it sounds. The average ballplayer can get from home plate to first base in 3 seconds. A fast man can do it in less. So you have got 3 seconds to field the ball clean, fire it to second, make the play there, keep clear of the runner, pivot and throw to first. That is a lot of work to do in 3 seconds. The shortstop and the second baseman have got to be like a fine machine, working together to the split of a second. They have got to know each other like a book. It is like they was 1 and the same man, not 2 different men. That is how Perry and Coker works, like they was 1 and the same man. It is beautiful. Then, too, it is a great help to any pitcher. It saves wear and tear on him. A good double play combination around second base will save you many a ball game. It can win a pennant for you or lose it."

"All this brings us to the very point of the whole discussion," said Aaron.

"I must say it is about time," said I, "for it is now 2 o'clock in the morning and we have jawed away at this thing for 7 hours. There is nothing left."

"There is still the main point left," said Aaron. "You have jammed it all in 1 sentence, but it is the main point," and he picked up 1 half of the last page that I had tore in 2, and he read what I had wrote. He read: "Well, the outcome was that I went up to the Mammoths in September of the second summer, and I pitched 1 inning in relief against Boston."

"You might just as well throw that out, too," said I, "for you cannot have a chapter that has got only 1 sentence in it."

"Yet that is the big point," said he, "for that is what you were aiming at from the time you first took a baseball in your hand. The rest of the chapter is full of dead matter that leads you nowheres."

"I will not write it over," said I. "I should of never begun it. It is chapter 12 and that is a bad number for me and always was." "That is up to you," said he. "If you wish to leave number 12 out of your book it is your right to do so. However, it seems to me that whatever chapter follows 11 ought to be about when you was sent up to the Mammoths." "Tomorrow," I said. "I will do it tomorrow. I thank you all for your wonderful goddam help."

Aaron and Pop went home, and I was tired, and yet I could not calm down and sleep. I lit the fire in the fireplace and shaved a new point on an Eagle #4. I thought I would write a few minutes and then turn in. Yet when you get to writing you run on and on, and it is hard to stop, and I have wrote 14 more pages front and back and *still* not got into the main point, which is when I went up to the Mammoths. I will do it tomorrow—that is, tonight. It is now daylight and I must first get some sack.

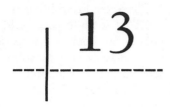

13

WELL, the outcome was that I went up to the Mammoths in September of the second summer, and I pitched 1 inning in relief against Boston.

The word come on a hot afternoon. Me and Perry was laying on our beds in our room in the Blue Castle Hotel in Queen City in the Four-State Mountain League when in come Coker and Canada in their shorts and bare feet. Canada said it was so hot he had took 4 showers since noon. Coker said you would never know what hot was until some summer's day you was down in a coal mine in West Virginia, and then you would know.

"I will tell you what hot is," said Perry. "If you was ever to be in the Ford Rouge plant of a summer's day you would know what hot is. When I lay me down here and I think it is hot I say to myself be thankful you are laying here in your under drawers with this pitcher of ice water in your hand and be glad you are not back in the Ford plant." He took a drink from the pitcher, and he passed it to me, and I drunk and I give it to Canada. "I only hope I can save my money and never go back to the factory," said Perry.

Just then in come Mike Mulrooney, manager of the Queen City Cowboys and 1 of the grandest men you will ever meet. He taught me more baseball then any man before or since. Pop set me up and Mike put the finish on. When I went to Q. C. the summer before I was a fair enough country ballplayer, and when I come away I was big-time, and Mike said, "Well boys, leave us phone down and have them send up some steam heat." This give us all a big laugh, for Mike was always ready with a joke. He flopped down in a

116

chair and begun to fan himself with the newspaper. We sat, and we waited for him to say what he come to say, for Mike seldom come just for the visit. He always come for a purpose. Maybe he would come to tell of a fault he seen in 1 of us, or he would come and wise us up on some trouble another fellow was having. He might say, "Now boys, I want you to help me out with Squarehead Flynn," meaning Squarehead Flynn the first baseman. "I do not think it is kind to Flynn to call him by the name of Squarehead, so if you boys will just call him Flynn or Bob it will be a big favor to me." We done it when we remembered, though "Squarehead" seemed to fit perfect. But if Mike Mulrooney was to ask it you could never refuse. Still and all he never jumped right into the business of his visit, and we always waited, and he would talk about the weather or last night's ball game or some old-time remembrance, and on this day he said, "I do not call this hot. Nowadays the ballplayer has got things better. It is cool at night, and we play so much at night nowadays, and the trains and the hotels is air-condition. I will tell you what I call hot. I remember double-headers in St. Louis when it was 110 in the shade."

"What would you say is the hottest city of all?" said Canada.

"St. Louis," said Mike. "Washington is close. All of them is hot. I remember hot days everywhere. Yet I was always a good hot weather ballplayer."

"The hotter it is the better Pop likes it," said I.

"I have played ball in cold and snow in Boston and wet and dry and thunder and lightning. I once played ball in the flood in Cincinnati. But the worst of all is heat," said Mike. "However, I did not drop in for story hour. The reason I come is because I just heard from Dutch." He took a wire out of his pocket and handed it to me. It was the wire I was waiting 20 years to see. It said:

R. DVA 165 SER PD WUX NEW YORK 12 1158A
MICHAEL J. MULROONEY
      BLUE CASTLE HOTEL
                    QUEEN CITY
SHIP ME WIGGEN FASTEST
          DUTCH

I have got the wire yet, and I could not believe my eyes, and the other boys come around behind me and looked, and Canada give a whoop and shot out the room and spread the news around. I sat froze to my bed, and the first 1 I saw was Pop in my mind, and I said, "I must send a wire to Pop."

"I have sent 1," said Mike.

"I better get moving," I said, and I begun to cram things in my bags.

Mike laughed. "Do not be in such a hurry, Hank. I have got your plane reservations for 11 tonight," and I sat back down, and Mike said, "I hope it is the right thing."

"I am ready," said I.

"Yes, you are ready," said he. "But you have still got many things to learn." He fussed and fidgeted, and finally he said, "I will tell you the truth, for you will hear nothing but lies from now on. You are a natural ballplayer. You have won 21 games this year. You are a regular horse for work. Yet you have got things to learn. When you get up to the Mammoths there will be 1 man that will be no end of help to you."

"That is Sad Sam Yale," said I.

"No," said he, "it is not Sam. Do not listen to a single word said by Sam Yale. Do not play cards with him. Do not drink with him. Do not lend him money nor borrow any. If you see him with a woman put that woman down in your book as a tramp, for if she is not a tramp at the start Sad Sam will make her 1. Everything that Yale touches will turn to shit. Except only 1 thing, and that is a baseball. When he is pitching you must glue your eyes to him and never take them off. You must learn to watch him and never listen to him, and you will learn much about baseball and much about life."

"Then who is the man that will help me?" said I.

"That is Red Traphagen," said he, meaning the Mammoth catcher. "When he says something that has got to do with playing baseball you must hang on his every word like it was the word of God. He is the smartest ballplayer in baseball today. If he did not have so much respect for his own personal self-respect he would be in line to be a manager. But he will not brown-nose. On the ball field he will talk only about baseball, and you must listen. If you can remember to do it write it down afterwards and study it once in a while. But when you are off the field do not pay him no more mind then if he was a pillar or a post. He is all full of chatter and nonsense. He does not believe in God. That is 1 thing I hold against Red. A ballplayer must believe in God." Mike was quite religious himself and went almost every Sunday. I did not know if I believed in God or not. I rather suppose I did not, but I said nothing.

I said, "It is sad to me to hear what you say of Sad Sam Yale."

"Yes," said he, "it is sad. It is always sad when a great ballplayer goes wrong as a man. I am not telling you these things out of anything personal. I am telling them to you because I want you to be a great and immortal ballplayer. You have all the makings. You learn fast and never forget. But never listen to Sam nor the men that is his pals. If they was once good in their heart they are good no longer, for Sam Yale has did them in. Steer clear of Knuckles Johnson and Goose Williams and Swanee Wilks." Mike grabbed the water pitcher and took a swig, and then he took some ice from the tray and dumped it in the pitcher and sloshed it around. "There is nothing more to tell," said he. "Remember that the parks will be bigger then in the Mountain League. But do not let this make you over-confident. Do not relax too much at first. When you are in trouble rely on your curve and forget the fast 1. Do not forget that the boys you will be throwing against will be hitting harder then any you have ever faced. Remember that you will be throwing against the very best ballplayers in the world. True, some of the best ballplayers in the world will be on your side, too.

"Henry, I will tell you the damn truth. The damn truth is that I can tell you no more about baseball. You are already a fine young pitcher. When you are up there you will be playing the same game you been playing all your life. The ball will be the same, and the bases will be the same 90 feet apart, and there will be 9 men to a side, and the game is still decided by who scores the most runs. The main thing is not half so much the other teams but your own men that you will be playing with and traveling with and be close to every hour of the day from February to October. I have told you what I know about the men. The rest I do not know so well. They are young men. Let me see," and he leaned back and begun to reel off the men on his fingers. "The Carucci brothers, they are Roman Catholics of the Italian race, and good boys, and they stick together. I do not know them, nor I do not know Lucky Judkins, for he is young and new. Scotty Burns and Sunny Jim Trotter is the rest of the outfielders. They do not mix in with the rest. They stay to theirselves and sometimes I think this is best.

"Ugly Jones and Gene Park are steady hands. You can depend on them. I do not know Goldman or Gonzalez. Gonzalez does not speak the language, and he is just as well off. They are the kind of young men that Dutch is trying to build a club around. That is your infield, for the rest will be cut loose." Mike looked at Coker and Perry and Canada. "Here is the rest of your infielders right there in their underwear if they show up good in Aqua Clara in the spring. That is a secret amongst us 5, but it is the straight dope from Dutch.

"Red Traphagen will catch about 135 games a year. I have spoke about him and Goose. Bruce Pearson is your other catcher. He was big-time when I sent him up, but he does not get enough work. This has knocked his spirits all to hell.

"The pitching is young. If the pitching comes through you will have a winner up there in New York in the next year or 2. It all depends. Sam and Knuckles and Horse Byrd is your only veterans. Carroll I do not know. Castetter was sent down today, and he will never go back up. That leaves Sterling and Gil Willowbrook and Macy, plus Lindon Burke and yourself. Tell Lindon that if he gives himself 10 seconds between pitches he will help his control." Mike kept looking off in the distance, like he was in a dream. There was more he had on his mind to say, and we knowed it, and we waited, and he did not say it. I always wonder what it was, and I wonder to this day. Yet he said nothing but only rose and said, "I will see you boys at the park tonight," meaning Coker and Canada and Perry.

"I will be there, too," said I, "for my plane does not leave till 11."

Mike laughed, and he said, "There is no need, but it is up to you." Then he left, and we begun to dress for supper.

I got in uniform that night and worked out. The crowd give me a fine hand when I come on the field, for they had by now read it in the paper, and I tipped my hat and played pepper with some of the boys. Then I moved down to first base and took a hand in the drill and kept pretty loose.

After the drill I ducked back through the dugout and into the clubhouse, and I was alone. I showered and dressed, feeling sad. I cleaned out my locker. The 4 of us had lockers together, 1 right after the other, and I stuck a note in their lockers, and it said, "I will see you in Aqua Clara in the spring, and we will be in the Series next October. Good luck. Your friend, HENRY WIGGEN."

Then out I went, catching a cab on Rocky Mountain Avenue. We heard about 2 innings along the way, the Cowboys pasting the hell out of Denver. Perry hit a home run with 2 on in the third. The cabbie asked me if I had ever saw the Cowboys play. He said it was the best club they had in Q. C. in quite some years. I said I had saw them play once or twice and thought particularly high of that fellow by the name of Wiggen. He told me that Wiggen was signed on by the Mammoths and had went off that very day to New York by air. "What is your line of work?" said he to me.

"I am a heaver in the horsehide plant," said I. That was a joke that me and Coker and Perry and Canada played on people. We would run into some people in a restaurant or a bowling alley or somewheres and get to talking, and they would say, "What do you boys do?" Then Coker would speak up. "We work in the horsehide plant," he would say. "This here is Henry, and he is a heaver, and this here is Perry, and he is a scooper. I work alongside of Perry. This here is Canada, and he works the far throw."

They would say, "What is the far throw?"

"Why," said Coker, "everybody knows what a far throw is. Only a particularly pinheaded person would not know."

"Oh," they would say. "A *far* throw. I did not hear you right at first."

The cabbie said, "You are a what in a what?"

"A heaver in the horsehide plant," said I. "Sometimes I am a swatter, but mostly I am a heaver."

"Where is that?" said he, "for I seem to forget."

"Why, it is over there near the ball park. Do you mean to say you are a cabbie and do not know where the horsehide plant is?" said I.

"Oh," said he, "the *horse*hide plant. Why do you not speak up when you speak?"

At the airport I picked up my tickets and weighed my bags through and bought some insurance out of a machine, 50,000 dollars made out to the New York Mammoths. What a simple soul! Then I read some magazines while they dillied and dallied until finally they left us on the plane. The last I heard we beat Denver 15-3, but I could not get the details, and I have never been back to Q. C. since.

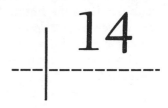

14

IT TOOK me about 10 minutes to get past the club-house guard. Naturally they post a guard there, for you have got any number of these kids that in the course of a year tries to worm through and tell Dutch Schnell what a great ballplayer they are. The guard gripped me like I was some sort of a crook and led me in the clubhouse. We seen Sid Goldman sitting on a bench putting laces in his shoes, and he looked up, and at first he did not recognize me, and I said, "Sid, why do you not tell this fellow just who I am?"

The cop said, "Do you know this boy?" and Sid squinted at me and said, "Yes, he is the new pitcher," and the cop left go of my arm. Sid stretched out his hand. "I hit a home run off you 1 time in Aqua Clara," he said, and he give me a smile.

"And last spring I struck you out twice in Jacksonville," I said, for we had played a couple exhibitions there, Q. C. and the Mammoths, and we shook hands and he said, "Boy, if you will pull us out of this slump you are my friend for life."

The Mammoths at the time was 6 games behind Brooklyn, which was in second, and only 2 games ahead of Cleveland, with Washington behind Cleveland, about 1½ games. There was the danger of falling back to fourth and maybe out of the first division money altogether. They had give up all idea of climbing higher. What they wanted now was to fight off Cleveland.

"Well," said I, "you have just shook hands with the best left-hander this town has ever saw," and he laughed, and just then Dutch Schnell come up behind me, and he said, "If you are 1 half so good as you say you are I will be 1 happy old man." Then he took me down the line and give me the locker Bub Castetter had before he was sent down. Dutch tore off Castetter's name and said they would put up mine, and I said he might as well paint it with paint that would last forever, for I had a mind to stay up in the big time for 20 or 25 years, and he said he was highly encouraged by my remarks, and he turned and walked back through the door to his office.

The boys begun to gather. Sid introduced me to them as they come in, and some of them shook my hand and chatted, and some of them shook it but never said a word. The gloom hung heavy. The 1 who spoke the most was George Gonzalez, and he blabbered away for 2 minutes in Spanish, and I never understood a word, and I said, "Do you remember when I struck you out on 3 pitches at Aqua Clara?" and he said, "Up yours, up yours," which is the only 2 words of English that he seems to know. It was the only time anybody in the clubhouse laughed all day. Me and Lindon Burke dressed side by side, and he asked me how everybody was back in Q. C., and I told him they was all fine and running away with the flag, and somebody said, "It is nice to hear that somewheres there is a Mammoth club that is winning a flag."

"Buck up your courage," said I, "for the tide is changing now that I am here."

"Shut up," said the voice.

"No, sir," said I. "I will not shut up."

But just then Lindon nudged me with his elbow, and he said, "You had best shut up."

In come Bradley Lord with a suit over his arm, and he brung it down to me. It smelled all fresh and clean like it just been took out of the moth balls, and I looked at the number on the shirt, and it said "48" and I said, "I cannot wear such a shirt."

"Why not?" said he.

"Because of the number," said I. "I cannot wear no number that has got 12 in it."

"That is ridiculous," said he.

Then the same voice come again, and it said, "Bradley Lord, God damn you, go back and get that boy a shirt with a number like he likes it or I will break your f---ing back between my 2 f---ing hands." The boys all call him Bradley Lord, for nobody likes him well enough to call him Bradley, and yet nobody would ever call him Mr. Lord, and then I knowed whose voice it was. It was Sad Sam Yale's, for I could tell by the way he said it—"God damn you"—which was the first thing he ever said to me at Aqua Clara that time. His voice was like thunder, and it rolled like thunder rolling in across the mountains, and you could feel it in your belly, for it made you shiver and shake, and Bradley Lord scampered off and come back with a different shirt, number 44, and he said real soft, "Is that a better number?"

"Yes it is," said I, and I took it, and away went Bradley Lord. I shouted out, "Thank you, Sam."

"F--- you too," said he.

Cleveland was in town, finishing up on a 3-game series. We had beat them the first day, and they beat us the next, which was the day before I come, and the day I come they not only beat us but massacred us as well, winning 9-1 and drawing up to 1 game behind. The scoreboard showed Washington beating Chicago, and that made us feel no better, and the clubhouse afterward was quieter then hell.

Generally the Mammoth clubhouse will be full of writers. But when we hit the slump that year Dutch give the order not to let a single 1 of them donkeys in. You cannot blame him. They are like the plague. There is not a 1 of them that has got the guts and gumption to get out there and play ball theirselves, yet they know just exactly how the game should be played. They will get the fatigue from climbing 6 steps, yet they know how Perry Simpson should steal a base. They will get a cramp in their arm from writing a few words down on paper, yet if a ballplayer pitches 7 innings and poops out they are as libel as not to decide he is a quitter. They tell Dutch how to manage the club, and if he does right they will crow in their column for 2 weeks, saying it was all their idea to begin with. They are like fans. Red says the only difference between the writers and the fans is that the fans have at least got the honesty to pay their own way in the park.

Yet ballplayers read the papers day and night, mostly buying

"The News" in New York. Red Traphagen will buy "The Star-Press," but I can't see it. I only buy it on Sunday when they run the pitching records and batting averages.

Cleveland lost the day after to Boston, Boston turning the trick again the following night whilst we was taking 2 in a row from Chicago. That give us our 3-game edge again and things begun to be more tolerable around the clubhouse. I got to know some of the boys, and half the club was my personal friends before the week was out. The west went back west, and Brooklyn moved in at the Stadium beginning on a Sunday, and a hot 1, with Sad Sam slated to work. There was a good crowd, for Brooklyn always draws well against the Mammoths, besides which they was still hopeful of overtaking Boston, which they finally done 2 days before the end, as you know. I was down in the bullpen as usual but I did not throw a ball all afternoon, just sitting and watching while Sam turned in a neat job. We scored 3 in the third and 2 in the fifth and that was enough. 5-0.

We still had the 3-game edge on Cleveland when Boston come in in the middle of the week with the flag hot in their nose and dumped us 2 straight, and we lost ground. Things was back to where the clubhouse was like a museum, so silent and still, the boys watching their third-place money about to float away, and maybe fourth as well, and I dared not speak above a whisper, for the tension was so high it was like you was sitting on thin ice and the least little rustle would crack it and down you would go in the drink.

Friday Dutch pitched Sam, hoping to beat Boston and hang on, Sam grumbling from overwork, but he had it that day, and the guts to go with it. I was in the bullpen again. He got in trouble in the fifth, and I got up and took off my jacket and begun to throw down to Bruce, and then he pulled out of his trouble and I sat down again. Then he was in trouble in the sixth, and then out of it again, and in the eighth Boston had 2 on and 2 down when a young kid name of Hillhouse, now no longer with Boston, hitting for the pitcher, clubbed a drive into right-center that Pasquale Carucci went halfway up the fence and pulled down or it would of went for a triple at least. It was 1 of the finest fielding gems that I ever seen, and I am lucky to have had the chance. Pasquale got a great hand from the crowd. It was still 0-0 and anybody's ball game.

In the last of the eighth Gene Park and Red Traphagen singled, and Dutch played the gamble and lifted Sam and sent Swanee Wilks up to hit. I knowed my turn had come, for there was only me and Lindon in the bullpen, and Dutch would not send a right-hander in against Boston if he could help it at a time like now.

I warmed up hard. I was really throwing, and Swanee lined a single into right, and Gene scored, and I knowed it was now my ball game to win or lose for Sam, and when the signal come from the dugout Lindon said to me, "You will do it, boy," and I started across the field. Pasquale Carucci, on his way out to right, he give me a slap on the rump, and then it come over the speaker. I will never forget it: "*Your attention please. Now pitching for New York. Wiggen. Number forty-four. Now pitching for New York.*"

Down around second base Gene Park give me a cluck-cluck with his mouth, meaning good luck, and Sid Goldman and George Gonzalez was waiting at the hill with Red and Dutch, and they said words to me, though I forget them, and then Red went down behind the plate and I throwed a few, and Dutch headed back for the dugout and Sid and George back to their spots, and Ugly come in from short and said something and then turned and went back, and then I was alone.

I remember. I remember I seen Sad Sam standing at the dugout door, and I seen Dutch on the bench with his legs crossed, and I seen the club all leaned forward with their elbow on their knees like they do, waiting and waiting to see if I was a man or just another boy, and down in the coaching boxes the Boston coaches was roaring insults out my way, saying did I happen to know I was now in the big-time and did I not know this and that, usually things of a rather low-down nature, and Red called down from behind the plate, "Give me what I call for and we will be back in the showers in 5 minutes," and I said to myself, "I will try. Yet at this particular moment I am not sure that I could hit the side of a barn with a basketball." I looked down at the ball in my hand, and it did not seem like my hand a-tall but like the hand of a stranger attached to my wrist, and the arm was not mine and I did not believe I could trust it. I wished I was anywhere but where I was, maybe down in Borelli's in Perkinsville, relaxed, *listening* to this ball game. And then I thought of Borelli's, and it flashed like a vision through my brain that probably this very minute Pop was down in Borelli's, and there was a silence amongst the men, and the barbers was standing with razors in mid-air, and I could just see old Borelli running out in the street and setting up the cry.

Then I wound and pumped and throwed. It was a ball, slightly wide, and just about then a cheer went up, and I did not know why. For an instant I thought Dutch was lifting me, and I looked around, puzzled, and Ugly Jones laughed and pointed to the scoreboard, and I looked, and it showed 5 runs in the second inning for St. Louis at Cleveland, and I knowed that if we won now we would be breathing easier again.

The batter was Black. I remembered the knee-high curve Sad Sam had throwed when me and Pop come down that day for the Opener, and Black had connected by sheer luck, and Red called for that kind of a pitch now, and it cut the corner, as clean a strike as you ever seen, and Hunt Glidden, the umpire, called it a ball, and I stormed down towards the plate and made a few remarks about how it was my belief umpires ought to be pensioned off once they went blind, and Glidden said to me, "You have throwed 2 pitches in the big time and already you are a hot head. Now get back out there and pitch," and I offered a few further bits of advice about the knack of being an umpire, and he turned his back. George shouted down from third, "Up yours, up yours," and Ugly and Gene come in and give Glidden a piece of their mind, and Dutch come up off the bench and told Glidden several things more or less harsh in tone. It seemed to bring the club to life. I think it was the first time in several days that it showed any life, and I went back out and throwed the same pitch again, and this time it was a strike and no mistake.

Then it was a fast ball, letter high, and Black never seen it, and the count was 2 and 2. Then I struck him out with the screw.

The crowd give me a good hand, and they give the razzberry to

Granby, the next Boston batter, for he was not popular in New York since 1 time he spiked Ugly Jones in a play at second. He tried to cross me up by bunting down the third base line. I seen him shift when the ball left my hand, and I went down fast, and Red yelled "Wiggen, Wiggen," meaning for George to get out of the way, and I fielded it clean and whirled and fired to Sid Goldman at first, and Granby was out by a full step.

Now I was relaxed. It was like I was always up there, like I was there all my life, with the Mammoths, and I went back to the hill and scrubbed around with my toeplate, and I fingered the resin bag, and I looked up at the scoreboard and out at the fielders, and I was no more nervous then if I was back in the Legion league in Perkinsville.

Fielding stepped in. Casey Sharpe, the Boston clean-up man, was kneeling in the on-deck circle. "Get on," shouted he to Fielding, "and I will drive you home," and then he shouted something out at me that I will not repeat, and I shouted down to him, "Go back to the dugout, Casey, for number 3 is at the plate." Fielding must of liked those shoulder balls I throwed him, for he went after 2. He did not have the good fortune to get wood on them, however, and then Red called for the screw, and Fielding got a slice of it, and he skied it up behind third base. Ugly and George both went for the ball, and Ugly called "George" and George took it on the lope, a very easy play, and that was the ball game.

You would of almost thought we clinched the pennant. The clubhouse was downright cheerful. We got a later score on Cleveland, and Cleveland was losing, and Dutch come by, and he said to me, "Good work," and then he went back in his office. That was the game we needed, and we knowed it.

Patricia Moors was all smiles. Bradley Lord give us the warning, and she come through on the way to the office. She stopped near the door, and she said, "Sam Yale, nice game," and he told her he thought so himself, considering that he was more overworked then a n----r, and she said, "Where is Pasquale Carucci?" and he come forward, and she said, "That was a fine catch. I never saw DiMaggio make a better 1," DiMaggio being Pasquale's hero since he was a kid, and Pasquale said "Thank you, ma'am," and then she looked around some more, and her eyes lit on me, and mine on her.

"1-2-3 they come up and 1-2-3 they went down," I said, and she laughed, and when she laughed all the diamonds jiggled on her ears, and she brushed back her hair with 1 arm, and I think there was about 4 pounds of bracelets on the arm, and she stood looking at me.

"You set them down fine," she said.

"I rather thought the same," said I.

And still she stood there and looked at me, and I at her. "The trouble with you," she said, "is that you do not have enough confidence in yourself," and she laughed and turned and went off towards the office, and I watched her go, and a fine sight it was.

That day we dressed slow, me and Lindon, and in the days after. We made the last tour of the eastern clubs, and I worked just about every day down in the bullpens, yet Dutch did not use me. He said he would pitch me the last game, which was Sunday in Boston, and we beat them Friday and Saturday and knocked them out of the top spot, Brooklyn taking 2 from Washington in Brooklyn, and then it rained on Sunday and I never got the chance. I guess nobody give a damn but me, the race already settled, Brooklyn, Boston, New York and Cleveland finishing 1-2-3-4.

We had a meeting in the hotel that afternoon, and the boys voted shares of the third-place money. They voted me 100 dollars, which was good enough pay for 1 inning of work, and then we broke up, and it was sad because you knowed there was some amongst us that had played their last games in the big time. Next year they would be on their way down, down and down to nowheres.

Yet I was happy, for I was on the way up, and I said to Lindon, "I guess we are sitting on top of the world, away up in the clouds, and the gate is open and the music is playing," and Lindon said the same.

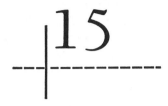

ME AND Lindon and Piss Sterling and Gil Willow-brook was planning to take in the start of the Series in Brooklyn together, but then I never went. I don't know why. Something just come over me. On top of that I promised Al Mellon I would get up on the TV between innings and reel off a little speech on razor blades, and I even learned it by heart like he asked me to, "Yes, Al, in my estimation these are the finest blades on the market. I have tried them all, and I know. These are my choice for a *smoother* shave, a *cleaner* shave, a shave that gives me that pleasant good-to-be-alive-all-over feeling. Fans, take my word for it, penny for penny THIS is your most dependable buy." (SMILE BROADLY), and then I was supposed to hold the package up in front of the camera and smile broadly like shaving to me was the equal of a broiled steak. But then I got thinking about Holly and Pop and I went straight home from Boston instead. I sometimes recite that speech in the clubhouse with a few little twists and turns in the dialogue, and then I hold up a jockstrap or a roll of toilet paper or something of the sort and smile broadly from ear to ear. The boys always get a great laugh.

I no sooner hit Perkinsville when Bill Duffy grabs me at the station and tells me there is this great spontaneous demonstration about to take place on the square. There was a banner flung across the waiting room saying "WELCOME HOME, HENRY WIGGEN," and a band in the street below playing "Take Me Out To The Ball Game" and the Perkinsville High anthem, and Mayor Real come forward and pumped my hand several times for the photographer

131

from the "Clarion" and give me a cardboard key to the city. I hadn't no particular objection to this sort of thing, but I was hungrier then hell and wanted to get home.

Bill said forget it. "Get in the spirit of things," he said, and he sat me on a platform on the square set up behind the statue of Mr. Cleves with about 15 big shots, storekeepers and politicians and such, and every damn 1 of them got up and made a speech. Bill was the m.c. Never a 1 of them forgot to mention their place of business, though about half of them forgot to mention *me*. 1 of them remembered me but had the idea I was with Brooklyn. They read off a list of things they was to give me, each from their own store, and some of the things was sent to me, too, although some of them I had to go down and fetch myself.

There was a terrific crowd at first, but then it begun to drizzle a bit and some folks took off, and frankly between the rain and the speeches I could not blame them.

Finally Bill auctioned off this picture of me, about 6 feet high all drawed in color by B. C. Donaldson, the top artist of Perkinsville. He had me all dressed up in a Mammoth uniform with the blue sky behind and an assinine smile on my face, the only thing wrong with the picture being that the word "Mammoths" was wrote across my chest. Actually "New York" is on the shirt, and Borelli bought it for 150 dollars and hung it in his shop over the coat-hooks where Sam Yale used to be. I do not know where the picture is now, and I do not care. To tell you the truth I thought it was corny.

Mayor Real called on me to say a few words. I did not know what to say. I stammered around awhile, saying I was glad to be home about 9 times. I suppose it was a stupid speech though no worse then some of the others. Then I signed about 100 autographs for the kids, and then I drifted off towards home.

After dinner we sat out front, me and Pop and Holly, on chairs in the grass. The rain had passed over, and it was a fine night, and cool, and I told them all that happened from the time I left. It was all new to them, for I had not wrote a letter all spring and all summer. Many a time I would sit down and start a letter, and then along would come meal time, or time to sleep, or time to go to the ball park, or time to catch a train, and the letter would stop dead where it was, and then when I looked at it again it seemed stale and out of date, and I would tear it up and throw it away. Holly sent me some letters with a postcard inside, all addressed, but it seemed like I lost them, or if I wrote them I never remembered to drop them in the box. So I had to tell them everything myself now that I was home.

After awhile Aaron Webster come over with some fireflies in a bottle. He sat down on the grass beside my chair, and he set the bottle of flies beside him, and he tucked his knees up under his chin, and he listened, and I talked on and on.

Then it was late, and Pop said, "I guess there is now nothing more I can tell you about the game of baseball, for Sad Sam Yale has told you all." I suppose I laid it on a bit thick about me and Sam, probably giving the impression that we was a good deal chummier then we was. Actually the whole month of September he had 2 bits of advice for me, telling me for 1 thing shut up and number 2 go f--- myself, and Pop straightened and stretched and went indoors, and Aaron upped and went off down the road swinging the bottle all lighted with flies.

Then it was quiet, and there was only me and Holly, and we talked that night about a million things or more, just talking to be talking, and I remember how quiet and peaceful it was and how I discovered for the first time in 20 years that I was beginning to enjoy a little peace and quiet in life about as well as anything else.

I guess that is the thing I remember most about the whole winter—how quiet it was—how nothing much happened and yet it was a good winter and I was not all in a dither to hurry it through like the winters before. Probably this sounds peculiar coming from a fellow that in the spring stood a good chance to land a notch with the New York Mammoths. Yet that was how it was, and no sense hiding it or telling it otherwise.

It was the winter of the blizzard. I was at Holly's when it broke. The snow piled up higher and higher and we built a fire in the fireplace, and I did not leave because I figured it soon would stop, but it did not stop, and I did not leave, and we burned the wood slow to keep from running out, and I laid on the sofa in front of the fire with my head on Holly's lap, and she sat with her legs tucked up beneath her. Her face looked upside down, yet even upside down I come to the view that it was a pretty face, and I liked to look at it, even upside down, and I laid there and looked up at her, and she read to me out of a number of books. Her chin waggled up and down and up and down when she read, and I watched it, and I laughed, and she said my face was just as upside down to her as hers to me, and I reached up behind her head and drug it down to me, and I give her an upside down kiss.

She read a good deal from the books. There was 1 on psychology and 1 on God, but not so dry as you might think. She also read to me from the book called "Huckleberry Finn" that I had read before and could not see much sense in plowing through again, but she said the second time was better then the first. Generally I would say it is a waste of energy to read a book once, let alone twice. But it is no chore to read a book any number of times if you can lay straight out with your head in somebody's lap and close your eyes and listen. You can picture all the action in your mind as you go.

There was 2 days of snow, and then it stopped, and I was even a little sorry. Yet I guess it was a good thing, for I had to keep moving and not put on weight, and we walked in the snow clear to Perkinsville in high boots and back, and after that every day we walked a little, 5 miles or so, and my legs stood as strong as they was in the summer, and my wind, and my weight stood put and my appetite was good, and I slept like a bear all winter.

The more I slept the faster the time would go. The next best thing to sleeping is keep busy and never look at the calendar, and the time goes quick. I refereed basketball at the Hebrew Association, and I went to some dinners and made a few speeches for boys and 2 lunch clubs. I pulled Holly on a sled with the rope across my chest like a horse, and we went skating down on the creek where I was bit on the elbow by the bug that time.

Then it was Christmas, and then it was January, and soon afterwards the sun come out strong, and the snow got lower and lower. You could see where it left a wet mark on the side of the houses, and every now and then you would look up and see a great cluster of snow come down off a roof or a tree, and you could see patches of ground peeping through.

And what clinched it for me was my contract in the mail on the fourth of February. There is a law which says that they have got to mail them out no later then February 1. Otherwise clubs would mail them late to keep holdouts down to a minimum. But I had no intentions of holding out, for it was a good contract—8,500 plus maybe a Series share—and we signed it and shot it right back.

The night before I left Holly read to me out of a book that I did not understand much of. The whole point was that the richer you are the better chance you have to get along in life, and if you are poor you had best go about mending your ways, which I did not need no book to tell me, and I said so, and I rose up and took the book away and throwed a heap of wood on the fire, and then I made her lay out the straight way on the sofa, and I laid beside her, and we talked a long, long time, half the night at least. I said a number of tender things which I need not repeat, for they are altogether too rich for the daytime, yet they was all true, and I meant them, every word, for now that I was leaving I knowed that I would miss her and I said so in so many words, and she called me "Henry the Navigator," which is what she calls me when she is in the tenderest frame of mind.

"Henry the Navigator," said she, "it will be a long time, and I do wish I would hear from you personal and not have to read about you in the papers." Then she give me the best advice anyone ever give me concerning baseball and how to play it. She said, "Henry, you must play ball like it does not matter, for it really does not matter. Nothing really matters. Play ball, do your best, have fun, but do not put the game nor the cash before your own personal pride," and I said I would. I loved her and would of said most anything, and in the heat of it all I asked her would she marry me. She said no. "But we will see what Old Father Time brings forth," she said.

In the morning I was up and gone. I parked in my slot in the depot, and I got the early train out. I had 100 dollars in my money belt, and I still had it tucked in my belly when I undressed the following night in the hotel in Aqua Clara. I was no more a green punk.

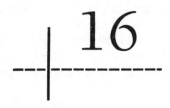

YOU can tell a ballplayer from a punk by the cut of his clothes and the way he walks and the way he handles himself, not only on the field but off. I remember the first morning in Aqua Clara last spring I was woke by the train and I went over to the window and stood there looking down when the train drawed to a stop at the station below. About a dozen got off plus 4 colored chaps way down in the last car, and you could tell they was punks by the way they piled off, spilling out like marines in a newsreel and standing there blinking in the sun, looking all dazed and bewildered. You could tell they was rooks by the seedy old bags they toted, all wore and cracked and hung together with straps and cord. You could tell by their clothes. Mostly they wore jackets, and there was names and numbers on the jackets standing for high schools and clubs where the boys played before, and some of them wore sneakers without no socks. They set out across town, straggling along together like you seen school kids do, going down the street in a pack.

There was twice as many on the noon train, and I watched them again, except that there was 1 that was different, and I knowed the instant I laid eyes on him that here was a ballplayer, and the way I could tell he was dressed in the best and his bag had a bright shine, and he walked cocky. He did not come diving off the train like a marine. He come down slow, after all the rest, and he carried his bag easy and swung away from the punks and towards the hotel.

It turned out that it was Bub Castetter that been sent down to Q. C. when I come up. He was back for another try. I never met

him before, but I knowed him when I seen him close, just before
he went under the awning in front. Except for me he was the first
of the club in camp.

I thought maybe we might grab a bite together, and I timed it
right and met him on the stairs coming up. There was a bellboy
with him, carrying his bags, all dressed up like an Admiral like
they do down there, and I give Bub a hello and a big pleasant
smile. "Hello punk," he said, and he went on past me and up the
stairs.

That first night I had the regular blues, lonesome as the moon
and not a soul to talk to. I halfway thought of going and asking
Bub what bug he was bit by. But I give up that idea and stripped
down. I read the Aqua Clara paper through twice, and I read some
in the hotel Bible, about 20 chapters. 1 thing I will say for that
book, a chapter ain't no trick a-tall. About 10 o'clock another
train come through, and I stood at the window. There was the
usual gang of punks, plus a dozen or more that headed towards
the hotel, but it was too dark to see who. I was sure there was
ballplayers amongst them, for I could tell by the way they walked,
and there was some writers, too, waddling along with their machines in their hand. Then I could see that 1 of the ballplayers was
Sad Sam Yale, and I dressed quick and shot out of there and met
him on the stairs and stuck out my hand, and he stuck out his and
give me a shake. "Hello punk," he said, and he went on past me.

I would of followed but I seen Red Traphagen behind, and he
seen me and winked and asked me how my flipper was.

I remember to this day Red standing there and asking me how
my flipper was. I do not know why I remember, yet I do. You will
have pictures in your mind of certain ballplayers doing certain
things. I remember Sad Sam with his hat over his heart and the
band playing the day me and Pop went to the Opener in New York,
and I remember him standing and watching from the dugout door
the day I relieved against Boston, the first inning I ever pitched
for the Mammoths.

And Red I remember coming back towards the screen, all loaded down in his gear, his mask and cap throwed off and his hair in the wind that very same day at the Opener, and I remember him standing there that night, his hair all red and asking me how was my flipper. Then he asked me up to his room, and we went. Red used to room with Monk Boyd until Sid Goldman eased Monk out of a job and Monk got traded away to Washington. Now he rooms with George Gonzalez, and they talk Spanish together. Sometimes I sit around and listen to them talk and never understand a word. George was not yet in camp, so there was only Red and me, and he asked me what I done all winter, and I told him, and he told me what he done, which was mostly play handball in California to keep his weight down.

He was in good spirits that night, and I forgot how lonesome I was. He said he believed we would have a good year. "If the youngsters come through," he said. "That is the big thing." He asked me did Ugly Jones sign yet, and I said no, not according to the papers, and he asked me who all was in camp, and I told him. He told me some stories about Ugly, and some about George, and some about the club in general. Some of them I could not follow exactly. Red is fairly deep, and sometimes he will set his tongue to wagging and I can no more follow him then Aaron Webster, and he might as well be talking Spanish to George for all of me. He asked me this and that about Mike Mulrooney—did Mike still head for church all the time? I said he went fairly regular. I remembered what Mike said about steering clear of Red off the field, but I said nothing to Red about that, besides which I liked him and like him yet, though many people do not. He told me he believed I depended too much on too many screwballs.

"Dutch says I throw too many *fast* balls," I said.

"When did he say that?" said Red.

"2 springs ago," said I.

"At contract time?" said Red.

"Yes," I said, "2 springs ago at contract time."

"That is what I thought," said Red. "The bastard. He knows better."

That seemed a poor way for a ballplayer to talk about his own manager. "He was just doing what he considered best," I said.

"Best for who?" said Red.

Well, that's Red for you. He can be very sarcastic at times. You got to get used to him. His motto is: never be cheery if you can possibly be gloomy, and I passed it off and went on to other things. Before we knowed it it was midnight, and we sent down for sandwiches and Coke, and then I went back to my room. I felt good.

By Monday all the pitchers and catchers was in camp plus Dutch and the coaches and Patricia Moors and Bradley Lord and Doc Loftus and Doc Solomon and Mick McKinney and about 2 truckloads of writers plus a slew of people that hung around the park and the hotel but never, so far as I could see, had any sort of a job to keep them occupied.

All except Bruce Pearson. Bruce is the third-string catcher. He might catch 5 or 6 games a year, but mostly he warms pitchers in the bullpen. Every year he comes 2 days late to camp because he ties 1 on on the way down. He don't drink except once a year, and then he goes the whole hog and drinks for 2 days in Jacksonville and Dutch has got to send Bradley Lord, and Bradley has got to hunt around for Bruce and find him and wait till he is done. Then he puts him on a bus to Aqua Clara, and when he gets there Doc Loftus works him over awhile and Mick McKinney works him over some more, and after about 6 hours Bruce is as good as new.

The sad part is that there is never much work for him. Yet a ballplayer has got to play ball like a singer has got to sing and an artist has got to draw pictures and a mountain climber has got to have a mountain to climb or else go crazy. That's the way it is, and that is why things look so dark for Bruce every spring.

Dutch called the first workout for 10:30 that Monday, and we worked 2 sessions, from 10:30 to noon and then again from 1 to half past 2, sandwiches and milk in between plus a special energy orange drink Doc Loftus invented. I guess you would hardly call it work. At least it did not seem to be work to me, although it hit some of the others harder. We done some exercises, and we jogged about a bit, halfway around the park and walked the rest. Then we laid down in the clubhouse awhile. Those that needed a rub from Mick McKinney got it. It is always the older fellows that need their rub the worst, Sad Sam and Hams Carroll and Knuckles Johnson and Horse Byrd, and 1 after the other they laid on the table and got the works.

The second day we went at it a little harder, and the third day harder still, and my arms and neck browned up a good bit from the sun. All the rot that gets in you in the winter begun to seep away. I could feel it, and I said to Lindon I could go 9 innings right then, and he said so could he, and Bub Castetter told Lindon he could blow it out his ass, and Lindon shot back with a smart remark, and then Knuckles took up for Bub, saying it was these damn punks that work so hard in the spring that throwed the whole thing out of gear every year. But we never got any deeper in the matter because we was back in the clubhouse by then, and it was just at that moment that Bradley Lord brung Bruce Pearson in.

You never seen such a sight. I could scarcely recognize him, for he did not look a-tall like the ballplayer that I had throwed to in the bullpen the September before. He is blondheaded, and it was pasted down over his eyes now, and there was blood in it, and the way I remembered him he was meek and mild and never said a word unless he was spoke to. But now he was ranting and raving. He had Bradley Lord by the back of the neck, and he called Bradley every name in the book plus a few that I suppose is special to Bainbridge, Georgia, and his shirt was tore clean in 2 and the fly of his pants was wide open and all the buttons gone. Bradley Lord was screaming at Dutch to take him off his hands. Dutch just laughed. "He will quieten down," he said.

Bruce give Dutch a ferocious look. Yet drunk as he was he knowed better then to mix with Dutch, Dutch being the skipper and all, and he looked around like he was trying to decide who to scrap with, and his eyes lit on Sad Sam, and he charged across at Sam, and Sam stepped aside as neat as you please and wandered out the door with his sandwiches and milk, and Bruce went down in a heap by the lockers and laid there a minute.

Then he begun to cry, and it was pitiful, and he cussed out Bradley Lord some more, and he cussed out the Greyhound Bus Company and the City of Jacksonville and the whole State of Florida and the game of baseball and Mike Mulrooney and Q. C. and all the cities in the Four-State Mountain League, cussing and crying all the while. Dutch said he never seen him quite so bad before, and he sent Bradley Lord out for Doc Solomon and for Mike Mulrooney, Mike being over working with the rooks.

After a little bit he stopped. He was sobbing and shaking, but he seemed better, and he rose and went rather wobbly over to the water fountain and took a drink and come back and sat on the bench in front of the lockers. He seemed deep in thought, and then he rose and went very deliberate to the water again, and he filled his mouth and shot a stream across at Red, and it caught Red square in the face, and Red wiped it away.

2 men come in for the empty crate of milk, and Bruce begun to give them hell and call them all sorts of foul names, "n----r" and such, and some of the boys made him quieten down and chased the men out of there so as not to cause any more disturbance then was necessary, and then Bruce begun a torrent, running down the colored people and milk companies and Bradley Lord. He dove for the bottles and would of upset the crate but me and Lindon pulled him off. He got hold of 1 bottle, however, and looked around for someone to fire it at, but by this time the clubhouse was cleared out and there was nobody left but me, for all the boys was eating their lunch on the grass outside. Bruce smashed the bottle on the floor, and I finally got him under a shower, and he shivered and shook and vomited something awful. Doc Solomon come then and said leave him vomit. I said there was little else you could do, for you can not give a man an order not to vomit. Doc Solomon left, and Bruce shook and shivered and vomited, and between times he laced into Doc Solomon, calling him a Jew and what not else.

He was at the heights when all of a sudden in walked Mike Mulrooney and it was Mike that calmed him down, handing out the sweet talk and saying what a great ballplayer Bruce was. He went right in there under the shower and turned it off and crouched down on the wet floor with Bruce, and they talked about the good times they had back in Q. C. Soon Bruce come out just as calm as if he was sober, and Mike talked to him some more and held his hand and patted his shoulder.

Then Dutch yelled "Back to work!" and I went.

That night I seen Bruce at the hotel, and he was as nice and polite as ever, and quiet, and when he spoke he spoke soft, and you could hardly believe it was the same man. From that day onwards he settled down and done his work like he was told, and you never heard so much as a peep from him the season through.

OTHERWISE it was mostly work. I mean work. I do not mean a dozen push-ups and a couple turns around the park and a shower and a rub and the rest of the day back in the sack at the Hotel Silver Palms or a round of golf or the dogs at night.

I will say this for Dutch: he laid down the rules and they stuck. He give us a speech before the Saturday drill, and he give another when the rest of the club reached camp—the infield and the outfield—and he give several more as time went by just in case your memory went bad.

"You will leave them goddam dogs alone," he said, and he would jump on a bench so you all could see him. "You will be in your goddam rooms at 11 o'clock and your goddam lights will be out at midnight and there will be no goddam monkeyplay afterwards and no goddam sneaking around them halls in the dark after these goddam women that would as soon steal you blind as not," and his face would get all red, and he would run his hand through his hair that had growed gray over all the summers and growed grayer yet before the season was out.

"You will steer clear of these goddam dudes that hang about. You will not play cards with them nor drink their drinks, not even a little drink, not even if it is such a little drink that it would not cover a thimble because them goddam bastards would as soon f--- up my ball club as not. They are on vacation and here for the kicks. But you ain't on vacation. If there is anybody that thinks they are on a vacation down here in the sunny goddam south I will give them a little extra work so as to help them get over the idea. I ain't worked you hard yet, but I mean to." A groan went up, for he had worked us hard all along.

"Why am I doing it?" Dutch said. "Am I just naturally some kind of a son of a bitch? No. I am working you hard because I aim to win a flag this year and I am not going to have it took away from me by the middle of August because my club give out from under me. I have saw that happen too often. And why does it happen?"

He did not seem to want no answer.

"Because of ballplayers not taking training serious enough," he said. "Because there is too many goddam ballplayers that think the spring season is set up for golf and the dogs. You men are here to work and I aim to work you. You know how long the summer runs? It runs to the last day of September. It does not run to Labor Day or the goddam Fourth of July or the middle of May. I have saw too many clubs that about the middle of August they are dragging their ass like a bunch of goddam gymnasium teachers. That is why you are here, to get in shape, and the harder you work the better it will pay you off in the end. Is that clear?"

It was clear. But the lecture wasn't over yet. Dutch would work up a head of steam, and once he got there he hated to see it go to waste.

"I am the boss," said Dutch. "Joe Jaros and Clint Strap and Egg Barnard is my right-hand aids. That has got to be clear once and for all. There can never be more then 1. If there is more then 1 man giving orders then you have not got a ball club but a mob, and I have never saw a mob win a flag yet and never will. When I say I am the boss I mean that I am the boss. I mean you take orders from me and not from any of the Moorses nor from any son of a bitch back home that writes you a letter and not from any goddam radio announcer that comes around and asks why you played it this way when you should of played it the other. By the Lord God Christ Almighty if I tell you to run the bases on your hands you will do like I say. Them goddam announcers is all mouth and 50 percent horseshit." (These are Dutch's opinions and none of my own.) "That brings up the writers," he said, still traveling on that same head of steam. "I do not want you hanging with them bastards any more then you can help. Okay, they want a story. Answer their

questions in a polite way. If they get too personal just tell them
you do not know. Listen to them when they got something they
wish to get off their mind. They always think they know more
baseball then the ballplayer himself. The only catch is that they
never do. If you was to show them a baseball they would scarcely
know what it was. If you was to throw it at them they would be
scared shitless and duck for cover and never come out till morning.
I am the f---ing manager of this f---ing club and not some damn
writer. If they write something in their paper that does not go
down just forget it. For God's sake do not argue with them. And
for the love of Jesus never hit 1 of them bastards because if you
was ever to hit 1 they would write about it till their fingers was
wore to the bone.

"I am telling you all this from 40 years of long experience in
baseball. I think I know what I am talking about. I was playing
this game when some of you was pissing your drawers and the rest
was no more then a fine and anxious gleam in your old man's eye,
so I know. There ain't a club that will win except 1 that works its
ass off in the spring so that by the middle of April you are not just
getting in condition but you are *in* condition. When I say in condition I do not mean 5 pounds over your weight or even 1 pound.
I mean you are *at* your weight. There is some of you that look
like you never done a thing all winter except shuffle back and forth
between the bed and the kitchen. If there is anything I hate it is a
fat man. I am near 60 years of age and never weighed more then
210 in my life." Dutch went over to the scales and climbed on.
"Red," he said, "you are a smart boy. Come over here and look at
these scales," and Red went over and worked the weights until
they balanced.

"210," said Red.

"That is what I mean," said Dutch. "Half of you has got the
look of a gymnasium teacher." He mopped his head, and he stood
there on the scales and talked some more, and the scales jumped up
and down, and the fiercer he talked the more they jumped. Dutch
was plenty fierce then and all through the summer. There was
never no question who was the boss.

"This year I am going to have a running club," shouted Dutch.

"Some of you may remember the Mammoths of 35. That was a running club. It begun running in February right here in this park and it never stopped until after the Series. You know who won that Series. We never stopped moving. We beat out hits we should of never beat out, and we made doubles out of singles and triples out of doubles. We caught fly balls we should of never caught and we stole bases we should of never stole. We hustled all the way. Do you know when we begun to hustle? It was in the spring. That was when we begun. This is my motto. Hustle. Every pitch counts, and every inning and every ball game, and you cannot relax and say we will start winning them in April. We have got to start getting in a winning frame of mind now, in the spring. Okay, now let us get out there and get to work."

He was as good as his word, for we worked that first week like our life depended on it. There was some boys that I think would as soon went on a 12-hour day in a boiler factory. That is what they said, although you can't believe everything a ballplayer gives out. Usually if you ask a ballplayer how he likes his job he will tell you, "It is better then carrying a lunch pail, ain't it?" He run us, and he walked us, and he give us exercises sometimes as long as an hour at a stretch, first Dutch and then Joe Jaros and then Egg Barnard and then Clint Strap, 10 or 15 minutes from each, rotating on and off. They was up on a high platform so you couldn't slack off, although there was some that tried. Bub Castetter was always careful to get back in a rear rank. He spent more energy figuring out ways to goof off then he would of spent doing them damn exercises in the first place.

Not me. Me and Lindon was up in the front row, and we never missed a beat. Sometimes I was such a damn Boy Scout I feel ashamed. Like 1 afternoon, the first real scorcher, Dutch and the coaches give out, and Dutch ordered me up on the platform, saying, "Wiggen, see if you can draw a little sweat from these boys," and I give 30 push-ups and 50 deep knee bends and side-arm flings combined, shouting as I went, "*Hup* 2 3 4, *hup* 2 3 4," over and over until even Lindon Burke slacked off. I could of went on I don't know how long but that Sad Sam Yale shouted up to Dutch, "Say, Dutch, how *about* this?" and Dutch called it quits. I guess I would not of won no popularity poles that afternoon. Dutch was all grins.

What did I care? You do not win ball games by votes. It is like Leo Durocher said, "Nice guys do not win ball games." Dutch knows it and so does everybody that ever laid hands on a glove.

I guess I was really in the best shape of my life. I could of shouted and sung, for I felt so good. Did you ever feel that way? Did you ever look down at yourself, and you was all brown wherever your skin was out in the sun, and you was all loose in every bone and every joint of your body, and there was not a muscle that ached, and you felt like if there was a mountain that needed moving you could up and move it, or you could of swam an ocean or held your breath an hour if you liked, or you could run 2 miles and finish in a sprint? And your hands! They fairly itched to hold a baseball, and there was not a thing you could not do once you had that ball. You could fire it like a cannon and split a hair at 300 feet, and you could make it dance and hop, and the batter could no more hit your stuff then make the sun stand still. When you feel like that you could sing in the street, and that was how I felt by the end of the first week in camp.

It wasn't until the middle of the second week, however, that we so much as touched a baseball. By then the whole club was in camp, and the writers was as thick as flies and the papers full of the news from the various camps, who signed and who held out, who looked good and who was over their weight, and what the managers was thinking. Also, there was a good deal of gossip on how the different rookies was showing up. It was too early to tell, there not being any ball games as yet. But a little thing like not having any information to go on will never stop these writers. There was an item or 2 concerning myself. It always sounded to me like they was talking about somebody else. 1 writer said I was "enthusiastic." I suppose I was.

But the biggest news I made was when I run in with the sap that runs the Hotel Silver Palms. The way it happened me and Coker and Canada and Lindon was roomed on the same floor, Coker and Canada together, Lindon with Bruce Pearson because Lucky Judkins was not yet in camp, and me all alone. Perry was supposed to room with me because all the regulars was in the hotel plus the promising rookies, and everybody knowed that Perry was ripe and ready to come up so he should of been in the hotel. But they have got these damn regulations, so he was over in the barrackses with the punks, and mighty lonesome, too. Me and Canada and Coker went down to see him almost every night. It was like he was in prison and this was visiting day. We would sit around and chew the fat. Lindon come along sometimes, and the Caruccis come once in awhile, for they had a kid brother amongst the punks name of Joseph, a first baseman. There is 4 Carucci brothers, 3 of them owned by the Mammoths system, 1 by Philadelphia.

On the way back, under the awning in front of the Silver Palms, we run into this joker. I told him what I thought of the damn regulations that a fellow of the caliber of Perry Simpson was holed up in the barrackses. He laughed. Well, 1 word led to another until finally he said he did not like to argue right smack in front of the main entrance, and he whirled around and started off so fast that his feet got tangled up in themself—and down he went. I rushed over, meaning to help him up, and Canada and Coker grabbed me from behind and told me to lay off, and the doorman come running over hollering "Gentlemen, Gentlemen!" and the fellow got up from the sidewalk with his nose all bloody, and that was all there was to it. I never hit him. The papers all said I hit him, though I never did.

About a half an hour later there comes a knock on my door. I was laying in the bath reading the paper. "Come in," I yell, thinking it was 1 of the boys, and in comes Dutch and Bradley Lord and 2 policemen and Mike Mulrooney and this hotel chap with a patch across his nose. They all come in the bathroom. It made for quite a crowd. 1 of the cops asked me some questions and the second cop took it all down, and then there was a big gabfest out in the room amongst the whole 6 of them, all except Mike. Mike come in the bathroom and sat on the John awhile and talked to me, not about anything in particular, and finally I got out and wrapped a towel around me and went out where the conference was, and Dutch made me shake hands with this fellow, and I done so, and he said he did not prefer any charges against me. The cops breathed easy, for they wanted no fuss with the Mammoths, nor did the hotel. The Mammoths bring more money to Aqua Clara in 1 month then the town sees the rest of the year through. Then they all left except Dutch. He seemed pleased with me. He said he liked a scrappy ballplayer, though he said he wished I could manage to save it for the ball park. He give me a couple pats on the shoulder, saying he liked my spirit and all, and he said he give a doctor 5 bucks for patching up the nose.

Naturally the writers got hold of what happened more or less. I think if you was to go by night to the darkest jungle of Africa and paint yourself black and dig a hole and climb in you would no sooner get to the bottom then there would be a writer there, asking you how come. It was in all the New York papers for a day or 2, all about this terrible bloody fight, and pictures of me and Perry and this hotel chap with the patch on his nose. I got a letter from Holly soon after. She said my heart was in the right place but I should of went about it different. It beat the hell out of me how much fuss was made. Everything is crazy. Sometimes I think the whole world is off their nut.

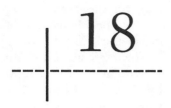

18

UGLY JONES was in the stands down the first base side, leaning forwards with his arms on the rail, watching the infield drill wearing a Palm Beach suit.

I was warming with some of the boys, just easy, no cutting loose as yet, and when I had enough I went over for water, and a kid brought me my jacket, and I slipped it on and went and stood down by Ugly. "Hello punk," he said, "how is the flipper?"

"Never better," said I, and he begun to chat. But suddenly I was not hearing Ugly a-tall, but looking past him, up in the stands, about 12 rows up, in a shady spot, and I seen Patricia Moors in shorts and a halter and beach shoes strapped about her ankles. Her jewelry glistered. She was smoking a cigarette.

"Keep your mind upon the doughnut and not upon the hole," said Ugly.

I tore my eyes off her and back to Ugly. Lord, what an ugly man he is, too. His lower teeth laps out over his uppers. "You are thinking you would like some of that," he said. He never looked back towards her. "You coming up this year?"

"That is right," I said. I tried to look at Ugly and get my mind on what he was saying. "I hope so," I said.

"We need another lefthander," he said. "We have always needed another lefthander. We have got too much righthanded pitching and too much lefthanded hitting. Poor little rich girl, she is down to her last truckload of diamonds. Is that Roguski at short?"

I looked out at the field. Dutch and Egg was running the drill,

Egg slapping out grounders and Dutch watching. By now Dutch was fairly well set on his infield, George Gonzalez at third and Ugly at short, Gene Park at second and Sid Goldman at first. Sooner or later Ugly would sign. Dutch spent a couple weeks trying to dig up a utility first baseman. He would of traded Sid away altogether if he could of got Klosky from St. Louis, and there was some talk that the deal was brewing, but it never come to pass. He tried Squarehead Flynn at first for awhile in the spring, but even if he could of learned Squarehead to play the bag he would of still needed to learn him to hit, so Squarehead was back in Q. C. in May. What Dutch finally done was use Canada at first when Sid needed a rest, or sometimes on defense in late innings of tight ball games. "Yes," said I, "that is Coker Roguski. We was together 2 years in Q. C."

"He is a nice ballplayer," Ugly said. "He can go to his right. Give me a shortstop that can go to his right. Keep your eyes off her, for she will only keep you awake nights. Dutch says no contract no work. He will not even leave me put on a suit. I suppose that is Smith on third."

Canada had took over for George. "Yes," I said. "He was in Q. C. too."

"Nice arm," said Ugly, "but his throws have got the habit of rising. You married?"

"He used to be an outfielder," I said. "Mike Mulrooney made him over into a third baseman. No, I ain't married."

"You got a girl?" said he.

"Yes and no," I said.

"I do not like them yes and no girls," he said. "What do the boys say about me not signing? Does Dutch ever say anything?" Ugly kept looking past me, out at the field.

"They naturally wish you would sign," I said. "All except Coker Roguski that naturally wishes you would drop dead and give him the chance at short."

"I can understand that," said Ugly. "Do the boys know that there is nothing but a lousy 2,000 dollars between me and the Moorses? She has got 5 times that amount riding on her wrist right this minute. There is only 1 thing she ain't got and that is her snatch ain't lined with ermine. She might tell you it is but it ain't. I like Sid Goldman. People say he is weak in the field, but I do not see it. You watch his feet. He will make bad throws look like good throws. Do not keep looking up at her like that." He laughed.

"She ain't looking this way," I said.

"The hell she ain't," said Ugly. "She can see through you clear to your cup if you got 1 on. I remember Perry Simpson stole a base off us in a camp game 2 years ago."

Perry was working out at second now in place of Gene Park.

"He is a nice ballplayer," said Ugly. "If I was Dutch I would keep him. I see where Roguski switch-hits."

"That is right," said I.

"What is she doing now?" he said.

"Just sitting," said I.

"This is like a goddam concentration camp," said Ugly. "What in the hell is the sense of turning thumbs down on wives? I like my wife where I can keep an eye on her. Sad Sam has wore the rubber shirt since the first day in camp I suppose."

"Yes," I said, "he has." We watched Sam throw awhile. I watched him every chance I got. He was throwing down to Goose Williams, easy. "His weight is up," I said.

"That is 1 thing I never worry about," said Ugly. "I was born skinny and spent my first 15 years staring up the ass end of a mule. What is she doing now?"

"She is leaving the park," I said.

"Me too," said Ugly, and he turned and went after her, and I shagged flies until Dutch shouted lunch.

Ugly signed the next day. The newspapers said that him and the Moorses had a long conference and split their difference. That ain't what Ugly said. Ugly said him and Patricia Moors had lunch at the Silver Palms and dinner in St. Pete and a midnight snack somewhere on the road between St. Pete and Aqua Clara in a little place called the Pleasant Dreams Motel. He said it was 1 of the most satisfactory conferences he ever had, but it cost him 2,000 dollars.

Coker took it in stride. He had the sense to know that you do not come up from AA ball and knock a man like Ugly Jones out of a job as quick as all that. You dream about it, but you never do it, for the age of miracles is dead. Everybody knowed that Ugly would sign anyways sooner or later. What else could he do? Once you are with a club you are their property. You either sign or you do not play ball. Besides which, no need to feel sorry for Ugly Jones at 20,000.

Coker would be up there anyways, and he knowed it. He might spend a couple years on the bench, waiting for Ugly to give out, but sooner or later he was in. So was Canada, and so was Perry. It was me they was worried about for awhile.

We used to talk about it almost every night up there in the hotel, all except Perry, and the way it looked there was 1 spot open on the pitching staff that would go to either Bub Castetter or me. Bub was probably through, yet maybe Dutch was figuring on him for steadiness. Bub had 10 years experience and knowed the league. I figured me being a lefthander would help, for there was only Sam and me. Old Man Moors would of give 100,000 dollars for somebody like Bill Scudder, say. But Brooklyn would as soon sell the park as sell Scudder.

I suppose it don't pay to worry or try to figure ahead. What it all boils down to is what you do in action and not what you jaw about up there in the hotel room. Deeds is mightier then words. But ballplayers are great talkers, though every now and then you run across a fellow that never talks from noon to noon but just plays ball. There's always a couple on every club. On the Mammoths it's Sunny Jim Trotter and Scotty Burns. They room together, and I suppose if 1 was to say to the other "Open the window" or "Shut the door" or "Where is my pants?" the other would eat him out for a barber. Many a day I seen them come down for breakfast together and sit side by side and finish their meal and then go out in the lobby and light a cigar and sit in a chair with their head back. They would still be sitting there when you come down for lunch, and then they would go for lunch and rush right back and still be there right up until time to go to the park. I believe they never open their mouth the whole time except to take the cigar out and look it over and put it back in. Maybe I would of been better off if I copied their style. I don't know. I would not

know their voice if I heard it in the dark. If you ever wish to tor-
ture your average ballplayer to death simply tape up his mouth. He
will not die from the lack of food. He will just go mad from the
silence.

Wednesday of the third week the worst of the training was over
and we begun to actually play ball. That afternoon we split up in
2 teams, the Eggs and the Joes, Egg running 1 and Joe Jaros the
other, and we played a game every day for 3 days. The pitchers
worked an inning or 2, just fogging it through the middle, and the
hitters had a holiday, whaling the ball to all fields and then loping
around the bases. Nobody was supposed to slide, and the outfielders was not allowed to throw far, only relay, and the infield
played deep so as not to get their head blowed off by a batted ball,
and most of us come loose all of a sudden, like a cold motor on a
winter's day that coughs and gasps and misses fire and then all of
a sudden begins to hit on all cylinders and straightens away and the
oil begins to flow and the sparks fire regular, so that by Saturday
we was ready for the first real game.

Mike Mulrooney brought over the boys that he lined up for
Q. C. There was a few familiar faces, but mostly they was youngsters fresh up from clubs far down in the Mammoth system. It
drizzled a little, but we played nonetheless, and Gil Willowbrook
started for us and pitched 3 innings, and Herb Macy 3 more, and
Bub Castetter finished it off.

These kids was mighty anxious, and they played hard, hoping
to show everybody what hot ballplayers they was. Oh, they was the
hustlers! I guess they thought if they won that ball game that Dutch
would fire all the Mammoths and hire them instead. When you
are a kid you dream. Then in the seventh Scotty Burns batted for
Herb, and he skittered a single into right. It was a real blow, the
first of the year that had the sound and the look of the kind of a
hit a top ballplayer delivers. It went on a line, about knee-high,
and the first baseman and the second baseman dove, and they
neither of them more then seen it go past. I guess Mike's boys was
still thinking that 1 over when George Gonzalez and Scotty worked
the hit and run, George punching it through in just about the same
place, and there was 2 on.

The hit and run is 1 of the prettiest plays you will ever see. The runner on first will break for second. The second baseman on the other team goes over to cover. The righthanded hitter hits behind the runner, right through the slot where the baseman was. Only he ain't there no more. It is the kind of a play where if you miss the sign things is fouled up, but good. If the batter don't hit, the runner will get throwed out at second, or if the runner don't run the baseman will stay where he was and gobble up the ball and turn it into a double play for sure. If anybody misses their sign, or if the other team spots it, the whole thing falls on its face.

Anyhow, these poor kids was rattled by now with 2 on and none out and the heavy end coming up. There is nothing worse then a rattled club. Mike come off the bench and went out and tried to calm them down. We give Mike hell from the bench. "Mike," I yelled, "Q. C. will just love that ball club. They will just *love* it, Mike, just *love* it." He acted like he never heard me, though I guess he did. Christ, what an ungrateful bastard I can be when I try.

But for all Mike's talking them kids was just not up to the situation. We finally won the ball game, 12-9, Bub Castetter pitching the last 3 innings and getting touched up quite a bit. I tried not to feel sorry for Bub, for it was his job or mine, yet I could not help it. It is sad to see an old pitcher that 3 or 4 years before could of set down punks like these without half trying out there now and working as hard as he can and just about barely standing them off.

We played Q. C. again on Sunday. It was sunny and hot and the club charged admission to the park. The Cowboys was in their regular uniforms now. There was 1 kid wearing the number I wore the year before, an infielder as I remember. There was quite a crowd out, maybe 5 or 600 people in the stands and a couple hundred colored fans behind the ropes down the left field side. Dutch started Sad Sam, telling me I would finish up, and that give me the chance to watch Sam work the first 3. I was glad for that, and I sat on the bench between Coker and Perry and watched Sam work.

He worked very slow. Here would be this kid at the plate waving his club and itching to go, and Sam was down on the hill just taking his sweet old time. When he finally throwed the kid was wore out from all the exertion. I don't think there was 1 of them kids that got any solid wood on the ball except 1 colored catcher by the name of Brooks. Sam almost lost him. He throwed him 3 balls, which was the first time he got behind a hitter all day, and then he throwed the cripple. Very few ballplayers will hit the cripple, which is usually a straight ball that the pitcher fogs through. It is almost a custom not to hit at it, but this kid done so, and he lined it between right and center. Pasquale and Lucky raced over, and Lucky called and took it on the run, and I bet Mike eat that boy out plenty afterwards for swinging on the 3-and-0 pitch. The colored fans behind the ropes clapped, thinking the kid done something worthwhile. That is the way it always is. The fans will clap and cheer at something that anybody knows is bad baseball. Then on a good play, something that is really hard to pull off, they will sit there like their arm was paralyzed and their jaw broke.

Beginning in the fourth I warmed up with Bruce Pearson, and in the seventh, when I begun to work, Dutch put Perry in at second and Sunny Jim and Scotty and Swanee Wilks in the outfield.

I worked it slow, like Sam done. It used to be that I went out there and fired them through. I always wanted to be pitching. But I learned to take my time and think about what I was doing and not just go ahead and fire like a lot of boys will do. You do not get paid by the pitch.

The first hitter I faced was this same Brooks. He wanted to hit real bad. Fine, thinks I. I see him standing far back in the box, and I see him wave that club, and the club just barely reaches the outside corner of the plate. Red sees what I see. So we throw him 2 that will maybe nick the outside corner and maybe not, and he misses the first 1 clean, and the second he tips back in Red's mitt. Now he is way behind. He is worried. You can see his mind work. He figures maybe he ought to get closer to the plate, and he leans in a little. So Red calls for a fast 1, close, and I really pour it through, and the kid twists away, and he feels the breeze on his wrist. Now he thinks maybe he was too close after all. So he backs back to where he was. Behind me I can feel the boys tense a little. They know that this kid will go after the next pitch. He has got 2 strikes on him, and he is worried.

Mike Mulrooney comes down from the box at third and says something in his ear. Everybody knows what Mike said. Mike said to stand closer to the plate. But the kid knows better. This kid been playing ball 4 or 5 years and Mike has scarcely put in more then 40. Oh, these smart kids! Nonetheless he crowds up a little. I give him time to think it over. I scuff the dirt with my toe. I pick up the resin bag to dry the sweat from my hand even though it ain't sweaty. I look at the ball, thinking maybe there is something wrong with it, even though I know there is not. By now the kid has come to the conclusion that Mike is wrong and *he* is right. So he moves back to where he was. Then I throw the curve, which is what Red calls for. The same thing is going on in Red's mind as in mine. It is going on in the head of everybody in the park excepting only that kid at the plate. *Oh boy,* thinks he, here comes a fat 1. He swings at the wide breaking curve. Red grabs it and fires down to third. George whips it to Ugly, and Ugly to Perry and Perry to Sid. The ball is halfway around the infield before the kid knows what happened. He feels stupider then he ever felt before. He walks back towards the Queen City bench, trailing his bat behind. He says in his mind, "Maybe I will listen to Mr. Mulrooney hereafter." Down behind the ropes the colored fans clap.

I got the first man out in the ninth. Then 1 of them kids rapped a single into center, and about 30 seconds later the ball game was over on a double play, Perry to Ugly to Sid on a hit-and-run that Perry stole the sign off Mike, the sign being kick the dirt twice with your left foot with your right hand on your stomach and your thumb looped over the belt. We kidded Mike about that afterwards. He said he forgot about Perry being in there and remembering the sign from the year before.

That was the last we seen of the Queen City bunch for awhile. We played them twice more in Jacksonville about 10 days later, soon after we broke camp and started north. They were looking smarter by then. So were we, and we beat them both days. Then they headed west and back towards the Four-State Mountain League. They won the flag again. What a man Mike Mulrooney is!

19

MONDAY we drilled, and Tuesday Dutch give us off. That was the first and only open day we got all spring in Aqua Clara. It was the day me and Coker and Canada and Lindon sight-seen around and about town by bus and went to the alligator farm.

When we got back to the hotel none of the boys was around. Usually you will see Scotty and Sunny Jim in the lobby, and if there is a pinball machine you will always see Gene and Sid and some-times Bruce. We went upstairs, and it was quiet all up and down the floor until about 15 minutes later Red come strolling through. He had sandwiches all wrapped up in a napkin, and 2 Cokes with the caps off, and a bottle of olives, not yet opened. He went in his room. I followed. He took off his shoes and set up his food on the table by the bed. He went to his suitcase and got out a book and went and laid on the bed with his book in 1 hand and the food in reach. There was 3 chicken sandwiches, all white meat. I said, "All set for the night, ain't you? You sure look comfortable."

He give me a broad grin. "Go up and get you some," said he. "There is enough food up there to feed all the starving Chinese and then some."

"Where?" said I.

"Up in the penthouse," said he. "Up at Patricia Moorses that she pays 75 dollars a day for."

Red hates that girl. "Why do you hate her?" I said.

"I do not hate her," he said. "I feel sorry for her, just like I feel sorry for you and for me and the whole stinking earth. She is all confused in her mind and in her body." Then he picked up his book and found his place and stuck his finger in. "Go ahead up," he said. "You look hungry and probably ain't ate in an hour or more." He screwed open the lid of the olives and took 1 out and popped it in his mouth. He sucked out the stuffings. It made a good sound. My stomach give a rumble and I knowed I would have to go up.

(Holly says, "What book was he reading?" She says if you was to keep track of the books a man reads you would know more about that person, what type of a character he was, and so forth and so on. But I don't know. I never thought to look. Even if I would of looked I wouldn't of remembered.)

You never seen anything like the layout up there in her penthouse, 4 tables all pushed together and piled halfway to the ceiling. There was a big chunk of ice with a fish froze inside. There was types of food that I did not even know the name of. Half of them scarcely even *looked* like food. Yet I ate them, and they was pretty tasty. There was duck and goose and chicken and ham and about 20 types of cold cuts. You just dug in and shoveled it down. I was sorry I had ate any supper, for after awhile I was so stuffed I thought it would do me a week. I ate my head off.

The whole club was there plus a number of writers plus a number of people from the town, most of them in high society. Krazy Kress of "The Star-Press" was there, 1 of the fattest men I ever laid eyes on. We was standing together, him with a beer and me with a Coke when Patricia Moors come over with a glass in her hand, never looking at me, only at Krazy, and she asked him was he getting his fill, and he said he was, and I said leave us hope so for poor Krazy was probably down perilously close to 350 and what with the hot weather and all might waist away to a mere 325. "This is 1 fresh kid," said she to him. "If Dutch was not needing a lefthander so bad I would sell him."

"Like hell you would," said Krazy, and he laughed and give me a clap on the shoulder.

"This kid might make a story," said she. She took a swig from her glass and shoved it off on a colored waiter passing by and told him bring her another. "He will tell you how he is going to win 20 games this year if Dutch has the sense to keep him. Mike Mulrooney thinks very high of Henry."

"Is that so?" said Krazy.

"I was at Q. C. last year," I said. "I won 21 games there and left the club with still a month to go."

"The trouble with him is he ain't got enough confidence in himself," said she. The waiter brought her a new glass.

Krazy begun to pump me now. We went over and sat on the couch together. Patricia drifted away, and we talked awhile. Krazy was taking it all down in his mind, and I knowed it, for I can read these writers like a book. "Go ahead and write it down," said I, "for that is what you are itching to do," and he took some paper and a pencil out of his pocket and took down all we said.

Soon she come back and sat down beside us. I think she done it to shake off Ugly Jones. Well, Krazy Kress is mostly hips, and he took up a good deal of that couch, leaving me and Patricia not far apart, and her thigh was up against mine. There was an ash tray on a stand out in front of where we was sitting, and when she leaned across to stump out her butt now and then she grazed along my arm with her breast, and the first thing I knowed I was dry in the mouth, and there was a kind of a heart or a pulse drumming in my neck, and on top of all that I begun to feel that if I stood up all at once I would of looked peculiar, and pretty soon I could no more concentrate on what Krazy was saying then knit a pair of stockings.

After a time he hoisted himself to his feet. That is practically a job in itself for Krazy. He went back and mingled amongst the people. He give me a first-class write-up about 3 days later.

Me and her just sat there. I moved away about 6 inches or so, and she drunk another glass or 2 and smoked a lot of cigarettes, and pretty soon she begun to babble. She said she wondered how Krazy Kresses wife and him managed, him being so big and heavy and his stomach out so far. She asked me what I thought about that. I said I had never give it a thought. She asked me if Ugly Jones ever spoke about her. I said no, which was a lie. She asked me did I think Sam Yale loved his wife, and she asked me the same of Red, and then every little while she come back to Ugly, asking me did he ever speak of her and did he love his wife.

This palaver went on for quite some time. I forget all the questions she asked. Some of them she asked over and over the drunker she got, and once or twice I got up and started to leave, for she made me nervous, and every time I done so she grabbed a hold of my wrist and pulled me back down, and then she would not leave go of my wrist for 2 or 3 minutes. She would hold on, and she would dig 1 of them long nails down in the heel of my hand, and the way she done it got me so all-fired excited I thought I would blow the lid right then.

She hardly raised her voice above a whisper, and it was husky and rough, and her lips were wet and her teeth white and her eyes a little glazey, and she begun to call me her boy, saying I would be her boy now, like all the rest, and we was all her boys and we would win the flag for her if for no other reason, and she said she remembered a long time back when Sad Sam Yale first come up, and she was just a kid, and he kissed her smack on the button and said he would win her the flag, and he done so, and after the Series he kissed her again, and she remembered most how his hair was black and thick, for that was years ago, before Sam went bald, and things was different now. Then she put her hand in my hair. I pushed it away.

Then she upped and started out of there, very wobbly, and I went after. She went out in the hall and down past the elevators and out another door that looked like a window, and I followed, not knowing why but only so heated up I suppose if she jumped off the roof I would of did the same. It was cool out there, for it was a balcony, and she was standing by the ledge and vomiting off the side, down in the hotel swimming pool. "All that good liquor," she said. "All that good liquor gone down the drain to nowheres, just like me. Did you follow me, Wiggen?"

"Yes I did," I said. "You can call me Henry. Or Hank."

"Thank you," she said. "I suppose you have now begun following me about. Where is your sense? I guess you boys have got no sense, for your sense is down below your belt," and she cried, and she asked for my handkerchief, and I give it to her, and she cried some more and blowed her nose in the handkerchief, and finally she sank right down where she was, and she sat there a long while, and I stood over her, feeling foolish and yet not knowing what to do nor how to help. "For having his sense below his belt it cost Ugly 2,000," she said, and she laughed in a most hysterical way.

After a long time she felt better. I raised her to her feet, and she stood there a few seconds testing the ground like somebody feeling the ice on a lake before starting out, and then we walked very slow together back towards the door that looked like a window, and she held my hand, and when we got near the door she stopped and turned, and she said if I did not mind stale vomit and strong liquor and salty tears she would kiss me. I said I would take my chances, and she kissed me, except it was not like a kiss a girl would give a fellow on a dark balcony but more like a lady would give a little boy. Yet I liked it well enough, and I thirsted for another, and I dreamed that night that I had got the other, and more, too, dreaming the dream that night and many another night, all that summer, many and many a time, right down to the wire.

20

PHILADELPHIA landed in Aqua Clara the morning following. About 9 Coker come barging in the room along with Canada and 2 boys that been with Salt Lake the year before in the Four-State Mountain League and now was up with Philly. Philly owns Salt Lake. "You remember these boys," said Coker.

"Sure," I said, and I sat up in bed and stuck out my hand, and they come over and shook it. 1 of them was an outfielder that we always throwed low curves to, and the other was a righthanded pitcher with a motion like Knuckles Johnson but none of Knuckleses stuff. "Have they learned you to hit a low curve?" said I to the outfielder.

"I been working on it," he said.

"You better," said Canada, "for after 1 time around the circuit they will all be wise to you." I sent down for some breakfast and an extra pot of coffee and we jawed away an hour or more.

Philadelphia is the regular springtime opposition for the Mammoths. We always play a number of games with them in and about Aqua Clara just before we break camp, and we meet them on and off all the way north, winding up with 3 either in Philly or New York, 1 year 1 place and the next year the other, about 14 games in all. We beat them 9 times last spring, and they beat us 5, and the boys get to riding them, saying we was going to write the Commissioner and ask him to please switch Philly over to our league on account of life would be so much happier that way.

We drubbed them good the first 2 days at Aqua Clara. Dutch pitched Piss Sterling and Knuckles Johnson and Lindon 3 each the

163

first afternoon. We had the usual little meeting in the clubhouse before, going over signs and such. I spoke up and told Dutch about this kid that could not hit the low curve. "What is his name?" said Dutch.

"I forget it," I said.

"You forget it," said Dutch, very calm. "Very well, Wiggen, will you please do me the favor of bringing me that bat over there in the corner."

"Which 1?" said I, for there was about 75.

"I forget," said Dutch. A big laugh went up. I seen Sad Sam Yale grinning. Red was talking to George in Spanish, telling him what happened. Then George begun to laugh, too. I looked over at Coker, and he was sitting there looking down at his shoes.

"Coker," said I, "what was that fellow's name?" Coker shook his head, for he did not remember, nor did Canada nor Perry nor Lindon. Squarehead Flynn said it was on the tip of his tongue, but he could not remember.

"Oh, that is too bad," said Dutch. "It is on the tippy tip tip of the tongue of Squarehead Flynn and 5 other goddam rookies that passes themselves off as ballplayers. Well, ain't this just grand. I suppose it will all come back to you some day." My face felt like it was on fire. "It may not come back until Christmas," said Dutch, "but that will be time enough, for you can write it on a Christmas card and give me something to think about over New Year's."

"He bats left," said Coker, lifting his head. "He has got the name Mother tattood on the back of his hand."

"Ain't that tender," said Dutch.

"I will watch for him," said Red, trying to get us off the pan.

"No you will not," said Dutch. "These boys here will watch for him. I want his name and the number on his back before the game starts. Is that clear?" He looked from me to Coker to Perry to Lindon to Canada to Squarehead, and we all shook our head yes. I wished that I never brung the matter up. I would rather get knocked out of the box in 1 inning then get eat out by Dutch.

The big surprise of the spring was Swanee Wilks. Swanee been around a long time. For about 3 years everybody expected it would be his last. But now he hustled like he was 19. He bought some special-made bats in the winter. He said this was what done it plus having some teeth pulled plus getting a divorce from his wife. He was like a new man, hitting along at about a .400 clip. We felt good for Swanee all spring.

We went down to St. Pete for 2 days, whipping Detroit on both, 1 day in St. Pete and the next day over in Clearwater, and then we split 2 games with Philadelphia in Tampa, and then we doubled back to Aqua Clara for 2 with Cincinnati. When we got there we found out that Bradley Lord had kindly checked us out of the hotel, saving 4 days in rates for Old Man Moors that of course he needed to save on, him being just about in the poorhouse. Bradley Lord had all our gear moved down to the barrackses, which was where we was supposed to sleep. You can imagine what we thought of that little arrangement.

Yet we was in good spirits. It come on us all of a sudden that we just won 7 games in 8 days, and of course it did not mean a thing, being only spring games and nothing riding on the outcome, and yet in a way it meant plenty, for it meant that a lot of things we was worried about was not happening, and things we thought might happen never did, meaning mainly that Sam Yale and Hams Carroll and Knuckles Johnson was all looking good, and the younger pitchers was showing up fine, and the hitters hitting, and a fellow like Swanee that figured to spend the summer on the bench was all of a sudden out there plastering the ball like nobody's business, and everybody was down to his weight or else very close to it. Gene Park had a muscle in his heel that give him trouble from time to time, but this spring it just laid there quiet, and Horse Byrd had a crick in his elbow that usually never thawed out till June, but now it give him not an instant of pain whatever, and that was the way it was, hardly a gripe or a bitch, and I guess some of the boys was already imagining in their mind the pot of gold that laid waiting at the end of the rainbow in October.

That was the first night me and Coker and Canada and Perry was able to get together on the quartet. We had not sung in a bunch since Q. C. the summer before. If we was rusty it never showed. We was all sticky and tired when we got back from

Tampa, and it was late, and some of the boys took another shower, and the 4 of us sat on Perry's bed all wrapped in a towel, waiting for the others to clear out of the shower. We always give the older fellows first crack. We got in tune, sitting there on the bed and humming "I Love You As I Never Loved Before" real low, and going over the words, and "Carry Me Back To Old Virginny," and the 1 about the nice girl, the proper girl, where her hair hung down in ringulets. Bing Crosby done it on a record. Then we went in the shower, and we showered, and then we begun to sing. I guess we sung for 30 minutes, and when we was halfway through we could feel how quiet it was out in the main room of the barrackses, I took a peek out once, wondering why, and I seen where most of the boys was just laying on their bed, some of them all naked, some of them fanning theirselves, some of them just sitting wet and letting the breeze come through the window and dry them off, yet all of them looking kind of peaceful, like they was enjoying the music. Gil Willowbrook and Herb Macy was playing double solitaire on an empty bed, and Herb looked up, and he said, "Go on and sing some more."

So I went back in and we sung some more. Later, when we got to New York, we went up in the Brill Building on Broadway at 49th where all the music people hang, and we went in 1 office and out the other, telling them who we was, and they give us free copies of all the best new songs, stamped all over "Complimentary." The night before the opener we was on a TV show, and we sang, and after that these music people called up regular at least every other day, just about down on their knees and pleading with us for God sake sing their song on the air.

I really loved singing in them clubhouse showers. The walls vibrated, and I think it would put everybody in a good frame of mind. If we lost a ball game we might not sing at first. Then someone would say, "Why not sing?" and we would sing 1 that was slow and sad, like "My Old Kentucky Home," and then we would pick it up and sing faster, maybe "The Camptown Racers" or "Old Susanna," and after a time we forgot that the game was lost, and we was thinking ahead to tomorrow, and I think that when you add up all the things that made the club what it was you have got to take the singing into consideration, for it done something, just like Dutch's lectures done something, just like the hard work down in the south done something to make us what we was.

We split 2 with Cincinnati. Dutch had the pitching rotated pretty good. The fellows that was in the best shape was going 5 innings at a clip by now with Dutch every so often splitting up a game amongst the relief.

Bub Castetter started the second game against Cincy and set them down fine for 1 inning. But he got in a pack of trouble in the second, though he give up only 1 run. He was sweating like a hot-dog stand when he come to the bench, and breathing harder then he should of been. I felt sorry for him.

And then I got to thinking. Supposing he snapped back. Supposing he went along like his old self all spring or maybe clear to the Fourth of July. Then what? It was only a matter of time until he would be sent down again, like the year before. It seemed to me the best thing Bub could do was quit while still on his feet.

In the third somebody drilled 1 back through the box into center. I watched Bub. I seen him give ever so slight a look down at Dutch on the bench. Ugly took the throw in from Lucky, and Ugly and Gene both shifted over towards second, hoping to plug the gap. But you cannot cover up for another. The game has got to be played 1 certain way, and old friendship cannot matter, even though you might of once roomed with a man and drunk his beer and dealt 10,000 hands of poker, and he told you his troubles and you told him yours. You might of wrote him a letter over the winter.

But none of it matters. Only the game matters, and that is why I felt sorry for Bub, and sad, and wished him well, and yet, at the same time, I seen him falter and fail and knowed in my heart it might as well be sooner for his own sake and the sake of the club.

He never got a man out in the third, and Dutch lifted him, and we lost because we could not make back what Bub give away. That was only the second spring game we dropped.

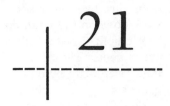

21

THAT night we broke camp for good and headed up by bus for Jacksonville.

The boys bitched about riding the bus. Red said every year they rode the bus all night from Aqua Clara to Jacksonville, and every year they bitched, and never a 1 of them thought to fuss about it at contract time. "But we have got to get these games in," said Red, "for it is a couple mighty good nights for Old Man Moors," meaning that since we played Queen City there, and then the Jacksonville club, and the whole works including the park owned by the Mammoths every dime got kept in the family except the electric bill, these being the first night games.

We sung for about 100 miles, me and Coker and Canada and Perry. It was the kind of a night you could sing your best, all clear, and the moon was big and she rode along beside, first in 1 window and then in the next, then disappearing over the top of the bus and coming down the other side, and now and again we would stop and pile out for a hamburg in some little town where they was all asleep except the people that run the diner and a few truck drivers and maybe a cop or 2 and a few old men. They would all be stunned to see us. We give out autographs, and 1 old boy in 1 of these towns grabbed a hold of my arm and he said, "Which is Sad Sam Yale?" and "Which is Ugly Jones?" and "Which is Swanee Wilks?" and "Which is Gene Park?" and there was 1 old colored man in 1 place come up and said he wished he could get the autograph of Lazybones Leo Newton, and the boys all laughed, for Lazybones was 10 years dead. Finally Red said, "Say there Lazybones Leo Dutch Newton, come over here and give this fellow your autograph," and Dutch caught on quick and come over and give out the autograph, forging it, and a dollar besides.

When we got back on the bus Dutch told us some stories of Lazybones, for they played together many a year on the old Mammoths, when they was called the Manhattans. Dutch said Lazybones could sleep 16 hours at a stretch. Yet give him a bat in his hand and he was not sleepy, not by a long shot, as the records prove. Well, you have probably read a good deal about Lazybones without me telling you anything you don't know. There is as many stories about Lazybones as about John McGraw or Ty Cobb or Shoeless Joe Jackson or Babe Ruth or Walter Johnson. I wish I could tell them like Dutch told them, sitting up there in the front of the bus with his feet stretched out on a suitcase, staring ahead at the road and thinking old memories and telling old stories. I moved up front. I took down a suitcase from the rack and stood it on end and sat in the isle, and I listened to them stories for 75 miles or better. They would just about make you weak from laughter. Or they could make you cry. If you ever heard Dutch tell about the death of Babe Ruth it would make you cry. I don't care who you are.

Mostly he told funny stories. I seen the driver, and I seen that he would smile. We would pass under a light in a half-assed sleepy town, or a car from the other direction would shine in his face, and he would be smiling. I guess for a bus driver it was a pretty big night. It was quiet, and I remember. Dutch talked soft, and we rode and rode and I never felt so peaceful and happy in all my life, listening there to the soft voices in the dark of the night. Then I heard a voice from the back. It was Swanee. "Dutch," he said, "suppose you was to do it all over again? Would you be a ballplayer all over again?"

Dutch thought awhile. "By God I would," he said.

"Not me," said Sad Sam.

"Bullshit," said Dutch. "What else would you be?"

"Bullshit is right," said Red. "There ain't a man on this bus that could eat like he eats in any other line of work. Leave us not kid ourselves. It is a stupid f---ing way of making a living but it is better than eating somebody's crap in a mine or a mill or a farm or an office. It is the gold we are after."

"This is all getting too deep for me," said Dutch. "Boys, let us have some music."

"Smith and Simpson is asleep," I said.

"You and Roguski sing," said Dutch.

"We cannot sing except all together," said I.

"That will sure play hell when it comes time to come down on the limit," said Sam, pretending like he was talking to Dutch' and I was not there. "Of course you might string up a radio between New York and Queen City. Then the 3 can sing at 1 end and Wiggen at the other."

Then Red said loud, like he was talking to Dutch and *Sam* was not there, "I was just telling George that if Sam Yale has not got some youngster on the club to razz and rag he considers the season a bust."

"I do not mind," said I.

"Boys," said Dutch, "why must we snipe at 1 another at a time like this? I certainly do hope in my heart that there will be no politics on the club this summer. Sometimes I think every ballplayer ought to be struck dumb at birth and kept like that until he has bowed out for good. If I had my way it would be done, for I sometimes think I would rather manage a squad of goddam gymnasium teachers. Talk talk talk. Politics, politics."

We got to Jacksonville early in the morning and slept all day in some damn hotel that did not have no air condition. It was so hot I could barely sleep. Perry slept with some friends and said they had a cool place.

Considering that I was tired I done well that night. Mike's kids was looking better, hitting harder and connecting more often. They scored 3 off me in the third on a pop fly home run by Brooks that in any ordinary park would of went for an out. All it was was a little looping drive that never sounded nor looked like a hit a-tall. There was 2 on at the time, both of them on singles that bounced off the wall in right, the wall being located about 6 feet behind first base, or so it seemed. Brooks went strutting around the bases like he done something unusual. Then I settled down and throwed wide to lefthanders and close to righthanders, and when I left the game after 5 innings we was ahead 7-3.

Afterwards Dutch asked me what that kid Brooks hit off me. "Hit!" said I. "He never hit nothing. His bat bumped into the ball."

"What in hell did he hit?" said Dutch.

"Just a fast ball," I said.

"Thank you," said Dutch, real sarcastic.

On the train to Savannah we seen a report in the papers stating that Dutch spoke long distance with Brooklyn, trying to buy Bill Scudder for 75,000 plus Gene Park and Goose Williams. That was why Dutch played Perry at second all 4 nights in Jacksonville, for he wanted a good, long look at Perry. Red told me. I never met a man that could figure the angles like Red. Red said that Dutch believed that for every colored ballplayer on a ball club there ought to be another to room with him, and that tied in with Dutch asking me about what Brooks hit, for if he sold Goose he would of brought Brooks up. There was another report in the Savannah paper saying that Dutch was ready to close a deal with Brooklyn, giving them Goose and Sid Goldman plus cash for Bill Scudder, and this made sense when tied in with the report the day after that St. Louis was ready to swap the Mammoths Jim Klosky for Gene Park plus cash, St. Louis badly needing a second baseman and Brooklyn feeling that Goldman and Williams would plug their gaps, though of course they was far from wild to part with Scudder. That would of meant that Perry Simpson would take over for Gene Park at second for us, Klosky at first, Brooks would come up and I would of probably been sent back to Q. C. Well, we was all in a nervous frame of mind and no mistake.

I pitched like a fiend the first game against Philly in Savannah. If they ever seen what I throwed they seen it too late to hit it, or if they hit it they never got a good piece. I worked 6 innings and give up 4 hits and no runs, and Bub Castetter finished and was wobbly all the way, but we won it on home runs by Sid and Gene Park. The trading talk sloped off some. That stuff goes hot and cold, and now it was cold, at least for a time.

Dutch probably turned cool on the trades. Maybe he was beginning to feel like I felt. I felt like this was a *club,* not just a bunch of ballplayers, but a *club.* Maybe there was politics and mutterings and mumblings, but it never mattered, for when you was out there it dropped away, and if Sad Sam Yale ain't spoke a word to Red Traphagen in years unless it be a dirty dig nonetheless you would of never knowed it watching them work together, and if George never spoke no English except his 2 favorite words it never mattered neither, for the lovely throw from third to first is something that got nothing to do with words.

I knowed that if anybody beat us they would go a long way to get it done, and when they was done they would know they been in a scrap. We could be beat. Sure! But beat us once and we would beat you 3 times back. We won easy and we lost hard all spring.

Philly beat us 2-1 the second day in Savannah, and we beat them on the third, 5-2. Savannah is where Perry was born, and he left when he was but a tot, him and 3 sisters and his brother and their uncle in an old 24 Moors with half the windows broke and no door by the driver. Perry says it was the coldest ride he ever took, going in the dead of winter from Savannah to Colorado. The uncle had a job in Pueblo, Colorado, and when they got there the job was took by another. Don't things like that just make you boil? Who would of thought that someday Perry would come back to Savannah and it cost you a buck just to see him from the bleachers?

Dutch played him at second on getaway night. He beat out a bunt twice and stole 2 bases. When Perry gets on base he gets the other pitcher rattled plenty. You can't judge Perry by averages. The way you judge him is by the number of times he gets on base, whether bunting or drawing a walk or beating out a roller that on most fellows would be an out, and you got to judge him also by the way he keeps the opposition worried. Then, too, every so often he will powder 1 plenty. As a defensive second baseman I consider him the equal of anybody in the league except Gene Park and possibly Pearce of Brooklyn, though I even doubt that Pearce can go so far to his right as Perry.

We took 2 out of 3 from Atlanta. I pitched the full 9 the third night, the first of the pitchers to go the route, and we lost 3-2.

It was the night I beaned this kid name of Scooter Lane in the seventh inning. We was leading 2-0 when Scooter come up, a right-handed hitting outfielder that seemed to like outside fast balls. So we naturally throwed him curves, close, that a smarter ballplayer might of expected, but he did not, and he leaned in, and the first pitch hooked and caught him full in the face, and it made a dull sound like if you was to drop a grapefruit on the sidewalk from 2 stories up, and he stood there looking at me, and it seemed a long time, and it seemed like he was smiling, and then his knees give way, and he leaned on his bat, and then he dropped.

When I reached him Red was bending over, and the umpire, and the crowd was still and silent, and then the doctor come, and the Atlanta trainer, and they stood the kid up. His face puffed up like a balloon, and he covered it with his hands, and they walked him off and out of the park.

Then I become terribly wobbly and give up 2 runs. Dutch give me a talking to between innings, saying "Forget it. Them things will happen. Steady down and do not be a goddam gymnasium teacher," and I steadied a bit in the eighth but got worse instead of better in the ninth, and the Crackers pushed across the winning run before I got a man out.

I showered and dressed quick and hustled out of there and over to the hospital. They had Scooter laying out in the hall on a stretcher, and his face was covered with wet towels, and I went in a little room and spoke with the doctor. The doctor said there was nothing broke. He said Scooter would be a little fatter down the left side of his head for a week or so, but otherwise nothing serious, and then we went out to where Scooter was, and the doctor took the towels off. "See," said the doctor, "does not Scooter look good all blue like that?" and Scooter tried to smile, but he could only work his lips in a very sickly way, and he did not open his eyes, and I said, "Lane, this is me, Henry Wiggen, that conked you," and he stuck up 1 hand, and I shook it.

"The doctor says you will be up and around in a week," I said. I could hardly look at him, for his face was an awful mess. Yet I looked at him square, out of duty. "Scooter," said I, "I have got a train to catch or I would keep you company awhile. I wish you would write me a letter and tell me how you do. I will be either with New York or Queen City. You can watch the papers and see. No doubt you will soon be up there yourself." This was a lie, and I knowed it, for he was not that good of a ballplayer. Yet I said it. "Scooter," said I, "you may be a little blue now, but you will be red hot by opening day." I thought that was fairly clever, and he gripped my hand again, and I loosened his shoes and took them off and carried them over to a basket and knocked the dirt out of the spikes and brung them back and laid them on the stretcher. Then I said "Goodby," and I went. He never wrote me the letter. But I followed the Southern Association averages in "The Sporting News," and Scooter done middling well, hitting about .260 on the year.

We whipped Philly 2 out of 3 in Knoxville. Swanee Wilks says once you are in Knoxville you are in the deep north. Sad Sam went the route the first night. That was his first full trick, and he set them down with 1 run on 5 hits, and Hams Carroll done as well the next, and Knuckles lost a close 1 the third night, and then we went over to Roanoke for a weekend pair with Philly, the last weekend but 1 of the spring. All we done most of the way over was play poker. There was a big game down in 1 corner, Sam and Goose and Knuckles and Bub and Ugly and that bunch, and another fairly big 1 somewheres in the middle of the car, Gil and Herb and Sid and the Caruccis and that crowd, and way down at the far end there was me and Perry and Coker and Canada and Squarehead and Lindon and Bruce playing a nickel limit. We played about 3 hours and Squarehead won a buck, and then he said this was too small potatoes for him, and he went up the line to where Sad Sam's game was, and we all went up and watched.

Them boys played it for blood. They played 5-card stud 50 cents the limit and none of your circus games such as the rest of us played, 7-card and draw and spit in the ocean and such as that. If the betting got down to 2 players the sky was the limit if they both agreed.

Sam always plays with a dead cigar in his mouth, and Knuckles always drinks water, and Ugly keeps clucking his lower teeth out over his uppers. If that ain't disgusting! They never say a word except whose deal it is and what was bet.

Squarehead dropped 25 bucks in 15 minutes, going clean broke when Sad Sam Yale drawed a 4 of clubs and filled a straight that nobody figured him for, least of all Squarehead.

Even now I seldom see a 4 of clubs but I think of Squarehead Flynn and Sad Sam Yale and the whole of that spring from Aqua Clara north, the singing, the bus ride, the trains, Patricia Moors and Scooter Lane, day games, night games, laughing and crying, Patricia crying in Aqua Clara, mostly a happy time, for it was a good club, maybe even a great and immortal club, and that was the best spring of my life, the spring when the dream come true.

22

WE FINISHED it up in Philly the Sunday before the Opener, Sad Sam Yale letting them down with 5 hits. I suppose I should of seen the handwriting in the cards right then and there, for Dutch must of already been planning to start me when the season got under way Tuesday. Else why would he of worked Sam Sunday? But I was so busy watching Sam I wasn't thinking ahead much. It was really beautiful. I sat betwixt Coker and Perry in the dugout, and we watched, and it was beautiful. It was the third straight time Sam went the full 9, and all in all it was the neatest, cleanest job anybody turned in all spring. The minute the game was over I ducked back through the dugout and in the clubhouse. Then in come the rest, all hilarious. Here is what it was like:

In comes Sad Sam Yale, and he says, "Mick McKinney, you Irish bastard, come here and give my arm a rub."

"Coming, pal," says Mick. Sam whips off his shirt and Mick goes to work.

In comes Goose Williams. "Nice game, Sam," says Goose.

"Goose," says Sam, "what in the hell did you do with my 9-inch raping tool?"

"I never seen it," says Goose.

"You lie, you bastard, for I loaned it to you in Aqua Clara."

"That is right," says Goose. "So you did. Sam, I must of lost it."

"Damn it," says Sam, "ain't that the way? You loan a thing to a fellow and you never get it back."

"Maybe Ugly will loan you his," says Mick.

176

"Ugly, you ugly bastard," shouts Sam. "Loan me your 9-inch raping tool. I will give it back to you in New York Tuesday."

Ugly never gets a chance to answer. In comes Bradley Lord. "Men," says he, as loud as he can, "nobody must get dressed, for Miss Moors wishes to come in and say a word or 2." He sits on a bench far from the rest.

"Get your ass off that bench," says Knuckles Johnson. "That is my bench."

"Your bench?" says Bradley Lord.

"That is Knuckleses bench," says Swanee Wilks.

Bradley Lord gets up and stands by the water cooler. In comes Red Traphagen. He sits down where Bradley Lord was, and he begins to shed his harness. He unstraps his protector and slips it off. He unstraps his shin guards. He reaches down in his pants and yanks out his cup. He looks across at Sad Sam Yale. "Nice game, Sam," says Red.

"Thank you, friend," says Sam. That is the longest conversation Sam and Red have had in years. Mick goes over to Red. He tapes Red's finger where a nail is broke and bloody. In comes Dutch. He is smiling. He goes to the trough.

"Miss Moors is coming," says Bradley Lord.

"She will have to wait until I am done pissing," says Dutch. "Nice game, Sam."

We all sit on the benches, talking quiet. Sam Yale speaks out above all the rest. "Dutch," says he, "Goose borrowed my 9-inch raping tool in Aqua Clara and never give it back. Could you loan me yours?"

Dutch stands there buttoning his pants. "I use mine yet," says he. "Joe Jaros never uses his. Borrow Joe's."

Everybody looks at Joe. He is sitting on a bench. He takes off his cap. He is old, yet there is not a gray hair on his head. He bends his head forward. "For every hair on my head I will use my 9-inch raping tool 1 more time," says he. "The same goes for Egg." There is a great laugh, for Egg is as bald as a baseball. Egg spits out a squirt of water from the cooler, and it lands on Joe. Sunny Jim Trotter goes to the trough.

"Miss Moors is about to come," says Bradley Lord. Sunny Jim

looks at Bradley Lord, but don't stop what he's doing. A great laugh goes up. Sunny Jim finishes and goes back and sits beside Scotty. They talk together in a low voice.

"I will be damned if I was out at first that time," says Lucky Judkins.

"Things was getting called bad all day," says Pasquale.

"Toft is getting old," says Clint Strap, meaning Dale Toft, the well-known umpire.

"Was that Toft umpiring at first?" says Canada.

"Yes it was," says Clint.

"Pasquale," says Sam, "loan me your goddam 9-inch raping tool."

"Pasquale never needs it," says Hams Carroll. "He might as well loan it to you."

"I will need it in the winter in Frisco," says Pasquale.

"Pasquale," says Dutch, "get Mick to give you a new sunshade if you need 1."

"Yes sir," says Pasquale.

"Bradley Lord, when is she coming?" says Horse Byrd. "I wish to take a shower and get out of here."

"Say," says Sam, "we have forgot to congratulate Bradley Lord."

"That is right," says Swanee. "We have forgot."

"Congratulations!" shouts out a number of the boys. Then there is a long time of silence. I wonder what Bradley Lord has done. Yet I am sure this is some kind of a gag, and I say nothing. Finally Squarehead speaks up. Poor Squarehead! "For what?" says he.

A great laugh goes up.

"He has stopped —— ——," says Sad Sam Yale.

"Why is everybody so down on Bradley Lord?" says I.

"Nobody is down on Bradley Lord," says Sam. "There has always got to be a pimp in the crowd. He would rather be a pimp then a man."

"He would rather be a pimp then a man," says Bruce Pearson.

Bradley Lord just stands there like he does not hear a word.

"That is enough," says Dutch.

"Vincent," says Sam to Vince Carucci, "loan me your 9-inch raping tool. I will give it back to you in New York Tuesday."

"Borrow Sid's," says Vince.

"Sid," says Sam to Sid Goldman, "I would borrow your 9-inch raping tool except it is of a different sort and might not work so good."

"Hell," says Sid, "you would never know the difference. Mick, come over here and look at my foot. It got stepped on by Jay Pringle." Mick goes over and looks at Sid's foot. There is a little nick from a spike. Mick cleans it and tapes it.

"Jay Pringle goes on and on," says Dutch. "He must be 42 at least. Yet year after year he looks like the year before. I honestly believe some men grow old fast and some slow. I never seen Pringle except that he was hustling. I admire that son of a bitch as much as I admire any man in the game today."

In comes Patricia Moors and 2 of the workers from the park, all dressed in white. They are carrying 2 cases of beer and 2 of Coke. They set the cases on the steamer trunk in the middle of the floor. They take can openers and bottle openers out of their pocket. "Thank you, boys," says Patricia. She gives them both a dollar.

Dutch opens the cases. He heaves a can of beer to whoever wants. Most want beer. I take a Coke, but there ain't an opener handy, and I go forwards and open the bottle in the lock of the steamer trunk. "Wiggen, sit down," says Dutch, "for Miss Moors wishes to speak."

She leans against the trunk. "Pzzz, pzzz," goes the beer cans. She waits until everybody is set. She lights a cigarette. "Up in New York everybody is talking about the Mammoths," says she. "I wish to say how much that pleases me. My father calls me up from Detroit. He says, I see where the club beat Baltimore something awful last night. I said to him did you call me just to tell me that. Call me when we lose, for when we win it ain't news. That is how everybody feels in New York. That is the way it ought to be, for this is as fine a club as was ever put together."

Bradley Lord opens her a beer. "Is there a glass around?" says he.

"Give me the can," says she, and she grabs it from him. "I mean every word I say," she says. "There would be no sense in trying to fool you, for you know it yourself. I just seen Krazy Kress," meaning Krazy Kress of "The Star-Press." She opens her bag and fumbles inside. "Krazy give me a copy of his column for opening day. I will read it," she says, and she reads it.

I will write it out in full at the end of this chapter.

The smoke pours out of her mouth while she reads, and every so often she stops and pulls on her beer. I keep looking at her and thinking how beautiful she is. My name is mentioned in the column, and I listen very close. When she is done reading she gives it to Dutch. "This is for your memory book, Dutch," says she, "for this will be the year you will want to remember, the year and the club. That is all. I just wish to add that everybody knows where my offices are, both at the park and then again downtown. I am not there only to go with the furniture. I am there to be a help to anyone that needs it, as well as Dutch and the coaches and the doctors. Feel free to call on me."

"I want my salary doubled," says Knuckles. This gets a great laugh.

"There will be a salary or 2 doubled," says she, "after we win the flag. I am anxious for you boys to see what we done with the park. We done wondrous things. There is a new scoreboard 135 feet in the air. There is all new grass and infield dirt. There is another Coke machine in the clubhouse and a coffee machine as well. There is 4 new towers of lights. Nobody in the league has got lights like us. Some of you boys complained about the beer sign in center field being too white. That sign is took down and the space painted green. The club comes first. The ballplayer is what makes the club. The outfield is sloped to drain better. There is 12 foot of black clay all around the outfield fences so you will know where you are at, and there will not be no more fielders crashing in the wall like Pasquale done that time last year."

"About that article," says I. "It is cockeyed in 1 respect. He says we could use 1 more lefthander. He must of been asleep like a bear all spring, for I lost but 1 ball game and would not of lost that but I beaned a kid in Atlanta and had 2 wobbly innings."

"That is true," says she. "These writers have got their cockeyed moments." She thinks a little. "I guess that is all. I am driving back to New York. Is there somebody would like to come?"

Ugly says he will go.

"Anybody else?" says she, and she looks around. "Red?"

"I will take a rain check," says Red.

She looks around still more. "How about George?"

Red speaks in Spanish to George, and George answers. "George says he will take a rain check," says Red.

"Patricia," says Sad Sam Yale, "I have got a problem. Down in Aqua Clara I had a beautiful 9-inch raping tool that was never used more then 20,000 times. I loaned it to Goose, and Goose lost it."

"A what?" says she.

"A 9-inch raping tool," says Sam.

"Oh," says she. "Well, Sam, see my secretary in New York." She says to Ugly that she will bring her car around to the clubhouse door. Out she goes with Bradley Lord.

"Maybe Henry Wiggen will loan you his," says Knuckles.

Sam says, "Henry, you punk of a lefthanded son of a bitch, loan me your 9-inch raping tool as I have need for it tonight in Upper Darby."

I am now positive it is a gag. In the beginning I did not catch the words too clear. I rise from the bench. "Yes, Al," I say, and I hold in the air an imaginary object, "in my estimation these are the finest raping tools on the market. I have tried them all, and I know. These are my choice for a smoother, superior product, a tool that gives me that pleasant good-to-be-alive-all-over feeling. Fans, take my word for it, penny for penny THIS is your most dependable buy." Then I smile broadly, and there is a great laugh.

Dutch sits on the bench and shakes his head. "Somebody ought to write a book," says he.

"Somebody ought to write a good book about baseball," says Sam.

"Somebody ought to write a good book," says Red.

Ugly is all naked by now. He goes across the floor and in the shower. "Nice game, Sam," says he. He runs the water, and the steam pours out. But he is the only 1. Nobody seems to wish to move. Everybody sits back and sucks on their drink. Everybody is relaxed, and everybody is happy.

I swig another Coke. "We had a kid drunk Cokes like that," says Gene to me. "All in 1 gulp. He was a first baseman in Queen City, a redheaded kid, and he begun 1 year with us and then got took by the Army. Dutch, you remember that kid. What in the hell was his name?"

"That was a kid name of Petey McCall that Mike made over from a pitcher. He was killed in the war," says Dutch.

"How many Cokes you drunk?" says Sam to me.

"2," says I.

"I bet you a dollar you cannot drink 1 more all in 1 swig," says Sam.

"Put up your dollar," says I, and Sam reaches for his pants and pulls out a dollar, and I do the same. I take a Coke, and I snap the cap. I stand in the middle of the floor and I put my right hand on my hip. Everybody is watching. With the other hand I pour it down, all in 1 swig. Sam gives me the dollar, and I sit back on the bench.

"What was the matter with sending Ugly home on Gene's hit?" says Egg to Joe Jaros.

"5 runs ahead what was the sense?" says Joe. "The first thing you know Ugly is sliding and busting his f---ing leg over a run we do not need in an exhibition."

"Roguski," says Sam to Coker, "I know what you are thinking, you bastard. You are thinking Joe should of sent Ugly home and left him bust not only 1 leg but his both f---ing arms besides."

"I was never thinking no such thing," says Coker.

"For thinking thoughts like that run over to the Philadelphia clubhouse and tell Jay Pringle Sam Yale needs to borrow his 9-inch raping tool," says Sam.

But Coker never makes a move. He is wise to the gag. He sees how Sam is working down the line to the rookies, trying to pull it on me, and now on Coker, looking for the 1 that will fall. "Maybe you might borrow Perry's," says Horse Byrd.

There is a good laugh at this, and the boys look down the line at Perry Simpson. He is shaving a bat handle, and he does not look up. Then he speaks, saying each word slow and deliberate. "It ain't the right color," says he.

All the boys roar. "That is 1 nifty kid," says Sam. "Perry, you are 1 great kid. For your sake I hope that Gene Park dies of the bloody flux by Wednesday."

"You boys are playing mighty free with my ball club," says Dutch.

"Dutch," says Sam to Dutch, "you do not need a ball club. You need only Henry Wiggen. He will pitch 4 days in every 5. He will pitch doubleheaders and batting practice and in his spare time mow the grass. I walk into the hotel in Aqua Clara the first night, and down comes Henry fresh as a daisy. He is all set to chew my ear. I do believe he was waiting at the window. I go past him up the stairs and flop in bed, all wore out from the trip. 5 minutes later he corners Traphagen. I hear him all the way down the hall. He is informing Traphagen the situation on Ugly Joneses contract, all about the home town and all about pitching. You do not need second-rate ballplayers such as Ugly and Gene. All you need is Henry Wiggen. Goddam it, ain't we ever going to clear out of Philadelphia?" He pulls off his shoes and his pants and his stockings. Then he sits down again in his jock, and he scratches his feet 1 against the other. "Squarehead Flynn," he shouts, "I would give a lot if you will run over to the Philly clubhouse and ask Jay Pringle to loan me his 9-inch raping tool."

Squarehead is not sure if it is a gag. He gets kidded so much he never really knows if it is a gag or on the level. 1 time in Q. C. the bellboy brung him a package, saying it was a gift. Squarehead chucked it in the basket, saying he was no longer a sucker for jokes. When it hit the basket it crashed all over the place. We opened it up. It was a set of 6 cocktail glasses for his wife, 5 of them broke and the other chipped clean down the middle.

"Why do you laugh?" says Sam. "If I was dressed I would go myself. That is the trouble with the average rookie. Tell him a thing and he laughs. That is why you do not get nowheres, Squarehead. Everything to you is a big joke."

"Sam," says Goose, "do not make Squarehead go over. I am the 1 that should go over, for it is I that lost it to begin with."

"You are truly a friend," says Sam. "I thought Squarehead was my friend. It seems to me that I remember I loaned him 5 dollars when he was broke in Savannah. Is that not true?"

"That is true," says Squarehead.

Everybody is absolutely quiet.

"Then when a fellow gets down on his luck all the world turns against him," says Sam.

Squarehead starts to speak, but Goose cuts him off. "Should I go, Squarehead, or you?"

Out comes Ugly from the shower. "Somebody loan me some goo for my arms," says he, "for I stink like a mule in the summer." Gene tosses him a bottle of Mum, and Ugly dabs in with his finger.

"Go easy," says Gene.

"Ugly," says Red to Ugly, "I know of a thing that stops a man from perspiration."

"What is that?" says Ugly.

"Death," says Red.

"Ha, ha, ha," says Ugly. "That is a real smart remark. Did they learn you many of them smart remarks at Harvard?"

"They never learned me a thing," says Red. "All I learned I got by myself. They give me a sack full of books and I read them through. Then they give me a diploma. Then I go down to New York. I go in 1 office and out the other. I have read a sack full of books at Harvard, say I. 50 dollars a week, say they. Up yours, say I, for I can make 50 dollars of an afternoon playing baseball. I sell the books. I send home for my mitt and my mask and my protector. I have lost my shin guards. I buy a ticket to Aqua Clara with the money from my books. Gussie Petronio is the Mammoth catcher at the time. He has an old beat-up pair of shin guards that he sells me for 2 dollars and 50 cents. Thank you, Gussie, says I, I will do something for you some day. You know what I done for Gussie?"

"You took away the bastard's job," says Dutch. Everybody laughs.

"I bought a car off Gussie in the winter," says Sam. "He runs a Moors agency in Dallas."

"To me," says Dutch, "Gussie was always 1 of them ballplayers that had all the makings of a great. Yet he never quite come to the full promise."

"Gussie is the kind of a guy that if he was here he would lend you his 9-inch raping tool," says Goose to Sam.

"Squarehead, old boy, run over and borrow it from Pringle," says Sam.

"Cut it, Sam," says Dutch. "If you have lost your tool it is your own damn fault. If I was Squarehead I ain't so sure I would run your errands. Squarehead ain't an errand boy. He is a first baseman."

"Ain't that the truth," says Sam.

"I will go," says Squarehead, and out he goes through the door. Nobody says a word. I wait for the laugh, but there is no laugh.

"He hits a long ball," says Egg. "The only trouble is that 9 times in 10 he hits it dead center."

"Mike Mulrooney done everything he could to learn him to pull," says Lindon.

"Usually it is against my policy to talk behind a ballplayer's back," says Dutch, "but just between us I will say it is a hard job learning Squarehead anything. You cannot blame Mike."

Ugly is dressed to kill. He usually always is. "Goodby, you bastards," he says.

Out he goes, and in comes Squarehead.

"Sam," says Squarehead, "Pringle says he has got 2 and does not know which you want."

"Either 1, Squarehead old boy," says Sam, and out goes Squarehead again.

"Somebody throw me a beer," says Hams Carroll. He is laying stretched out on the floor. Gil Willowbrook opens a can and carries it to Hams.

"St. Louis bought Jimmy Lusk off Cleveland," says Joe Jaros to Dutch.

"Who says?" says Dutch.

"I seen it in the paper," says Joe.

"I never seen it," says Dutch, "though I believe the change might do Jimmy good. Boys, there will be no more trades."

Everybody hears this and is pleased. Then it is quiet. A little breeze comes in through the window. The boys that smoke smoke, and the smoke floats out through the window, and now and then somebody goes over and lifts out a beer and opens it. "Pzzz, pzzz," goes the cans. A few of the boys get up off the bench and begin to strip down. It seems to me like somebody ought to speak. Yet there is nothing to say. There is nothing left to say or do, for it was all said and all did between Aqua Clara and Philly, and all the weight was shed that needed to be shed, and the mob that was at Aqua Clara is now no longer a mob, but a *club,* all narrowed down, and all the dead wood is cut away except for the last slash in May, and that would be Bub and Squarehead, for the boys could figure it out for theirselves, and the boys was all fit and ready to go and waiting only for the cry "Play Ball!" on Wednesday, all brown and fit and itching to get started, and nobody hurt and nobody sick and nobody mad at nobody.

In comes Squarehead Flynn. He has got a package in his hand, about the size and shape of a Coke bottle, all wrapped as neat as could be in toilet paper and tied with the lace of a shoe. He carries it over to Sad Sam Yale, and Sam says "Thank you, Squarehead my boy. I sure appreciate what you done for me."

"That is okay, Sam," says Squarehead, and he stands there looking. "Ain't you going to open it?"

"Open it?" says Sam. "Would you want it to get all saturated?"

"No," says Squarehead, "I guess not."

Sam lays it very gentle on the top of his locker, and everybody watches, and yet nobody says a word, and yet we are laughing to ourselves. Red is talking in Spanish to George, and George busts out in a fit of laughter. But George is the only 1, and we take our shower and dress, and little by little the clubhouse empties out, Scotty and Sunny Jim, Vincent and Pasquale and Sid, Herb and Gil, Dutch and the coaches, Red and George, Lucky and Gene, Squarehead, Bruce and Piss, Hams and Horse, Knuckles and Bub and Goose and Swanee and Sam, then me and Canada and Coker and Perry and Lindon. I am the last. There is nobody left but Mick McKinney. I am always the first to the park and the last away. The final thing I see is the package, still tied all neat and trim, sitting on top of Sad Sam's locker. Whoever found it afterwards must of wondered.

Following is the article wrote by Krazy Kress in "The Star-Press" on Opening Day but read to us beforehand by Patricia Moors in the clubhouse in Philly. Pop tore it out and saved it. He saved everything that was wrote in the papers from February through September. He bought all the New York papers every day in Perkinsville, plus the Perkinsville "Clarion," and he clipped them with a razor and pasted them up in 6 different scrapbooks. The article is as follows:

OUT ON A LIMB

I returned yesterday to this littered desk from a delightful weekend in Philadelphia, historic home of such wonders of the modern world as Connie Mack and the Liberty Bell. It was not, however, the charm of the Quaker City that contributed to the pleasures of my stay so much as the edifying view I obtained of our own Mammoths. What I saw gratified me, however much it may have dismayed the 61,385 Philadelphians who witnessed the three contests.

Now, as constant—bless 'em—readers of this column are aware, I am constitutionally opposed to pre-season predictions. It is a dangerous practice, leading to severe cases of embarrassment after the fact. But I hereby break my own rule. I predict. I say, and you may quote me, that the pennant flag will fly from the center-field mast in Moors Stadium this very summer.

No? Okay, you are entitled to your own opinion. But who's your choice? Boston? Boston is the most obvious suggestion. It has the pitching, to be sure, but it lacks power. It owns baseball's most fearsome long-distance hitter in Casey Sharpe, but its attack ends there.

Brooklyn, you say? No, I can't see Flatbush repeating last year's triumph. Can Bill Scudder pitch every day? Hardly. Those of the Greenpernt persuasion must therefore doff their rose-colored glasses and face up to reality. Brooklyn looks like a shoo-in—a third-place shoo-in, that is.

Cleveland: a fourth-place finish.

St. Louis: will top the second-division, garnering such honors as may go with that position, honors (not cash) being about all the Mound City lads will enjoy this year.

Pittsburgh and Washington: these two clubs will battle for the sixth-place berth.

Chicago: the cellar, as usual, until a certain club owner I could name overcomes his excessive zeal for money and becomes willing to buy the ballplayers only money can buy by building a farm system that extends beyond the playgrounds of the Windy City.

That Certain Age

There is, it seems to me, an age factor involved in the sensational spring showing of the Mammoths, and it is this age factor, too, that will fortify the club through the long campaign. At first glance one might opine that it lacks balance, that its old dependables are just a shade too old, its youngsters a bit too young. This, however, is more than likely to work in favor, rather than against, the boys who will be playing under that amiable gentleman, Dutch Schnell.

Let's look first at that outer garden. The pickets who will patrol the far reaches of Moors Stadium along about mid-afternoon today—Lucky Judkins and the Brothers Carucci—are seasoned ballplayers who have not yet begun to slow down. Is there a better outfield in the league? Name it, please. And you might almost say that the second-best outfield in the league is sitting on the Mammoth bench. Swanee Wilks, the grand old man of the Mammoths, will be thirty-five in June. Nevertheless, our Swanee is still a better than fair country ballplayer. He led the club in hitting this spring with a resounding .395.

Behind the plate, too, the Mammoths are the class of the circuit. The learned Berwyn Phillips Traphagen, at thirty-two, may find himself sitting out the second game of double-headers now and then, but the tempestuous redhead, popular again with the fans after his eccentric wartime behavior, is the league's wisest backstop. Williams and Pearson have the necessary equipment to serve as able replacements when, as, and if, needed.

In the infield, George Gonzalez and Sid Goldman are young men with futures. Jones and Park, if they are older than ever, are also more dependable than ever. Both boys hit hard, and they, with Traphagen, provide that punch in the lower half of the batting order which has won so many ball games for the Mammoths in the past and can be expected to do so again. It

is only on the bench that the infield is weak, Roguski, Flynn
and Simpson being untried and untested, with Canada-born
Earle Smith slated to return for further seasoning at Queen
City under Mike Mulrooney, the jovial gentleman whom Red
Traphagen has described as baseball's Harvard and Yale.

A Kingdom for a Southpaw

A strange phenomenon often commented on by baseball-
wise observers has been the inability of the extensive Mammoth farm system to produce first-rate left-handed pitchers.
Sam Yale, he of the lugubrious physiognomy, almost alone,
year after year, has carried the brunt of the Mammoth's southpaw chores.

Skipper Dutch Schnell seems to have a certain amount of
faith in young Henry Wiggen. Wiggen was the sensation of
the Four-State Mountain League last year, and he has twirled
creditably this spring. But whether he can carry his load
throughout the summer is a moot question. It is well-known
that Dutch would give his right eye, several ballplayers and a
barrel of Moors cash for a left-hander of the caliber of Brooklyn's big Bill Scudder. This failing, the Mammoths will be
forced to rely upon Sam the Sad and Wiggen, the latter a
doubtful quantity. In any case there are a battery of formid-
able right-handers—Johnson, Carroll, Sterling, Macy and Willowbrook, Horse Byrd, the dependable fireman, Castetter and
Burke. Burke's tendency to wildness after three or four innings is a regrettable affliction which Dutch and his corps of
aides have sought in vain to cure all spring. But Burke may
yet settle down and pitch winning ball.

A crackerjack ball club, you must admit. The crackerjack-
est, you might say. That's why I fully expect, come October,
to be viewing portions of the World Series from the elegant
press box at Moors Stadium. And I'm not afraid to say so,
even at this early date, and even despite my constitutional aver-
sion to the ancient and honorable—but frequently embarrass-
ing—practice of crystal-gazing.

Play ball!

23

MONDAY we drilled from 11 till a little after noon. I come up through the dugout with Perry and Coker and Canada, and we stood on the steps. "There she blows," said I.

"*This* is a ball park," said Canada, for he never seen it before, nor did Perry nor Coker. Perry whistled between his teeth. Coker said, "I suppose if you was lost up there in the stands somewheres they could send a dog out after you."

For a drill that was supposed to be closed to the public there was certainly a large number of people present. There was men on scaffolds riding up and down along the fences, putting in a last little dab of paint here and there. There was about 100 more sweeping and scrubbing in the stands and bleachers. There was a bunch of men crawling up and down on the towers, testing all the lights. There was 3 men on power mowers, and about another dozen down on their knees clipping with a scissors what the mowers missed. There was 1 man painting the top of the visiting dugout. You could hear hammers and saws in all corners of the park, and there was a fellow testing the loud speaker, "testing, 1, 2, testing, 1, 2," and the lights on the new scoreboards was flashing on and off. That scoreboard shows just about anything, up to and including a running box score, plus a line score, plus how other games are going in both leagues, plus of course balls and strikes and hits and errors, plus even the names of the umpires. It takes 3 men to run it.

And then of course on top of everything there was the usual plague of writers circulating around the clubhouse and the dugout and the batting cage. Me and Perry no sooner hit the field then a colored photographer run up wanting a picture of the 2 of us with our arm around each other. It come out quite nice in the Harlem paper later on in the week. Other writers come around asking questions and trying to get somebody to say something worth writing down. Soon Dutch come up out of the dugout and made them all clear off the field.

We got some work done. There was a good infield drill plus some mighty impressive hitting. Some of the boys parked a few in the stands. Sid hit 1 over the Gem sign, a mighty blast when you consider that the cage was moved clear back to the screen, and Red walloped 1 that went in just above the Blatz. Squarehead hit the longest of the morning, a drive that went 450 feet that I took without moving, for me and Gil Willowbrook was shagging flies in center. It seemed like I waited 20 minutes at least, for it went so high before it dropped. I said to Gil, "I guess I know where Squarehead hits them." When Squarehead finished hitting me and Gil moved in about 50 feet.

After awhile Dutch yelled at me to come in and hit a few. I suppose it should of made some impression on me at the time, for since when does a lowly relief pitcher take batting practice? But it did not, and I trotted in and took a bat and went in the cage. Lindon was throwing. "Now," said I, "not too hard, Lindon old boy, for I am no hitter."

Bruce Pearson was catching. "Dutch says to throw fast," he said.

"Okay," said I. "If I catch a glimpse of it I will stick out the bat."

I poled the first 1 a terrific drive that Lindon picked up with his bare hand when it stopped rolling. Then I swang at 5 and missed them all. Lindon give me a twist of the wrist, meaning that he would throw a couple curves. I swang at 3 and missed. I poled the next 1 a gigantic clout that went about 150 feet in the air and come down on the screen above my head. "Bunt a couple," said Bruce, and I bunted 3. I consider myself just about a perfect bunter. A pitcher has got to know how to lay them down.

When me and Coker and Canada and Perry got back to the hotel a fellow come to see us from the TV show put on by Fireball Gas called "People, U. S. A.," and he said he would give us all 100 each to sing on the air that night. The m.c. of the show is Larry Hatfield. Larry would throw a few questions at us and then we would sing 2 songs.

This fellow was a very swishy sort of a character. I notice that there's quite a few like that in and around TV studios. Just before he left Canada made some little remark, using a nasty word. "That reminds me," said this fellow, "you have got to watch your language on TV. If someone was to cuss there would be the most awful consequences."

"Cuss?" says Coker. "Why, dear me, nobody on this ball club ever says so much as the nastiest little word. Heavens to Betsy, if we was to be vile or not act like gentlemen Dutch Schnell, our sweet manager, would wash out our f---ing little mouth with soap." Coker never cracked a smile, and this fellow did not know if he was being took for a ride or not. Perry cut in and made Coker lay off. Perry said it is okay to ride a man, but not when you are libel to get him mad and it cost you 100.

We went down to lunch, and then I telephoned home. I could hear the Perkinsville operator switching in, and the next thing I heard was Pop's voice.

"Pop," said I, "this is Hank."

"Hello, boy," said Pop, "how is the flipper?"

"Never better," said I.

"Why do you never write a letter?" said he.

"I am too busy," said I.

"I guess you are at that," said he.

"Listen," said I, "the reason I called is that me and Perry and Coker and Canada is going to sing on the TV tonight."

"Sing?" said Pop.

"Sure," said I.

"What time?" said Pop.

"8," said I. "We get 100 each."

"For singing?" said Pop. "Maybe you ought to quit baseball and go into singing." He laughed. "We are coming down to New York tomorrow."

"Coming down?" I said. "What do you want to come all the way down just to see me sit on the bench?"

"I got a hunch you might pitch," said he.

"You are nuts," said I.

"Dutch would want to get off to a fast start with a win," said Pop. "His best bet would be a lefthander, would it not? And Sam pitched Sunday."

"Who all is coming?" I said.

"Me and Holly and Aaron," said he.

"After the game come up to the hotel," I said.

"Hank," said Pop, "I got a letter from the club. It said you done well and listened to what you was told and never spoke back and kept good hours and no monkeyplay. You keep that up. Study Sam and listen to Dutch. I am convinced that Dutch will use you as a starter."

"Do not pay no attention to that piece by Krazy Kress," I said.

"What piece?" said Pop. "I never seen it. When the hell was it?"

"That is right," said I, "it will not be out until tomorrow." Perry was laying on his bed. "You want to speak to Perry?" said I.

"Sure," said Pop, and I give the phone to Perry.

"Howdy," he said. "Do not forget to see us on the TV tonight." He went bippy-de-bop-boop-bop in the phone a few times, and Pop got a kick out of that.

"Get to bed early afterwards," said Pop. "Gene Park is libel to bust his leg."

"Leave us hope so," said Perry. "Hank told me all about you, playing ball yourself and all."

"I played a bit with Cedar Rapids in the Mississippi Valley League," said Pop. "Then I played a lot of semi-pro. I am still at it."

"Hank says you were pretty fair," said Perry.

"Well, maybe so," said Pop. "I see where you stole a good many bases this spring."

"That is me," said Perry. "I do not like to stay too long in 1 place. I am 1 of the roving kind." Then he done the bippy-de-bop-boop-bop again, like Bing Crosby done on the record, and Pop laughed and asked for me back, and I took the phone.

"I do not want to run up your money," said Pop. "I hope you ain't throwing the screw too much. You got time for that."

"That is what Red says," said I.

"You follow Red and do what he says," said Pop. "Say," he said, and he lowered his voice a bit. "Is Flynn in the room?"

"No," I said.

"Why does he not hit?" said Pop.

"He does not pull," I said. "It ain't like Q. C. where we had that short center field. These parks is big, Pop. Big! We drilled this morning and he done the same."

"That is too bad," said Pop. "It seems like he would learn. We got seats square behind home about 15 rows up. We wrote away in the middle of March. If Dutch does not start you tomorrow he will start you Thursday. I will stake my life on that. We will lay over till Thursday if need be."

"That is crazy, Pop," I said. "But if you wish to come and see me sit on the bench that is okay with me."

"You will work," said Pop. "Listen, boy, I do not wish to run up your money. Get your sleep tonight. Well, we will see you tomorrow. We will be pulling out of here with the birds."

"Pop," I said, "is my car still in the depot?"

"Still sitting there," said he. "I pass by now and then and take a look. Hank, Perkinsville is gone mad. Business stands still when they get the Mammoths on the radio. They stopped the show when you was down in Baltimore the other night. Bill Duffy telephoned it in play by play. I guess you seen Bill."

"Yes," I said. "He was in Baltimore and then again in Philly. He done "Casey at the Bat" for a crowd of us up in the hotel in Philly."

"Well," said Pop, "I do not want to run up your money. Good luck, son. We will see you tomorrow."

"So long, Pop," I said.

"Goodby, son," he said, and then we hung up.

Me and Perry and Coker and Canada spent the afternoon deciding on what to sing. We chose "I Love You As I Never Loved Before" for we liked it and knowed the words, but we could not decide on another. We thought about "On Top of Old Smokey" but Hams Carroll was always singing it to the tune of these very vulgar words and we would of probably busted out laughing in the middle. We liked that 1 about the girl where her hair hung down in ringulets, and finally Perry remembered that it was on the juke in the Manhattan Drugs in the lobby, and we went down and played it a few times, copying off the words. By about 5 we had them down pat. We ate early so as to get the burps out of our system, and about 7 we caught a cab in front of the hotel. "Radio City," said I to the cabbie, and away we went.

"Who is going to win the ball game?" said the cabbie.

"Heavens to Betsy," said Coker, "Notre Dame, I suppose. Notre Dame *always* wins."

"Oh," said the cabbie, "I thought you was ballplayers. The ballplayers stay up in that hotel."

"Ballplayers?" said Coker. "Lordy me, that is too strenuous. We are singers."

Well, Coker been on that kick ever since we spoke to the swishy fellow from the show early in the day.

"It is pretty strenuous," said the cabbie.

"I bet at the day's end them poor ballplayers is all wore down to where they ain't got enough energy to trim their nails," said Coker.

"Yes, they get worked pretty hard," said the cabbie. "It is a tough life."

"Heavens to Betsy," said Coker, "they start playing ball in February and sometimes they play clear into October. Then them dear boys have only got November and December and January and part of February to theirselves."

"That is right," said the cabbie. "It is a rough life."

"Good gracious but I would never be a ballplayer for all the perfume in Paris," said Coker.

"It is sure tough," said the cabbie.

"What hours do you work?" said Coker.

"I work 12 hours a day with every other Sunday off," said the cabbie.

"You lucky stiff," said Coker.

The program was fairly corny. Larry Hatfield is rather flatnosed, and he said if we was to make a remark or 2 about his nose he would not mind, for it always brung a laugh. There was 3 acts before us.

Then the band swung into "Take Me Out To The Ball Game,"

and we was introduced. "Well," said Larry Hatfield, "I see where Brooklyn is leading the league." That was true, for Brooklyn opened down in Washington that afternoon. The opener is always a day earlier in Washington, the President throwing out the first ball and all that crap. Bill Scudder won it, 6-1. The audience give out with a great hand for Brooklyn.

"That is right," said I, "and they better make the most of it, for just as soon as the Mammoths get rolling there will be little to clap for over in Brooklyn." This remark got a tremendous amount of applause. Hatfield give me the sign to keep on talking. "It ain't where you stand the first day," said I. "It is where do you stand along about September 30. Now, if it rains 3 days until Scudder rests up Brooklyn is safe. But it ain't going to rain 3 days in 4 the whole summer through, so these folks that clap so hard for Brooklyn might just as well save their breath." This just about brung the house down.

"How about you other boys?" said Larry. "What is your opinion in this matter?"

"It is about like Hank says," said Coker.

"Hank give it to you straight," said Perry.

Canada give a grunt.

"It looks like Henry Wiggen does the talking for this quartet," said Larry Hatfield.

"I do not believe in hiding the truth under a basket," I said. There was so much applause it sounded like even some of the Brooklyn people was chiming in.

Then we tore into the music. Frankly speaking, I think we was a little flat here and there. Somehow we was geared to the shower room rather then to an open place. We sung 2 songs. Perry forgot the words halfway through the girl with the hair hung down in ringulets, but he filled in with a couple bars of bippy-de-bop-boop-bop and it sounded exactly like it was planned that way. On the way out we was give 100 each in an envelope.

Canada and Coker went for a ride on the subway afterwards. I wanted to go along, even though I been on the subway a number of times with Lindon the September before. But Perry grabbed me. "Back to the hotel," said he, "for you might work relief tomor-row."

"It ain't but 9," I said. Nonetheless he steered me in a cab, and back we went. We grabbed a couple sandwiches and milk down in the Manhattan Drugs, and then we went up. "It sure is earlier then hell," I said.

"It is nearly 10," said Perry.

"I ain't tired," I said.

"Take a bath and relax," he said.

"I took 1 this afternoon," I said.

"Take another," he said.

But I did not. Red and some of the others stopped by and said they seen us on the TV. Red said we sounded a little flat. Most of the boys seemed to think we sounded better in the shower, which was true. I wish to make this clear, for I don't want nobody to think we sing so flat as we done on the air. Dutch come by. He asked us if we got the 100 as promised, and we said we did. "Well, get to bed," said Dutch.

"What the *hell!*" said I. "I never before seen so many people so hot after getting to bed at 10:30 in the evening in my life."

"Everybody goes to bed early the night before the opener," said Dutch. Well, if Dutch says a thing it might not always be true, but it's the law. I begun to undress. I must of fell asleep about 11.

Along about 9 I woke up, and I laid there looking out the window. It looked cloudy and cool, and the sun went in 1 minute and out the other. I laid very quiet, for me and Perry never would stir around until the other 1 did. I laid there thinking. Lots of times when I lay still like that my mind catches a hold of things that it misses completely when I am up and moving. That is what happened, for all of a sudden it flashed upon me that if you will read in Sad Sam Yale's book called "Sam Yale—Mammoth," pages 196 through 199, you will find a description of the first Opener he pitched, and how they rushed him to bed the night before and never told him a thing for fear he would be nervous and lose out on his sleep, being just a rookie and all, and how he got up about 12 midnight, thinking he would go down for a sandwich, and then he was no sooner out of his room then Dutch Schnell and Mike Mulrooney, both coaches for the Mammoths at the time, collared him and asked him where he was going, and then they went along and sat with him like 2 guards over a prisoner, and then they steered him back to his room and straight to bed, and Mike sat on a chair outside Sam's room half the night, guarding it.

I remembered that. And I remembered all the dreaming I done as a kid, maybe whilst laying in bed, and how I would dream that that was what they done to me the night before the opener. I must of dreamed that dream 500 times. Now here it happened to me, like in Sam's book and like I dreamed it, and I never suspected.

I got up and opened the door. Right smack across from the door, up against the opposite wall, there was a chair. Beside it on the floor there was an ash tray choked with cigarettes, cork-tip like Clint Strap smokes, and I knowed where Clint spent most of the night.

I closed the door. Perry was awake. He had a gleam in his eye like he just stole home. "You bum," said I. "You knowed all the time."

"Knowed what?" said he.

"Ain't it true?" said I. "Ain't I going to pitch today?"

"It is true," said he, and he give me a grin from here to St. Louis. "Now you know. Everybody in the United States knowed it by midnight last night, all but you."

"Well, I cannot go to the ball park naked," said I, and I begun to dress, and along about halfway through my heart begun to pump something fierce and I got so excited I could barely button my shirt. I guess it was a good thing they did not tell me after all, for I would of never slept.

Dutch and Red come in about 1 minute later. "I suppose by now you know," said Dutch. I said I did. Then Dutch went out and me and Red and Perry went to breakfast together. There was a picture of me in all the papers, saying such things as ROOK TO HURL and MAMMOTH'S SURPRISE STARTER, and Red read Krazy Kresses tripe and said that Krazy's crystal ball was muddy already and the first game yet to be played. Red reads "The Star-Press" every day but says it is cockeyed. 1 time I asked him why he did not read another, and he said "The Star-Press" was the biggest and give you the most laughs for your money.

Then we spent most of the breakfast going over the Boston hitters. Red knowed them all but Heinz, a young kid up from the

American Association. He said that if we got the chance we should try and watch Heinz hit in practice. Perry done so, and that was a help, although we would of got his number sooner or later. There's people that say Heinz is a coming immortal, but I got my doubts. We had a good book on him all year.

About 11 me and Canada and Perry and Coker and Lindon and Squarehead piled in a cab. The more you get in the less you each pay. The traffic got thicker the nearer we got to the Stadium, and when we got out there was a mob of kids waiting there where I first seen Sad Sam Yale in the flesh that time with Pop. The cops tried to clear a way, but the kids ducked under and around. They spotted me, for my picture was all over the morning papers, and they spotted Perry, for that was no trick, him being the first colored Mammoth since Mark Jackson in 47. Besides which they seen us on the TV the night before. They come charging at us, crying "Sign my book, sign my book," pushing their books under our nose. The way to do is grab 1 and sign it and keep on moving. You just can't sign them all. I usually say, "Look, kids, if I was to sign all your books my arm would be broke and I could not pitch. So if everybody will meet me here after the game I will sign them then and it will not matter if my arm is broke or not." When the game is over it will take awhile to get dressed, and when you come out there will only be a few kids left that would rather have your autograph and never mind the whaling they might get for not getting home to dinner.

If you lose there might not be no kids a-tall. I seen that happen, too.

24

I WATCHED hitting practice from the dugout. You could hear folks "oooh" and "aaah." Sid and Squarehead blasted a couple long ones. Finally I got up and took my swipes, and I could feel folks quieten down a bit and studying this punk that would be working instead of Sad Sam Yale. I hit a couple puny fouls and bunted 3.

After awhile I moved down to the first base side to the warm-up slab. Over on the other side I seen Fred Nance warming for Boston. Fred is an older man, 32 or 3, and he was already at work, the day being cool.

I felt good, although I might of liked it 5 degrees warmer, and my teeth chatted, and I was nervous. But the more I throwed the more I warmed, and after a time I could feel that folks was not looking at me so much. Goose caught me in the beginning, and then Red took over, and when I had enough we went in. I sat on the can awhile, and then I washed up and changed my shirt. Mick give her a few rubs to keep her loose, and the clock on the wall inched nearer and nearer the time, and the nearer it got the more my teeth chatted and the more I wished I had went in some other business besides this.

Sam was whistling and gay, and he stripped down and laid on

the rubbing table in his jock. "Rub me slow, Mick," said he. He hummed and whistled and joked with Mick. Yet though he was whistling and humming and joking and gay and making remarks at everyone, kidding them along and all, his face was nonetheless sad. It was like a man was to be whistling whilst carrying a coffin.

Soon the place quietened down, and Dutch begun to speak, and there wasn't a sound but Dutch, and dim in the background you could hear the noise of the crowd, and you could hear Red taking whatever Dutch said and putting it in Spanish for George, and the only other sound was Sam laying on the table, whistling.

"Okay, boys," said Dutch. "There is a kid name of Heinz. We looked him over. He hits everything. He hits at bad balls, too, so be on your toes.

"I do not wish to be a gymnasium teacher, but I am going to carp again on this matter of calling fly balls loud enough for all to hear and then everybody else get out of the way. Ugly will call as usual, plus Lucky in the outfield, plus Red around and about home on both pops and bunts and such, and the first man that f---s up in this respect is going to get hit in the pocketbook and hit hard. Sam, stop that goddam whistling." Sam stopped.

"I got my rotation f---ed up in Baltimore which is partly why Sam is resting today and Henry working. If I can possibly do it every pitcher will get a full 3 days of rest and possibly 4 to begin with. Then we will not be so hard put when doubleheaders and such pile up. They give you 154 f---ing ball games and set the schedule up like it is never going to rain and wash you out and pile up your doubleheaders. You are supposed to do everything except shit ginger snaps and win a pennant besides. Well, I ain't complaining.

"I have not got the faintest f---ing idea why Fred Nance always gives us so much trouble. Make him work. Unless there is a different sign I do not want anybody to hit until at least 1 strike is called. Is that clear? Red, tell it to George.

"That reminds me. Red, there is this goddam Porto Rican with Boston so you will have to keep George up on the signs and not be shouting them out loud.

"We might manage to tire Nance. We are going to bunt some

and keep him moving so keep your eyes peeled careful for your sign. To start with George will bunt, and if he gets on Lucky will swing bunt. I think we can jump off to a fast lead.

"Henry, we have got 7 minutes yet if you wish to warm some more."

"I am ready," said I to Dutch.

"I want to hear plenty of music. Henry is a first-class big-time pitcher. We all know that. Yet nobody is not shaky the first time, so I wish to hear plenty of chatter out there, and on the bench as well, and I do not aim to take him out the first little bit of trouble he might get in so you better figure on keeping tight and seeing things through if it gets rough.

"It is a little cloudy. That should hurt them more then us," meaning that I was fast and Nance more of a curve-ball pitcher.

My hands was all a-sweat, and my teeth chatted. I kept my jaws clenched.

Dutch rubbed his chin, trying to think if there was anything more to say. He paced up and down. "Sam, stop your whistling," he said, "for I am trying to think. Yet that is all I got on my mind. Is there anybody else got anything else to say?

"Oh yes, 1 other thing that has got nothing to do with baseball. After the Saturday game in Philly I get a call from some goddam gymnasium teacher wants to know why in hell you boys cannot stand still and give your attention to the anthem. I meant to tell you and forgot. I watched you Sunday. Up and down the dugout here is what I seen. Lucky is standing there scratching his ass. Ugly is fiddling with the lace of his glove. Gene is picking his goddam nose. Some is leaning against the wall and some got 1 foot up on the bench. Now I do not think it is too much to ask to stand up with your hat over your heart for 2 minutes and not give no gymnasium teachers something to squawk about. Is that clear?"

"My lace was loose," said Ugly.

George spoke in Spanish and Red put it back in English. "George says tell Ugly lay more over closer towards second on lefthanded hitters. George says he goes to his own left like a shooting star. George says he feels fine and hopes the rest is the same. He says he loves everybody and wishes them good luck."

The boys fired back "Good luck" and "Adios" and "Hasta la vista" and "Manyana" and all such. George gets the drift by the tone. I wished they would stop their fussing and get out of there. "Okay," said Dutch at last, "leave us go," and out we went through the door and down the little tunnel to the dugout, and some of the boys patted me on the shoulder and elsewhere and said the things you say to give a fellow courage. I guess I know how a poor beggar feels when he walks the last mile.

We sat on the benches in the dugout. The big clock in center field showed 3 minutes to go, and they seemed like 3 weeks at least. The scoreboard showed Washington and Brooklyn 0-0 after 1 inning of play. The groundsmen pulled their smoother 1 last time across the infield, and the umpires come out and was booed, as is the custom, and the band played "Three Blind Mice" in their honor, and just when it seemed like all was set the loud speaker called out the license of some cluck that parked his car on the sidewalk and was told to move it or get tagged.

Then Dutch said it was time and out they went on the double, starting in a bunch and then fanning out to their positions, Sid and George to first and third, Ugly and Gene down around second, Vince and Pasquale and Lucky off on the long jog to the outfield, and the crowd stood up and give them plenty of reception, and me and Red strolled out together, and the rest of the boys stood in the dugout, and the loud speaker said, "Ladies and gentlemen, our national anthem." I took off my cap and held it over my heart and stood facing the flag like we was told, and Red done the same, standing like a knight in his gear, his cap and his mask in 1 hand, and the anthem was played and a lady sung.

Red jabbered all the way through, and when it was done a mighty shout went up, and he said, "Land of the free and the home of the brave. There ain't a 1 of them free, and there ain't 200 of them brave. 25,000 sheep."

"My old man is up there," I said. "Also my girl."

"Ain't a 1 of the whole 25,000 brave enough to sit it through with their hat on," he said.

"I notice you took yours off," I said.

"By God, I did," he said. "That is the last time. Hereafter I will never stand for the anthem. I will wait in the alley betwixt the dugout and the clubhouse," and he done it ever after as you will notice when you see the Mammoths play.

"Throw anything you want the first pitch and after that listen to your old redheaded papa," said Red. "Good luck, Henry, this is for the money."

I throwed about 6 to loosen. Then the Mayor of New York throwed out the first ball. Sid copped it and run over and got the autograph and rolled it down to the dugout. Morty Zinke was behind the plate, and he give Red another, and around it went, Red to George to Ugly to Gene to Sid, and then to me. My hand sweated, and I picked up the resin bag, and then I tossed it down, and Black stepped in, and I throwed the first pitch, wide, and Red whipped it back to me, and I was set.

Black went after the second pitch. He lifted it up behind second, and Ugly called "Gene" and Gene gathered it in.

Now I begun to hear the music. It was sweet, believe me. You hear the crowd, but they ain't really with you. They are just a lot of people and a lot of noise, and they shout things at you but you never hear much. What you hear is your own boys. You hear the dugout, and you see their face, and now and then Dutch will raise his voice above the rest and tell you something. I heard Perry and Coker and Canada and Lindon, and I heard Squarehead loud and clear, and out behind me I heard the music, and in front of me, from Red.

Red says, "To me, Henry, to me, this is my sign, to me, to me."

George says a flood of words in Spanish, and then he says your name.

Ugly says, "Baby boy, Hank is my baby boy, baby boy, baby boy, Hank is my baby boy, baby boy," over and over.

Gene says, "All you got to do is throw, that is all. All you got to do is throw. Just throw, Hank. Just throw. All you got to do is throw."

Sid sings a song. He sings different songs, but the words is always the same. He sings, "Oh they cannot hit my Henry boy oh they cannot hit my Hank oh my Henry oh my Hank my Henry Hank Hank Hank." He might sing the same song 1 inning or a whole game or a week.

You know they are there. You have got to know. When you are a kid you think you don't need nobody behind you, for when you are a kid you think you will strike out whoever comes along. You will gobble up the whole blooming world and you do not need no help. But in the big-time it is different, and you have got to know they are there. You have got to know that if you make a mistake there is someone behind you to cover for you and help pull you out. You are always going to make mistakes. The idea is to not make too many.

I made a mistake on Granby and throwed 1 too fat, and back it come like a rocket, about ankle high, right at me. I could not of stopped it if I tried, and it burned past me with "1 base" wrote all over it. Gene was moving fast behind me. He took it backhand behind the base, and still off balance he whipped it down to Sid. Perry or Lucky or George might of beat the throw, but Granby stays longer in 1 place and he was out by half a step. Gene got a great hand. He deserved it.

Now I heard the music clear from the outfield. I never hear Lucky much, but I hear Vincent and Pasquale, and their voice floats in, saying, "Nuttin to worry, nuttin to worry, no hitter boy, no hitter boy, never worry, nuttin to worry," and I stopped worrying right then and there, with 2 down and none on, knowing from then forwards that it was my ball game to win. I had the old confidence, and I never lost it, not then nor any other day. Give me a baseball in my hand and I know where I am at. Give me a piece of machinery and I may be more or less in the dark. Give me a book and I am lost. Give me a map and I cannot make heads nor tails, nor I could no more learn another language then pitch with my nose. But give me a baseball and I know where I am at, and I fired down to Fielding twice, 2 blazing fast balls, and then I changed up and throwed him a jughandle curve that he went for like a fool and bounced down to Sid. I raced over to cover. Sid waved me away and beat Fielding to the bag in plenty of time.

Fielding rounded the bag and went over for his glove. "Say

boy," said he to me, "I hear that they have got you rooming with a n----r."

"That is right," said I to him, and I dropped my glove along the line, and the kid run up with my jacket and held it while I slipped it on, and I went in towards the dugout. I got a good hand on the way, and I touched my cap.

Then the running begun. George was on first quicker then you could tell it. He bunted down third on the second pitch, and Nance went over and fielded it and never even bothered to make the throw.

They figured Lucky for the sacrifice. Lucky swung around for the bunt and Blodgett tore in from third, but Lucky chopped at it, the swinging bunt, and it popped down the third base line where Blodgett was but wasn't no more, and Granby chased over from short and Blodgett turned and started out after it, too. That was where he put the knife in his own back, for George rounded second never busting his stride and come barreling down for third. Nance come over to cover as soon as he seen what was happening, and Joe Jaros give George the slide sign, and George hit the dirt. Nance took the throw from Granby from short left, and George brung him to earth with the slide, and Nance was still trying to get up off his back while Lucky went streaking to second.

Vince Carucci worked the count to 3-and-2 and then lifted 1 about 410 feet into left center that Black took, and now we was running again, George tagging up and scoring easy enough from third, which was what everybody expected. The only thing they did not expect was what Lucky done. Lucky tagged, too, and he broke for third on the catch, which neither Black nor all of Boston expected, and he made it in a very close play with a neat slide. That is how ball games are won, doing the unexpected.

We wasn't through yet. Dutch ordered the squeeze, shoving his right foot up on the dugout step. That's the bunt sign, not bunt and run but run and bunt. The suicide squeeze. It means get moving and not worry about getting doubled up or trapped. All or nothing. It means the batter has got to bunt no matter what.

Thinking back on it it all sounds simple. But Dutch figured it all in a flash. They would be throwing low to keep Sid from hitting in the air where Lucky could score after the catch. The infield would lay in a little close for the possible play at the plate, though not *too* close. It would never expect the bunt from Sid, for his specialty is the long drive. Joe Jaros flashed the sign to Sid and Lucky, shouting, "Okay, Sid, leave us drive 1 about 650 feet." You will notice that the name "Sid" is the second word. So between the bunt sign from Dutch and the word from Joe both Lucky and Sid knowed that Sid was to bunt the second pitch.

The second pitch was low, the best kind to bunt, and Sid pushed it along first, neat enough for a man that don't do it much. Fielding took it, but he seen he had no chance in the world to make the play at the plate, for by now Lucky was across. Chickering covered first, and Sid was out. But we had 2.

That was how it stood when we batted in the last of the third. I come up first. I got a good hand, partly because I done well up to then and partly because I was a rookie and folks always like to see a rookie make good. I touched my hat.

"Well, well, well," said Toomy Richardson, the Boston catcher, "if it ain't Henry Wiggen that rooms with the n----r." He crouched and give his sign.

"That is me," said I, "and it will not be many weeks before you will be dizzy trying to throw that n----r out stealing."

Nance sailed 1 past me for a called strike.

"Is that so?" said Toomy. "Well, n----rs was always fast runners. They ain't honest so they got to know how to run."

"That is so," said I.

Nance breezed another by, and Zinke bawled out, "Stee-rike!"

All of a sudden I got a notion maybe I could get on base. I figured Nance would waste 1 and then fog 1 through. He figured I would never take the bat off my shoulder. He throwed wide. "What in the world is the sense in wasting pitches on me?" said I to Toomy. "I wish you would throw it through good so I can go back and sit down."

"Oh," said Toomy, "we always play around a little bit with punks before we strike them out."

"Well, hurry it up," said I, "for I would like to get back and put my jacket on and keep my flipper warm," and Nance reared and throwed. I swang. When I have a mind to do it I can cut pretty good at a ball. I caught that 1 nice, with the fat of the bat, and I drove it down the line in right, and Casey Sharpe loped over. I seen him waiting to play it off the wall, and I thought, "Well, Casey old boy, how is your arm this fine day?" and I rounded first, and I dug, and I churned down the line and got them legs moving about as fast as they ever went before, and I went on down towards second like there was the flag itself resting on the outcome, and Granby come over to cover, and I hit the dirt about the instant he took the throw, and I went under him, and my foot hooked the bag just as snug as could be, and Neininger called me safe.

I think this must of upset Fred Nance's ideas of what was proper. He walked George. Lucky moved us along with the sacrifice. Vince Carucci popped out, but then they walked Sid to load the bases and have a play at every bag, figuring they had a little better chance with Pasquale then with Sid. But Pasquale lined 1 into right center that was still on the rise when it left the infield. We was all running, of course, with 2 down, and the drive hit the Gem sign about 10 feet off the ground. I jogged in, and George was right behind, and Sid was rounding third when Heinz begun his throw. Nance cut the throw off, seeing there was no chance on Sid, and that kept Pasquale from taking third. It did not matter, for Ugly singled him home anyways, and that was all for Nance. Nippy Lewis come on to relieve. Gene almost kept the rally going with a smash down third, but Blodgett took it backhand on the bag, and that was the end of the inning. 6-0.

That was how things stood through 6. In the top of the seventh Dutch lifted Sid Goldman and sent Canada in at first. Sid is a fair enough fielding first baseman, but he tends to weight, and the weight slows him down. He says if he lived in the hotel with the boys he might keep his weight down better, but he lives with his mother on Riverside Drive when the club is home and she feeds him too much. I ate up there 1 Friday night and must of put on 2 pounds betwixt the time we sat down and the time we tried to get up. So Dutch lifted Sid and played Canada at first so as to bolst the defense. It was a good hunch, like all Dutch's hunches that day, like pitching me in the first place and then again jumping off to a fast lead by bunting. Everything was working. I do believe if we sent the batboy up to hit he would of rapped a triple.

I been going good up to the seventh. I was really enjoying myself. The boys was singing behind me and threatening at bat almost every inning, and the sun come out bright and strong about the fifth, and the crowd was with us all the way, for next to beating Brooklyn they love best to beat Boston.

I felt a little sorry for Squarehead. I guess when Dutch sent Canada in poor Squarehead knowed for sure what was in the cards. Yet he kept booming out from the dugout like he never thought a thing about it. Soon I was too busy to worry about Squarehead. I was up to my eyeballs in trouble.

Fielding opened the inning with a single. Canada sung to me over from first, "It does not mean a thing, Hank, does not mean a thing," and I throwed down to first a couple times, not half so much trying to pick Fielding off as give Canada a chance to loosen and get over being nervous. I knowed he was nervous. Casey Sharpe followed with a Texas League single that Lucky and Ugly and Gene all raced for, yet it fell between them in short center. Canada went down to cover second, and I shot over to first. Fielding took third.

Heinz was up. We had got him out twice before, mixing curves and the fast 1. Red give me the sign for the curve, and I shook him off. Okay, he signals, throw the screw, which was what I wanted to throw. Red don't like me to, though. He says I'm too young and will ruin my arm. I throwed it, and Heinz popped it foul down by the Mayor of New York's box, and Canada streaked over. Sid would of never made it. I did not think Canada would neither, but over he went, and about 5 feet from the barrier he left this earth and took off. I caught a glimpse of Kellogg racing over to call it. Then I lost sight of Canada, for down he went behind the rail, and Kellogg jerked back his thumb, meaning that Canada made the catch, and the next thing I seen the ball was flying back out of there. It was a pretty good throw, considering that the poor boy was laying on his back all tangled up with the seats and the spectators, and I took the throw about halfway between the line and the stands, and I wheeled and whipped it to Red, figuring that Fielding would of tagged by now and been headed for home. That was what he done, never expecting Canada to get the ball back in play like that, and now he was trapped betwixt third and home. Red run him back towards third and flipped to George. George run him back towards home and flipped to me, for I was backing up Red by now. I run Fielding back towards third and flipped to Ugly, for Ugly come over from short to back up George. Ugly run Fielding down towards home. Red was waiting, and he stuck up his hands like he was expecting the throw, and Fielding seen the hands go up and naturally reversed again and started back towards third. Only Ugly never throwed a-tall, and Fielding tried to reverse still again, but Ugly was roaring fast down the line, and he tagged Fielding and turned and wheeled and fired back to George at third and damn near caught Casey Sharpe besides.

I was out of it now. Chickering drove Casey home with a single, but I got Blodgett on strikes.

In the top of the ninth, with 2 gone and none on and the crowd moving towards the exits, Casey Sharpe hammered a homer into the upper stands in right. Then Heinz rolled to Ugly, and that was it. That was my first.

We had dinner together that night in the hotel, me and Holly and Pop and Perry and Aaron and Red and Rosemary Traphagen and George. I suppose I might of hogged the conversation somewhat, hashing over the afternoon about 5 times. Nobody else got much of a word in edgewise until towards the end I noticed I was talking and nobody was listening. Pop and Perry was gassing together, and Aaron and Red was discussing I do not know what and now and then turning it in Spanish for George, and Rosemary was telling Holly about some of the problems of a ballplayer's wife. It used to be that when I won a game I spent hours and hours jawing it over again for the benefit of anybody that cared to listen, though I got over the habit as time wore on. When I lost I never considered it worth discussing and still don't.

Finally we broke it up, and me and Holly went walking, and after a time I said, "Well, Holly, I hope Rosemary has filled you in on some of the fine points of marrying a ballplayer."

"She told me of the problems," said Holly.

"You are putting me off again," said I, for I could tell she was stalling like she done that night in February just before I shoved off south. "What problems? There is 20,000 girls that would give their right arm to be married to such problems."

"I am not of the 20,000," she said. "It takes thought."

"To hell with thought," said I. "I must have the answer, yes or no."

"Now is not the time for big decisions," she said. "You are sitting on top of the world, and it is too easy to be in love when you are sitting on top of the world. How about on afternoons when the chips are flying all wrong? How about on afternoons when all does not go so smooth as it went today? Will you then be in love with me and all the world? Rosemary Traphagen has told me about such afternoons."

"Why so gloomy?" said I, but she went on being gloomy none-theless, and after about 6 blocks we turned around and went back, hardly saying a word the whole time. Later her and Pop and Aaron grabbed the 11 o'clock. I seen them off, and I walked clear back to the hotel. I felt sore.

But walking cooled me off some, and I kept thinking about the dinner that night and what a fool I probably was. At least that's what I *think* I was thinking. Yet maybe it wasn't until some time later in the summer that I begun to wise up to myself, for I soon seen where it is easy enough to be in love with all the world on a fine spring night after you have just throwed a 6-hit win but maybe not so easy come steaming August and the September stretch. A lot of things Holly ever said begun to sink in, and I learned a lot about such things as love, and actually, when you think about it, it is a wonder that she didn't cut me loose then and there, for I was so stupid, and so green, that it makes me sick to mention it.

The box score:

BOSTON	ab.	r.	h.	po.	a
Black cf	4	0	0	1	0
Granby ss	4	0	1	2	1
Fielding 1b	4	0	1	7	2
Sharpe rf	4	2	2	2	0
Heinz lf	4	0	0	2	0
Chickering 2b	3	0	2	2	3
Blodgett 3b	2	0	0	3	1
Richardson c	3	0	0	5	2
Nance p	1	0	0	0	1
Lewis p	1	0	0	0	2
aHampden	1	0	0	0	0
Tawney p	0	0	0	0	0
Total	31	2	6	24	12

NEW YORK	ab.	r.	h.	po.	a
Gonzalez 3b	4	2	1	1	2
Judkins cf	3	1	1	2	0
V. Carucci lf	4	0	1	2	0
Goldman 1b	1	1	1	7	0
Smith 1b	1	0	0	3	1
P. Carucci rf	4	1	2	1	0
Jones ss	4	0	2	2	3
Park 2b	3	0	0	3	3
Traphagen c	4	0	1	5	1
Wiggen p	4	1	1	1	2
Total	32	6	10	27	12

aHit into force play for Lewis in eighth.

```
Boston .......... 0 0 0   0 0 0   1 0 1 — 2
New York ........ 2 0 4   0 0 0   0 0 - — 6
```

Error—Chickering.

Runs batted in—V. Carucci, Goldman, P. Carucci 3, Jones, Chickering, Sharpe.

Two-base hits—Wiggen, P. Carucci, Goldman, Granby.

Home run—Sharpe.

Double plays—Jones, Park and Goldman; Chickering, Granby and Fielding; Smith, Wiggen, Traphagen, Gonzalez and Jones; Gonzalez, Park and Smith.

Left on bases—Boston 3, New York 7.

Bases on balls—Off Wiggen 2, Nance 2, Lewis 2.

Struck out—By Wiggen 5, Nance 1, Lewis 2.

Hits—Off Nance 5 in 2⅔ innings, Lewis 4 in 4⅓ innings, Tawney 1 in 1 inning.

Winning pitcher—Wiggen. Losing pitcher—Nance.

Umpires—Zinke, Kellogg, Neininger and Bowron.

Time of game—2:32.

Attendance—29,812.

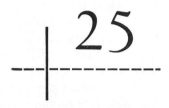

ANY kind of a race, whether dogs or ponies or boats or cars or men or baseball clubs, begin the same. All are bunched at the start. Then the gun goes off or the flag goes down or, when it is baseball clubs, the first ball is throwed out, the openers played, and they are off.

At the beginning, for a week or 2 weeks, or maybe a month, they run neck and neck, and the eastern clubs meet the eastern clubs and west meets west, and then the east goes west or the west goes east, depending on the schedule, and soon each club has played the circuit round. You have got a look at the new hitters that come up in the spring, and your own hitters have saw the new enemy pitchers, and some of the kids that come up with all the fanfare finds out they cannot hit the big-time stuff, and some of the new young pitchers finds out they was pretty flashy down in AA or AAA, but now they cannot get a man out, and down they go, out of remembrance.

Now, after the first swing west and the first swing east, after the first turn of the course you might say, the field straightens away. Them that have it sticks, and them that don't begin to fade. Quality begins to show, for it is a long pull, and over the long pull your day-in-day-out clubs move out ahead of the field, maybe only 2 clubs, maybe 3 or 4, and on the other clubs the weaknesses begin to shine through, and a second-rate bench begins to hurt because fellows get injured aplenty in this game called "Baseball." And the club that might look good over a week or 10 days begins to look poorly and weakly over the longer haul.

It ain't the short series that means a thing. It is how are you fixed when July comes round. Is your bench strong? Have you got the kind of ballplayers that when the pressure is on, when the heavy cash rides on every pitch in every ball game will they still have their nerve? Will you hustle in August like you hustled in May?

Things started last spring according to form. We got away fast. Sam Yale beat Boston the second day, though Knuckles lost on the third, and we split 2 with Brooklyn and went down to Washington and took 2 out of 3. The rotation was working nice, Hams and Piss rounding out the staff and the relief coming on when needed, mostly Horse Byrd, sometimes Lindon, Dutch juggling once and skipping my turn so as to throw righthanders against Washington and keep me and Sam ready for the series up in Boston. I beat Boston the first day there and Sam done the same the second, and the third day it snowed, and we moved out on the noon train and back to New York for 3 with Brooklyn in Brooklyn before the first trip west. We was in second place then, with Cleveland leading by a game. If anybody was worried it never showed.

1 thing I begun to notice, and that was this. When you are a top-flight ballplayer you do not go around collaring everybody you lay your eyes on and tell them so. We was doing our ballplaying on the ball field and our jawing amongst ourselves. If there was anybody we give a riding to it was the opposition, or umpires. As for cabbies and bellhops and such we done our business with them and give them the time of day and a good tip and thank you, and that was that.

I do not mean that you could of confused us with a squad of chess players. Show me a ball club with nothing to say to nobody and I will tell you where they are in their league, for they are probably in seventh place with the cellar door open. I only mean that we was tending to business and tending it good. Off the field there was no water bags dropped out of windows, no nailing nobody's shoes to the floor nor shortsheeting the bed nor any of the things that you read about in books.

We got back from the first trip to Boston early in the evening.

Me and Coker and Canada and Perry and Lindon and Squarehead
went down in the Manhattan Drugs for a late evening bite, and we
lazed around and played the juke and read the comic books off the
stand. It was a cold night out. It looked more like the middle of
December then the last of April, and we ended up just sitting there
looking out the window at the people rushing by, not talking much,
and finally Coker piped up, saying, "Sgurd Nattahnam."

"Who?" said Lindon.

"Sgurd Nattahnam," said Coker again.

I caught it right away, for I noticed where Coker was looking.
He was looking through the window where the words "Manhattan
Drugs" was painted facing outside, reading it off backwards, and
I played along, saying "Syadnus Nepo."

Then Perry caught on and he said "Slaem Tnellecxe," and soon
Canada picked it up, saying "Scitemsoc." This must of went on
for a long while, for even Squarehead latched on to what was being
did, saying at last, "Oh, now I teg ti," and we all got a great laugh
out of that. Then we went back up.

There was a big card game down in Sam's room. I guess everybody was there but Red and George and Scotty and Sunny Jim that
never mix in much plus the boys that their wives had a place in the
city. Also plus Sid that lives up with his mother on Riverside Drive.
We drifted down and watched, lugging in chairs and sitting on the
backs so as to see. They had 2 tables shoved together, and it was a
nice quiet game, everybody talking low and chatting about this and
that, not worrying the cards, and I felt like playing and I said so,
and Sam said through the cigar, "Go ahead and get in. All of you
boys get in. We will take your money and keep you from spending
it careless."

"There is too many already," said Goose.

"Hell," said Sam, "we will play with 2 decks and make it wild
and woolly."

We went and lugged another table and sat in, and we played
awhile a dime limit. The wind slapped in against the windows.
You could hear it whistling up and down betwixt the buildings. It
was all nice and cozy, nobody trying to win, just throwing in their
money and running the cards. Along about the fifth hand Coker
said, "Check to Esoog."

"What is that?" said Sam.

"I said check to Esoog," Coker said.

Sam looked around. He looked at me and I was all a-grin. "Say it 1 more time, you imitation of a shortstop," said Sam to Coker, and Coker said it again, Sam taking his cigar out of his mouth like that would help him hear. "That is what I thought you said," said Sam, and he put the dead cigar back in his mouth.

"Beats the shit out of me," said Goose. "Everybody has throwed down, so I guess he means my bet. Bet a dime."

"Esoog bets net cents," Sam said.

"You and that goddam cigar," said Goose.

"It ain't the cigar," said Sam. "It is your ears. I talk as plain as the eson on your ecaf."

"Say it again," said Goose. Sam said it again. Coker took the pot with 3 jacks. "Goddam it," said Goose, "I had 3 sneves," and he showed his hand to prove it.

Then it wasn't a poker game no more. It was saying names and asking what was said, and saying it again, and then maybe asking again, and then saying it again, 3 and 4 and 5 times.

"Whose deal?"

"Nodnil."

"Who?"

"Nodnil. It was Das Mas Elay just dealed, so now it is Nodnil. Next it will be Ylgu. Next after that Yrrep Nospmis. Next after that Ecurb."

1 by 1 the boys come in. Gene caught on the quickest after Goose, and after him at least 1 fellow come in on every hand, and sometimes more, and them that was in batted it around plenty until there was none but Bruce Pearson still in the dark. I think we was on the train west before Bruce caught on to what was cooking.

We opened in Pittsburgh on a Wednesday, still trailing Cleveland by 1. I worked, my third start of the year.

It rained the night before, and now and then a few drops spreckled down. The boys complained the outfield was sloppy. Dutch started Swanee in left in place of Vincent Carucci on account of

Vince wearing glasses. He can never keep them clean in the rain.

In the fifth, with 2 out and nobody on, Lucky Judkins grounded down to Mills and it looked like the inning was over. But Morty kicked it around some, and Lucky was on, and Pittsburgh was soon to know that when you can get a Mammoth out you best do it while the doing is good, for Swanee followed with a hit into left, sending Lucky to third, and Sid shot another into right, scoring Lucky and moving Swanee to third. Then Pasquale drilled 1 back through the box into center, Swanee scoring, Max Gurwell, the Pittsburgh pitcher, going off to the showers, and the score now 2-0.

It was still like that in the last of the seventh. I had 2 strikes on Steve Baker and Red called for a curve, nothing too good, thinking maybe we would just nick the corner and get the call. It was in there, and Frank Porter, an old-time immortal, now an umpire, called it a ball.

Red flipped his lid. Red never argues unless he feels he is right. I believe that was the first squawk he raised all year. Many a ball-player squawks loud and long 3 times a week, but not Red, and it makes it all the worse on the ump because everybody knows that Red never beefs unless he has had a raw call. He got up out of his crouch and said something to Porter, and Dutch bellowed out from the dugout, and I come down the line, and Ugly and Gene and Sid; and George shouted down from third, "Up yours, up yours," and we ganged up on Porter and give him an awful nasty talking to, and then we cooled down a bit and the boys started back to their positions, Red putting in a last word. "You know," said he, "you got to keep awake even on the 0-and-2 pitch. That was a good pitch and this here man should be out. There is 1 thing that burns my ass over and above all other things in this world and that is to have a man struck out and then have him still up at the plate," and he banged his fist in his glove and stamped his feet and growed all scarlet in the face. Finally Porter turned his back.

I shouted down that in my opinion when an umpire went blind he should be pensioned off, and Porter turned around again. "Ain't you the smart 1?" he said. "Did some big-league ballplayer teach you that clever statement?"

Red crouched down and give me the sign, and with it the music, and he shouted down to me, "We will get him anyways, Henry, even if Porter is a Knarf Retrop." That done it!

"Time! Time!" shouts Porter, loud as he can. "Stop the goddam game! Traphagen! Out! Out I say! Off the field!" and he give Red the thumb, jerking it back and pointing to the dugout. Red got up and looked at Porter and then begun to laugh, and Dutch come off the bench shouting, "Why? Why?" and the whole rhubarb was on again. Joe Jaros come out to me. "What did he say?" said Joe.

"He called him a Knarf Retrop," I said, and Joe begun to laugh and went back to the bench and told the boys, and they all laughed and begun shouting at Porter, "Knarf Retrop!" for about 1 inning until finally he come over and ordered the whole bench into the clubhouse, all except Dutch and 1 coach to be named by Dutch, and the bench went off laughing, and the boys in the field was laughing, and even Pittsburgh was laughing though they did not know at what.

What it amounted to was it give us all such a laugh and relaxed us so much that we loosened up and begun to play ball like it was all in fun, like it was hitting practice where you are all loose and limber and nothing counts but take your swipes and leave the next man bat.

George opened our ninth with a single. Dutch was coaching third now, with Joe Jaros shifted over to first, and Dutch signed for the sacrifice, playing for 1 insurance run, the score still 2-0, and Lucky stepped out of the box and looked down at Dutch, pleading like, and Dutch switched it and give Lucky the sign to hit away, just playing a hunch, and Lucky rammed a double down the line in right, Dutch holding George at third, there being none out, and Swanee hit, sending George and Lucky home, and Sid followed with his third home run of the year, a drive into the stands in right that was still rising when last I seen it. With Ugly on and 2 gone Goose lifted 1 into the bleachers in left. I fanned to end the inning, and we got them out quick enough in the ninth to take the ball game 8-0. That was number 3 for me. I was the first in the league to win that number.

Lindon Burke pitched and won Thursday, his first start of the year, and his cause was helped when Squarehead pinch-hit and connected for his first and only big-time home run.

In my opinion Lindon has got all the makings of a first-rate pitcher. I will not say an immortal, for he has not got that kind of stuff. The main thing is wildness. It don't crop up so long as he has got only the batter to worry about, but as soon as men get on base he begins to worry about his runners, and then he starts throwing too quick, and the first thing anybody knows he has blowed and the only thing left to do is take away the ball from him and say you are sorry and better luck next time. Then the new man comes on from the bullpen to clean up the wreck that Lindon left behind.

As it turned out, Lindon had the honor of pitching us into first place, for Boston whipped Cleveland that afternoon, and that tied it, Boston 1½ out, Brooklyn 2½, and the rest beginning to fall behind according to form.

It was this same day in Pittsburgh that Sam Yale got in some sort of a wrangle with a fan hanging over the barrier just off to 1 side of the dugout. Nothing come of it, but the band struck up "The Old Gray Mare," which is what they always play when they hope to get Sam's goat. Pittsburgh has got the biggest band in the league. "Well," said Sam, "they got no ball club so I guess they must give the customers their entertainment 1 way or the other." That got a good laugh up and down the bench.

I shouted down at Sam, "It looks like you have now got another bandleader to take a poke at," for on page 105 of the book called "Sam Yale—Mammoth" it tells where Sam gets all riled up when that song is played and pastes the bandleader if he don't cut it out.

"I suppose that is another thing you read in my book," shouted Sam to me. I said it was, and he thought it over a little. Then he said, "Say there, Knah, how about you sending home for that book," and I said I would.

We fell behind the next day temporarily. Knuckles tangled in a beauty with Les Chapman, the Pittsburgh ace, and it went into extra innings tied at 2-2. Dutch's strategy fell flat in the first of the tenth. He sent Squarehead up to hit for Knuckles with 2 on and 2 out and Squarehead fanned, and Bub Castetter come on in the last of the tenth and lost the ball game right quick. Bub said he

was not warmed enough. Cleveland beat Brooklyn and was back
at the top by 1 full game. We seen a little item in the paper where
they was getting orders for World Series seats in Cleveland. That
give us a laugh.

On the train to St. Louis I begun a letter home. It is wrote on
railroad paper, and it says, "Dear Pop, Would you send me Sam
Yale's book that is laying on the . . ." That is all the letter writing
I done from Aqua Clara through July. Perry come along just then
and said there was a card game down in the other car, and I shoved
the letter in my bag, thinking I would polish it off later, but then
I telephoned from St. Louis instead and never thought about the
letter again until I found it amongst my gear a long time later. It
is 1 of the souvenirs now, and they come in handy, for they bring
back memories of all that happened day by day. There is Pop's
clips in the scrapbooks, which is how I remember how the ball
games went, plus a good deal of stuff having nothing to do with
ball games a-tall but plenty to do with memory. There is an ash
tray that Pop swiped out of the hotel the night of the Opener and
a spoon we et with down in the hotel dining room, me and Holly
and Pop and Perry and George and Red and Rosemary and Aaron,
and a hotel glass and a towel and 2 baseballs, 1 signed by the
Mayor of New York and 1 that Heinz hit for Boston that Ugly
throwed him out at first with the last play of the opener that Canada
tucked in his pocket and give to me in the clubhouse after.

I remember that first St. Louis series on account of the weather.
It was the first real baseball weather we seen since Aqua Clara,
neither too hot nor too cold, and the sun come out warm in the
morning and went the distance. We seen the first shirt-sleeves
crowd of the year. The boys shed their jackets and sat in the dugout soaking up the sun, and at night, up in the hotel, you begun to
see more and more walking around in shorts and less. I guess the
reason I remember the St. Louis weather so good is because it was
never like that after. We was back in early June and again in July
and again late in August, and ever after it was blistering hot. Red
says if Old Man River was to spill up Olive Street and wash the
town away there would be no comeback from him. He would stand

there and cheer the waters on. But you can't go by Red, for he says the same of all the towns.

Hams Carroll twirled the first game. He stood by the clubhouse window, looking out. "Shine, you old sun, shine away," he said. "Heat up old Hamses soupbone." He had it rocky the first 2 innings. Yet Dutch left him in, and we come back in the third with 3 and tied it up. In the first of the seventh Swanee hit a homer with 1 aboard, for Dutch been playing Swanee regular ever since the Pittsburgh series, and Sid done the same 1 minute after, and Hams blanked St. Louis the rest of the way.

Sam worked the day after. It was warm, though not so warm as he might of liked it, but everybody was hitting and he got by without much trouble. In the middle of the game a wire come for Pasquale and Vincent that their father was very sick in Frisco, and they took off. Dutch played Sunny Jim in left and moved Swanee over into the sun field. That give us only 1 outfielder on the bench, so the following day Dutch made Canada work in the outfield the whole of the drill, just in case. This bothered Canada, for he was beginning to get a big bang out of first base. However Dutch said that the club was not run for the purpose of helping Canada Smith to get a big bang out of life, and that ended that.

Piss Sterling turned in a nice job against St. Louis the third day. It was a tie game, 2-2, going into the ninth. Scotty pinch-hit for Piss and singled, and Perry pinch-run for Scotty and worried St. Louis to death. They had never set eyes on him before. He kept dashing up and down the baseline and making Owen Fischer throw over to Jim Klosky, and every time Fischer throwed Perry dove back in head first until finally Fischer throwed 1 that got past Klosky and Perry was up like a grease of lightning and down to second. George untied the whole affair with a single into short left, and Perry come home like a tornado with the run that counted. Gil Willowbrook pitched the ninth and done what needed to be done. Cleveland lost to Washington and we was tied for first again.

We seen in the Cleveland papers in the morning where Vincent and Pasquale's father died, and we all felt sad and sent a telegram and flowers. In the clubhouse Squarehead said we must go out and murder Cleveland for Vincent and Pasquale. How corny can you get? It reminded me of how it always was in the books about Sid Yule by Homer B. Lester where somebody would be sick and Sid Yule would go out and win the ball game for the sick 1. I do not believe nobody ever actually *died* in them books, however, and I cannot remember that Sid Yule ever bumped up against Cleveland on a day in May along about the time they had the bug in their brain that they might win the pennant.

They was mostly a very young club, rough and ready, and they hustled, and they fought with the umps and they fought with the opposition and played a good brand of ball up through August or thereabouts until they begun to go down in a heap and wound up fighting amongst themselves. But in May they was still a scrappy outfit that if anybody was to beat they had to hustle and fight and scrap as hard as them.

Dutch give me the assignment, and that pleased me fine, and I told the boys in the clubhouse, "Get me a run or 2 and we will have these lads a good deal quietened down by supper time."

We got no runs in the first, however. For about 4 innings Cleveland shouted theirselves hoarse trying to rattle me until finally I pulled this little stunt that cost me 25 dollars in fines by the League. "Say boy," said they, "it cannot be true that you are roomed with a n----r." "Maybe Henry is a n----r himself," said another. "Say there, Wiggen," said yet another, "I run into your brother this morning. He shined my shoes at the barber shop." I scarcely minded what they said. It is all a part of the game, and I never answered them, though 1 time they said something that was just a little bit *too* nasty and I stopped working and faced the Cleveland bench and give them the old sign, 1 finger up.

Neininger, umping behind the plate, warned me not to do it again. The League considers it a vulgar gesture detrimental to the best interests of baseball, and I done it no more that day though I relied on it several times later in the year for 1 reason or another. It cost me 25 each time, and I always paid it quite cheerfully. To me, it is worth 10,000 words, for when no words will say what it is in your heart to say you have said it all with that simple sign— the crooked arm and the old 1 finger up.

Red made me work very slow. These boys was all jitterbugging, hoping to get off to a flying start, and the slower we worked the itchier they got, and Red said it is a well-known fact that a club that is itching must scratch, and as soon as their hand is occupied with scratching they are playing 1-handed baseball. "So leave us take all the time in the world," said Red, "for in the long run your turtle will beat your rabbit." This tied in with what Dutch said in the lecture. "Play steady ball," he said, "and leave these young kids make their own mistakes."

I begun to wonder along about the fifth when they was going to begin making them. They jumped me for a run in the third and another in the fifth. I was hooked up with Robin McKenna that next to me is the youngest pitcher in the league. He was blazing them through, and for 5 innings we never got a man past first.

In the sixth he begun to make a mistake here and there. Lucky Judkins got on. Swanee fouled off about 5 and then McKenna tried to fog 1 through. You never want to try a stunt like that on an old hand like Swanee. He slammed it up against the wall in left for 2 bases. Another foot and it would of went in. Lucky scored. Perry pinch-run for Swanee, and Sid looped a single into right. There was a young kid in right name of Levette Smith that must of had a mighty high opinion of his own arm, for he heaved home, thinking to catch Perry at the plate. He would of never done it if he thought about what he was doing, but he got all flustered I guess, and not only did he miss Perry but Sid went down to second. Then Sunny Jim drilled a hit into right, scoring Sid, and we was ahead 3-2.

I was very wobbly in the eighth and would of been in trouble but Lucky went clear to the wall in center and brung down a drive off the bat of Nat Lee. Red told Dutch he believed I was tired, and Dutch asked me and I said I was, and he lifted me in the ninth for a hitter—Coker—and Coker drawed a walk. McKenna kept looking over towards his own dugout, and I caught him looking, and so did Dutch and so did Red, and Red shouted out to George to wait him out in Spanish. McKenna was puffing hard and stalling for breath, playing with the resin, taking off his cap and studying it like he never seen such a thing before and generally behaving like a kid will do when he is tired and don't want to show it. But that ain't the way to hide it. The only people he hid it from was his own club. Anyways George followed orders and drawed the walk.

Rob had nothing left to throw but a wish and a prayer that Lucky Judkins stepped into and clubbed on a line into right that Smith never moved for but waved it "goodby" whilst it sailed to the stands beyond. It whammed into the scoreboard and dropped down in the lower deck, and that was all for McKenna and Cleveland and dreams of the Series in October, for I do believe it was Lucky's blow that busted the back of Cleveland.

Horse Byrd finished up, and I got credit for the win. I had yet to lose a game.

There was a wire from Vincent and Pasquale that night. Dutch passed it around, and it said that their father died and everything would be squared away in a day or 2 and they would meet us in Chicago, and thanks for the flowers, and congratulations to Henry and Lucky and all the rest for the nice snappy win over Cleveland. It was signed "Tnecniv dna Elauqsap" and we all got a laugh out of that. I guess they could feel it way back there in Frisco, like we felt it in Cleveland, that we seen the circuit round, all but Chicago, and there was nothing to fear but fear itself, like the fellow said.

In Cleveland the visiting clubhouse is smack up against their own. There is only a wall between, and on the first day, whilst Dutch was giving us the lecture, you could hear the Cleveland boys a-whooping and a-hollering. On the second day you could hear them again, not quite so loud. On the second day we whipped them again, Swanee and Sid blasting doubles after 2 out in the ninth for the run that decided. That was Knuckles Johnson's ball game, a very nifty 5-hit job.

On the third day there was nary a peep from behind the wall. It was silent and still, and all we could hear was Joe Lincoln giving them hell, a low hum to his voice, and we could not hear the words, of course, yet we knowed the general pitch, and they was meek and mild that afternoon like a kid that got whaled and sent up to bed and along about the middle of the night come down looking for his supper. In the sixth, trailing by 2, they rallied and tied it up, but that was the last of the fight that was in them. In the seventh our big guns opened up, and we peppered the walls, and the few faithful fans that stood to see the inning out needed both hands to count it up, for it come to 7 runs on 6 hits, 2 walks, 2 wild throws and 7 or 8 mistakes in judgement. The game run 4 hours, and the score wound up 14-4 and would of been worse but we got tired running the bases.

Winning pitcher: Hams Carroll.

We split 2 in Chicago. We left Chicago at 7 of a Sunday night. We played about 20-handed poker quarter limit throw in your money and run them and don't worry your cards from 9 o'clock that evening until daylight. We had took 9 out of 11 in the west. We landed in New York 2½ games ahead of Boston.

STANDINGS OF THE CLUBS
May 12

	Won	Lost	Pct.	Games Behind
New York	17	6	.739	—
Boston	14	8	.636	2½
Brooklyn	13	8	.619	3
Cleveland	13	8	.619	3
St. Louis	10	12	.455	6½
Washington	10	15	.400	8
Pittsburgh	9	17	.346	9½
Chicago	7	19	.269	11½

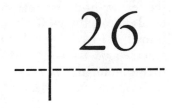

I NOTICE that both the last chapter and the 1 before wound up with statistics. I had this book all full of them, batting averages and fielding averages and the standings of the clubs day by day. But Holly said too much was too much.

Red Traphagen come through for a couple days last week, and he said the same. He read over what I wrote, and he says it is good but too much statistics.

Well, I used to be fairly hot on statistics myself. But I do not believe statistics tells the whole story. I could give you a run-down right now on every ball game the Mammoths played between the time we got home from the west the first time, played the home stand, played the east, played the west again and come home again, right up through July 4th. I could tell you my won and lost record (13-3) and how many I fanned and how many I walked and my E. R. A. (2.74). I could go through these clips that Pop saved up and tell you who hit what and where and when and how. I could give you a day by day report on Swanee Wilkses hitting streak that had the league agog. I could tell you everything, and you could read all the statistics and still not know the true story. Red says the same.

It is like the stars. I could tell you that Sirius is 8.6 light years, for Aaron Webster happened to mention it only last night. Yet what in the name of thunder do you know about Sirius that you never knowed before? I said so to Aaron, and he said I was right. A light year is how far can light go in a year, about 6,000,000,-000,000 miles. I said to Aaron if that is a light year I would hate to see a heavy 1. He laughed until he dropped. "You are right," said he, "for it is not the statistics that tells the story. It is what went on in your heart." That was put rather neat.

Many of the things that went on never got in the records. A good many more never took place on the ball field a-tall, but elsewhere. Folks say to me down in Perkinsville, "What was your biggest thrill? Was it the All-Star Game, or was it that Brooklyn game?" Perkinsville ain't down on me a-tall, though I thought at first that they might be. They might sometimes look at me a little bit like they don't quite trust me all the way, but for the most part people seem to forgive and forget.

Well, that Brooklyn game was quite a thrill at that. I was hooked up with Bill Scudder in a night game on May 14. I was plenty fast that night and working without my full rest besides, Dutch having pitched me 1 day out of turn, figuring that I was a better bet then anybody else in a night game, being fast and all. The night is not so good for the batter no matter what anybody says. Electricity ain't sunshine. Anyhow, I was plenty fast, and we was getting to Scudder without too much trouble, but then he would tighten up in the pinches, and it wasn't until the first of the sixth that we pushed over some runs. Swanee and Sid singled, and Sunny Jim drove them home with a double. The Caruccis been on the bench since they got back from Frisco, Swanee and Sunny Jim hitting like mad and there wasn't no sense in doing otherwise then leave them in the line-up. Consider that 2 such ballplayers as Vincent and Pasquale was sitting on the bench and you get some idea how hot the Mammoths was.

In the last of the sixth, with 2 down, Scudder come up. He is a fair hitter for a pitcher. We usually pitch to him fast, about letter high and close, and I thunk back over what he done the first time up, and I remembered that he popped to Ugly. Then it dawned on me that if this was the last of the sixth and Bill Scudder up there only for the second time they must not be hitting much. I checked with the board, and it was the last of the sixth all right. Well, thought I, then we must of pulled a couple double plays. But I could not remember any. Then I said to myself, "Why, you idiot, you just ain't give up no hits so far." We throwed fast under the armpits, and Scudder fouled down the third base line, and George took it on the run, close to the boxes.

I come in to the bench and the kid brung me my jacket. There was a hush over the crowd, and on the bench as well. "Why so quiet?" said I. "Ain't a guy got a right to pitch no-hit ball?" Nobody said a thing. There is a superstition amongst ballplayers and fans alike that if a no-hit game is in the works nobody must mention it.

We was ahead 3-0 in the ninth, and *still* no hits for Brooklyn. In the last of the ninth Gibby Reeves was sent up to hit for Pearce. The loud speaker blared it out, and the crowd booed Arms a-plenty, Arms being the Brooklyn manager, for the crowd wished to see the no-hitter completed. I could understand Armses viewpoint. He is paid to win ball games and not be sentimental. Dutch sent Canada down to first and Vincent and Pasquale into the outfield, hoping to tighten the defenses. The park was quiet.

I got Reeves on strikes.

Arms sent Marriner up to hit for Wynn, the Brooklyn catcher, and the booing took up again, "Boo-oo-oo-oo-oo-oo," long and loud and drawed out like a train whistle in the night. When it let up a little I throwed down fast, nothing too good, and it nicked the outside corner, and Marriner slammed it back at me like a rocket, 1 of them drives that you stick your hand up without ever thinking about it. If you had time to think about it you would fall flat and get out of the way. It whammed in my glove and popped out, high in the air, and Ugly come in from short and dove after it and took it about 1 foot off the ground.

That was 2 gone and 1 to get. Arms sent Paul Sanders up to hit for Scudder, and the booing was terrific now. There has been no-hit games ruined with 2 out in the ninth, and some of the language that come floating down in Armses direction was of the best brand of Brooklyn vocabulary. Some of the things said included the fact that he would eat certain things as well as do certain things to his own mother, and there was several promises made that if he was caught on the streets of Brooklyn he would die. These fans are always very brave from a distance. I wished they would shut up and leave me concentrate.

Red signed for the screw, and I throwed it, and Sanders whistled 1 down the line in right. I held my breath. It hooked foul about halfway between first base and the fence.

Red called for the screw again, and I shook it off. I figured Sanders would expect it. Red give me the go-ahead, and I fogged 1 through, a powerful fast pitch, and Sanders left it pass. It was a strike.

We wasted 1, and then we throwed the screw again, and he drove it on a line towards right. I seen Canada leave his feet, but he had no chance whatever to grab it, and Pasquale come tearing in, and he dove but never quite got his glove on it, and the whole park groaned. Schoolboy Wenk popped out a minute later, and the ball game was over, 1 hit for Brooklyn, and a clean 1 that couldn't of been scored otherwise if I had scored it myself.

True, that was a great night in my life and I will always remember it, but it was also the night that Bub Castetter was let loose, and Squarehead was shipped back to Q. C., and in the clubhouse, whilst I showered and dressed, I caught a glimpse of Bub now and then, taking off his uniform that he wore 10 years or so with the number 31 on the back and dropping it where he stood and leaving it there. The writers milled about as thick as thieves, and they shouted in to the shower, "What did you throw Sanders on that pitch?" and "Do you feel very bad?" and "When did you first notice you had a no-hitter going?" and all such as that, and all the time I was thinking of Squarehead and Bub.

Me and Bub was never chummy. Yet I was sad for him, for nobody took up his waiver and he was too proud to go back and play AA at Queen City. There was no club now that was willing to fork over the piddling 10,000 waiver for a ballplayer that not many years before would of brought 50 or 75,000 on the market if the Mammoths cared to sell him. They never would, of course. The last I seen of Bub he was on his way out the clubhouse betwixt Sam and Swanee. I suppose they went and had a drink together.

We sung in the shower. Squarehead come in, and we sung "Old Lang Zine." "Never mind," said Squarehead, "sing me a happy song, for Mike Mulrooney will learn me to pull hit, and I will be up again next year, and Sid Goldman can then go and coach at Evander Childs High School in the Bronx, for there will not be no need of him around the Mammoths." Sid always said he wished to go and be a coach at the high school where he went.

"That is right," said Perry. "I believe this is the year that Mike will set you straight," and me and Coker and Canada said the same. Yet I knowed in my heart that it was a lie. I suppose even Squarehead knowed it was a lie, for he is 25 and played 3 years under Mike, and if he could not learn yet he would never learn. He gets up at the plate and forgets all he ever learned. He just hits away, never scientific, all meat and muscle. Dutch give him all the chance he dared, and the record reads 10 times at bat, 1 hit, 1 home run, 1 run drove in, for a .100 average. Dutch played him 1 inning afield, and the record reads 1 putout, 1 assist and 1 error, and the error cost a run, and the run canceled out the 1 run Squarehead batted in. So Squarehead left the Mammoths no better and no worse then he found them, even Steven. He is a first-rate friend but a second-rate ballplayer.

We had supper that night at Dempseys over on Broadway and then we seen Squarehead off on the train, me and Canada and Coker and Perry and Lindon, and it was sad, and he wished us luck and we said the same, and I was sorry for all the things I ever said and done, all the gags we pulled on Squarehead. He said he never minded, but he must of. Squarehead is 1 of them people that you knock them down and they get up and ask you did you hurt your hand. I am sorry if I run down Squarehead as a ballplayer anywheres in this book, but the main thing you must remember is what I said a few lines above, that Squarehead is a first-rate friend. That is the *most* important thing about Squarehead Flynn. Sometimes I think friendship is more important then even being an immortal.

It was about this time that the discussion begun over whether Perry Simpson was a faster runner then Heinz, the Boston left fielder. I don't know how it begun. It is another 1 of them things that took place off the ball field. Things that start in hotels and amongst the writers I got no way of tracing them down.

There was a piece in the "Mirror" saying that Joe Jaros said that he believed Perry was faster then Heinz. Joe said he never said no such thing. He said that what he said was that he believed Perry *run bases* better then Heinz, which is a different thing, not so much a matter of speed as brains. A writer in Boston told Heinz what the writer in New York said Joe Jaros said, and it was then wrote up in the Boston papers that Heinz said he could beat Perry any old time. Heinz told me later that he never said no such thing. 1 day Krazy Kress said to me did I think Perry or Heinz was the fastest. I said I did not know. I said I believed they was both fine ballplayers, Heinz a harder hitter but Perry maybe a better all-around ballplayer. Krazy wrote that I said Perry could beat Heinz in any department any day of the week. I told Krazy a day or 2 afterwards that if he was just going to write what he pleased why in hell come to me in the first place. He just laughed. "You know," he said, "I been thinking it over, and I believe anybody would be crazy to bet 100 on a white man to run **faster then a n----r** anyways." I said who bet 100. "Oh," said he, "some of the boys up in Boston."

"Well," said I, "I will match that 100." Then he wrote it up, saying that I said I would put up 100 on a race between Perry and Heinz.

Before a week was out there was 1,000 in the pot. Boston matched my 100, and then the boys come around, saying they would cover me, and they done it so enthusiastic we had 400 collected. Boston matched it and went 150 better. By the time it stopped there was 1,000 on the line with everybody in that was coming in, meaning all the Mammoths plus 100 from Patricia Moors. Folks started sending it in through the mail. The club sent it back. If there was no return address they give it to the cripple soldiers to buy chewing gum and such.

Perry was against it from the start. He went around and told the boys to draw out and stick to baseball. But it had went too far to draw out now, and 1 of the writers was holding the money, and the time was set for between the games of the doubleheader in Boston on Memorial Day in baseball suits but running shoes. We bought Perry a pair and he busted them in a little bit every day in drill. The writers fought over whether it should be against the clock around the bases or man against man in a straightaway. Then they argued if it should be on grass or dirt. It was decided that it would be part on each, man against man in a straightaway, and whoever umpired that day would be the judges. It got so that there was so much talk about the running race that nobody noticed the baseball much.

We moved into Boston for a night game on the Wednesday before the holiday, the holiday being scheduled for Friday. We went in 5½ games to the good, Boston second, Brooklyn third, Cleveland fourth and beginning to fade. The lead was cut to 4½ Wednesday night, Piss Sterling dropping a close 1.

About 100 folks come up from Perkinsville that night and give me a Day. They give me a wrist watch and a traveling bag and a suit of clothes and a lifetime pass to the Embassy Theater in Perkinsville and Government Bonds worth 300 plus 100 more in credit coupons on the Perkinsville stores plus 4 new tires for my Moors. They also brought along that corny picture of Borelli's where it says "Mammoths" on the shirt. It looked like I had rouge and *lipstick* on, for Christ sake. I was hoping Holly and Pop and Aaron might come, but they did not.

After the ball game the Perkinsville crowd come to the hotel to a party give by Patricia Moors. She says whatever they spent on the trip and gifts they drunk back 2 times over. I said I believed she could afford it, and she said she could. She had a lot of friends up from New York, all a bunch of regular snobs, plus about 60 of the same from Boston itself, and they drunk Perkinsville under the table. I will say 1 thing for Perkinsville, it ain't full of a lot of snobs. I said to Patricia I believed there was as many rummies in high society as there was in Perkinsville. "More," she said. She said they fornicated less, however. She said she read in a book where the higher you go in society the less you fornicate, but when you fornicate you take off more clothes then the lower classes. She asked me if this was true in my opinion. I said I had no opinion. I do not believe she would of went into the matter with me at the time if she had not of been so looped. She said I was the first man she ever met that did not have no opinion on fornication.

I said I would certainly like to fornicate with her.

She slapped my face.

After she slapped it she said she was sorry, and she rubbed my cheek.

Everybody was falling-down drunk, folks from New York and folks from Boston and folks from Perkinsville and writers from both places and a few ballplayers as well, tomorrow being an open day and all.

I remember seeing a high society lady flat on the floor and Mayor Real of Perkinsville beside. Somebody picked them up and sat them straight in a chair. Wherever Patricia went I went. Everything she told me to do I done. "Move that body out of the line of march," she said, and I done so, and the longer things went on the more people was strewed about. There was 1 society girl from New York that about every 20 minutes tried to jump out the window. There was 3 or 4 big society ladies that give me their jewels and bracelets and such. Patricia told me keep everything that they give me lest the hired help grab it off, and she give it all back the next day. "Just follow me," she said, rather thick of tongue. But later, when I was not looking, she slipped off. I had the feeling that I had got the gate.

I wandered around a bit, munching on the food, not drinking, for I never drink. Bill Duffy of the Perkinsville "Clarion" was there. He was standing with a glass in his hand reciting "Casey At The Bat," and I listened to him awhile, and then I drifted off. Here and there a lady would give me her jewels.

There was 1 girl, no more then 19, high in society in Boston and formerly married to a San Francisco Seal. She snaked up to me and asked me if I believed she had the nerve to strip down and go walking on Beacon Street. I said I believed she did, for she was drunk enough, but I said she would only get hauled in and I could not see no sense in that. She agreed there was no sense in it, but she said she never done anything in all her life that you could call distinguished. "I wish I was a ballplayer," she said, "for a ballplayer is a man that lives by what he does in life."

In the morning I took all the jewels to Patricia's room. She knowed who they all belonged to. She give me a tall glass of seltzer water with different pills in it, saying this would fix my hangover. I told her I was not hung over, having drunk nothing the night before but Coke, but she did not seem to hear. I drunk 1 glass slow while she drank 3 or 4. She told me we was busting all attendance records, with Boston sold out for tomorrow and the Stadium sold out for the 2 with Brooklyn before the club headed west again. The telephone rung all the while, and people asked her this place and that, and she told them no, saying she was in conference with 1 of her ballplayers.

I cannot understand it now, but at the time I would of give anything I owned or could beg or borrow or steal to fornicate with that woman, and every time I thought I might be able to edge around to the subject the telephone rung. Finally the call come that she was waiting for, and she hung up and she said, "Well, Henry, I guess that winds up our business for the morning," and she went inside to another room, and I sat there awhile clinching and unclinching my hands and not knowing what to do next. I had half a mind to go after her. I thought I might charge in there and do with power what I could not do with strategy. After awhile I got up from the chair and turned and heaved the glass against the door that Patricia disappeared behind. It smashed to pieces. The door opened cautious, and she looked out, all bare at the shoulder. "Somebody knock?" she said, and I picked up the nearest thing, an ash tray, and she closed the door quick and locked it, and I went back up after Perry and Coker and Canada and Lindon, and we went out to the ball park to give Perry the chance to stay loose for the race tomorrow.

Friday the park was full by noon, with as many standing as the law allowed, plus about 2,500 more roped off in the right field corner. Any balls hit in the crowd behind the ropes was declared doubles only, and it turned out fine for us, for Sid and Lucky and Ugly and Sunny Jim between them popped about 12 in the crowd during the afternoon.

Sam Yale worked the first game. Goose caught him, leaving Red rested and free to handle me in the nightcap, and Sam coasted through, and we took it 9-4. Perry was beside me on the bench, so nervous he could scarcely see, sitting with his glove in his hand that by the end of the ball game he twisted the lacing until at last it snapped in 2. You should of saw him try to work a new lace back through the holes with his hands trembling like a schoolboy asking a girl for his first date.

After the game I begun to warm with Bruce, and the umps laid out 100 yards, stretching in from left, cutting across the skin of the infield and finishing up at the first-base line. 3 writers come down on the field, 1 from Boston, Krazy Kress from New York and a neutral from Washington. They had the 2,000 wrapped in a silken handkerchief. Perry and Heinz practiced starts. 4 umps worked the race, 1 at the start, 1 in the middle and 2 at the finish. The boys run without their caps.

There was 2 false starts. Heinz jumped the gun the first time and Perry the second, and then they was off, neck and neck until the very last. About 5 yards from the finish Heinz give a spurt, and he won it, and Perry kept right on going, circling around and heading for the dugout and disappearing through the door, never even stopping to shake hands. He got booed a-plenty by the crowd, almost as much as Heinz got cheered, and Boston come rushing over for their money, and the Mammoths turned and ducked back in the clubhouse. I stood and warmed with Bruce 15 minutes or so before going in.

Perry was crying and laughing at once. The boys was sitting around jawing, drying off, taping theirselves, getting a rub from Mick. I told Perry he run a good race and it was all over now, so forget it. I guess that was what all the boys been saying. What was 900 dollars to a bunch of fellows that figured to cut up a Series melon in October coming close to a quarter of 1,000,000? Now and again 1 of the boys would come past Perry and swat him 1 or spit water at him or call him a name, all in fun, and when they done so he laughed and the tears run down his cheek, and Dutch took him by the shoulder, and he said, "You took up his challenge. You done the best you could. You run a good race. Take off them mean-looking shoes and put on your shoes, for you are starting at second." That give Perry back his good spirits, and he dressed and went out and drilled.

Dutch juggled the order a bit, batting Perry second and shoving

Lucky down to the number 3 spot, Swanee 6, and it never bothered us a bit, all that patchwork, for we bunted Boston crazy, and when we was not bunting we was dropping doubles in the roped people. Perry got booed in the first, in thanks for which he ripped off a single, stole second, and then come home on a single by Lucky.

Heinz got all the cheers and none of the hits. He got on base once on a cheap single and tried to steal, and Red throwed him out by a good foot and a half. Running bases is more then simple speed. If you wish to learn how to run the bases watch Perry Simpson, not Heinz. We won the ball game 8-2 without straining, and we left Boston sadder then it was when we come, and 6½ games behind besides.

We swung west and then again east. We was 8½ to the good after the Washington doubleheader July 4th. The band played "Happy Birthday to You" to me, for it was my twenty-first birthday. The boys chipped in and bought me a couple very beautiful shirts with a note inside saying now I was 21 and a man like all the rest. I am the youngest fellow on the club, though to tell you the truth I believe many of them still act like kids about a lot of things. We split with Washington, Boston splitting with Brooklyn.

We had hopes of maybe clinching the flag about early September. We made up a pool, writing down dates on shreds of paper and throwing them in a cap, all the dates from September 1 through 30, enough for all the players, 3 coaches, Dutch and Mick. Clinching the flag is where you have got the mathematics beat, so even if you lost all your ball games and the nearest team won all theirs nonetheless you would win, because of the mathematics. We all throwed in a buck and drawed a shred of paper. I drawed September 5. It seemed a little early, yet possible. Then Ugly said we ought to throw in more, for what was a pot of 30 dollars to some fellow that had a share of the Series melon coming up. So we throwed in 2, and Sam said "Goddam it, how about 5?" and we all throwed in 5 and wrapped it in a towel, all 150, and laid it up on the shelf in Dutch's office, and everybody wrote their name on the shred they drawed and put it in a glass. Somebody figured to have 150 extra come September. Red said it would pay a part of the tax on a Series share. The boys all gripe about taxes. Aaron Webster never pays any taxes, saying it all goes for the wars.

Around this time the votes was in on the All-Star squads. There was about 4,000,000 votes from every state and a number of foreign countries, the fans voting for all the players but the pitchers. The manager picks the pitchers, the manager always being the man that won the flag the year before, and this year it was Frank Arms of Brooklyn, and he chose me and Sam from the Mammoths and Bill Scudder from his own club. All the rest was righthanders. Mammoths that won in the voting included Red, Ugly, Pasquale, George and Swanee. We all felt especially good for Swanee, for he been off the squad for 3 seasons. He led the voting with 1,294,-792.

That was a great thrill, too. I pitched the middle 3 innings and give up 1 run on 4 hits. That was the best job turned in, though I cannot say I would like to try it very often. You really sweat, for you are up against the absolute tops. The big leagues is tops enough, where you got 400 ballplayers weeded down from the whole wide world, but in All-Star play you have weeded the 400 to 50, and every man you face is a big man with a big bat. I always dreamed of working in an All-Star game since the first 1 I ever heard down in Borelli's. It seemed like there was getting to be no dreams left, only the Series.

The game was at Philadelphia, and afterwards we left for St. Louis, me and Sam and Red and George and Pasquale and Ugly and Swanee. Some of us was in the poker mood, but Red and George will never play and we could not find Sam, and I went in search of Sam and found him in the diner. The dinner hour was over, but Sam knows all the porters and all the conductors, and they admire him and give him pretty much the run of the train. He was sitting at a clean table reading a book, and I told him come and play poker, and he said he could not. "I am improving my mind," he said. "Say there, Hank, did I not have my picture in front of this book?" He was reading out of "Sam Yale—Mammoth" that Pop sent like I asked.

"Maybe you did at that," said I. I had that picture at that very moment folded in my wallet. But I could not tell Sam. "Some kid must of tore it out," I said.

"I am glad to be reading this," he said. "It is pretty goddam long. I been reading 2 and 3 pages at a time."

When I was a kid I would wolf that book down once a week regular.

"But it is all a pack of horseshit," he said.

"You should of thought of that before you give Murray Miller the go-ahead," said I, for Joe Jaros told me that a writer name of Murray Miller on the "News" wrote the book.

"It was not Murray," said Sam. "It was Krazy Kress. Krazy wrote it up and sent it down home 1 winter all typewrote on yellow paper. I begun reading it 2 and 3 pages a night but never finished it, and then I give it to Hilda to send it back, for I went hunting with Bub Castetter."

He studied the book, smiling and turning it over in his hand. "If I was to write a book for kids I would not write such trash as this," he said. "This is a good book and teaches them all the right things about smoking and going to church and such. For most kids that is all right. It will get them where they wish to go. They never aim very high. Those that aim high when they get there finds out that they should of went somewheres else. You think you want money and then you get it and you piss it away because it ain't what you really wanted in the first place. You think you want your name in the headlines, but you get it there and that ain't what you want neither. You think you want this woman or that woman, and then you get the money and the headlines and the woman besides. Then you find out you do not want the woman no more and probably never wanted her in the first place."

"That is right," said I.

"How would you know?" he said. "It will take you 15 years to find out. You get so you do not care. It is all like a ball game with nobody watching and nobody keeping score and nobody behind

you. You pitch hard and nobody really cares. Nobody really gives
a f--- what happens to anybody else." He looked very sad, exactly
like he looked in the picture in my wallet.

"*Sad* Sam Yale," I said.

"I ain't sad," he said. "I just do not care. I just play for the
money I do not need and fornicate for the kicks I never get. Some
day there will not even be the kicks. If I was to write a book they
would never print it. It would be 5 words long. It would say, Do
Not F--- With Me. I would send it to every church and every
schoolhouse and tell them to hang it up over their door. It will not
get you anywheres in life. But it is the best you can ask for *out* of
life. The best you can hope is that everybody else will just leave
you alone. This book is all horseshit." He shoved it across the
table, and I took it.

"Ain't it the truth?" I said.

"Leave us go play some cards," he said, and we pushed back the
chairs and went.

It was either on this train or on another very soon after that
Krazy Kress brung up the tour to Japan and Korea. I forget which,
but now is a good place to write it in, this chapter being mostly a
collection of odds and evens anyways. He was supposed to take
about 20 ballplayers in October on this tour against clubs such as
the Yomiuri Giants and the Nankai Hawks of the Japanese leagues.
Then we was to go up to Korea itself and play squad games for the
soldiers behind the lines.

I never said yes and I never said no. I sat looking out the window and remembering the hand to hand combat at Perkinsville
High. Just thinking about it set off these noises in my stomach. I
begun thinking about all the boys in Korea that never knowed from
1 day to the next if they was slated to live or die, and I felt sorry
for them. Yet I could not see where if I was to go to Korea it
would do them any particular good.

"It will do them much good," said Krazy. "It will buck up their
spirits and give them the idea that folks back home are thinking
about them. There is nothing like the sight of baseball to make
them think they are home."

"I see baseball every day," I said, "and never get the idea I am home."

"This is all expenses free, Henry. Maybe I did not mention that. It will not cost you a nickel."

And then it seemed to me that if I was too much of a coward to go and fight in the war against Korea myself I had no business going over and playing ball for them and encouraging *them* to be fighting it.

"Hell," said Krazy, "not only expenses but maybe a little extra cigarette money for your pocket as well."

"I do not smoke," said I, and I looked out the window some more. I thought about Holly and I wished she was around to give me some advice. And I wondered what Aaron would say to me going to Korea and egging the boys on in their war, for Aaron was against it from the start. Him and Pop had a regular knock down squabble when I was even supposed to go and be *examined* for Christ sake at the Vets hospital in Tozerbury. "Ain't it awful cold to be playing ball over there that time of year?" I said.

"Cold?" said Krazy. "Why no. Have you never seen Korea on the map? Korea is more south then St. Louis." Actually I never saw it on the map until just this minute. I went over to Aaron's and looked it up. I always had the idea it was out around where Alaska and Russia come together. I wanted to tell Krazy no and I wanted to tell him yes, both at the same time. I wanted to go to Korea if it would do the boys any good, but at the same time I couldn't see where it would.

"Ain't you behind the boys over there?" said Krazy.

"I am behind the boys," said I, "but I am against the war."

"You know, Henry, you must not forget the fun you are libel to have on such a tour. You know how these Japanese girls are. Why, they ain't got no more morals then a cat. I understand that for an American buck you can get the works and a meal besides."

Finally I said no. I just wasn't interested. Krazy asked me again 2 or 3 more times over the summer, and every time I told him no. I don't know why, but my heart just couldn't of been in it. Yet I believe I am as much of an American as Krazy and probably wouldn't like the Russians any better then the next fellow if I ever met 1. But I said no, and I said no every time Krazy brung it up.

Another thing, too, is I will bet that somewhere under the haystack you will find that Krazy had some angle in it that he forgot to mention, some cash to be made most likely. I do not mean that he is a crook or anything like that, but he has got so many irons in the pie that you sometimes begin to wonder. In his column he is always promoting 30,000 things on the side, and if you keep a close watch you will see where whatever comes along Krazy is somewhere where the cash flies. If it is some kind of a benefit dinner who is handling the tickets? Krazy. If it is a collection being took up for some sick kid in the hospital who is all of a sudden the chief collector? Krazy. Is it a new suit of clothes you wish to buy? Or a car? Who will get it for you cheap? Krazy. Or if it is a book you wish to have wrote he will write it for you out of the goodness of his heart, wanting none of the glory and only 66 and ⅔ percent of your take. I was a full year catching wise to all this, but I done so at last, and I believe I know Krazy well enough by now to know that Korea to him is just another benefit dinner, just another sick kid in the hospital, for he has yet to turn Boy Scout and do 1 single deed out of pure love for the next chap.

SWANEE WILKS got his streak snapped the first night in St. Louis by a kid name of Tony Tiso, born and raised on Dago Hill. Somebody was due to stop Swanee sooner or later. Tiso was wild that night, not too wild but just wild enough, and the boys never dared dig in, and we lost it 5-4. Up to that time Swanee hit safe in 29 games plus the All-Star Game. He said he was just as glad to get handcuffed at last, for the pressure gets great.

He got in a terrible scrap with Wes Jenkins in the third on a close play at first, spitting at him and calling him some extremely nasty things, and Wes would of throwed him out of the game, particularly after Swanee give him the old sign, 1 finger up. The League frowns on this, saying it don't look good before women and children, but Wes took no action, giving Swanee a warning only, thinking Swanee might yet collect a hit and keep the record going.

Sometimes I almost wished I was an umpire. I remember, the Saturday after, looking down at Wes, for he worked the plate that day, and wishing I was him. I was getting lumped up plenty and I thought how nice it must be to be an umpire when it makes no difference who wins and who loses. It was dreadful hot that weekend, and I think I drunk too much water, and time after time, when I throwed, full speed come out half speed, and curves never curved enough, and my control was sometimes off a full six inches. Dutch finally lifted me, and I walked out without no argument.

We split a doubleheader Sunday, Sam losing the first but

Knuckles winning the nightcap. We was glad to pull out of St. Louis that night. It was the first series we lost all year, and the first time we lost as many as 3 in a row.

We damn near lost the Chicago series as well. Piss dropped the first game, and Hams won the second, and I was behind 3-2 in the ninth inning of the third when Red begun our half with a single, old Red so cool and collected and always playing ball right down to the finish and never saying "Die," and Perry pinch-run for Red, and Pasquale Carucci swung for me and pumped a hit to short center. Jeff Harkness took it on 1 hop. I suppose the sensible thing would of been for Perry to hold at second with none out and the heavy end coming up, but he was playing the long percentages, and he went right around second, never stopping, never looking behind, and Harkness hesitated just the fraction of a second, knowing that if he tried to cut Perry off at third that Pasquale would move down to second anyways and we would still be in scoring position. Well, he throwed towards third, and Lindsay cut off the throw at short and tried for Pasquale at second, and they got him easy enough, except that whilst everybody was watching the play at second Perry was turning third and flying home at 90. The throw come in, and he slid safe under Millard May and tied up the ball game. Horse Byrd collared Chicago in the ninth and we later won it in extra innings.

We went on to Cleveland in the morning, all but Ugly. Ugly stood behind to see a Chicago doctor that he had good reports on. Ugly was all run down and weakly, and Dutch give him permission to stay.

Lindon said, "Ugly, why do you not merely tell Dutch that you need a rest?" Lindon was dead serious, but a laugh rose up from many of the boys.

"It been tried," said Gene. "Dutch only gives you a song and a dance and tells you how it was in the olden days."

"Why," said Swanee, "back in the olden times ballplayers *never* rested."

"That is true, though," said Goose. "I believe they was tougher."

"Bullshit," said Red.

"If I was to take a rest your pal Roguski might take away my job," said Ugly to Lindon.

"I do not want your job," said Coker. "I want to win the flag. I do not care who plays and who does not."

"I have heard that song before," said Ugly.

Yet Coker was speaking his true feelings. Naturally any ballplayer would rather play regular then sit on the bench, but Coker did not care how he won his share of the Series melon just so long as he got it. He was planning to build a house for his folks in West Virginia. He said they lived in a tar-paper shack for 25 years and would as soon live in a brick house, just for the change. You may not believe this, but Coker never seen an indoors toilet until he was 18 years old 1 time in Clarksburg, West Virginia, when he went there to play in the Legion tournament.

We figured Coker would take over at shortstop in Cleveland, but he did not. Dutch moved George over to short and played Canada at third. Sam turned in a fine game, needing a little help from Herb Macy in the eighth but getting credit for the win nonetheless. Lindon lost a 2-1 ball game the following night, Rob McKenna going all the way for Cleveland. When Rob is hot he is hard to beat, in particular at night. He give up only 4 hits, and the only run we got was a homer by Ugly, for he caught up with us just before game time. He said the doctor in Chicago said if he busted Ugly's jaw and set the teeth right Ugly would digest better and feel top-notch all through his system. Ugly said, "Goddam that noise." The doctor give Ugly a bill for 50 bucks. Ugly said send it to the club and make it 500 for all he cared. It was terrible funny the way Ugly told it.

Dutch eat us out before the Saturday game. He said maybe we was too busy figuring out ways and means of spending the Series checks, but in case we had not noticed we lost 5 out of 9 since coming west. He was real sarcastic. Naturally we noticed. But them things happen. Boston picked up a game on us. Dutch said if we was to fall back a game a week we would be spending second place money instead of Series cash and watching the Series from the grandstand. "Of course," said he, "it is very pleasant to watch the Series that way, for you do not get sweaty. Then, too, it is really grand fun to keep score on a card. You might also pick up 100 or so putting in a plug for razor blades on the radio. 100 is not 6,000, but then again there is nobody on this club that cares anything about such a thing as money. We just play for the fun of it on the Mammoths." Then he was silent for a space. "Well, I got nothing more to say," said he. "Johnson will pitch and Vincent Carucci go back in left." That was the outfield we begun the year with, Lucky and the 2 Caruccis. Sunny Jim was hitting poorly since the beginning of July. "Anybody got anything to say?"

Nobody did.

Knuckles was back in the shower by the end of the third. Horse Byrd joined him 2 innings later. Herb Macy was back there before the seventh was out, and Gil Willowbrook finished up. We lost the ball game 12-5. The scoreboard showed Boston whipping Chicago.

Dutch never said a word. He went in his little room and dressed fast, and then he passed back through and out the street door. "Has he went?" said Gil, peeking out from the shower, and we laughed. The talk took up a little, and we got the quartet going, and I believe that picked up spirits some. The boys was not worried.

"Hell," said Knuckles, "Dutch is not worried neither. He is a regular John Barrymore that puts on the long face to carry out the act."

I come out of the shower just as Dutch come back in. "Boston beat Chicago," he said. "A fellow told me there was some ballplayers in here and I thought there might be 1 or 2 with an interest in the pennant races." He went out again.

"Up his," said Goose.

"Still and all," said Lindon, "that is only 6½."

"Punks is to be spoke to and not heard," said Sam.

"Okay," said Lindon.

It rained the first day in Pittsburgh. We drilled in the drizzle, and the game almost begun, and for 5 minutes or so the sun come out and took a look and did not like the weather and went back in, and the umps called it off and we went in and dressed and shot back to the hotel and laid around. We caught St. Louis and Boston on the radio. It was 1 of them recorded deals where the Pittsburgh station took it an hour or more before and put it on tape.

Along about the third inning Sam Yale come in the room. He never come in our room before, and I knowed he was up to something, and he asked how the game was going, drawing a chair up by the window and sticking his legs on the sill. It was 1-1 with Boston batting. "They ought to go ahead this inning," he said. There was 2 down and none on and the lower end of the order coming up, and I doubted that they would. But I said nothing. Bruce Pearson said, "Not this inning, probably."

"Bet you half a buck," said Sam to Bruce, and he took 1 from his pocket and flipped it in the air a few times. Bruce pulled out a dollar. "You are on," he said. Toomy Richardson singled and Nippy Lewis doubled, scoring Toomy, and Bruce give Sam the dollar and Sam give him the half in change.

The telephone rung, and Sam picked it up. "Well, well, well," said Sam, "if it ain't my dear girl Suzy. How did you know I was in here? Me and some of the boys is listening in to a ball game." He kept up a running fire, and finally he told Suzy call him back later, for the ball game was very exciting, and he hung up. He sat there staring out the window and creasing the dollar bill, and Klosky come up for St. Louis. "Jim ought to hit a home run," said Sam.

"Bet you half a buck," said Bruce.

"You are on," said Sam, and Klosky hit a home run and Bruce flipped Sam the 50 cents.

Suzy called again. "Goddam it, Suzy," said Sam, "leave a fellow alone once in awhile when he gets a day off. Maybe I will see you next time I come through Pittsburgh. Sure I love you, Suzy, but I am listening to St. Louis and Boston on the radio. Me and Wiggen and Simpson and Roguski and Smith and Burke and Goldman and Pearson. Klosky hit 1 in the fourth and the last of the fourth is over now so call me back another time." He hung up. "Suzy figures Heinz might hit a home run inside the park," he said.

That is the hardest kind. There probably ain't 10 hit all year.

It has got to be a long drive and a fast runner in a big park. Bruce said he doubted it. If Bruce had any less brains he would be in Squarehead's class.

"It is your privilege to doubt it," said Sam.

"Half a buck," said Bruce.

"You are on," said Sam.

Heinz done it sure enough. Bruce must of lost about 3 dollars before he had the sense to quit. The half would go from him to Sam and then back to Bruce in change for a dollar and then back to Sam free and clear, and finally Sam rose and said he was off to see Suzy (she had called twice more in the meanwhile). He said he figured Boston to win by a score of 7-2, and they done so. Actually it was Goose on the phone all the time, over at the radio station playing the tape before it was put on the air. There was never no Suzy a-tall. I do not think Bruce knows it to this day. I believe Sam done it just to see if he could.

I was in bed that night before it dawned on me that Boston was now only 6 behind and plenty hot. They was winning 2 out of 3 in the west.

I pitched the opener against Pittsburgh. Hams was slated to pitch the day it rained, but then we grabbed off the rest and Dutch figured I was ready. He was getting so he relied on me more and more. The assignment suited me fine, and I won it. That give me 14 and 4 on the year, which was more wins then anyone else had. Scudder had 12 and Rob McKenna 11. It looked like I was headed for 20 for sure. That would be another dream come true. We picked up a game on Boston, for they lost to St. Louis that day, and the 7 looked a lot better then the 6 of the night before. But it was shrunk to 5 when we left the west, for Sam and Hams both lost their starts in Pittsburgh, Boston winning 2 in St. Louis. On top of everything else Lucky Judkins wrenched his back skidding on the wet grass going after a fly ball. Mick taped it up. Lucky figured it would work itself out in a couple days.

I do not like Washington nor ever will. I am minus a roomie there for 1 thing, for Perry must go sleep in Howard University. Red says it is a pretty good school, though not Harvard. Red says

99 colleges in 100 is run by boobs. Anyways, in Washington I have got to room alone in the hotel. In the beginning I never minded, for once you are asleep it don't matter, but after awhile I begun to sleep bad and worry, and I had the backache all through September, and Perry done me plenty of good, talking to me and cheering me up and telling me things was never so bad as I imagined. "Things is getting better all the time," he would say. Him and Red got in these damn arguments about whether things was headed up or down. Perry said "Up" and Red said "Down." Perry said Negroes are better off then ever before, and Red said true, but they are better off in a worser world. Perry said he don't care about the world, just about Negroes. Red said Perry don't care about Negroes, neither, just about himself, Perry Simpson. "Ain't that true?" said Red, and Perry said he supposed it was at that.

Yet he seemed to care about me, and that was why I hated Washington, for I was all alone. It would of been the same in St. Louis but Dutch knowed the owner of the hotel. I could of roomed with Piss Sterling in Washington, for Piss roomed alone on account of his sinuses, but I done so 1 time in September, and then in the middle of the night I got up and went out and slept in the park, for between the racket Piss made with his nose and the backache and the heat I could not sleep. It is important who your roomie is. It has got to be somebody that will listen to your troubles and tell you the way out, and sometimes we would talk far in the night, and I told him my troubles and he told me his, and time and again, laying there, we would figure it out. Perry is always thinking. He always has ideas. It is true that he sat on the bench most of the year, but he did not just *sit* there. He studied. Mostly he studied pitchers, for that was how he learned to steal on them so good. But he picked up plenty about hitters as well, and what he picked up he passed along to me. Some day he will have Gene Park's job, and you will see smart baseball from Perry. He is studying and thinking all the time.

Lucky Judkinses back still hurt him from where he fell and wrenched it on the wet grass in Pittsburgh. He took the drill on Saturday with about 12 feet of tape wrapped about his middle.

Mick said it would help. Lucky said it would help Washington maybe. He said Mick was no better then a horse doctor. Mick said he only done what Doc Loftus said, and Lucky said that made 2 horse doctors, and Mick said most horses have got more brains then certain ballplayers he could name. But Lucky could not get the full power in his hitting. He kept chopping them off to left and center all right, but when it come to the full swing he could not go all the way around, and Dutch made him take the day off, playing Scotty Burns in center.

Dutch give us a lecture before the game, saying we had bad luck in the west, and now we was to turn over the slate and start anew. He was not sarcastic, and he eat nobody out. He said Scotty would bat in Lucky's spot because this was the kind of a club where we was all hitters and it did not matter who hit where, and we would go out there and not worry and just wait until Buderman blowed.

Piss pitched and turned in a fine job. He got nicked for 1 run in the third, and that was all. The only trouble was that Buderman never blowed a-tall, and when it was added up we got 4 hits on the afternoon, and Piss lost it 1-0.

Boston split a doubleheader in Brooklyn. We was 4½ ahead. The clubhouse was so quiet you would of thought we just lost the pennant. Krazy Kress come in and said to Sam, "What is the matter with the boys?"

"I do not know," said Sam. "Ask the boys," but Krazy never done no asking, for Dutch throwed him in the street, not throwing really, just telling him nice to get out of the clubhouse and tell the other writers the same for awhile.

Maybe we was trying too hard. I begun to notice out there in the west, in St. Louis and Chicago and Pittsburgh and then again in Washington, how the second division clubs played it free and easy. They was earning their check, but they was out of the money, and they played like kids on a lot, you hit and then I hit and then the next man hits and when it gets dark we go home. They was not setting no records nor busting no fences nor stealing no bases, just playing ball the best they knowed how, and sometimes it was pretty bad ball, and what was happening was you had a bad team playing free and easy and beating a top-flight team that was all tightened up. Over the short pull them things will happen. Perry said the same.

That night I got to feeling blue. I got it in my head to write a letter, and I begun 1 to Pop, and then I tore it up and begun another to Holly, telling her how blue I was, and along about the second page I run out of material. I wrote down that I loved her, giving 1 page to that, and then I got to looking it over and it sounded like I was saying it because I was so blue and there was nothing better to write. I did not wish it to sound like that. I laid the letter aside. I dug out a bunch of things from my gear, thinking to send them home and travel lighter, some newspaper clips that I thought Pop might of missed and "Sam Yale—Mammoth" and a book Red give me to send to Aaron Webster that Aaron asked for the night of the Opener when we all had dinner together and Indian moccasins that I bought in Aqua Clara and meant to send to Holly and never did and then forgot to give her in New York. I wrapped it all up, and then when I was done I seen that I forgot to put the letter in for Holly. You ain't supposed to put letters in parcel post, but I always do. So I tore up the letter and fluttered it out the window.

Finally I just wandered in the street. I walked a good long ways, and soon I come to a park. There was a band there and a lot of people laying on the grass, trying to beat the heat. I laid on my back, and after a time the band packed up and went home, and many of the people cleared out, and it become cold on the grass and I went and sat beside what they call the reflecting pool. People sit there and reflect and think about their trouble, mostly alone but now and then 2 and 3 people together. It is quiet there, and you can get a little grip on yourself, like when you are in hot water and you slow the game down and let the opposition cool and go over the hitter in your mind because for some reason or other your brain works better when your body lets down and gives it the chance, and I sat there reflecting. I suppose that is where your big-time Senators might go when the going is rocky, and they might sit there and think things out. All the world has got trouble. Yet I believe if they would all sit still awhile and reflect they might get to the root of the matter. Aaron Webster says the same.

I thought to myself that what was wrong with the club was they was thinking too much and counting too heavy on the melon in October, and we ought to let down and relax. That was how we done when we was winning, beginning in Aqua Clara and straight through the early part of July. When we was winning we was relaxed, and I thought to myself if I was Dutch I would give the boys a lecture, telling them to ease off. It all seemed simple, and then I got up and strolled back through town to the hotel. It was cooler now, and I felt fine. I thought maybe with night games coming up more and more we would be beating the heat some and hustling better.

I dropped in the coffee shop for a bite. Dutch and Joe Jaros and Clint Strap and Egg Barnard and Swanee and Sam was at 1 table drinking coffee and smoking cigarettes. They had a bunch of napkins spread out, and they was writing things down all over the napkins. I slid in behind a far table and give the waiter my order, and then Dutch shouted at me, "Say, Henry, come on over," and I went, and I drawed up a chair in the isle. Dutch folded the napkins and put them in his pocket.

"What are you doing out so late?" said Dutch to me.

"I been in the park reflecting," I said. "Do you know what I think is wrong with the boys? I think they are too tight."

They all looked at 1 another. "That is just what we been saying," said Joe.

"Maybe we hit it right," said Dutch.

"That is all it is," I said.

"Goddam it," said Sam, "I bet that that is all it is."

The waiter brung me my food and Dutch paid, though I argued some. Then Dutch took the napkins out of his pocket again and leafed them through and found the 1 he was looking for. "Okay," said he. "How is this? Simpson, Roguski, Smith, Goldman, Carucci, Carucci, Wilks, Bruce Pearson and Burke. How does that look? That moves Swanee down to the 7 spot and takes the pressure off him. It gives Red a rest and also gives an extra day to my rotation. It gives all but a few regulars a real chance to catch up on their rest. By Tuesday we should be back in shape. How does that look?"

Everybody said it looked fine. Dutch crumpled up the napkin and throwed it on the floor. "Make Red explain it to George," said Joe. "George been playing good ball and you would not want him to think he is getting benched."

"Red is a big problem to me," said Dutch. "I feel like Red tells George what I tell him to tell him, but he puts on a different twist."

"That is Red," said Clint.

"I could of swapped Red for Bill Scudder," said Dutch. "I would do it if I had the chance again." Joe Jaros give him a big scowl, meaning there was a little pitcher with big ears in the crowd. I looked down in my cup like I wasn't listening. "This is all under your hat, Henry. Then I would of swapped George to Chicago for Millard May. I would have Smith to take over in George's spot. I like young Smith. He is my kind of a ballplayer, and in 2 or 3 years he will be the equal of George. Chicago will take these here Cubans. Then I would of got hold of Klosky some way or other. Goldman ain't my kind of a ballplayer."

"He has got 5 years of youth on Klosky," said Egg. "You would of made a bad deal."

"I would rather face Klosky then Sid any day in the week," I said.

"Maybe so. Well, this is all under your hat," said Dutch. "I get so damn sick and tired of different ballplayers with different kinds of personality. Why in the hell do they have to have all different kinds of personality? Why in hell ain't they all the same?"

After a time we broke up and went to bed.

The next day Lucky showed up at the park and got in uniform and drilled. I stood beside him and we shagged flies together. Them that you needed to run for Lucky said, "All yours, Hank," and off I went and dragged them down, and them that just floated out to where we was standing Lucky got under and let it drop, and then he flipped to me easy and I tossed it back towards the infield.

He said his back was worse then ever. He said he was over to the Navy Hospital but all they done was tear off Mick's tape and plaster on their own.

Lindon did not begin warming until very late. It was terrible hot, and there wasn't no need, and Dutch give us a lecture whilst we sat around drying off. It was real short, and all he said was as far as he was concerned he did not care if we won today or not, but just go out and play the best we knowed how and then Tuesday we would be back home and rested and all set to dig in for the stretch. He was sweeter then honey. He went around the room slinging compliments. He was like your old grayheaded grandfather, all gentle and kind.

Lindon done fine, and so did they all. If you squinted a little and took in only the box and the left side of the infield it looked like Q. C. all over again. The boys sung, and I remembered all of a sudden that all across the west they was not singing, and I think that helped Lindon plenty, for he is the sort of fellow that lacks confidence. He has got to be told time and again how good he is. If you tell him something bad about himself you have got to square it with something good. I never tell him he pitches too quick but what I tell him I wish my fast 1 hopped more, like his, even though I actually know mine hops the better.

In the top of the sixth we rolled. Swanee and Bruce hit, and Lindon flied deep, scoring Swanee. Perry slashed a single off Jack Klausner's glove and Bruce took second, and Coker pushed them along with a bunt that he almost beat. It was too bad he did not, for Canada followed with a blast high in the upper bleachers in left. It was a mighty swat, and we was 4 ahead. It was Canada's first round-tripper in the big-time.

The board showed Brooklyn swamping Boston. It seemed like we might all enjoy the open day better if we was to go home 5½ ahead instead of something less.

In the sixth Dutch sent me down to the bullpen to warm. Lindon was just the faintest bit tired, though never in trouble to speak of, and we picked up another run in the seventh and things looked safe.

In the Washington ninth, however, after 1 was out, both Klausner and Monk Boyd singled. Lindon could of pulled out of it fine, I believe, but Dutch never give him the chance, yanking him in a hurry and sending me in to relieve. I believed at the time that it was a mistake, and I still believe it, for he should of showed more faith in Lindon and left him finish and made him feel like he trusted him. What it was he lost his nerve—Dutch did—and put no faith in nobody.

Anyways, it was Lindon's game to save, and I saved it easy enough, and the only reason I mention it a-tall is because it was 1 of them games that had a *meaning* to it that the box score never showed.

First off, it come as a crusher to Lindon to get lifted that way. As for the rest of the boys, they took it as the sign from Dutch that he was now wearing his worrying clothes. All the little things —Lucky's ailing back, Ugly feeling poorly, Lindon and Piss never too dependable, Swanee Wilks somewhat in a slump—all these little things and more now added up to the fact that with the race still far from over there was the first small signs of trouble ahead in the wind, and Dutch could give us 45,000 more lectures saying "Go out and relax and play ball and never mind who wins," but we knowed all the same that he meant something else again, for winning is meat and drink to Dutch, and losing is the bitterest of pills.

And amongst the boys it was the same, not only on account of the money (though we never passed payday by) but also as a matter of pride, because I don't care who they are—Sam Yale or Red Traphagen or anybody else—deep down they play ball to win for winning's sake, not only for the cash but also for the glory. There was a lot of Dutch Schnell in all of us, and I believe that when Dutch stepped into his worrying clothes we put our own on, too. And I believe it was that Sunday afternoon in Washington that for the first time things took on a dangerous look.

28

POP says, you remember, there is too much dirty language in this book. This gives me rather a jolt, for I been wondering right along whether there wasn't too *little*. Him and Holly argued it over, and we asked Red when he was here. "Well sir," said Red to Pop, "you been a ballplayer and you know how they talk. If that is the way they talk should not Henry put it down like that?"

Pop said that was the way they talked back in the Mississippi Valley League, but he rather thought there might be a different class of ballplayers come of age in the meanwhile that talked in the higher style. "After all," said Pop, "there is a rash of ballplayers that went to college."

Red said to Pop, "Do you not want Henry to write a true book so as to explain everything that happened just like it was? Why, a book about baseball without no swearing would be like "Moby Dick" without no whale or "Huckleberry Finn" without no Huck."

Well anyway, you know what happened later on if you read "SPECIAL WARNING TO ALL READERS!!!"

We played poker all the way home from Washington. It was only a short trip and we did not play long. We had got out of the habit of playing all together any more. Things run in streaks like that. For awhile we was calling everybody by their name backwards, and then that left off just as sudden as it begun. Anyways, we was back to playing poker in little groups on the way home from Washington, me and Perry and Canada and Coker and Lindon up at 1 end of the car, what you might call the Queen City bunch. Maybe also Bruce Pearson. I forget about Bruce. It was either then or soon after that the boys took to riding Bruce. Him and Lucky had a scrap and that was the beginning. 1 day Swanee called Bruce a name in the clubhouse and Bruce could not think of 1 to call Swanee back. When Bruce gets riled his mouth don't work. Lucky laughed, not meaning no harm, just laughing, and Bruce said it was a mighty sad note when a fellow got laughed at by his own roomie, and Lucky said he would as soon room with someone else anyways. So Lucky switched over and roomed with Lindon, and Bruce with Sid, and then when the club was in New York Sid lived with his mother on Riverside Drive and Bruce was all alone, and the more alone he was the bluer he become, and the bluer he become the more the boys rode him.

Tuesday night Cleveland moved in. There was a big crowd, 45,000 or better, and they got their money's worth, both as to the time they put in and the brand of baseball they seen. Dutch give us a lecture beforehand. He praised the boys to the skies, and when he got done he ripped out against the writers and the announcers and the organization—the Moorses—and the schedule and the weather and the umpires. If I was to tell you some of the names he called these people you would never believe me. They was rip-roarers, just about everything in the book plus a few that was too spectacular for any book. Dutch said there wasn't a thing wrong with the club itself, just with the people that messed in from the outside. He said he heard that a few of the boys was snapping amongst themselves and talking about changing roomies and all. He said he did not believe any such stories, for he had hand-chose the club with an eye to fellows getting along together come hell or hot water.

He said he was pitching me tonight because he wanted to get his rotation back on schedule and not because, like some writers said, the staff was off its form. He give Sid a rest and played Canada at first, saying Sid deserved the rest for the way he hustled all year, and he put Lucky back in center so as to let him work out the kinks and get used to the tape. The boys sung that night, and we hustled, and we would of had it easy but for a couple bad breaks.

I was hooked up with Rob McKenna. That was partly what brung the crowd, I suppose, for there was much said by the writers over which was the best young pitcher in the league, me or Rob, and 1 writer said in the St. Louis "Globe" 1 morning that it would probably be either me or him for Rookie Of The Year. As it turned out Rob won Rookie Of The Year because I won Most Valuable Player Award when the election was held around November 1 and they could not give me both. Actually MVP tops them all. I also won the Sid Mercer Memorial Award of the baseball writers association as Player Of The Year in case you're interested.

Rob was a different pitcher at the end of July then he was back in May. He still made mistakes, but never so soon nor so frequent.

We played the kind of ball we always played against Cleveland, waiting for the mistakes. On this particular night they almost did not come, and it irritated hell out of me because we had the game sewed up 2 different times and then missed fire. It seemed like we lacked the punch when we needed it.

In the seventh Nat Lee slammed a home run off me that cleared the wall in right that if there was another coat of paint on the wall would of bounced back in play. When I come back to the bench after the inning Dutch was in a mood and the boys was mostly shoving down towards the far end and trying to look invisible.

We still trailed 1-0 when Ugly worked himself a pass to open our ninth. Perry went in to run. The crowd begun to sidle towards the exits by then, although a good many of them stopped in their tracks and leaned on the rails and watched. I don't know why they come in the first place if they are all in such a sweat to get home. Perry kept prancing back and forth off first. Rob McKenna throwed over a few times and Perry slid back in safe on his chest. I was praying for him to play it smart and not do nothing that would get him eat out.

Gene struck out, and the crowd begun to move again, and it was here, 2 outs from what would of been the finish, that Rob made his mistake. He went into a full wind-up. We all seen it on the bench, and we screamed, but Perry already seen it and was off like a bullet, and it was too late for Rob to check, or else he would of balked and Perry gone down anyways, and the only hope was to throw to the plate and pray that Perry busted an ankle on the way down. But he did not, and Rob felt like a fool. He must of felt a good deal miserabler 2 pitches later, for Red lined a single to left and Perry come home on wings, and the ball game was tied.

I would like to see the face of some of them boobs that cleared out of the park and got home and then maybe flipped on their radio and found the game still going. It was still going in the eleventh, and yet again in the twelfth. Coker was down at short now in place of Ugly. Sunny Jim was in center in place of Lucky, Lucky's back stiffening up on him in the cool of the night. It was past midnight. Horse and Gil was down in the bullpen, and they called on the phone and said don't forget to send them down breakfast.

I cooled off awful fast between innings. Doc Loftus said later that maybe that was when my backache set in, but I doubt it. I wore my jacket to bat in the twelfth. I do not believe I ever done such a thing before or since.

Dutch asked me every inning did I need relief, and I said no. I said if McKenna could keep going I could. We was making him work, nobody swinging until there was at least 1 strike called, and still he kept pouring them through, and I admired him for that. In the last of the thirteenth Sam come over and sat beside me on the bench. He hardly ever done that, usually staying down at his own end, but he come and squeezed in betwixt Perry and me, and he give me a special salt pill all wrapped in silver paper, saying swallow it. I did not swallow it right away. I don't know why. I put it in my pocket.

The crowd was so still my ears itched. Everything seemed unnatural, like everybody was told be quiet and the noise would be filled in later, and every sound carried far, and it was like a dream where you knowed it would all stop happening real quick, and yet it went on and on, the fourteenth, the fifteenth.

In the first of the sixteenth Barkowski opened with a single. It sounded like he hit it with a hollow bat. He danced back and forth up and down the line, and Canada covered, moving up and back with the pitches, trying to keep the runner close and at the same time play the bunt, and I throwed high to Taggart, and he tried to bunt, first fouling 1 off, and then bunting on the second pitch, and it trickled down the line towards first, and I moved over after it, and my legs was heavy and I felt like I was carrying around a sack of lead on my back, and finally I reached the ball and made the throw to Gene at first, for Gene was covering, but Taggart beat it.

McKenna batted for himself. He got a hand, but this time it was me that got the break, for he tried to bunt but popped it in the air, and I moved a few steps to the left and took it, and the runners scrambled back to their bases.

That brung up Reynolds. He is the Cleveland shortstop and been their lead-off man as long as I can remember. The books say he is 36. That would mean he broke into pro ball at 14. I would of rather it been a younger man that would maybe do something real dumb and help me out this late at night. It was the old veterans that worried me and give me the most trouble all year. Red signed for a fast 1, just blaze it through, and it seemed wrong to me but I was too weary to shake it off, and I throwed it, and Reynolds just looked it over, and Neininger called it a strike. He was trying to wait me, and tire me, and somehow that made me mad, and I remember that right about then I seen a little knot of people moving towards the exits, and that made me mad, too, for it seemed like when a fellow is in trouble people ought to at least stick it out and watch and not be in such a hurry to rush on home because it looks a little late. It was after 1 now on the center field clock, and Red called for the same, but neither so fat nor so good, and I throwed it, and Reynolds sliced it off foul down the line in right. It hooked into the stands and clattered amongst the seats, and a lady in a white dress strolled over and picked it up and stuck it in her purse.

I took out the pill Sam give me. I tore off the paper and popped it in my mouth, and it stuck in my throat, and after awhile it went down, and I remember thinking maybe Sam was giving me poison for all I knowed, and I remember that I wondered if anybody ever wrote a murder story where 1 ballplayer murdered another. This was about the time I begun to read murders quite a bit. Then Red give me the sign, and I throwed, and Reynolds swang and lashed it into right, and I knowed that I should of been backing up a base somewheres, but I could not think where to go. So I just turned around and watched the play. I seen Pasquale come charging in and diving and skidding along on his belly and making what they call a shoestring catch, and then all in the 1 motion he was up on his feet and firing down to second. Barkowski was halfway to third, not thinking Pasquale could make the catch, and now he was stopping short and turning and heading back towards second, and Coker took the throw, stretching out toward right with 1 foot on the bag like a first baseman, and Barkowski was doubled easy and the inning was over. I never told Pasquale what the catch meant to me, and I never asked Sam what was in the pill. I always meant to. But soon it was another day and another ball game and I guess I never did.

Sunny Jim opened our half of the sixteenth with a single. Lindon pinch-run for him, and Canada bunted Lindon along.

Pasquale was up there it seemed like years. He run the string out and fouled off a couple. And then I seen him shift his feet just the barest trifle, and I seen where Reynolds seen it, too, and shifted over himself and shouted to the rest of Cleveland to do the same, and Joe Lincoln yelled from the bench. But it was too late, for Pasquale drove 1 into right, and it fell close to the line and Levette Smith come over as fast as he could from where he was playing Pasquale more or less straight away, and he grabbed it and done the only thing he could do, firing it home with all he had, and the ball was still in the air when Lindon slid across.

I looked out at Rob. He was standing with his hands on his hips and his head bowed. He took 1 very deep breath, and then he looked over towards me 1 time, and then he turned and walked towards the Cleveland clubhouse. I felt very sad for him.

In the night I felt a little crick in my back. I noticed it several times before, beginning in the west, but never like this. I turned over a couple times, thinking maybe it was just from the way I was laying, but it did not go away, and I woke Perry and told him so, and he said what did I expect after working 16 innings. He laid in bed with his arm over his eyes. Then he said several dirty words and pulled the pillow over his face and fell asleep again. I pulled the pillow off his face and told him did he remember waking me in the middle of the night in St. Louis to crack his neck. He said he did, and he stumbled up out of bed and stood there swaying and trying to open his eyes, and he said there was some liniment on the shelf in the bathroom, and I went in and brung it back. It burned, and he rubbed it on where the crick was, mumbling and swearing and saying it could of waited till morning, and after a bit I felt that he was not rubbing, and I turned, and he was sitting there dead asleep with the bottle cockeyed in his hand and dripping down over his leg. I waited to see how far up it would drip. If it dripped far enough he would of woke again in a hurry. But it did not, and I give him a little push and he fell backwards on the bed and never woke up.

The next day I drilled a little, but it still hurt, and I went back in the clubhouse and down the stairs where Doc Loftus has his office. On a hot day it is the coolest place in the park. Piss Sterling was laid out on the table with 2 cotton sticks up his nose. He has sinuses something awful, and it got worse on the trip west. He laid there reading a paper with his arms stuck in the air. He give me a hello and Doc said for him not to talk or the medicine would all run down in his mouth. "Well, Wiggen," said Doc to me, "I do not see you here very often."

"I got a crick in my back," I said.

"That was a great game last night," he said. "It is no wonder you have got a crick."

"It sure run long," I said.

"Leave me see your back," said Doc, and I pulled off my shirt and he felt around with his hand where I told him to. He said he could not feel nothing, no bump nor no break. He said if it did not clear up in another day or 2 he would shoot some X-rays.

"Maybe it is all in your mind," said Piss.

"Shut up and lay down," said Doc, laughing. That was a big joke amongst the Mammoths. When Doc Loftus could not find something wrong with somebody he sent them down to the Navy hospital or some other big hospital, and it usually wound up with a report that it was all in your mind. Then you went and seen Doc Solomon. They said that Pisses sinuses was all in his mind. Sometimes Piss would run at the nose for an hour or more, and if you told him you would be glad to do something if you could he would say, "Oh, it is nothing. It is only my mind that I am blowing out my nose."

"Maybe it is at that," said Doc.

"Nuts," said I, and I put my shirt back on.

In come Patricia Moors for a bottle of pills. "I have not slept in a week," she said. I believe that was the first time I seen her since I heaved a glass at her over Memorial Day in Boston. "You ain't ill?" she said.

"I got a crick in my back," I said.

"Dutch says he hears by the grapevine that some of the boys is beefing about a doubleheader after a night game," she said.

"They got a right to," I said. "It was 3 o'clock before anybody got to bed."

We went out of Doc's office together, and then instead of going back up in the hot park we sat on the ledge there and looked out through the little slit in the fence where Doc himself generally sits. It give us a sort of a worm's view, and we seen 2 rough and ready ball games plus a fist fight betwixt Goose and Johnny Libby on a play at third plus some dandy language from Dutch on the play that cost Sam the first game. Sam lost it 5-4, a tough 1. Somebody on the Cleveland bench brung along a trumpet and every little while give out with "The Old Gray Mare She Ain't What She Used To Be" and then quick hid the trumpet until Carrera went over and found it and made them put it back in the clubhouse.

"Poor Sam," said I.

"I do not feel sorry for Sam," said she. "Sam is 1 of the few people I really and truly admire." She was in a very confidential mood that afternoon, though dog-tired after not having slept in a week. "Is it not odd that after putting thousands of dollars in sprucing up the park I wind up down here?" she said.

"It is out of the hustle and rush," I said. "Though Dutch will probably wonder where I am all day."

"I will square it with Dutch," she said. "Dutch is another I admire."

"Do you admire me?" I said.

"It is too early to tell," said she. "1 thing I like about you is you say what you think. You are a very frank type of a person. Most ballplayers I admire as ballplayers only. I admire Red. I admire Red as both ballplayer and man."

"I admire them all," said I.

"You go around admiring everybody you lay your eyes on," she said. "That is 1 of the things I admire about *you*. Yet you need not do it, for you are in debt to no man, and you never need be. In your job you need only deliver the goods. You are not forced to act like you admire those who you do not. I am your boss, yet you are frank with me. You do not admire me, yet you make no secret of it."

"I admire you as to sex," I said.

"Well, that is something," said she. "There goes the Boston score," and we crouched down for a better look at the board, and Boston beat Chicago, and that meant a full game sliced from our lead.

"Boston is getting the pitching lately," I said.

"A ballplayer need only do his job," she said. "He need never throw a party for a politician by way of selling the army the product of Moors. He need never entertain the owner of a paper so as to get a decent treatment in the press. It does not matter what the press says. A home run is a home run and no 2 ways about it. A pitcher pitches a 16-inning game and not 5,000 writers can take it from him. He never need care what people think or say. All that he does is open and public."

"Yet there must be people to keep the organization running on all fours," I said.

"That is the part that is closed from sight," said she. "That is the part that any cluck can do. There is 5,000 people in this park this minute that can step in and do what I do. But it is mine because I was born to it. My name is Patricia Moors. What gives me the chills is suppose my name was Betty Brown."

"You need some sleep," I said. "You ain't slept in a week."

"Nor am I libel to sleep for another," she said. "My mind is too full of a number of thoughts, and none of them pleasant." Then we rose and headed back up. Knuckles Johnson was coasting through to a win in the second game, and I suppose that might of put her in a better frame of mind. Yet I don't know. She is 1 of these women caught halfway between keeping house for some cluck and really *doing* something in life. Holly says the same.

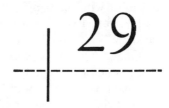

29

THE crick in my back got no worse but no better, so Thursday I had the X-rays shot, going clear down to some hospital on 26th Street. The nurse that worked the machine said her little nephew spoke of me often and would be pleased to have my autograph, and I wrote it down over my picture that was in yesterday's paper laying on the table in the waiting room, and then I beat it back in a cab to the Stadium. I missed the drill and never throwed a ball all afternoon, and that helped some.

But we dropped the ball game. Boston and St. Louis was to play that night, but it rained in Boston and that chipped another half a game off our lead. That was July the 24th.

Cleveland moved out and Chicago moved in. Dutch give us a lecture before the Friday game. He said we ought to done better then split the series with Cleveland. He hit hard on the fact that .500 ball was good enough most any time but not right now with Boston as hot as they was. He said what he wanted to do was make them cry "Uncle" as soon as we could and clinch it and have the mathematics beat and then maybe take things easy 2 weeks or so the end of September until the Series opened. "This is the class of the league and there is yet a flag to win, and we are going to win it all right, for there is no question in my mind. But I would like to get it over with." He mopped his brow whilst he talked. "Red," he said, "does George know anything about this Lavalleja?" meaning the Chicago pitcher.

Red spoke to George and George give him a long spiel. "George says he comes from a town nearby his own," said Red.

265

Dutch mopped his brow some more and spit on the floor and ground it with his toe. Then he said very quiet. "That ain't what I asked you, Red. I am not interested in the personal history of Lavalleja."

"George says he is plenty fast and got good control," said Red. "He has got a fast curve."

"Thank you, Red," said Dutch. "You boys heard what he said, so stand right up to him and figure on good control. We ought to pick up a game or so over the weekend." He walked up and back. "These doubleheaders are driving me out of my mind. Sunday is another. Well, that is my worry and none of yours. Okay, is there anybody got anything on his mind?" Nobody did, and we all filed out, all but Red and Dutch. Dutch called Red back, and they had a little conference all their own, and I do not know exactly what went on, for I got my story second hand from Coker who got it from Mick. Mick said they was not exactly a couple lovebirds in a cage. Dutch told Red not to be so smart, particularly around the younger men, and set a bad example, and Red said that George said that he heard that Dutch would as soon trade him off and never have another Latin on the club, and this made Red mad, George being his roomie and all. Dutch said why in the devil did not George learn the language of the country that was making him rich. Red said why in the devil did Dutch not learn *George's* language. Dutch called Red a gymnasium teacher, and Red said if Dutch did not want a gymnasium teacher on his club it could be arranged, and he begun to peel off his shirt until Dutch said to not take everything he said in heat so serious. Dutch said many of the Latins in the league picked up the language by going to the movies and the TV every spare minute they got, and Red said him and George both hated the movies and the TV both. He said George was better off not knowing the language in the first place.

As for Lavalleja, I believe he speaks enough English to order a meal and shine his shoes, and that's about all. But he fires a baseball good enough. On a better club then Chicago he could win 15 games or more a year, for his E. R. A. is up there with the best. He is a slow worker. He might scrabble around out there 2 minutes between pitches. The crowd will holler and the opposition bench will complain to the umps, but Lavalleja don't give a hoot for neither. He takes the attitude that if the fans is in a hurry to get home they should not of come out to the ball game to begin with, and as for the other club the more he takes his own sweet time the more they boil, and the more they boil the worse ball they play. I admire him for that. I got so I could be almost as slow as him by the end of the summer. I could keep 60,000 howling people and the other club waiting whilst I tied a shoe that never needed tying or blowed my nose when it never run, not to mention thousands more on radio and TV. I guess I growed a tough skin over the year.

Lavalleja kept us in agony that afternoon. It was like trying to make time on a highway where every mile there was a full stop sign. Dutch moved Pasquale to center and played Canada in right. It looked odd to see Canada in the outfield. Yet we expected it. Krazy Kress wrote that Dutch was about to cut loose 1 outfielder and bring up a pitcher from somewhere, maybe Dolly Peterson from Q. C. I always liked Dolly and hoped it was true, for we needed another pitcher.

We kept getting men on base almost every inning. Then Lavalleja would drop off in his wintertime sleep, and by the time he was ready to throw again we scarcely remembered our signs, and the batter would back out and look for his sign again, and the runners would wear theirselves thin running up and down the baselines. Piss turned in a fine job, and it was 2-2 going into the ninth. They scored 1 time, and we tied it up right away, Sid lining 1 into the stands in right just over the bullpen, and we went into extra innings.

In the first of the tenth Jeff Harkness beat 1 into the ground in front of the plate. It was an easy play, and I do not know what happened except that Piss went for it and it rolled up his arm and over his shoulder, and Harkness beat it, and then Pisses sinuses begun to trouble him. Vasquez singled. We expected the bunt, and then he whaled 1 that would of crippled George if he did not leap up out of the way. It was stupid baseball, but I guess when you are as low down in the standings as Chicago you will try anything once. Harkness held second, and Leif Lindsay pushed the runners along with a bunt, and Piss throwed 2 wide pitches to Joe Fredericks, and then Red went out and talked with Piss, and then they called for Dutch, and Dutch went out and spoke awhile and finally signed down to the pen for Horse. Horse walked Fredericks on purpose, and we played for the double play on Millard May. We almost got it, too, but "almost" ain't enough. May rapped down to George, and George fired to Gene and Gene to Sid, and May beat it by a hair, and Harkness scored from third. And that was the ball game, for we could not do a thing in our half of the tenth.

That night I went up with Sid for dinner at his mother's on Riverside Drive. I was glad to have the invite. Tempers was short in and around the hotel. Sid has got the right idea about living at home if you can.

Friday night is a special time at Sid's. He has got 1 brother and 2 sisters, and they come and bring their family, 5 kids all told, and Sid sometimes brings 1 ballplayer up. He brung Piss and Lindon and the Caruccis in the past, and Monk Boyd when Monk was a Mammoth. He said he would bring Perry Simpson, but he did not think it would sit well with his mother. He said it took him a long enough time to whip her in line and let him bring Christians much less a Negro. I told his mother I might as well be a Jew for all I was ever anything else, and she got a big boot out of that. I told her that many of my best friends in Perkinsville was boys I played with on the YMHA basketball club. I did not tell her who they were. They was 2 Irishmen, 2 Italians, 4 Jews and Cal Robertson that I don't know what Cal was. The kids all fell in love with me at once. The oldest was a girl, 16, name of Sylvia, and I tried to shove in beside her at dinner but the other kids would have none of that. There was 1 boy on either side of me and 1 about 7 that wanted to sit on my lap, but his mother yanked him off and his father said if he did not do right he would not take him to the doubleheader Sunday. The 4 youngest kids was named Oscar, Irving, Joseph and Helene. I kept looking across at Sylvia, and her at me, and I had her on my mind a full 2 days afterwards.

There was a maid that damn near run her legs off back and forth betwixt the dining room and the kitchen. I felt sorry for her. Her name was Mary, and after dinner I snuck back in the kitchen for some milk, for it was against the regulations to have it with the dinner, and she asked me was I not the boy that roomed with Perry Simpson. I said I was. She give me 2 glasses of milk. I must say that you have got to admire anybody like Sid that is willing to give up his milk for his religion.

We begun with a prayer said in Hebrew by Sid's older brother. Everybody bowed at the neck, the men and boys covering up their head with a napkin. Then we sat down and begun to stow it away. There was filter fish with horse radish, and soup with a couple doughy balls floating around, and there was roasted duck and cold slaw with a slice of ice on top and bread without no butter and finally cake and tea. I drunk about an inch of red wine, although it was against my rules to drink but Sid said it would never hurt me. Sid's sisters pointed out to them kids how careful I was to eat and drink all in the right amount. It was all delicious. Mostly we talked about what was causing the club to slump.

Whatever I done them kids done the same. They hung on my every word, and they felt of my muscles and made me spread my hand, and they studied it. Actually my hand is not too big, spanning about 10½ across. Sam has got the biggest hands on the club, about 12 inches. "I will bet you that Henry does not bite his fingernails," said 1 of the sisters. "Do you, Henry?"

"No," said I. "I do not. Who bites their fingernails?"

"Irving does," she said.

"Why," said I, "ain't that terrible?"

Irving said he would never bite his fingernails no more.

"I will bet you that Henry does not need to have chocolate syrup in his milk every time," said the other sister.

"No sir," said I. "I drink it plain."

"I hope Joseph heard that," she said.

He did. He said it would be plain white milk for him forever after.

Then they wanted me to go out in the park with them and play ball. I said I just spent the whole afternoon playing ball. Then this brat Helene says no I did not, for she seen the game on the TV and never seen me even in the bullpen. Sid said I had a crick in my back and needed the rest. This turned the trick, for these kids was Mammoth fans from the word "Go," and it give them a real feeling of helping the club by not tiring me out. They clumb on my shoulders a little and made me hoist them up and see how much weight they gained, but otherwise they took it easy on me. Irving wished to wrestle with me and show me how strong he was on the living room floor. Finally the kids all went in the other room, all but Sylvia. She was shy and very timid. Every time I looked at her she would blush and look in her cup. Her father, name of Abner, had many theories on the causes of the slump, all of them cock-eyed, and afterwards things begun to break up, for they had to get the kids home to bed, promising them if they would hurry they might catch a part of the Brooklyn game on TV.

Me and Sid and his mother went in the other room. She flipped on the TV and watched Brooklyn and Cleveland. Sid and me stuck our feet up on the window, and the breeze drifted in from the river, and we ate up the few chocolates that the kids somehow missed in the dish. Sid said he believed we would pull out of the slump fairly soon. I said I hoped so, and along about 10 I said I would be nosing along. They said there was cabs down in front of the house.

But I walked. The night was cool, and the river smelt good, and I strolled in a casual way down along the Drive. There was people on all the benches, old and young, men and women and boys and girls, and after 10 or 12 blocks I come to a bench where a young fellow and his girl was sitting with a battery radio listening to the Brooklyn game, and I sat on the end of the bench, leaning and resting for the walk roused the crick, and after a time the fellow left out a whoop and walloped the girl on the back, and I heard cheering over the radio, and I said to the fellow, "What happened?"

"It is all tied up," he said. "Reeves done it. I knowed he would. Did I not say he would?" and the girl said yes that was what he said, and she slammed *him* on the back.

"Have people really got their hopes up for Brooklyn yet?" I said.

"What are you?" said he. "For the Mammoths?"

Then they bent over the radio again, and soon I heard applause of a familiar kind. "Pitcher up?" I said.

"That is right," said the boy. "Scudder up and Reeves on third and Wynn on first and none down and shut up a minute for I do not wish to miss a thing."

"I am dying," said the girl.

"You are too young to die," I said.

"What are you?" said she. "A wise guy?"

"Shut up the both of you," said he, and they listened, and they looked like they was in pain, for they closed their eyes and hunched their shoulders, and the girl put up her hands like she was praying, and Scudder was called out on strikes, and I heard the crowd booing the decision, and the girl said that was a raw call, and she went "Boo-oo-oo-oo" in the radio.

That brung up Schoolboy Wenk, the Brooklyn lead-off hitter. He was 29 by now, but they called him Schoolboy when he first come up 10 years or so before, and the name stuck. He cannot hit speed. "That is 2 down," said I, for Rob McKenna was pitching for Cleveland.

"What are you?" said the boy. "An expert?"

"A little hit, Schoolboy," said the girl. "1 little hit and I will love you forever."

I sat back and listened, but I barely heard what followed, and I cared less. It did not seem important, and I did not seem to be myself. It was like I was somebody else, looking at it all from the outside, just leaning back and listening to 2 clubs on the radio. They was just 2 clubs and nothing more. It seemed funny to me that Rob was pitching with only 2 days rest after the long game Tuesday night, and I said so to the young fellow, and he said the long game was not Tuesday night but Monday, and I did not argue, and after a long time the boy and girl snapped the lid on the radio, and the quietness brung me back to where I was, and the boy give the girl a hug, and she hugged him back, and they seemed very happy, and they drifted off in the dark and out of sight.

I lifted myself off the bench and sauntered over towards Broadway and caught a cab back to the hotel, and the cabby said did I hear the ball scores, and I said no, and he said Chicago beat the

Mammoths this afternoon and Brooklyn just this minute whipped Cleveland while Pittsburgh was being smothered by Boston in Boston. He said in case I was interested the Mammoths put up in my very hotel. I said I knowed it. I said they seemed to me like a quiet bunch, however. "Even a little long of face," said I. "Maybe things is going bad for them."

"Oh," said the cabbie, "I doubt that they have got much to stew about. I am the first to worry if things do not break right for them. And I am not worried."

I suppose he wasn't, neither. Nobody was—only us Mammoths.

STANDINGS OF THE CLUBS
Saturday Morning, July 26

	Won	Lost	Pct.	Games Behind
New York	60	32	.652	—
Boston	56	35	.615	3½
Brooklyn	53	39	.576	7
Cleveland	49	42	.538	10½

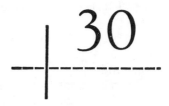

30

FOLLOWING is a string of letters that come to me in New York during the last home stand before the last trip west of the summer. Some run longer then others, but even so they make for a rather short chapter. Do not think that I am sticking them in here just so as to get out of writing a chapter. After you have wrote 29 1 more or less don't make the slightest difference. The letters are according to date, first come first served. I never answered a 1 of them.

Following is not a letter but a note probably taped on my locker by Mick McKinney or Bradley Lord or maybe Doc Loftus himself. It is from Doc, date of July 26, wrote with pen and ink on official Mammoth paper. It says:

Wiggen: The X rays are back from the hospital. Nothing shows. If there is something wrong with your back it should show in the X rays. If it does not work itself out I would suggest you see Dr. Solomon, as it is more in his field than mine—something mental, "in your mind." You may drop down and take a look at them if you wish. I will speak to Dutch about them.

ERNEST I. LOFTUS, M.D.

Following is a letter from Mike Mulrooney to Lindon Burke, date of July 30, wrote in pencil on the paper of the Blue Castle Hotel in Queen City. Lindon come in when I was not there and give it to Perry to read and said show it to me and then give it back. I forgot, and I found it amongst my gear when I got home. It says:

Dear Lindon,
 Dutch has sent to me a report on you, along with a report on Stdys game against Chi. He seems to feel that some word from me might help you to get hold of yrslf. I had been meaning to write to you anyway. I am complimented that Dutch thinks that I can do something from a distance of 2,000 mi. that he cant do right there on the spot.
 I dont know exactly how to procede. Lindon, what can one man say. All that one man can do is steer you along when you are under his wing. In the final analisis you are alone in the box, & if your control fails you at the crucial time you are the best judge of the whys & wherefores. I have before me a chart that Egg Barnard prepared on Stdys game. Dutch has a great faith in charts which I do not share. Every man to his own system. I see by the chart that with men on base your tendancy is to get behind your batter. That was always your tendancy & I did not need a chart to see it. When you are in hot water you are wild. You should not feel that simply because a man gets on base you are in hot water. You must forget the runner & pitch the batter. I have told you this many times.
 Dutch had the faith to pitch you Stdy. Just between us you are the best righthander on the club if you only knew it, & I am fully aware of Johnson. But you must not let rough water upset your control over yourself. You boys are going down the stretch now, & the responsibilities will be great. Here is where the weak go down & the strong win out. I believe, & have always believed, that the winning club is not always the best on paper but it is the club that refuses to go all to pieces in the crisis. Things will get worse before they get better. The heat is on, Boston is crowding, 3 games behind as of last night. You boys are the best on paper if only you are the best in your heart.
 Lindon, that is all that I can tell you. Everybody in QC watches their ex-boys with intrst. We are running a good second to Slt Lk & I believe we might yet beat them in the stretch. There is nobody here ready to go up, & that ought to ease your minds. The nwsppr

said Dutch was about to send for Dolly Peterson. This is false. I
have had word from Roguski & Smith, nothing from Wiggen or
Simpson or you or Pearson or any of my other ex-boys that I remember with fondness always.

Yrs,
MIKE

Following is a letter from Holly, date of July 31, typewrote on
plain white paper. It says:

Dear Henry the Navigator,
I sit for my twice-weekly letter to my favorite baseball player,
he who never replies to my letters and who, were it not for the
wonders of newspaper, radio and television, would be lost to my
sight, at least for the summer. The thermometer hit 95 today. I
melt.
I saw you on television this afternoon at Black's in Perkinsville,
against Pittsburgh. I saw Perry Simpson score the run that won,
and I was informed by a gentleman who stood at my shoulder and
who seemed to know whereof he spoke that "that boy don't run, he
just flies close to the ground." At times, particularly after com-
pleting an inning, you seem to look up into the television camera—
a more or less unconscious gesture, as if you were surveying the
grandstand prior to returning to the dugout—and you seem to be
looking directly at me. But you do not see me: I am not televised.
Only the great are televised.
This letter will be short, for the heat is terrible and I should like
to visit outside and breathe the night air and swat mosquitoes.
Swat. Was it Babe Ruth who was called the Sultan of Swat?
Your father says that you are diligent, that today's triumph was
your eighteenth, and that you are certain to win more than twenty
—twenty being the number which the newspapers and the books
on baseball describe as magic. A pitcher who performs this magic
feat becomes a member of "the charmed circle of twenty-game win-
ners." I promise you that I will be charmed as well.
Take care of your back. The announcer said this afternoon that
you have been spending some time in a whirlpool bath—what's
that?—and that you say your back is better. You pitched as if it
were, too. And you had only a very little rest, having pitched Sun-

day and in relief Tuesday. Your father pitched several innings Sunday against the Columbus Clowns. He fared ill.

Well, enough. Please know that you are in our minds constantly, and in mine in particular, such as it is.

Love,
HOLLY

Following is a letter from Pop, date of August 10, wrote on this very same sort of paper that I am using. It is in pencil by hand, and the words have the same slope as mine, the old lefthand tilt. Give it a quick look and you would think it is my writing. It says:

Dear Hank,

How's the flipper?

Son you have racked up number twenty, there is no need me telling you what I think about that or the way you been working all along, I bust my buttons with pride every time I go anywheres, though to tell you the truth my heart was in my mouth yesterday afternoon. But you pulled out fine, and between yesterday and to-day I am confident New York has busted the back of Boston, the boys in Borelli's back me up in this, I seen yesterday's on the television down in Perkinsville and watched for signs of the backache, I believe you have got that whipped as well as Boston, for you were a picture of beauty out there, Sam turned in a crackerjack job to-day, so you will polish up in the east OK and start west with four games as a cushion, yesterday and today busting the back of Boston I am sure.

I have not worked since the Sunday before last three innings against Bobo Taylor and his crowd, same old bunch with a new face here and there, me pitching the last three when Jimmy Dubrow petered out, I was sorry for that for I praised Jimmy high to Bobo and told him to get somebody from the Mammoths out here to see that kid work, as well as another kid that you never met, Ernie Hoyt, a boy that hits them a mile and roams the outfield like Judkins. Sorry about Judkins being laid up. Hoyt looks a lot like Lucky in all ways, even down to hitting the slightest bit with his foot in the bucket. I think this will be the last season for me with the Scarlets, I will hang up the glove and call it quits, youngsters coming in and teeing off on my stuff that a few years back they never could touch, but the club keeping me on I know because I am a sort of an attraction, being your old man and all or they would have let me go by now. Bobo said he seen you in Cleveland and never seen two such look-alikes, right down to toeing off the first base side of the rubber, and I said that was to be expected since who in the hell learned you from the very first, he said you and him and some of the others had dinner. I want you should always be nice to Bobo, it was him that first put Jocko Conrad wise to you, the rest is history.

I am sure pleased about number twenty and can't get over it yet and probably will not actually believe it for a day or two, Fish kept the Mammoth score coming in over the loudspeaker this afternoon, the crowd payed more attention to that than to the ball game going on in front of their eyes, I felt good for Sam in particular, that was a nice job and no mistake, also Jones walloping the ball like he done, maybe he does not need a jaw operation after all.

If I was Dutch I would leave things go a week or more and not be switching things around so dam much, give a guy a chance to work out in a new spot, I can't see playing Smith in the outfield, that kid the best natural infielder I ever seen from all reports, why not leave Wilks play more, an old veteran like him just the kind of steadiness you need at a time like now, and use Burke and Carroll more and give you more of a rest between starts, no wonder you have got the backache, well, Dutch knows best. Aaron says it is probably your nerves, I said hell, Hank has got nerves of steel, Aaron says steel busts and bends like nobody's business under pressure.

Son, Holly is worried about that boy getting beaned in Detroit, still in a coma according to the radio. She is afraid you might get a dose of the same, I said hell, nobody pitches hard to Hank, they just throw to him easy, he never hits. I said look at the paper, she follows the sports like a hound, he is hitting .109 on the year and nobody throws hard to a hitter that connects only one time in ten, this all got me to thinking you could help your own cause a bit with a hit now and then, yesterday if you would have connected in the eighth the suspense would have been over with right then.

Holly and I sends her love and wish you could be here, but business before pleasure, I am at the bottom of this page and must give Aaron a hand, I will close.

POP

Following is a letter from Aaron Webster that come pasted in an envelope on the outside of a package. It is typewrote on the back of the pages, the front all scratched out, date of August 15. It come just before we took off for the west. It says:

Dear Henry,

The accompanying package contains a book which belongs to Red Traphagen. I return it through you. Thus we make the play, Webster to Wiggen to Traphagen, three noble athletes, two of them big-leaguers, the third still in the bushes but showing promise. I shall be eighty years old in a few weeks, however, and I suspect that my age will count against me. I am not so spry as once I was, and it may be that on hot afternoons in St. Louis I shall be forced to request that my duties be assigned to others.

As I write this letter I look from my window into the yard behind your house where, not so long ago, you were busily engaged on many an afternoon in throwing a rubber ball against the wall. You may recall that on numerous occasions the ball responded in an eccentric way and bounced into my flower bed. You bounced after it, much to my horror. The larger you grew the more you endangered my shrubbery. Nevertheless I was, at one time, your cheering crowd, your New York and your Boston, your Cleveland and your Pittsburgh, and I cheer for you yet in my silent way. I pay no Federal Tax for the privilege. I paid it reluctantly when we went to New York in April. I shall not pay it again, and therefore I shall not see you play again in the uniform of the Mammoths.

I have been constantly concerned over this continuing pain in your back. I hesitate to diagnose your ailment at this distance, though I am perfectly sure that I know both its causes and its cure. Perhaps we will have a chance to talk of this over the winter. Meanwhile I leave you and your back to the mercies of professional physicians, specialists, trainers and others of that array of medicine men employed by the Moors "empire." (Even though, as I say, it is I, not they, who know your trouble.)

I follow you with fascination: a whole new field of endeavor has come into my view. Win, lose or draw (is draw possible in baseball? I think not) you are already a monumental success. Whether you participate in the World Series in October is (to me) a matter of indifference. You would have been a sufficient success had you returned home from Aqua Clara in March—or had you never left in February. Only sorely troubled human beings need success in the accepted sense; the wise are content to turn their backs upon it and to own, if not the Moors "empire," the love and respect of a few neighbors of moderate means, little "success" and no visible ambition.

Please remember to thank Traphagen for the book. I have not read it as carefully as I had hoped to: concentration is difficult. Despite daily resolutions to the contrary I am glued to my radio afternoons and evenings; today, for example, I must follow Mammoths vs. Washington this afternoon and Boston vs. Brooklyn tonight.

I know the announcers well by now. I am intimately acquainted with the speech mannerisms and favorite phrases of every baseball broadcaster. Their occupational slang is no longer a mystery to me (thanks to your father), and I am quite certain that I could conduct a sports column for the Perkinsville *Clarion* without arousing the least suspicion among my readers that I am seventy-nine years old and that a very few years ago I thought a dugout was a small boat which American Indians fashioned by hollowing a log.

I remain, now and forever,

Your neighbor,
AARON

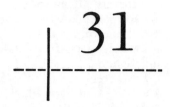

31

I WAS in the lobby in Pittsburgh when the news come concerning Dutch. I begun to ride the lobbies an awful lot by now. No more hanging with the boys for me, snapping like they was, 1 against the other, all kinds of little squabbles springing up over nothing a-tall.

I was in the middle of these arguments twice, and twice was enough for me. 1 time it concerned Cuba, of all places. George told Red to tell me I should come to Cuba in the winter and pick up some excellent money in the winter leagues down there, and Goose heard that and said, "Keep your mind upon the summer leagues and leave the winter take care of its f---ing self," and then he turned on George and told him the same, and the 2 of them stood chin to chin in the shower arguing with each other, both in different languages. Any other time it would of been funny.

Scarcely 2 days later Krazy Kress come around and spoke to me further concerning Korea and Japan. Well, mention Korea and Red hits the roof, and mention the winter and Goose hits it, and between the 2 of them and Krazy there was a 3-way spat. In fact, mention anything a-tall and somebody had a strong opinion on the subject in those days, and every time there was an argument I got weak all over in the middle of my stomach. So it was really the safest thing for me to start riding the lobbies, and ride them hard, and be out of the way of the fireworks.

I would find a soft chair in a far corner, and I would buy a murder or 2, them quarter books with the girls on front and their breast all practically bare and the murder generally in the first chapter and the chap that done it revealed at the end, although I pretty soon learned to spot him early, and I spent days and sometimes nights like that because it seemed safer.

It was a Tuesday. The train was late to Pittsburgh, and we missed lunch and grabbed red-hots outside the park and dressed like 60 and drilled without the red-hots digesting, and we no sooner finished the drill then the rain come down in buckets, and the game was called. We went back in the clubhouse, and the rain was beating against the windows something fierce, and Dutch bellowed over the noise of the rain, "The day ain't over yet, so nobody get dressed." We waited, and when it let up a little Dutch led us back out and we drilled an hour. That was the first of the extra drills, and the boys bitched, not only about drilling in the rain but about drilling a-tall, for we still had the 4-game cushion when we left the east and it seemed like the slump had run itself out. Yet we drilled, the bats and the balls so slippery your life was in danger, and nobody could scarcely run 50 feet but he skidded and went down in the mud, and the boys went about saying all sorts of murderous things against Dutch (always when Dutch was 300 feet away at least) until finally he called the halt and we went back in all covered with mud to where you couldn't see the number on a fellow's back, and afterwards we went back to the hotel, and I ate my dinner and bought a murder and took up my post in the lobby, and that was when I first heard the news on Dutch.

I was sitting there, and after a time the elevator starter come past, and he asked me was it true about Dutch. I said that generally speaking 75% of the things you hear about Dutch is 90% hogwash. "But what did you hear?" I said.

"Oh, nothing," he said. "Boston beat Cleveland."

"That I know," I said. "What did you hear? About Dutch?" and he stummered around a bit, and then he said that he heard that Dutch was canned. "Who told you that?" I said.

"I seen it in the paper," he said.

"What paper?" I said, for I seen them all, and he said he did not see it *himself* but he heard it from the clerk, and I said it was the bunk, for I did not believe it. By the end of the evening 6 different people asked me was it true, and I said I did not know.

In the morning the papers was full of it. There was more writers on that trip then ever before, most from New York, and Bill Duffy was along from the Perkinsville "Clarion." Perkinsville was so fired up over the Mammoths it would of took fire and flood on the square to get folks interested in anything local. Bill dropped in the room the first thing in the morning smelling of whiskey, and he asked me what was the poop on Dutch, and I said all I knowed was what I seen in the papers.

The papers said that reliable reports said that Dutch been let out and either Mike Mulrooney or Red Traphagen would take the club over.

So they were trying to hang it on Dutch! That give me a laugh. We was slipping, not only Dutch, not anybody in particular, and yet they would hang it on Dutch if they could, and there was long pieces in the papers showing where Dutch was a failure, how he done this when he should of done something else, them smart writers with their smart machines. From the sound of what they wrote you would of thought a ball club was as simple as a train on a track, 25 cars and an engine up front, and if she did not roll all you need do was cut loose the engine and hitch up another. But it ain't that simple, and these damn writers do not know what makes a club roll or not roll, no more then Dutch knowed, no more then I knowed. I did not know. All I knowed was that we blowed a big lead and Boston was hot on our tail, but I did not know why and I never pretended I did.

If I could tell you why a club slumps I would have 16 big-league owners running after me with pen and ink, and I could name my price. But I am a ballplayer and not no genius, and I did not know then and do not know now. I know only that when you slump you slump, and there is nothing to do but ride it out and play your tops and hope for the best. If you are the type that prays I suppose you pray, or any other superstition you believe in you cling to.

As for me, when the skid took hold I found myself a corner of the lobby, and I crawled in and hid my face behind a murder and sunk as low as I could in the big plush chairs. Then, when tempers broke, when quarrels rose, when the squeeze was on and the clamps was tightened and every day was a new crisis, a new quarrel, I was more or less off by myself. I was never in the middle. It may of been the coward way. But it was safer.

Wednesday afternoon we drilled, the usual little pepper games and 4-way catch, easy-like, until Dutch showed up soon after. We heard him come up out of the dugout. First we heard him before we even seen him. He was shouting to the coaches, carrying a bat in his hand and pointing and saying what he wanted done. "Strap!" he shouted. "Drive them boys *close* to the fences. *Close,* goddam it. Any son of a bitch can stand out in the middle of an acre of lawn and grab a fly ball. Close! Close to them goddam fences," for Clint was lofting flies with a fungo, and the boys in the field shifted over towards the fences, and Clint begun to hit them so they sailed high and then dropped almost straight and skinned the cement, and the boys raced for the walls and turned and took what Clint hit smack up against the concrete, and I stood and watched a minute, and then I heard my name, and it was Dutch, and he said that for the benefit of Henry Wiggen *spectators* was not admitted to the park until 6 o'clock. I hustled over to the cage and swiped at a few that Herb Macy throwed down, and Dutch stood by the cage and said through the screen he was sick to death of pitchers that got it in their head that they could not hit. "Stand up there, Henry, and swing like you was swinging at a baseball, like you was a ballplayer, not like some goddam gymnasium teacher on a butterfly hunt." I hit a few, and then I grabbed a glove and trotted out and parked myself deep in center, keeping my eye on Dutch. When he looked my way I pounded my hand in my glove and shouted and made it look like I was hustling out there at 5 in the afternoon and game time 3 hours off.

I believe those extra drills was a smart move. It kept the boys busy. Otherwise they would of sat back in the hotel moping and feeling sorry for theirselves and squabbling with 1 another for lack of anything better to do. I seen it happen time after time, the flare-up over nothing. I remember in Pittsburgh I was sitting in the lobby when Sid come out of the elevator and started for the door and then seen the pinball machine, and he felt in his pocket for change and went over, and just when he got there Gene Park was sliding a nickel in the slot, and Sid watched, and the bells rung a few times, not enough I guess, and Gene give the machine a kick and the sign flashed TILT, and Sid laughed. Gene turned on him with murder in his eye. "Why do you laugh, you Jewish horse's ass?" asked Gene, and he pushed past Sid and went his way, and Sid moved in and slid a nickel in the slot. But he did not play. He looked down at the machine, and then *he* kicked it, and the TILT flashed again, and he went out the door.

But on the field there is no time for grudges, no time for touchy nerves, no chance to clam up and say you will not speak to the next fellow. On the ball field you are the fingers of the 1 hand, and you take your sign or your throw from your worst enemy. You need not speak to him once the game is over with but you damn well better love him like a brother whilst the ball is in play, and I suppose that that is why Dutch called the drills.

I begun to warm with Red when the lights went on, and we done so until the boys come out from changing their shirts and told us there was sandwiches and soup inside. Me and Red went over the hitters eating off our knees on a bench in the clubhouse. Dutch give 1 blister of a lecture, and afterwards Mick give me the works, the whole back, all the way up and all the way down.

If you will feel behind your neck you will notice a bump. That is the uppermost hinge of your backbone or your spinal column. Doc Loftus told me which, but I forget. That bone runs down to a point just below your belt-line. It has got a lot of little ridges on it like the inside of a steering wheel. That was where it hurt, X rays or no X rays. I do not give a damn what the X rays said, neither the X ray in New York nor the X rays we took later in Chicago. If I say my back hurt I do not want no goddam hospital photographer telling me different, nor Doc Loftus neither, although he is a grand fellow, nor Doc Solomon neither, another grand fellow. If I say I have got a pain in my back I have got 1, and it is in my back and not in my mind. I guess I ought to know.

Everybody in the world become an expert on the pain in my back. After we hit the east again I got a baby chinchilla in the mail from a man in Arizona that had the same kind of a pain in

his back until he took up the raising of chinchillas, and he said
the little baby that he sent would do the trick. There was a picture
in the paper. A man from the Human Society come down and
took it away, and then things come hot and heavy in the mail, a
snake, about 2 dozen boxes and bottles of pills and lotions and
all kinds of lucky gadgets ranging from a hand-carved statue of
an Indian lady with her little baby in a sack on her back to the
usual things such as horseshoes and rabbit's feet, plus a flood of
letters and wires from people that knowed the sure cure for the
backache until finally I could spot that kind of a letter before I
ever opened it, and out it went in the basket. I have the statue
yet of the lady and the baby.

But all that was later, and generally the back let up long enough
to see me through my assignments, for when the ball game is on
there ain't the time to think about anything except what you are
doing, or what you are not doing, and I was fine and fast with good
control and all my stuff in Pittsburgh. That was number 21 for
me, a quick, neat job, 2 runs for Pittsburgh on 7 hits nicely scattered, and 8 runs for us, 4 of them on a drive by Sid with the bases
loaded in the fifth. It cleared the barrier in right. They stay hit
when Sid hits them. We had our 3½-game cushion again though
it was skinned away to 3 the following day when we split 2 with
Pittsburgh whilst Boston swept its third in a row in Cleveland.

My back felt pretty much okay on the train out of Pittsburgh.
I do not mean to harp and carp about my back. That is all over
with now, and you can believe that the pain was real, or you can
believe it was all in my mind, for I do not care what you believe,
nor what anybody believes. It is a free country. There was a doctor in Cleveland that called me and said what I had was a ruptured
spinal disk. I asked him if that was something that could be fixed
up quick, and he said he would need to take a fluid test, and if the
fluid test turned out like he thought it would I would have to go
under the knife, and I said I would think it over and maybe do it
in the winter, and he give me his number and I wrote it down
across Hams Carroll's picture in the Cleveland paper, for Hams
pitched Friday there and turned in a 4-hit job, and it was Saturday
morning that his picture was in the paper, and it was that after-

noon, in the first game of a doubleheader, that Lucky's back give
out on him for good. And losing Lucky was just about equal to
the death blow. He opened our seventh with a 2-base wallop, and
Vincent Carucci followed with a drive that raised the dust behind
second base, and the next thing I seen was Reynolds taking the
throw from Barkowski and wheeling and throwing home, and I
wondered had Reynolds went mad because surely Lucky was in by
now. But he had wrenched his ailing back making the turn at
third, and he was 20 feet from home and moving ever so slow,
and in pain, and Taggart took the throw and come down the line
and tagged him, and Lucky plunged forward and down on his
knees with his hands over his face, and then he rolled over on
his back and let his legs down gentle and laid there straight out.

When they brung him in his face was all white and his lip all
bloody from where he bit it to stop the pain, and Doc Loftus
rushed him off to the hospital, and Mick took his clothes and stuck
them in a canvas sack and wrote on the sack with the iodine stick,
"Judkins," and under it he wrote in small letters, "also the flag."
Then he scratched that out.

We lost the game 5-2.

Between games I warmed with Bruce, and I latched on a way
to let the screw slide more off my hand. I had less power, for
there was not so much weight behind it, but it broke just as good
and was easier on my back, though tougher on my wrist and arm.
It made my whole motion different. Red took over from Bruce
about 10 minutes later. He said what was I doing different, for
he noticed it quick, and I told him, and he said I better not tamper
with my motion, and I went back to the old way and the back
did not bother me until late in the game.

I breezed right along, and twice we busted out with a cluster of
runs. Sunny Jim hit 2 home runs that day, playing in center in
place of Lucky.

The last 2 innings I throwed the new way, and Red give me
hell, and I said it was my back and not his, and he said I would
throw out my arm in 5 years if I kept putting all the strain in the
arm and not get no help from my body. I said it was not the 5

years I was worried about, but the coming month of September, for I would go under the knife if need be in the winter.

Lucky caught up with us in Chicago. He traveled with the club until we hit the east again. Then Dutch sent him off to watch Boston, wherever Boston would be, giving him charts to keep on pitchers and hitters, for it begun to look like there might be a showdown with Boston in the end. Cleveland was out of it now, for Boston swept 3 up there and we took 2 out of 3. Brooklyn was barely an outside possibility, 4½ behind Boston and Bill Scudder down with the grip and missed part of the western swing.

Who would of figured us to drop 3 in a row in Chicago? But we done it, first Sam, then Knuckles, then Hams, the Sunday doubleheader and Monday, and the writers all scurried for the records and we took what little pleasure there was to be had from the fact that Chicago was long overdue for a stunt like that. They had not beat New York 3 in a row since 1939, had not took a doubleheader from the Mammoths since 1943, and no Chicago pitcher had throwed a shutout against the Mammoths since 1945 until Lavalleja on Monday.

Boston copped 2 out of 3 in St. Louis, and our cushion was only 1½ now, and I knowed, and most everybody knowed, that it was due to shrink some more, and there was not much left to shrink, and somehow we was in a terrible spin, and even if you pull out of a spin it takes a little time, and there was not much time left neither, and nobody knowed exactly when or where or why the spin begun, nor how much more downwards there was to go before the spin would stop and the tide would change.

We left Chicago Monday night. I was sitting and looking out the window when Goose come down the isle, and Goose said I had best go and look after Bill Duffy and quieten him down before the railroad tossed him off, and I went back and found Bill standing on the seat in the car behind reciting "Casey At The Bat" whilst 2 conductors tried to coax him down like you try to coax a cat out of a tree, and I laughed and said why did they not just drag him down, and they said it was against the rules of the rail-road. I said I was not under railroad rules myself, and I grabbed Bill's ankles and pulled his legs out from under him, and down he come, still reciting, and I stretched him on the seat with his legs draped over the end, and he slept that way all night.

I remember when I left him the line of the poem begun to beat in my mind, the opening line that Bill never got very far beyond any more. The poem goes as follows:

"Oh, the outlook was not brilliant for the Mudville 9 that day,
    For the score stood 4 to 2 with but an inning left to play,
    And so when Cooney died at first and Burrows did the same,
    A gloomy silence fell upon the patrons of the game."

That is the first stanza. There are many stanzas, but they come harder and harder for Bill the older he gets, and the drunker. Sometimes he will get to "Cooney," and sometimes to "Burrows," and sometimes as far as the "gloomy silence," but generally he never gets very far beyond the "outlook," where "the outlook was not brilliant," and that was what beat in my mind, over and over, "Oh the outlook was not brilliant," for that was how it was, not brilliant a-tall.

I believe the words of the poem run around in my mind 3 or 4 days, probably until after we hit the east again, and I never re-membered it till now, thinking back on everything that hap-pened.

Yet as far as that goes nothing ever really *happened* a-tall, at least nothing to *write* about, and probably that was what the trou-ble was, that nothing happened, that all was quiet. The things that was eating away at our mind was never mentioned. The rumors about Dutch was pretty much at an end, yet it hung over our head, though we never spoke of it, just like it hung over our head that the fat lead we had not many weeks before was now scarcely a lead except on paper, and Boston was coming on in a rush, and the Series melon that dangled before our eyes might 1 of these days move clear out of reach, and yet we never mentioned it nor ever admitted that we was nervous and afraid.

Now, in the spin, there was nothing but silence, and nobody had a good word for the next 1, and tempers was short and you waited around expecting any minute that somebody would blow their top, and all you hoped was that you was somewheres in a far corner of the lobby when it blowed.

Lindon drawed the assignment the first day in St. Louis. He had my sympathies. It was supposed to be Piss but his sinuses dripped like crazy and his bladder acted up. He has a bad bladder, which is how he got his name, and when he is nervous he cannot control it. It would of been my turn after his, but I had worked Saturday and so it was Lindon, and he blowed up at Piss in the clubhouse beforehand, and Piss never answered but just stood there at the trough with 2 cotton sticks up his nose, leaning with 1 hand against the wall and standing maybe 5 minutes and then going back and laying down on a bench and then getting up and going back to the trough, and you could see he was in no shape to pitch, and I said so to Lindon, and Lindon said if he worked regular like me he would not care, but here he was supposed to go out and turn in a job after not working for weeks except an inning in relief just before we left New York, and he called me a dirty name, which he would not of ordinarily did.

Lindon kept getting in trouble and then pulling out. Red steadied him and made him take things slow, and Lindon wore a worried face and frowned and scowled and done 100 useless things that sapped away his energy, mopping his face 2 and 3 times between pitches and picking up the resin and throwing it down and picking it up again, and he balked once in the eighth and it damn near cost the ball game, but he pulled out of that, too, and after every inning he come in the dugout sweating like I never seen him sweat before, his eyebrows plastered down to his head, and I fanned him with a towel between innings and told him I never seen 1 man throw so much stuff as him.

The score was tied 2-2 when Jim Klosky come up with 2 down and none on in the last of the ninth and lined 1 into the corner in right center, square in the angle of the wall where they come together, and Swanee and Pasquale give chase. Both boys have played St. Louis many a time over the years, and they know the walls, but it was a hard 1 to play nonetheless, and Pasquale got his glove on the ball, but it spun out, and Swanee trapped it and begun the throw about the time Klosky steamed around second, and Gene Park took the throw in short center and fired in, and Ugly yelled "Burke," meaning Lindon should cut it off because Klosky made third standing up, and Lindon cut it off behind the box about halfway to second.

What got in Lindon then I will never know. Klosky made the turn at third, edging a few steps in towards home, and Lindon cocked his arm, and Klosky made a faint for home, though of course he had no plans whatever in that direction, and he edged off a few more steps, and then a few more still, and still and yet a few more. Then all at once he broke for home. I do not know why except that when your club is in fifth and headed neither up nor down you might try anything just for the laughs, and Lindon stood with his arm cocked, like he was a statue froze to the spot. It seemed like years. It might of been as long as 1 second, and there was still plenty of time to nab Klosky at home, and then he throwed, except he did not throw home to Red, but down to George at third, throwing to the wrong base like you will see kids do on a playground 9, and George come out for the throw as fast as he could and took it and fired to Red, and Klosky hit the dirt and made it by the split of a second, and that was the ball game.

There was never a sound in the clubhouse, never a word spoke nor a laugh laughed. There was only the sound of water in the shower, and the sound of Mick tearing tape. If somebody was to snap the cap on a Coke it would of amounted to a noise.

Chicago beat Boston that night. I caught the score on a newscast at 11. I never care much for them newscasts myself, but beginning along about the end of August when the race growed so hot the first item on many a newscast was the ball scores, never mind the wars and never mind the politics, and we would catch that much and then tune out, and I went down the hall and dropped in on Lindon, thinking I might cheer him up, and the room was dark

and Lucky said do not turn on the light for he had give Lindon
some pills to go to sleep. Lucky said the last thing Lindon said
before he went under was tell me he did not mean to call me that
name he called me in the clubhouse. Me and Lucky talked in the
dark. He said Lindon was all broke up over the boner he pulled,
and he cried and cried and carried on plenty, saying he had ruined
Coker's plan to buy his folks the brick house and ruined all the
plans all the boys made to take trips in the winter or buy a house
or do what they planned with their Series money, and he said that
on account of him Hams Carroll's little girl would be a cripple.
Hams has a little girl with a twisted leg that he would have fixed
in Minnesota in the winter with the Series money. Finally Lindon
was just about hysterical and Lucky went and got some pills from
Doc Loftus and put him to sleep.

    I worked and won on Wednesday night with my arm sore from
my shoulder partway to my elbow where I strained it trying to
shift some of the heavy duty off my back. Red kept nagging me,
saying he seen too many arms throwed out by youngsters with more
ambition then brains. Yet I suppose he was as relieved as the rest
that I won it, for Boston smothered Chicago 11-1.
    Sad Sam Yale went the distance on Thursday, and he won it,
and Boston won again in Chicago, and the east headed east for the
final time, Boston still hot and the Mammoths glad enough to have
1½ games to go home on because there was times when it looked
like we might have even less. We figured to do better at home
then we done on the road, and Dutch said the same, and the writers, too. Things could of been worse, I suppose.
    When we hit New York I got a call from the Perkinsville
"Clarion" asking me where was Bill Duffy. They had not heard
from him in a week, and I remembered that the last I seen of Bill
he was planning a trip across the river for a drink with a friend in
East St. Louis. But I did not tell them that in Perkinsville, nor I
did not tell them Bill was in his cups from the time we left Chicago.
    Bill always drunk heavy, but never like that before, and the

greater the pressure got the harder he drunk. Under pressure you squirm out the best way you know how. For me it was the far corner of the lobby with a murder. For Bill it was the bottle.

STANDINGS OF THE CLUBS

Saturday Morning, August 30

	Won	Lost	Pct.	Games Behind
New York	78	45	.634	—
Boston	79	49	.617	1½
Brooklyn	72	52	.581	6½

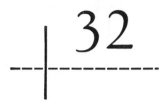

32

LABOR DAY fell on a Monday. In the morning, before we was out of bed, there come a knock on the door, a very chipper sort of a knock—Boom, diddy boom boom, BOOM BOOM— like somebody was in high spirits. We could not imagine who.

The door opened and in walked Keith Crane, his grips in his hand and his face all a smile, and he set his grips on the floor and come over and shook our hand. "How is the flipper?" said I to him, "and what in the world are you doing in New York?"

"I been brung up," said he. "Judkins been put on the inactive list." I shot Perry a quick look. We always liked Keith and wished him well, but we always considered him strictly AA, a good ball-player but never really the tops, a southpaw with a crossfire delivery that is very puzzling to hitters until they catch on to it, good control and a fair curve but not much speed. He come to Q. C. our second year there with a great record in the Northern League, which is where the Mammoths send all colored ballplayers until they are ready for AA under Mike Mulrooney. Perry seemed pleased, however. "Maybe you will bring us out of the slump," he said.

"I believe you are out of it already," said Keith. We had just took 2 over the weekend in Washington and picked up a full game on Boston. "However, I must admit I was in a sweat yesterday," and he went on to say that the hostess on the airplane kept reporting the scores on the Mammoths in Washington and Boston in Brooklyn inning by inning all during the flight. He said half the plane was for Boston and half for the Mammoths, and they hardly talked about anything else. "How is your back?" said he to me.

"Not so good," I said.

"Mike Mulrooney says it is your nerves," said he. "Who will pitch today?"

"Anybody is libel to," I said. "For all you know you are libel to work yourself."

"I am just barely off the plane," said he. "I just got off the plane last night." He was pretty fidgety at the suggestion.

Me and Perry laughed. "If Dutch works you you had better work and not be full of explanations," I said.

I was a little late to the park that day. Traffic was slow between the hotel and Brooklyn, and the jam around the park was thicker then I ever seen it before. I got out of the cab and walked the last few blocks through all that crush in the broiling heat. There must of been thousands come over from New York plus of course thousands and thousands from Brooklyn itself. Brooklyn was just about counted out by now, and I suppose they give up on their own chances. What they was really hoping to see was the skids put under us and the road made easy for Boston. Next to seeing Brooklyn win the great joy for Flatbush is seeing the Mammoths lose.

Crane worked and won, fogging them down crossfire and having the good sense to do what Red said on every pitch. Canada turned in a nice job in center field, playing there in place of Lucky now, and it looked like Dutch might have that problem licked.

Boston lost its first game to Washington, and our cushion jumped to 3½ again with 1 game less to go. We was in better spirits in the clubhouse between games then any time since the western swing, and the quartet sung.

I thought I might work the second game, but I did not. Dutch was saving me for the Boston series coming up. That suited me fine. Knuckles Johnson worked it and lost it 4-3 to Bill Scudder, 2 of Brooklyn's runs unearned on a bad throw by Bruce Pearson. Bruce took over for Red. It would of usually been Goose when Red needed a rest, but Goose had 2 floating cartileges in his elbow that kept him on the bench. Dutch eat out Bruce something awful afterwards, and Boston took the nightcap from Washington, so our cushion was back at 2½.

Tuesday was an open day, but we drilled in the afternoon in

all the heat. I throwed some, but mostly I stretched out bare to the waist deep in center field, and I left the sun bathe the back, and it was good.

When we left the park after the drill there was already a line at the bleacher gate, 40 or 50 people sitting up against the wall, the stands mostly sold and only the bleachers left.

The club roomed Keith with Perry, and me and Bruce went in together, Sid living at home now that we was back in New York. That was pretty much the final break-up of the old Queen City gang, Coker and Canada having split some weeks before over a matter I never knowed the inside story of, Lindon fairly chummy with Lucky now, and *them* 2 roomies, and Perry with Crane as stated above.

It was in the cards. We still sung in the shower, me and Coker and Canada and Perry, but we did not run together like once we done. We was Mammoths now, no longer Queen City Cowboys, swallowed up you might say, though never swallowed up really, being neither Mammoths of the old school—Sam and Knuckles and Swanee and that bunch—and yet not green rooks neither, rooming more or less together and drilling more or less together but still and all not tight and close like we was at the first, not like some weeks before when wherever 1 was there was the others 9 times in 10 like these twins that you see pictures of in the paper joined at the hip. Perry and Keith went their own way, and off the field I almost never seen them. They went uptown a hell of a lot. Lindon and Canada developed a very fancy taste in restaurants. They spent a lot of time at Toots Shorses, and Coker put in a hell of a lot of hours at various clothing stores. He soon begun wearing a different suit every day, and I never seen a guy so worked up if his tie didn't match his socks. Well, that was okay, too.

I figured I could put up with Bruce for a month. Mostly he would sit and stare out the window, and then again he would trail me to my place in the lobby and sit near by, and I would be lost in a murder, and when I put it down he was still there, just sitting. Sometimes he would fall asleep. Sunny Jim said that me and Bruce was not *real* lobby sitters, for your real lobby sitter will neither read nor sleep, but merely sit. That was the most conversation I had with Sunny Jim all year.

Wednesday morning about 6 A.M. Bruce woke me and told me the radio said there was a wreck on the train from Boston. He said they put on a number of extra sections to bring down the crowds, and 1 end of the railroad forgot to tell the other what was up. I told him to turn off the radio and get back in bed. He said he always got up early, ever since he was a boy in Bainbridge, Georgia, and he asked me would I come and go hunting with him in the winter, and I said I would if he turned off the radio, and he done so.

But that was all the sleep I got. I was jumpy, and I was worried about my back, for it was tight from the knob behind my neck to the knob of my spine, and I dreamed all night that we dropped 3 to Boston and lost the lead, and Bruce said he believed that dreams come true because he dreamed 1 time that there was rabbits in a certain meadow, and he went there and there was. I said I believed it was impossible that we could drop 3 in a row to Boston. I said if we took even 1 we might scrape through, for I knowed that as long as we had the lead we had hope. Once we fell behind we would never make it back.

Sam worked. I had not worked since the Wednesday before in St. Louis, and I do not know what the strategy was, but Dutch picked Sam. Fred Nance was on the hill for Boston. Me and Keith Crane kept warm in the bullpen.

Sam was in trouble now and then. He give up 1 in the fifth and another in the sixth and steadied down for the seventh, and in the last of the seventh Canada and Vincent singled after 2 was out, and Sid blasted a home run and we led 3-2.

Sam was rocky again in the eighth. Here and there amongst the crowd the song took up whenever Sam was in trouble, and groups of people would sing, "The old gray mare she ain't what she used to be, ain't what she used to be, ain't what she used to be," most of them down from Boston or over from Brooklyn, and generally they was drowned out by the rest. Nonetheless the song come through. It never bothered Sam, or if it did he did not show it, knowing as well as anybody that he was not what he used to be.

Nobody at 34 has the stuff he had at 30, or 25. The crowds begun
to sing that song in Washington the weekend before Labor Day,
and they picked it up in Brooklyn and sung it a number of times
during the holiday doubleheader, and it was with us yet on Wednesday and all through September right down to the wire.

Casey Sharpe begun the trouble for Sam in the eighth with a
single, and Heinz moved him along with a bunt. Chickering
slammed 1 back towards the box and it went through into center, and Canada come in fast and fielded it with his bare hand
and uncorked the long throw home, and it bounced once near the
box and kicked up the dust, and Red took it at the plate and
slapped it on Sharpe, Chickering going to second on the play, and
the telephone rung in the bullpen, and it was for me. I walked
the long walk across the green.

Tubs Blodgett was the hitter, Chickering on second, 2 down,
and still the 1 run lead for us. Tubs reminds me of Mike Mulrooney. I do not know him in a personal way except to say "Hello,"
but he is the friendly type, and he looks like Mike, red of face and
jolly. He hits with a black bat, and he waved it and looked as fierce
as he could, though it is hard to look fierce when your face is a
natural smile and you look like Santa Claus without the beard. I
throwed a few down to warm, and then I was ready, and Red put
his mask on and signed for nothing but curves. We always throw
curves to Tubs, and I checked Chickering, and then I throwed the
curve, and it did not break, and Tubs whaled it down the line in
left, and a great cry rose from the people. I did not look. Then
the cry all of a sudden stopped, for the ball hooked foul, and the
new ball come out and I checked my runner again, and then I
throwed a second curve, and it broke better then the first, though
not very good a-tall, and Tubs whaled it again, trying to pull it
close, aiming for the wall in left, and this time it hooked but not
so soon, and finally it done so and landed in the upper deck a bare
5 feet foul or so. Red come down and asked me what was the
matter. "Nothing," I said. "Only my back. I do not seem to get
the full motion."

"I do not think he will expect another curve right away," said
Red, "so we will throw him another," and he went back behind

the plate and settled in his crouch, and a drop of perspiration rolled down off my nose, and I stepped off the rubber to itch it before I throwed, and I felt of my face, and it was wet like I was fresh out of the shower, and I toed back in and tugged at the peak of my cap with my thumb and first finger, and with the other fingers I took the sweat of my brow and rubbed it along my fingertips, and then, with my fingers still wet, I throwed the curve.

That is what you call a spitter. It is outlawed from baseball. A player can pull a suspension for a year if he throws it, for you can kill a man with a spitter if you hit him right. You do not have it under full control. All this I knowed, and I did not care. I did not wish to kill Tubs Blodgett, but my curve was not breaking on account of my back, and I throwed quick before I had time to think about consequences, and the curve broke big and sharp, for my fingers was slimy and wet, and Tubs swang and missed, striking out and ending the inning. Red whipped it down towards third, like he was making the play on Chickering coming down from second, and George never even reached for the throw but left it roll to the outfield, for the rolling dried it off, and Boston stormed from their dugout and beat their chest and raged and swore and howled and stamped their feet, for it was plain to all that I had throwed a spitter. But Frank Porter could not call it a spitter because the ball was laying out in left, dry, like new, because the rolling dried it, and I was all a-tremble, knowing that I done wrong according to the rules and could of been suspended and might of killed Tubs Blodgett besides. The crowd give me a hand when I come to the bench for the way I fanned Tubs on 3 pitches, and they give Canada a hand for the fine throw on Casey Sharpe from center, yet I hardly heard it I was so scared and shaking.

We scored twice in the last of the eighth, and I coasted through the ninth, and the cushion was 3½ again and the quartet sung in the shower.

Boston protested to the League on the spitter I throwed Blodgett, and the League turned it down on grounds of lack of evidence though warning Dutch if I done it again I would be in hot water, and Dutch told me and said I must not do it again, and he laughed, for he was in a good frame of mind that night, which was Wednesday night, and he pitched me Thursday.

The heat hit the peak on Thursday. 1 fan dropped dead. I wished I was anywheres else but here, though I turned in a good job for 7 innings and left the ball game with 3 on and none out in the top of the eighth and the score knotted 2-2 on account of my back.

It was not so much the pain. But I could not get the full motion, and the curve and the screw broke crazy, not like they should of broke a-tall, and I worried so much about my motion that I believe I give myself away on several pitches, particularly on the 1 to Blodgett that opened the eighth. He singled, and Toomy Richardson singled, and I finally walked Devereaux after he bunted foul twice. Then Dutch come out from the dugout. We could barely hear each other speak, for the noise was so great, and Red said he believed I ought to be lifted because the curve never broke and the fast 1 did not hop and my control was off, and Dutch said that was reasons enough for him, and Keith Crane come down from the bullpen and I give him the ball and said I was sorry to leave him in such a fix, and I walked off.

He pulled out of it that inning, fanning Black and getting Granby to hit into a double play, Gene to Ugly to Sid, and he got a terrific ovation from the crowd. But then he lost it in the eleventh after throwing 3 innings of perfect baseball on a home run by Granby that cleared the fence in right by 3 feet, if that much.

Dutch done away with the extra drill beginning on Friday. We did not even begin to warm until just before the lights went on. It was cooler, and the tenseness seemed to lift with the heat. The crowd was quieter though the figures showed that it was about as large as the day before, not capacity but a good 55,000 at least, and Keith Crane drawed the assignment, the second straight day he worked.

The boys did not seem so tight, nor Boston neither. There was lulls in the game, times that you would of thought everybody lost interest, times when there was no insults floating back and forth, sometimes 2 and 3 innings at a stretch and not a beef against an umpire. There was times on the bench when there would be laughter, and something might come under discussion having nothing a-tall to do with the ball game, and then you was brought back sharp because suddenly you remembered that the melon was riding on every pitch and every hit, and everything anyone was ordered to do they tried to do it perfect at least just this once because it was not only their piece of the melon but also the next fellow's, and every man's hope hung in the balance.

Yet we must of been tight all the same. I remember along about the sixth inning, when Dutch sent me down to the bullpen, I looked at him and he sweated so free you would of thought it was the middle of yesterday afternoon when the heat hit the peak, and Joe Jaros beside him was as wet as Dutch, and Clint and Egg the same, their faces glistering under the lights, and up and down the line, 1 after the other, I studied their faces, and all was wet and shining, and I felt of my own, and the same was true.

We was 1 up after 6, but in the first of the seventh Boston got to Keith. Sharpe walked and Heinz singled and Chickering powdered 1 high up, high in the lights and down again, and Pasquale raced and stood with his back flat against the wall, waiting, and then he dropped his hands and walked forwards, back towards his position, and that was the end, as quick and as sudden as I give it to you here, and Boston had it, 6-4, and the cushion was 1½ again.

There was nothing said. There was no lecture. There was nobody eat out. There was only silence, and I suppose you would call it a peaceful silence except that it was not peaceful neither, and I do not know what sort of a silence it was, only that it was thick and heavy. Dutch went through to his office in back, and soon he come out again, and he called 5 names, looking down in his hand at 5 shreds of paper. He called, "Simpson, September 1—Park, September 2—Wilks, September 3—Gonzalez, September 4—Wiggen, September 5," and we each come forward and took the shred of paper with our name and the date that we wrote down on the shreds and put them in a glass way back around the first of July, betting 5 apiece on the day we would clinch the flag. I took my shred and folded it and give it a flip with my finger, and it bounced off the wall and landed amongst Hams Carroll's gear, and he scowled and swore.

"There is 150 wrapped in a towel on the shelf in my office," said Dutch. "If nobody wins it we will send it off to some f---ing charity or other," and he turned and disappeared through the door.

33

YET it begun to look like the 150 would fall after all somewhere amongst the club. Boston moved out and the west moved in, Cleveland for the weekend plus a make-up game on Monday, and Knuckles won the opener, and Hams lost the second, but Sam Yale beat Rob McKenna on Monday. Boston split 2 with Pittsburgh and then was idle Monday, so the cushion was 2 with an even 20 games to go, and Cleveland moved out and Pittsburgh moved in, and I lost on Tuesday night, and Crane on Wednesday, but Hams come back and won the final. Boston lost 2 out of 3 to Cleveland, and the cushion still was 2, Boston muffing their golden opportunity and Alf Keeler roundly eat out and told to resign by the Boston writers according to information brung back by Lucky Judkins. Lucky spent the week in Boston seeing what he could see and keeping the charts for Dutch. But Dutch called him back after the Pittsburgh series and made him drill regular and sent Clint Strap up to Boston with the charts because if Lucky could whip the trouble in his back and be put on the active list again he figured to be no little help. Lucky come home with a cold. He was sneezing in the clubhouse Friday before the first Chicago game, and Dutch seen him sneeze and told him go down and get a shot of penicillin from Doc Loftus, and then, on further thought, Dutch made *everybody* on the club go and get a shot and keep it from spreading.

It was this same Friday, not long before game time, that Holly hit town. The first I knowed of it Dutch was in the middle of the

302

lecture when the clubhouse cop come in with a note. Dutch eat the cop out. But nonetheless he took the note and looked at the name and give it to me, and it was from Holly, saying she was in town and would see me after the game.

She was there till Monday morning, putting up at the hotel with the club, 3 floors downstairs. The Mammoths picked up the bill. Anything that might possibly have a good effect on the club they was happy to pay for, including shelling out 5,000 dollars right about that time for Hams Carroll's little cripple girl to get worked on by the doctor in Minnesota.

This had a good effect on Hams. He beat Chicago that day, the first time we won 2 in a row since the weekend in Washington just before Labor Day, and afterwards Holly was waiting out under the El tracks where the wives and the girl friends wait.

It was really terrific to see her. I had not saw her since the night of the Opener in April after having just won my first big-time victory and my head was about 97 times the size it ought to been. She was standing and chatting with a number of the others. When the club wins it is a happy little group out there. Days we lose they are libel to be sitting alone, each in their own car, like strangers. We drove back to the hotel with Red and Rosemary Traphagen, and we had supper together, the 4 of us, and then we went our different ways. Holly and Rosemary become fairly thick over that weekend. Also Holly and Patricia Moors. Holly takes this morbid interest in Patricia.

I told her I had considerable interest in Patricia myself, though probably for different reasons, and then I was sorry I said it. I am always sorry for things 10 seconds too late, and I apologized about 11 times, and she said forget it. There was a kind of a tightness between us that I do not know if it come from the general atmosphere around the hotel or what. It wound up in a brawl, the first really *big* brawl we ever had, which I will discuss further on in this chapter if I do not wander off too far on other things.

Friday night we went to an open-air concert. Actually it was my idea, for Holly is not 1 of them girls you can simply lug off to the nearest movie, and she said she was happy to see that life in the big-time was drilling a little culture in me. I suppose I must of told her that going to concerts was practically a habit, though to tell you the truth I only went once before—1 time with Red and Rosemary. I said I not only went to concerts but read about 14 books a week. I did not tell her they was these quarter murders, for I knowed she would think them trash, which they was. But I begun to understand—along with 1,000,000 other things I was beginning to understand—that time was running out with her and me and that I had best begin to show that I had more in my head then just baseball.

We heard that Boston beat St. Louis on the way back to the hotel, and the cushion was 2 again, and Saturday she sat back behind home plate and seen a wonderful job turned in by a wonderful ballplayer name of Sad Sam Yale, no runs for Chicago on 4 scattered hits, only 1 man reaching second, and we took it 6-0, and the cushion was 2½, Boston rained out in Boston.

It was your old Sad Sam that day, not Sam of 4 years ago or 6 years ago but a full 10 years back, all speed and wicked curves and the screw to boot, all control, all brains, and the sad, sad face and the limber arm, and he made it look easy, and you would of thought it was easy except that you seen from his face between innings that it was not easy, that it was harder work then most men done of an afternoon, and he spoke never a word all day, for he was breathing hard and needed the wind, and he wrapped it up in the ninth with 2 strikeouts and a weak pop to the box. He took the pop with his bare hand and laid the ball in his glove and folded it over and stuck the works in his pocket and broke for the clubhouse like a fellow in an office might pull down the top of his desk at quitting time and break for the streetcar, a great job by 1 of the greatest that ever pulled on a pair of baseball shoes. Maybe his last great job. I don't know. We will see what the spring brings.

Afterwards, in the hotel, she asked me 500 questions, why did Sam do this and Red do that, why did Sid do this and George do that, and I told her, explaining the game of baseball backwards and forwards, and she said it was marvelous how 1 head could know so much about so little. That was when the brawl begun. "So little?" said I. "Do you call it little? Ask Red Traphagen if it is all so little that a man with a Harvard education cannot bring the price of a man with a good hopping curve."

"Is that how you have learned to measure things?" said she. "Do you now measure a man by the size of his pay?"

"I measure people like everybody else measures them," I said. "This is a rich man's world, and the richer the better. I will draw down 8,500 this year plus a Series share if we make it, second-place money if we do not. I will hit the club for 15,000 at contract time in the spring. I believe it all adds up to slightly more then I could get pumping gas for Tom Swallow."

"I am not asking you to pump gas," said she.

"Then what are you asking?" said I.

"Nothing," she said. "You are no property of mine and I have no right to ask nothing."

"Damn right," I said. "Damn right. I am nobody's property."

"You are the property of the New York Mammoths," she said.

"Like hell I am," I said. But then I thought about it and realized she was right.

"Are you not, Henry? Are you not a little island in the Moors empire?"

"At 8,500 a summer," I said. "For 8,500 I can belong to somebody a little. I will hit them for 15,000 next year. Who would not belong to somebody at prices like that?"

"I," she said.

"So who is asking *you?*" I said.

"You," she said.

Well, that was true, too, for I had asked her Friday at the concert if she would marry me, and she said we would talk about it. And now we was talking about it. "Okay," said I. "Go ahead. Go ahead and marry some gas pumper. I am sure they are the salt of the earth."

"Henry," said she, "you are a stupid goon. Could you try for 5 minutes to listen to somebody that loves you? Not somebody that cheers for you, and not somebody that simply pays you your salary, but somebody that has lived next door to you off and on for a number of years and does not really care if you are a New

York Mammoth or a Perkinsville Scarlet." She was awful mad
and at the same time extremely pretty, though I did not particularly
care for her calling me "a stupid goon." "It is not a matter of me
marrying either you or a gas pumper. It is a matter of marrying a
man. I do not much care what he does, so long as he is a man.
You are 21," she said, "and under the law you are a man, and
your height and weight is that of a man. In the bed you are a
man," and she smiled a little. "But you are losing your manhood
faster then hell. Pretty soon in bed will be the *only* place you are
a man. But that is not manhood. Dogs and bulls and tomcats do
the same. Yes, you are losing your manhood and becoming simply
an island in the empire of Moors."

"Crap," said I.

"I suspected it," she said. "And then I knowed for sure a week
or so ago. I really did. I seen you on the TV. I seen you throw
that spitball at the man from Boston. And your Pop seen it clear
up in Perkinsville, and he said only a few words. He said, "I am
sorry to see Henry stoop to do a thing like that," and he cried a
few tears right there in the midst of all the people in the Arcade
Department Store.

"Is it worth it, Henry? Suppose you killed that man? Where
is my Henry Wiggen that I remember could never even swing his
fist at a man? Where is my Henry that used to go down in his old
Coward Crouch rather then lay a hand on his worst enemy?"

"Things are tight," I said. "Terrible tight. Every pitch is cash,
Holly. Big cash. Not only my cash but the cash of all the boys.
It is a brick house for Coker Roguski's folks and a new start in
life for Hams Carroll's little girl. This is for keeps. This ain't
playground baseball."

"That reminds me of something," she said. "I run across it and
stuck it in my purse." She went over and got her purse off the
hook and fished around. "It is a statement by Leo Durocher in the
"Times." I suppose you probably know Durocher personally."

"Just to say "Hello" to," I said. "He is a great hustler. He was
a great ballplayer's ballplayer in his time."

"Durocher says the following," she said.

"What're we out for, except to win? This is professional, not amateur. If I'm losing, I'll be bleeding in my heart; inside, I'll be dying. I'll congratulate you, but did I like losing? Hell, no. Look, I'm playing third base. My mother's on second. The ball's hit out to short center. As she goes by me on the way to third, I'll accidentally trip her up. I'll help her up, brush her off, tell her I'm sorry. But she doesn't get to third. That's just an exaggeration. But it's an illustration of what I mean. I want to win all the time. If we're spitting at a crack in the wall in this office for pennies, I want to beat you at it. Anybody can finish second."

I laughed. "That is pretty good," I said.

"Save it for future consideration," she said, and she give me the hunk of paper and I stuck it in my pants. "I will quit the club first thing in the morning," I said, joking.

"No, you will not," she said. "You will go on playing baseball till your feet trip over your beard. It is a grand game. I love to see it, and I love to hear you talk about it. It is a beautiful game, clean and graceful and honest. But I will be damned if I will sit back and watch you turn into some sort of a low life halfway between a sour creature like Sad Sam Yale and a shark like Dutch Schnell.

"You are a lefthander, Henry. You always was. And the world needs all the lefthanders it can get, for it is a righthanded world. You are a southpaw in a starboarded atmosphere. Do you understand?"

"Sure I understand," said I. "I am not such a stupid goon as you might think."

"Exactly," she said. Then she begun to cry a little, and she fought against it, and when she had control over herself she spoke further. "I hold your hand," she said, "and your hand is hard, solid like a board. That is all right, for it must be hard against the need of your job. On a job such as yours your hand grows hard to protect itself. But you have not yet growed calluses on your heart. It is not yet hard against the need of your job. It must never become hard like your hand. It must stay soft.

"In most places of the world hardness is a mark of credit. I do not believe that. I believe the best hand is the soft hand, the best heart is the soft heart, the best man is the soft man. I want my old soft Henry back, Henry the Coward Navigator." And then she busted out crying all over the place.

34

SHE seen a beauty on Sunday. I beat Chicago, the first game I won since the tail end of the western trip in St. Louis 17 days before, and Boston took a doubleheader, and the cushion was 2. She went home on Monday, and Knuckles and Hams beat St. Louis on Tuesday and Wednesday, and the winning streak stood at 6, though St. Louis snapped it on getaway day, blasting Sam from the box, and we moved out for Friday and the weekend in Washington, Boston hot but a 2½ cushion between us.

We had time on our side, and the 2½ looked big. It looked a good deal fatter then it looked on Labor Day, even fatter then the 3½ after the first game of the Boston series on the third of September.

It was 2½ almost all the month, a little 1 way, a little the other, and the later it got the better it looked. We was ready to settle for 2½. We would of loved 4 and we would of been in heaven with 5, but it was 2½ most of the way and we got used to 2½.

You have got to hand it to Boston. They clung to our tail, refusing to be shook, hanging on, hanging, hanging, knowing that with every passing day their chances took a downwards dip, yet clinging, fighting, tore through the middle with friction and illness (at 1 time there was 6 Boston players with a cold in their head because the weather was miserable up there all through September) yet never saying "Die," but seeing things through to the bitter finish, and you have got to admire them for that.

The west went west for good and the east settled down for the last 10 days, and we worried, for worry was a habit by now, and we fretted and snapped, and Dutch rode us, first pleading then scolding then pleading again, and I counted the days and the hours until it would be over and settled 1 way or the other, and sometimes I hardly cared which.

I beat Washington Friday night. That was number 25 for me. I was the first and only pitcher in the league that won 25, the first Mammoth that done so since Sam Yale turned the trick in 45. Outside of Sam I was the only Mammoth in history that won 25. The nearest anyone else ever come was Egg Barnard in 1920, with 24 wins, and Peter Rosegrant in 1916, also 24, Peter now a turnstile turner in the grandstand section back of the plate. Boston beat Brooklyn, and it was still 2½.

It turned hot in Washington, like summer again, and World Series seats went on sale at the Stadium. The front office seemed to figure that the 2½ would be good forever, and most folks figured the same, I suppose. According to a pole that was took at the time 66% of the people considered the Mammoths would win, 26% thought otherwise, 8% had no opinion.

Keith Crane went after his second win on Saturday. He had not won a ball game since Labor Day, his first and only big-time win, and he needed relief in the sixth, first putting the winning runs on base, and Boston beat Brooklyn again and the cushion was 1½.

But even then nothing broke, nothing flared. There was only a quiet amongst the boys, a silence and a quiet, and for fear of breaking silence you did not speak except when spoke to, and the safest thing to do was find yourself a corner in the lobby and slouch down and pull it in after, and that is what I done.

I sat in the lobby until half past 1 that night, and then I went up, and even then I could not sleep. Bruce sat by the window and said he knowed now we would lose for sure, and I did not answer. I got up and wrapped my sheet about me and went down the hall to Pisses room, and I laid on the empty bed with the pillow under my back, and I could not sleep on account of the heat and on account of my back and on account of the noises from Pisses sinuses, and I went back and dressed and laid in the park near the reflecting pool, and I slept a bit and was woke by the sun.

Lindon pitched the first game of the Sunday doubleheader. He had not worked since St. Louis when he froze and throwed to the wrong base and lost his own ball game. Dutch had no faith in him ever after, but he was trying to work out his rotation so as to aim with his lefthanders against Boston the last 3 days, and he gambled on Lindon, and he lost the gamble. Lindon was as wild as his wildest day back in Q. C., and Boston beat Brooklyn in the first of 2 at Boston, and the cushion was *one half* a game.

There was actually a period of nearly an hour that afternoon when in a manner of speaking Boston led the league. Dutch had no choice in the nightcap but throw Sam with only 2 days rest, and 2 was not enough and he fell apart in the fifth from simple weariness. We trailed 4-1 when he left the game, Boston leading Brooklyn at the time until Brooklyn busted loose with a big sixth inning and sewed it up, and a little while later—in the top of the eighth—the Mammoths come to life.

I will never forget that half inning. We played a desperate kind of baseball, Gene opening with a ground ball deep to short that he beat by an eyebrow, moving as fast as I ever seen him do before, Perry then pinch-running for Gene and going clear to third on a very shallow single by Red that Teddy Cogswell almost took over his shoulder going away. God, what a difference a couple inches can make!

Dutch took a long time deciding on a pinch-hitter for Horse, and finally he settled on Swanee, and he sent Coker down to pinch-run for Red. Swanee was a good choice, having been through fire many a time before, an old war horse without a nerve in his body. He finally worked himself a pass and loaded the bases, and Bruce rushed down from the bullpen to pinch-run for Swanee, and Red hustled down to the pen and kept Knuckles warm, and everything looked crazy, nobody where they ought to be, Red in the bullpen, Knuckles warming for relief, Dutch throwing his strongest card at every turn of events, the boys playing now with their back to the wall as tight and close as ever it was or ever it could be, and knowing it, every 1 of them, knowing it was now or never because if once we fell behind we would be behind forever, no Series melon, no rich and happy winter, nothing only drag home your

unhappy ass and explain to the folks and the friends how come
you was tops on paper and second in the standings.

George clubbed 1 in the dirt, a weakly little bounder. But it
bounced the long bounce towards short, and Cogswell brung the
play home, and Perry actually *beat* the throw to the plate, Coker
and Bruce moving up 1 base apiece, the bags still jammed. Coker
scored a minute later when Canada hoisted a long fly to left, and
1 thin run now stood between us and a tie ball game, Dutch fuming and swearing because Bruce had not took third on the play
and sending out Herb Macy to run for Bruce, something I never
seen before—a pinch-runner running for a pinch-runner—and
Bruce slinking off down along the fence to the bullpen again.
Vincent Carucci singled, scoring Herb, and it was 4-4.

Sid run the count out and then fouled off a couple. There was
points while Sid was at bat where I thought my heart would absolutely give out from the suspense and excitement. I would not
of been Sid for I don't know what. He kept rubbing his hands
with the resin, they was sweating so, and finally he got what he
was looking for and punched it into right, and George roared in
from third and give a leap like a broad jumper and come down
on the plate with both feet with the tally that busted the tie, and
we met him in front of the dugout, all of us, every goddam 1 of
us, up on our feet, and he was grinning and blabbering away in
Espanyol (Spanish). You would of thought the flag was clinched
right then and there. The relief from the tension was almost more
then a fellow could bear.

That was the end of the scoring. Knuckles pitched 2 perfect
innings and we squeaked through 5-4 and then dashed back in
the clubhouse and listened in complete and absolute silence to the
last inning of the nightcap in Brooklyn, won by Brooklyn. The
cushion was 1½ when we boarded the train out of Washington.

So we settled for an even split on 4 in Washington, and we
done the same in Brooklyn on Tuesday and Wednesday and the
Thursday doubleheader, almost the whole staff working but me
and Sam and Keith Crane, and Boston took 2 out of 3 from
Washington, chipping another half a game off of what was left of

the cushion. There was just that 1 game between us when Boston moved in at the Stadium. Homer B. Lester, in the Sid Yule story books, could not of set it up so neat if he tried.

We was favored in the betting. We had 3 lefthanders rested and ready to go, Henry Wiggen with an ailing back, a tired old man called Sad Sam Yale that had not won a start in 2 weeks, plus a AA ballplayer name of Keith Crane. I do not know who figured the odds. I doubt that much was bet.

STANDINGS OF THE CLUBS
Friday Morning, September 26

	Won	Lost	Pct.	Games Behind
New York	95	56	.629	—
Boston	94	57	.623	1

Games to Play

New York: With Boston, 3
Boston: With New York, 3

I SET down the first 7 men in a row in the Friday game, including the fanning of Casey Sharpe to open the Boston half of the second that brung a great ovation from the people, a louder noise then I ever heard before. I could feel the ground shiver beneath my feet.

You could not of brung your pet cat to the park. In the beginning it was a quiet crowd, considering the size, opening up once when I fanned Casey Sharpe, then quiet again until Toomy Richardson singled with 1 down in the third, the first Boston hit. Horse and Piss and Gil and Herb all went to work in the bullpen. There was no such thing no more as saving the staff. What would you be saving them for?

I got set to pitch to Fred Nance when there was a commotion behind our dugout, and I stepped off the rubber and 2 umpires went over towards the dugout to see what was up. It seemed that Sam Yale got up for a drink at the water spout and somebody potted him with a peach or a pear and the crowd become very abusive towards Sam. Zinke talked over the top of the dugout at the crowd, and they hooted and jeered until finally Zinke got a hold of some cops and ordered them up in the stands in the section behind the Mammoths. They insulted Sam all day, ignorant farmers from Brooklyn and Boston mostly I suppose, though probably some from New York as well that thought we should of clinched it weeks ago and lit on Sam as the main cause of the slump.

Nance bunted, not a good bunt, too much towards the box, and I pounced on it and made the play at second, the long throw that

Ugly took, forcing Toomy Richardson and putting Nance on first. It was a gamble but I tried it, hoping to keep Nance on his feet, not to mention keeping Richardson from being in scoring position. Dutch said he believed we would get to Nance if we worked him hard.

Sid played wide of the bag, and Nance led off long. Then Sid cut back in and Nance had no choice but follow. Sid done this twice until Nance finally stood resting with his foot on the bag and never led a-tall, and I went to work on Black. With a 2-2 count Black caught a hold of 1 and drilled it in the hole between Sid and Gene. Sid dived and missed, and Gene come over fast and took it deep in the hole and fired to me, covering at first, the kind of a play you seldom see, and the throw beat Black by a half a step and the crowd come to its feet applauding, for they had saw good baseball that inning, and they knowed it for once, which they so seldom do, and Dutch said "Good boy" to me when I come in the dugout, referring both to the play on Black and the quick thinking on Nance's bunt.

I believe we tired Nance at that. Red opened our third with a cannonball blow that Tubs Blodgett leaped for at third. It nicked his glove and skittered over in foul territory, a fair ball, however, on account of Tubs making contact with it, and Red went clear to second.

I tried like hell to hit, but the best I could do was a fly to short left that Heinz took on the run, holding Red at second.

Nance kept throwing low to George. I don't know why most clubs have got the idea that George ain't a low-ball hitter. Boston and Brooklyn both try to low-ball George and never seem to get wise to theirselves. The second pitch George walloped to the opposite field, a real drive that climbed up the bullpen awning, good for 2 bases, and Red scored and the ice was broke.

Neither Canada nor Vincent could bring George home.

I struck out Casey Sharpe for the second time to end the Boston fourth.

I also struck out Heinz to open their fifth, but Chickering followed with their second hit, a sharp blow that got past Ugly by inches, and I lost Tubs Blodgett, passing him and getting in hot water for the first time that day, having previously give up only 1 hit. Tubs grinned at me with that Santa Claus face on his way down the line to first, and then he said 2 words to me.

I will tell you exactly what he said to me, for folks have asked me many times since. "Thank you," he said, but Chickering, jogging down the line from first to second, must of thought something different passed between us, and he shouted at me—no need to repeat it. Ugly was over behind me, moving in for a conference at the hill, and he glared at Chickering and said the same thing back. Ugly was never much on thinking up original remarks. Then Chickering come sauntering towards Ugly, and I merely stepped over and tagged him out. He did not seem to care. He kept walking towards Ugly, and they stood head to head for several seconds, never a word passing between them, and Ugly slid his glove off his hand and begun to swing. But Chickering swang first, just once, and he busted Ugly's jaw in 2 places.

I moved out of it quick. I shouted at Perry, "Grab a glove," and we stood in front of the dugout throwing back and forth to keep warm whilst the players and the umpires and a whole hoard of cops moved out on the field, and the Commissioner come down out of his box, for he was there that day, and I stood warm, just throwing. The noise was almost too much to bear. The crowd comes for the ball game, but give them a busted jaw besides and they feel like they doubled their money.

They led Ugly off with his face in his hand, his jaw broke at last and later re-set in the natural way, Coker going in at short, taking up a great burden at a most strenuous time, and the game commenced again. Chickering was thumbed out. He was later fined and suspended. I pitched 2 pitches to Tocmy Richardson, Tubs then trying to steal second and getting throwed out, Traphagen to Roguski.

In the sixth the wind shifted. It blowed in from center and washed against the back, and the back tightened, and in the seventh I throwed 1 very bad ball to Granby to open the inning that he went flat on the ground to get out of the way of. He turned and said something to Frank Porter, and Porter said something to Red, telling Red to warn me there was to be no monkey business, and Red shouted out something that seemed to satisfy Porter and squatted quick, hustling me now, knowing that if I could keep warm we would get through the day on the long end, and we pitched high and fast to Granby, fast because it was cloudy and high because we did not care if they lifted them in the wind because the wind was in strong from center now. There is a factory not far from the park belonging to the Mendenhall Nut & Bolt Works that you can see the smokestack standing on the dugout step, and Red always watches it, for it blows smoke every day but Sunday and Red can tell from the drift of the smoke which way the wind will hit the park, and Granby poled 1 high that the wind took and played with and dropped it where Pasquale was standing and waiting.

We worked with the greatest care on Fielding. Except for Casey Sharpe he is the only first-class power hitter in the Boston line-up, and we finally got him on a roller to Gene Park, and Casey Sharpe himself come up. "Leave us get him," said Red, "and then maybe not face him again today," and we mapped the strategy, and then Red went back and settled down in his crouch. We did not work long on old Casey. He is not usually a first-ball hitter, but he went after it now, and he caught it good with the fat of his bat—a high, fast curve—and it went towards the sky, and far, and Pasquale and Canada moved backwards and forwards under it, according to the ways of the wind, and then Canada called and lunged, for when it dropped down out of the wind it come fast, and he took it, and it seemed like the worst was over, 6 men to get and the lower end of the order coming up. The crowd stood for the stretch.

Only Horse Byrd was warming now. Dutch moved Canada to first in the top of the eighth, Scotty Burns going to center with full instructions concerning the wind, the crowd silent again, the back aching in a dull way. But I was sure it was good for the 2 more innings. Dutch asked me, and I said I was sure.

Heinz opened the eighth with what seemed to be orders to tire me if he could. He did not take his bat off his shoulder until the count was 2 and 2, and then I struck him out with the screw. Plainfield, playing second now in place of Chickering, went down in the same way on 4 pitches, coming full around on the last and throwing himself to the ground by the power of his own swing, and he swore a mighty oath and hurled the bat clear to the screen behind home.

Tubs Blodgett come up, hitting with a heavier stick now, the only time I ever seen him use anything but the black bat, hoping maybe to beat the wind with extra drive. We played him straight away, Vincent Pasquale maybe a few steps more towards left then usual, but never more then a few, Tubs a cool and veteran customer, the crowd still very quiet, or at least as quiet as 87,572 people can be in 1 place, nobody budging nor moving for an exit, the loudest sound being a couple jet planes overhead that come and was gone before you could glimpse them. I looked up, and there was 1 plane writing in the sky. Then I looked up again, holding my head that way because it seemed to rest the back where it hurt at the knob of the neck, and I went to work on Tubs, full speed and screws, twice speed that he swang at and missed though my heart give a tumble each time he come round with that overweight bat, and then 1 screw, and he nicked the screw and it popped in Red's mitt, and then out, and up, and Red went after it with his bare hand and juggled it like a chunk of slippery soap and then clapped the big mitt over the hand, and that was all for Tubs, and the crowd give out with a thunderous din. For an instant I did not know why the ovation had a certain extra energy to it, and then it occurred to me that I had fanned the side.

There was 3 men to go to clinch the tie.

We went down in order in our half of the eighth. "3 to go," said Perry when I got up and slipped out of my jacket, and I said "Yes, 3 men to go," and the hill looked far away, and high, a long climb up, and I strolled out, knowing that 1 way or another in the next 10 or 15 minutes the pressure would be off for good—off *me* at least—and that was something to look forward to.

The wind whipped in from center, and it was dark. The lights went on.

A speck of dust blowed in my eye, and I called time and worked around in my eye with my finger, but I could not get it out. Red looked in my eye and seen it and yelled for Doc Loftus, and Frank Porter come down and looked in the eye and said there was no speck. He said it was all a stall. I said I was every bit as anxious as him to be out of the park, and the crowd howled for action, all in a hurry to get it over with, and finally Doc come with cotton sticks and a little bottle and dabbed in the eye and got hold of the speck once or twice but could not draw it out. His hands shook, for the howling of the mob made him nervous, and finally he hooked it, and I held my head back and he poured the bottle in my eye. "Good luck, Wiggen," he said, and off he run like he was glad to get out of sight again.

Alf Keeler had sent Hampden up to hit for Toomy Richardson. Hampden is a young kid, barely 20, and he was up there with a good deal riding on what he might do, tight and tense and anxious. He is a righthanded pull hitter, and we played him pretty much to the left side, throwing close. The count leveled at 2 and 2 and then we gambled with the jughandle curve. He did not swing, and it nipped the corner, and it was good and he knowed it was good and he turned in a fury on Porter and opened his mouth and never said a word, just closed it again and walked off, trailing his bat behind. That was the fourth straight man I fanned.

Bob Boyne hit for Fred Nance, a man of near 40 that I bought bubble gum as a kid with a card in every chunk and once had a card for Boyne, his picture and his history. He was a cool customer, like Tubs Blodgett, a switch-hitter, swinging righthanded now. He choked way up on his bat and stared at me and tried to face me down until it was like my eyes was glued to him, and I stepped out and broke the spell, and then I stepped in and *he* stepped out, and the mob howled and the wind whipped my back, and the back ached like blazes.

We stuck mostly to curves. Boyne choked up, hoping to punch 1 through and get a man on base and play for the breaks, a wild throw or an error or some sort of a general collapse in the field. He lashed at 2 curves and sliced them foul, for I throwed them with the full motion of my whole body and they broke sharp and fast, 2 pitches as good as any I ever delivered, and he fouled them along the line in left, George and Coker and Vincent all giving chase and never quite making it.

Boyne moved his hands an inch or more down towards the handle of the bat, and he shifted forward in the box, hoping to meet the curve before it broke full, or the screw if we throwed the screw. But we done neither. Instead we poured the fast 1 through, and he drilled it back and a little to my left. I got the tip of the middle finger of my left hand on it as it went by. It bloodied the nail. Gene come clear over and speared it backhand close to second, and the play at first was close, Canada stretching and splitting and Boyne not so young no longer or he might of had it beat. Toft called him out. I believe it was the right decision.

Boston thought otherwise. Boyne pulled up quick and turned and raced for Toft and spit in the old man's face, and Keeler stormed out and stood wrangling with Toft until he throwed them out, Boyne later fined by the League besides. Toft has heard plenty over the years but I rather imagine that this was the equal of any, and he took out his watch and give them 30 seconds to be out of his sight, and 20 they spent in further discussion and the other 10 drifting back towards their dugout and through the door to the clubhouse.

The Boston bench was loud. Toft heard them, too, and after a minute it become too much and he went and cleared the bench, all but those that was still in the game plus 2 coaches, and they went back behind the dugout door and now and then flung out a remark and then closed the door quick before you could see who it was. Every oath was wilder then the 1 before. I got so interested in seeing what they could possibly come up with next that I forgot about my bloody nail and never thought about it until after the game was over. And then it didn't matter.

The boys sung. I had not heard them in many weeks, and now they sung at last, and I could hear them clear from the outfield, their voice carried in on the wind—"1 more man, Henry baby, 1 more man"—and above them the voice of the crowd rolling like waves in an ocean. It would rise until I thought it could rise no more, and then it would rise even higher, and then as I pumped and pitched it died, and it was like every man and woman in the park was holding their breath, and then after the pitch there was the noise of all hell broke loose, beating against me like it was a solid thing, like waves in a genuine ocean, and when it hit I felt it in my back from knob to knob, from the back of my neck to the base of my spine.

I pitched 1 pitch to Black. I do not know if I could of throwed another. I pitched it in noise and pain that I will never forget, letter-high and hard, the full wind and the full pump and the full motion, and he swang, and the wood on the ball made a thin slim sound like a twig you might break across your knee, and the ball went upwards and upwards, almost straight up, halfway down the line between home and third, and Red called, not that you heard him but that you seen his mouth move, and the ball hung in the air and then fell, down through the lights, Red weaving, dancing first 1 way and then the next, his big mitt waiting, and then it hit, soundless, and he clapped his meat hand over the ball and turned and raced for his mask and picked it up and headed for the club-house, and I followed, and a dozen hands held me—George and Coker and Perry and Canada and Sid and I do not know who all—thumping me and lifting me clear of the ground, and then they set me down quick because the crowd busted loose from the stands and come swarming down on the field until in 5 seconds or less the green field was covered with people, and the boys turned me loose and we raced for the dugout and forced our way down and through the door to the clubhouse. Somebody amongst the crowd stole my hat for a souvenir.

I feel that that was the greatest game of my life. I had it all the way, the little old pill doing what I wanted it to from first to last. It was greater then the 1-hitter against Brooklyn, greater then the 16-inning duel with Rob McKenna, the tops. Above everything else it was the 1 that had to be won no matter what, and no 2 ways about it, and the cushion was 2 with 2 to go.

Ugly was lost. That was for sure. Doc Loftus was back from the hospital and said there was no question that Ugly was lost, his jaw hanging loose on his face, broke as neat and as clean as the best of your big-time doctors could of did, and I was glad for Ugly in a way I can not explain, envying him that the pressure was off, like maybe you would envy some poor soldier that in the midst of a fierce battle got a little nick and was carried back by the ambulance out of action. I figured that as far as Ugly went he already done what he could do. Win or lose the blame was off his shoulder now, and there was nothing left for him any more but lay there in the clean white bed and follow the papers.

"They will re-set it, and in the spring he will be handsome," said Doc, and the boys all laughed.

Gene said, "If there is 1 thing that eats on Ugly it is the fact of being ugly. I cannot imagine him different."

"We will change his name from Ugly to something more fitting next year," said Hams.

Then the whole thing begun to eat on Gene. Gene was Ugly's roomie for many a year, and probably in the excitement of winning the ball game he forgot, but now he said he was about to pay a visit to a fellow name of Chickering, and he started out the door and down the alleyway that leads under the stands to the visiting clubhouse. Many a fight has took place in that alley in years gone by. Dutch and a Pittsburgh catcher name of Roy Pink many years ago had 1 of the bloodiest fights on record down there. In August of last summer Coker and Canada had a date to meet there and battle out a personal argument that to this day I do not know the reason for. But I got there first and busted it up. I think they was both just as pleased. I did not want Gene getting involved neither, and me and some of the boys blocked his way and closed the door and told him forget it and keep his mind on the business at hand, and right about then Clint and Egg come in by the alley and told us that Chickering was fined 500 and suspended by the Commissioner. That squared things a little as far as the boys was concerned, though Gene swore he would murder Chickering when next he seen him, and the boys all swore the same.

Yours truly swore right along with the rest, and this hands me a laugh because of the following:

I left the park alone after the crowds cleared off some, and on the way I stopped to pick up some cleaning at Gordon's Quick-Way Cleaners, located down the block from the hotel. It is owned and run by a fellow name of Gordon that the boys all call "Flash" after Flash Gordon. I walked up to the counter and slid him my ticket, and about 1 second later in walked Chickering himself.

"You son of a bitch," I said.

"Flash?" said he. "Did you hear what the boy just called you?" He slid his ticket across the counter after mine.

"No fighting, boys. No fighting," said Flash.

"Who is fighting?" said Chickering. "We ain't fighting."

"You son of a bitch," I said. I was really at a loss for words and couldn't think of a damn thing else.

"I have just been fined 500 dollars and suspended by the Commissioner," said Chickering, "so do not call me another name, for my nerves are on edge."

"You son of a bitch," I said.

"You must have a fairly small vocabulary," said Chickering.

"No fighting in here boys, please," said Flash. "Mr. Chickering, have you not done enough fighting for 1 day?"

"Yes," said Chickering, "I have done enough fighting for 1 day. It is all over for me for the present time. The Commissioner says I must not even be at the park tomorrow. But I will buy my way in with dark glasses and sit like a gentleman. The Commissioner says my action is detrimental to the best interests of baseball."

"You son of a bitch," I said. That was the fourth time. But this time there was no sting to it, and Flash laughed, relieved, and Chickering stuck out his hand, and before I could even think what I was doing I stuck out my hand and was shaking the hand that busted the jaw of Ugly Jones.

"Easy, Wiggen," he said, "for I believe I sprained a knuckle," and I stood there shaking hands in a tailor shop with the fellow that an hour before I swore I would kill him if ever I seen him.

But it dawned on me that me and him was more or less in the same happy boat, and all of a sudden I was feeling good and would of shook hands with anybody. I would be sitting it out, like him, because it was all over for me, like it was for him, like it was for Ugly, and besides all that it never cost me nothing, neither a busted jaw nor 500 cash, and I felt good, and I stood there pumping his hand like he was an old friend that I had not saw in 8 years. He give me a queer look. "They tell me you are an odd sort of a kid," he said. "I believe them."

Then I took the pants that Flash give me, and I went out the door and up the street towards the hotel, whistling like a madman.

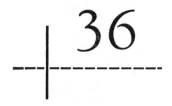

WELL, if I had knowed what was still in the cards for me I wouldn't of been whistling so damn hard, for I no sooner hit the hotel then I seen in an evening paper where the guess was that if we lost tomorrow I was slated to work Sunday. I read the same thing in 2 more papers, and then I heard it on the radio twice, and every time I seen it or heard it it was like somebody stuck a knife in my back. My back hurt worse that night then any night before or since and I hardly slept a wink except maybe a few hours towards daylight.

Saturday I did not drill. First off I took about an hour getting dressed, and then when I got dressed I had no hat, for some fan swiped it the day before. Mick went rummaging on a shelf and come down with a stinking old hat that was too tight to begin with, and then finally I told Mick forget it and give me a rub instead, and I stripped halfway down again and stretched out on Mick's table on my stomach. "Actually," he said, "it is no use. Do you know what I think you are? I think you are 1 of them people that thinks they are sick but never is."

"You are paid to rub," I said.

"I have saw many like you in my time," said Mick. "It is all in your head."

"Then rub my head," I said.

The boys floated in and out, Mick stopping now and then to do whatever somebody asked, saying there was boys with *real* aches and *real* pains and *real* complaints that a man could put his *hands* on and massage them out.

Dutch's lecture was not so much yesterday's mistakes and today's strategy as it was a plain old-fashion pep talk, sweetness all the way, not spreading it on too thick and yet at the same time leaving no doubt in your mind that this was Christmas and he was jolly old St. Nick. He said if ever a club was ready to step out and cop a flag this was it. He said that even with Ugly and Lucky both out of action there was no doubt in his mind and had never been no doubt that man for man we stood head and shoulders over Boston. He said that this particular moment would live in his memory in the years to come, for it was now, this moment, that he felt that he was addressing the finest collection of ballplayers ever brung together under a single roof.

"I rate this club with the Mammoths of 35," he said. That was high praise, coming from Dutch. He said many a time, in and out of the newspapers, that he considered the Mammoths of 35 the best club ever put together. "I told you in Aqua Clara in the spring that I expected to win the flag this year. I have expected it every minute since, and I expect it this moment. I swear to God and call upon him to strike me dead on this spot if in the deepest corner of my heart I speak anything else but the truth.

"We have had bad breaks. We hit a slump. We lost Judkins. We lost Jones. We have had rotten weather and doubleheaders. But have there been good breaks to match the bad? Have we had 1 *good* break all summer? Name me 1! No, I guess not. Even so, we are *still* at the top of the heap, and there will be a flag tucked in our pocket a couple hours from now."

Sam and Red come in from warming. Dutch asked was there any questions, like he always does. There was none. There hardly ever is, and then, after a long time of waiting, I spoke up. "Dutch," said I, "I might as well say it. Naturally I doubt that we could possibly lose today. But if by some miracle we do I doubt that I could pitch tomorrow if my life depended on it."

He looked down at me a long time from where he was standing. He was throwed off his guard a bit, I guess, for that was the first time anybody ever brung up such a question. I could see his wheels turning. I do not know what they was hammering out, but they was turning awful fast, and he started to say 1 thing and then he said another. "Who says you are going to pitch?" he said.

"The papers and the radio," said I.

"The papers and the radio are not managing this ball club," said he.

"Well, I am glad to hear it ain't true," said I. "It would be the wrong move."

"Who said it ain't true?" said he.

"I doubt if it could possibly be true," said I. "It would be the wrong move."

It was really terrible how quiet it was. I did not know what he would say next, but I was sure it would be something for the memory book. I was ready to settle for a fine and a suspension or get traded to Chicago or anything. He got red, and then he got white, and you could hear the boys breathing. I thought maybe somebody would say something. Yet nobody did. Whenever the boys got anything on their mind they say it amongst themselves, never to Dutch. All you could hear was a drop of water from a leaky shower in the shower room, "Ga-lup, ga-lup, ga-lup."

But when he spoke he spoke very quietly. "I do not make wrong moves," said he. "I make a couple hundred moves a day of 1 sort and another, and most of them is right ones. This club has been missing fire since the middle of July. It has proved too old in places and too young in others. It has got gaps a mile wide wherever you look. But I been making right moves."

"You just said we was the best since 35," said I.

"I said nothing of the sort. What I said was I said we would pull it out so long as we had no quitters and nobody dragging their feet amongst us." He was speaking louder now.

"You said we was the best since 35," I said again.

"Do not tell me what I said," said he, and he turned red again and wheeled around and folded his arms like an umpire and clattered off in the other direction, his spikes rattling on the cement. That was the only sound. I seen Red, and he was fumbling with his guards, and his jawbone was working but no sound come forth. I seen Perry, and he was looking down at his shoes. I seen Sad Sam, and he was standing by his locker wiping his face with a towel. Except for Dutch he was the only 1 standing, and he looked at me like he was saying, "Remember, Henry, what I told you on the train. *Nobody really gives a f--- what happens to anybody else,"* and he lit a cigarette and sat down and waited to see what would happen next.

"Okay," I said. "Okay. I am glad to know the score. Sam told me it would take me 15 years to find it out, but I have found it out in 1. I am 15 times as smart as Sam. Piss on you, Sam," said I to Sam. "Piss on the whole lot of you. Pitch me tomorrow. Pitch me *today* for all of that."

Something snapped in my back. I did not give it a thought at the time, but I remembered it afterwards.

"Pitch me any old time," I said, "but do not call me a quitter or tell me I am dragging my feet. We won 96 ball games through yesterday and 26 of them was mine. On a staff of 9 pitchers plus Crane tell me who dragged their feet and who did not. There may of been right decisions, Dutch, but there was also some boners, and any of the boys will tell you the same."

Dutch looked up and down the line at the boys, and they all become suddenly extremely interested in their shoelaces. "Time is running short," said he, looking up at the clock, "and I do not plan to turn this clubhouse into a debating society for Henry Wiggen. I have heard about clubs which was run like debating societies. But I cannot say that I remember seeing any of them win a flag. Has anybody got anything to say in the 2 minutes left?"

Gene Park cleared his throat. "Roguski," said he to Coker, "you laid a little too deep yesterday. If I was you I would position myself and then move up 2 steps. You have not got the arm of Ugly Jones."

"I will remember," said Coker.

Then they filed out, and finally I hoisted myself off the bench and followed, meeting Red in the alleyway where he was waiting until the anthem was done. My back felt much better. "Thank you, Red," said I, "for backing me up like you done."

"It did not seem like a good time for a clubhouse fight," he said. "Somebody always comes out with his neck dangling loose. It would never be Dutch's, so why should it be mine?"

"But why mine?" said I.

"You are young and single," he said, "and there is 15 other clubs that would jump at the chance to grab your contract. It ain't true of many of the rest of us."

"Red," said I, now noticing for the first time that the pain was pretty much gone, "I will appreciate you hitting about 4 home runs today."

"I will try," he said. "We must win it. I do not think that if we lose today we will have the strength to win tomorrow, and I know for sure that we cannot last through a playoff," and then the cheer went up and the anthem was done, and Red strolled out, and I slumped in a seat flush in the corner of the dugout with my back braced against the walls where they come together with this stinking old hat about 15 sizes too small sitting on top of my head.

It was less of a crowd then on Friday. The weather was warm and clear but there was football games here and there that drained it off, and the Friday record stood, the Saturday figures just barely hitting 75,000, Tawney on the hill for Boston, the best they could do, their staff shot, Sam Yale working for the Mammoths and looking good—at least at the start.

But he was wobbly from time to time, and Dutch lifted him in the last of the fifth for a hitter. The score was 3-3 then. Red, with 1 out, just singled a minute before, and now Swanee pinch-hit for Sam and also singled, and Perry pinch-run for Swanee and stole second, a bit of legwork that worried Tawney no little. George singled, scoring both Red and Perry.

Horse Byrd was in and out of trouble for 2 innings and finally was lifted for a hitter in the last of the seventh—Sunny Jim it was—Gene Park on second and 1 down. Sunny Jim batted left-handed against the righthanded Tawney and sent a screaming line drive into the bullpen in right. Knuckles and Piss and Keith Crane was all warming there with Bruce and Goose, and when Casey Sharpe come charging in after the ball you can imagine that these boys was hardly a model of co-operation in helping him get it. They stood their ground while Casey went scrambling around between their legs. Alf Keeler claimed interference and demanded that Gene Park be sent back to third, but nothing come of it.

So it was 6-3 when Keith Crane come on to relieve in the eighth,

Dutch forced to the gamble with Keith, Keith being the only left-hander left to throw. Boston rode him hard, calling him all kinds of a n----r. But he stood up under it fairly well, having been coached in the matter by Perry, and he blanked them in the eighth. Dutch moved Canada in to first base and sent Scotty Burns in center. We now had no reserve outfielders on the bench, and no reserve infielders neither, the barrel scraped clean, the long trip almost done but the tank just about dry.

That Boston ninth was murder. With every pitch I whispered to Keith Crane, and I prayed for him, and I twisted and turned on the bench, helping each pitch along, working at least as hard as him, until after what seemed like 25 minutes at least he had 2 down, but 2 on, and Granby the hitter. We all remembered when Granby clubbed a home run off Keith at a crucial time a few weeks before, and Dutch and Keith and Red and the whole of the infield had a long conference. A home run now would knot the score.

Then Dutch come back to the bench, and then Keith pitched—a ball, wide—and Dutch was flying out on the field again and arguing with Toft, and then when that was over with he come back, swearing and fuming and claiming he would see Toft put on the retired list in the winter if he had to murder the Commissioner.

Everybody always asks me, "What kind of a man is Dutch Schnell?" I never know exactly what to say. I think he is a great manager, and the statistics back me up in this. His first and only aim in life is winning ball games, and more often he wins them then not, sometimes doing it with worse material then the next club has got. He brings out the best in a fellow if the fellow is his type of a ballplayer. He is always in a fight, right or wrong standing by his guns. Red says if Dutch was Noah in the Bible he would not of took to the ark but would of stood arguing with the goddam flood. There is nothing Dutch will not do for the sake of the ball game. If he thinks it will help win a ball game by eating you out he will eat you out. If sugar and honey will do the trick out comes the sugar and honey bottle. If it is money you need he will give you money. And if he has no further need for you he will sell you or trade you or simply cut you loose and forget you.

And then it was over—the ball game, the race, the long long haul from Aqua Clara to the flag. Most of all what was over was the backache.

For Granby lifted a shoulder-high curve to dead center field, and Scotty Burns turned and run back 10 or 15 feet and then turned again and camped and waited, and as the ball come down so did the pain in my back, starting from the knob at the back of my neck, down,
      down,
         crunch,
            FLASH!
              Crunch
                FLASH!!
                  CRUNCH
                    FLASH!!!
                      knob by
knob, hitting the lowest knob at the moment the ball snuggled in Scotty Burnses glove, and out through my spine—gone I do not know where and do not care. But gone, and for good and ever.

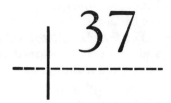

37

NO NEED to describe the clubhouse afterwards. Such a noise I never heard before nor since, nor such a crush of writers, nor such a flashing of bulbs, nor such a flood of beer, and in the midst of it all Alf Keeler come in from the Boston side, tears running down his cheeks while he pushed through the crowd and reached for Dutch's hand and shook it. "Congratulations, Dutch," said he, and then he turned quick and started out, and Dutch called after him, "Good try, Alf," and this made me laugh a little because I wondered what Dutch would of said if the table been turned, would he of been satisfied with a "good try," and Krazy Kress come along and slapped me on the back, all 350 of his stupid pounds behind it, and he asked me why so quiet, and then he pushed on.

After about a half an hour things calmed down a little and Dutch stood on a bench and asked would the writers and all others kindly withdraw while the boys transacted some business, and they done so, and we all sat pulling at beers and Cokes and franks, listening to the sweetest lecture ever heard.

"Boys," said Dutch, "I will be quick. I will say only God bless you 1 and all, for this is the happiest moment of my life. God bless Keith Crane for some cool work in relief and God bless Swanee Wilks for a hit at a time when the cash was on the barrel and God bless Sunny Jim Trotter for the same. God bless you all for being the right man in the right spot at the right time.

"I do not wish to be a gymnasium teacher, but there will be a slight celebration in the Moorses sweet this evening and I would like to request that at least 9 men stay sober more or less, for according to the rules of the Commission we must play tomorrow's ball game. Soberest man pitches."

This brung a terrific laugh. Then Dutch hauled out this towel with the 150 cash inside, and he reached in the glass and drawed forth several slips of paper and found the 1 he wanted. "September 27," he said. "Jones. Who will take this 150 to Ugly Jones at the hospital?" Nobody said nothing. Gene said he would take it but he doubted that he would have the time until after the World Series. I thought about taking it myself, for Ugly was always good to me and helped me out of tight spots whenever he could. It was always a good sight to see Ugly coming in towards the mound from short with a word or 2 of advice. If Ugly had of been in the clubhouse before game time he might of spoke up for me, too, and I said I would take Ugly the money and best wishes from all his friends that was too busy to go down and see him theirself.

The boys laughed, and Dutch give me the money and told me go straight to the hospital and not get tangled up with any young ladies along the way. This brung another terrific laugh. "Okay boys," said he, "now on to your business," and he went back in his office and Red took over, Red acting captain in place of Ugly, and we voted shares, 29 full shares for 25 ballplayers plus Dutch and 3 coaches, 1,000 each for Squarehead Flynn and Bub Castetter and Keith Crane. Practically every name that anybody could think of we voted them a small slice of the melon—batboys and clubhouse watchmen and specials that guarded the doors. After the Series when the books was balanced my full share come in the mail—5,876 and some change.

But on the way to the hospital I knowed that Ugly wouldn't of spoke up for me in the afternoon against Dutch, not in 1,000,000 years. The more I thought about Ugly the more I realized that he would be the *last* man on the club to help a fellow out. Ugly Jones and Ugly Jones and Ugly Jones are the first 3 things on Ugly Joneses mind and always was, and finally what I done I shoved the money at this nun at the desk on Ugly's floor and told her it was from the boys.

"I will give it to Mr. Jones," said she. "And who shall I say brung it?"

"Thank you, Sister," said I to her. "Wiggen."

"How is your back?" said she.

"100 per cent better," said I. "In fact, it has disappeared altogether."

"It was all in your mind," she said.

I ate a bite of supper downstairs in the coffee shop near 2 doctors telling 2 nurses about the ball game today and such things as what it meant when the flag was clinched. Then this 1 doctor explained how Henry Wiggen pitched and what he throwed and the various reasons for his success. I hope he knows more about his own line of work then he does about mine.

Between thinking about Ugly all alone up there in the hospital and hearing all that jabber from that cockeyed doctor I begun to sink in the foulest of moods. By the time I hit the Moorses sweet I was so blue, and so down in the mouth, and so disgusted I could hardly see. By all the rules I should of been riding high, yet I was not, and a whole raft of things was threshing around in my mind, and I tried to look them over as they swum past in a jumble and pick out the single thing that was causing the trouble.

But I could not, and the Moorses and their fancy celebration only made it worse, old Lester T. Moors, Jr., showing me off to his society friends and telling them I was practically his personal discovery, and then probably telling them later how he got me so cheap at contract time in Aqua Clara in the spring of 50, and Patricia wandering around like she was everybody's mother loaded with jewels to the armpits, and the writers flocking around Dutch that back in August they was yowling for his blood, and Dutch with 1 arm around Lindon crying "God bless Lindon Burke" when a few weeks before what he could of did for Lindon was show a little faith in the boy.

And Perry Simpson and Swanee Wilks clinking glasses together though from beginning to end Swanee hated and detested Perry and hated and detested me even worse for rooming with Perry, saying how could I do it and still hold my head up in public, and all this Perry knowed, for Swanee even told him 1 time to his face like the straightforward fellow he is. Yet here was Perry buttering up to old Swanee.

And the top of it all was Red and Sam, the 2 of them, their foot up on the bar rail murmuring sweet little things in 1 another's ear like a couple lost brothers that hadn't saw each other in 19 years.

Oh, winning heals many a wound in the flesh! And I could not help thinking, "What if we lost? What if 6 games between April and September had went the other way? What then? Would Perry and Swanee be drinking together? Would Red and Sam Yale? And suppose I only won 13 games instead of 26? Would I then be the little golden apple in the eye of Lester T. Moors, Jr.?"

I turned and left. When I reached the door I heard a most familiar voice back in the distance. "Where is Henry Wiggen?" it said. "God bless Henry Wiggen."

But I kept on going, and out by the elevators who should come out of the shadows but Krazy Kress. "Henry," said he, "could I see you a minute?" and I said he could, and we went down in the Manhattan Drugs. "Now Henry, concerning Korea," said he, "it is more important then ever that you go along. Sam Yale says he might come."

"I would not cross the street to see Sam Yale hung," said I.

"What in the hell is wrong with you?" said he.

"Nothing," said I. "Nothing and everything."

"A little good old Japanese air will set you up in the other alley," said he. "You can relax on the long boat ride."

"I doubt that the Japanese air is any better then America," I said.

"Tell me what is wrong," said he. "I will only find out in my own way if you do not. What was the blowup in the clubhouse this afternoon?"

"No blowup," said I.

"I understand that you had words with Dutch and Sam. A few rolls in the hay with them Japanese girls will clean the poisons out of your system."

"Leave us forget Korea and the girls," said I. "I have got a girl of my own," and I thought about Holly, and then the only place

I wanted to go was Perkinsville, and I remembered Mort Finnegan that got shot to death in Korea for what reason I do not know.

When the waiter brung us our food Krazy wished to pay, but I said no and paid my own, and when I took out my wallet I seen the old picture of Sam that I stuck in there so many years before. "You ever seen this?" I said. "It was in the front of Sam's book that he wrote."

"What book?" said Krazy. "Sam never wrote 6 words in his life," though a second later he remembered what I was referring to—the book "Sam Yale—Mammoth" that he—Krazy—wrote. "Grab a couple books and catch up on your reading on the boat ride over," he said. "These ocean voyages get wearisome."

"That book was a pack of lies," I said.

"I would not say that," said Krazy. "I thought it was a good book and read it several times myself."

"It is horseshit," I said. "Sam says so himself."

"Then why did he sign his name to it?" said Krazy.

"Why, he *wrote* it," I said.

"He did not," said Krazy.

"Well then," said I, "whoever wrote it certainly piled up the horseshit thicker and faster. I could write a better book then that lefthanded. Furthermore, if I ever wrote a book I would write it myself and not hire some lug to do it for me. Why does not somebody write 1 decent book about baseball, Krazy? There never been a good book yet."

"There been dozens of good books," said he.

"There has been only fairy tales," I said.

"It is a fairy tale game," he said. "You are 21 years old, Henry, and you have very few brains in your head except with a baseball cap on. Yet you will draw upwards of 10,000 this year for 40 afternoons of work. Is that not a fairy tale game?"

"40 afternoons," I said. "That is all *you* seen, Krazy. The pain in my back you never seen. I can see the point in a man falling down stairs and coming up with a pain in his back, but I cannot see too much sense in walking around half the summer with a pain from sheer tension. When we sewed up the flag this afternoon the pain melted in a minute. That is too crazy for me, and it made me a little wise to myself. After this I will be Old Take It Easy Wiggen. I bust my ass for no man after this."

"That is not how greatness is made," said Krazy. "That is not how a man gets his name in the Hall of Fame with the immortals. Nor that is not how a man cops the big green."

"Then I will not be great," I said. "Nor rich." He looked at me and laughed. "Laugh, you fat fool," I said.

"Jesus, Henry," he said, "do not shout at me. I done nothing. Furthermore, I can not help it if I am fat. My mother and father was fat before me."

"I apologize for saying you are fat," I said, "though you certainly are. And I guess there is really no sense in blowing off to you. I have really learned a lot this year, and it never really added up until this afternoon. But I will tell you 1 thing, Krazy. You have f---ed up the game of baseball. You have took it out of the day time and put it in the night. You have took it off the playground and put it in the front office."

"It is the same old game," said he. "There has hardly been a rule changed in 25 years."

"You have mixed it all up," I said. "I do not know how. I know only 1 thing. I know only that from here on in I play baseball for the kicks and the cash only, for I got to eat like you do, but as for the rest—Japan and Korea and society bastards like the Moorses, writers and fans and spontaneous demonstrations cooked up by drunks like Bill Duffy, fancy celebrations and the wars and the politics of it—all this I leave to them that glories in it. I bust my ass for no man. I get my head shot off for no man like this Mort Finnegan I was telling you about. And I will never wind up forgotten in a stinking hospital like Ugly Jones."

"What?" said he. "What about Ugly? What is all this you are saying in connection with Ugly?"

But by then I was off my chair and halfway out the door, and it takes Krazy Kress so long to get rolling that the elevator was closing by the time he hit the lobby.

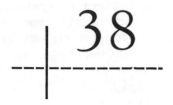

38

THAT night I slept like I probably didn't sleep in 2 months, feeling pretty good about everything, my back in particular, and never giving so much as a thought to my chat with Krazy. Sunday afternoon we finished up, just going through the motion, many of the boys drilling hard and sweating out their hangover, Boston with their bags half packed and ready for the long trip home. There couldn't of been more then 4 or 5,000 people in the stands, out for the afternoon sun and a little relaxation. Herb Macy and Gil Willowbrook shared the pitching assignment and we won 7-6. Or 8-7. I don't remember exactly and see no sense in digging through the clips.

I seen neither hide nor hair of Krazy, and that night me and Bruce Pearson went to this baseball movie around the corner from the hotel called "The Puddinhead Albright Story" that even Bruce could see for the usual slop that it was where nobody sweats and nobody swears and every game is crucial and the stands are always packed and the clubhouse always neat as a pin and the women always beautiful and the manager always tough on the outside with a tender heart of gold beneath and everybody either hits the first pitch or fans on 3. Nobody ever hits a foul ball in these movies. I see practically every 1 that comes along and keep watching for that 1 foul ball but have yet to see it.

Monday we sat for our picture, everybody all smiles, the batboy up front on the ground, 1 row sitting and 1 row standing and 1 up high on a bench, everyone there but Ugly. The picture is hung in a frame on the wall. I am looking at it now. Over the picture it is wrote, CHAMPIONS OF THE WORLD. Then we drilled a light drill, and by now the farthest thing in the world from my mind was Krazy Kress until about 9 o'clock Tuesday morning Patricia Moors woke me up rapping on the door, and I said come in and in she come with the paper folded back to Krazy Kresses column. "Have you read Krazy's column?" she said.

"I been sleeping," I said. "I hardly ever get up at the crack of dawn just to read the papers."

"Well, read it," she said, and she give it to me.

First off there was this smart-aleck picture of me that was first took back in September of the year before when I come up to the Mammoths with such a confident attitude about everything, and over the picture it said

"LEAVE US FORGET KOREA"

The column was as follows:

HENRY THE WHINER

We have had just about enough of Henry Wiggen, southpaw extraordinaire whose feats on the ball field have been nothing short of miraculous but whose drawing-room manners leave much to be desired. We are sick and tired of pampering and coddling and finding in our hearts the love that surpasseth understanding for a young man whose impudence and arrogance and downright orneriness deserve not the rich purse which he has just won, but, instead, a powerful kick in the seat of his togs.

We hardly know where to begin this sad history. Shall we begin far back when Henry the Whiner complained to his draft board that due to a constitutional disorder he found it inconvenient to enter military service? No, for such a comment on this ridiculous state of affairs might embarrass the soft-headed physicians who fell hook, line and sinker for such a yarn.

Instead, let us travel together to Perkinsville, N. Y., in which pleasant burg young Henry the Ungrateful first saw the light of day. Let us inquire on the streets and in the shops

the reasons for Henry's latest outburst against reason. I did
so. I went to a man named Borelli, and a man named Levine,
and to a sportswriter named Bill Duffy, as able a scrivener as
ever set pen to paper. "Tell me," I said, "Henry Wiggen
complains that folks up thisaway don't appreciate him. Oh,
you gave him his start in Legion ball and so forth and so
forth, but he says that these things, and the Welcome Home
celebration of a year ago, all had nefarious and mercenary
motives behind them. Can it be that you have not been duly
appreciative of the honor and the glory he has won for Perkinsville?"

They protested, and well they might.

"Thees ees not so," said the genial Borelli, wielding an
angry razor as he shaved a customer in his popular barber-
shop.

"Not true," said Levine, proprietor of the adjoining con-
fectionery emporium.

"Henry sometimes pops off before he thinks," said Duffy
from behind his littered desk in the "Clarion" office.

Too Much Is Too Much

Or let's look at it another way. As constant—bless 'em—
readers of this column are aware, I am opposed to members
of the Fourth Estate intruding upon the privacy of clubhouses.
But there was a blowup in the Mammoth clubhouse shortly
before gametime Saturday, and I felt it my duty to ascertain
its causes and consequences.

Its cause: Henry the Whiner. Reason: he took issue with
that amiable gentleman, Dutch Schnell, on a question of
strategy. (One might note in passing that in 1931, the year
of the birth of Henry Know-It-All, Dutch was a Mammoth
coach and had recently brought to a close a glorious and honorable playing career.)

Its consequences: Henry shunned his teammates that evening at a simple but well-intentioned celebration staged by
the Mammoth management. (Dutch's strategy apparently
succeeded that afternoon, the sage advice of Henry the Hooli-
gan to the contrary notwithstanding.) Not only did Henry
shun the shindig but he took the opportunity to pour into the

startled ears of this long-suffering scrivener a veritable bar-
rage of epithets and profane observations on the probable
ancestry of his teammates. I shall mention no names. I am
sure they know who they are.

It seems that they somehow betrayed him, deserted him. I
should like to ask who betrayed and deserted whom in a mid-
town establishment after Friday's game—or is it possible that
Henry, when he buddy-buddied with Boston second-sacker
Chickering shortly after Chickering broke the jaw of Mammoth captain Ugly Jones, was simply putting into practice
the injunction to love thy enemies as thyself?

But if Henry so loves his fellow man I should then like to
inquire how, earlier this month, in plain view of a packed
Stadium, he found it in his ever-loving heart to hurl that most
treacherous of all weapons—the spitball—at the jolly Tubs
Blodgett of Boston.

The League tolerated this. The evidence, in any case, was
circumstantial rather than concrete, due to quick thinking by
the learned Berwyn Phillips Traphagen.

But how much longer can we go on tolerating? How long,
for example, can the Mammoth front office continue to pay
medical bills for Henry the Whiner's nonexistent backache?
And how often, when Henry is lonesome for his girl, can
the Mammoths bring her to town and house her comfortably
so that Henry, when he needs his hand held, can trip down
three flights of stairs to be at his maiden's side?

The Unkindest Cut of All

However, all this is as nothing in view of his most recent
performance.

It seems that a group of public-spirited citizens have seen
fit to sponsor a post-season exhibition tour of baseball players
to the Orient where, on foreign battlefields, young men who
would much prefer to be home playing ball are fighting to
protect, among other sacred things, America's baseball diamonds.

Henry Wiggen was invited to join this entourage. But the
sacrifice, it seems, is too great. Money? No, his expenses
would be paid. Time? No, he will have little to occupy him
once the World Series is concluded.

"What then?" you ask.

I ask the same. I ask by what right a young man who has been generously pardoned from service can then refuse to participate even to this modest extent. I ask by what scale of simple justice do young Americans die on foreign battlefields while other young Americans are permitted to remain at home tossing a horsehide pellet back and forth on sunny afternoons for a salary far exceeding the wages of the mud-spattered soldier.

I should like to know—now—the whys and wherefores of this unspeakable state of affairs.

It is my sad duty to bring these matters to light at a time when all of us are intent on tomorrow's Series opener. But when Henry Wiggen told me, as he did the other night, "Leave us forget Korea," I felt that it was my duty to make these facts known.

When Henry was critical of his home town I was willing to laugh off the charge. When he berated his teammates I was willing to believe it was a temporary peeve. But when he calls on us to "forget" Korea and the sacrifices being made there, thoughtful people can only conclude that we have, in Henry Wiggen, a young man who is downright obnoxious.

An apology is in order. On behalf of myself and thousands of indignant Americans I demand that Henry Wiggen make such an apology. And he ought, as an earnest of his sincerity, express immediate willingness to correct past errors by fulfilling obligations he has thus far been unwilling to fulfill.

Is this too much to expect? Is it too much to demand that Henry Wiggen, whom a generous nation has showered with riches and fame, reward that nation with a token of esteem? I think not.

Disa and Data. I-Love-Me-I-Think-I'm-Grand Dept: in this space, last April 15, I predicted the following finish— New York, Boston, Brooklyn, Cleveland, St. Louis, Pittsburgh, Washington, Chicago. That's how they finished, too. . . . Plenty Friday and week-end tickets still available at the Stadium. Scalpers need not apply: two pasteboards to a customer only, and congrats to the Moors folks for this. . . .

Dutch Schnell will work on a book this winter. Look for it in April. Title: "Dutch Schnell—Mammoth."

Play Ball!

"Is it true?" she said.

"Part is and part is not," said I.

"I have wrote out an apology," she said, and she give me a paper with a big long apology typewrote out on it. Half of it said that everything Krazy said was true, and the other half was practically an invitation for a squad of marines to drag me off by dawn and shoot me.

"I will not apologize," said I.

"Then perhaps you will deny it," she said, and she hauled out another paper typewrote like the first, saying that everything Krazy said was lies from beginning to end. "This is the kind of a rhubarb that brings on a crisis for the organization," she said.

"I am not worried about crisises," I said. "I am through with them. I been through 1,000 crisises since I was a kid—high-school ball, Legion ball, semi-pro tryout, my first semi-pro game, camp games at Aqua Clara, my first games at Q. C., my first relief job with the Mammoths, Opening Day. How many crisises is a man supposed to go through? Does there not come a time when a man must simply say that nothing is so important that he must forever fight against crisises? No, I will not sign them, neither of them, neither apologizing nor denying."

"Yet could you not at least keep these thoughts to yourself?" she said. She sat down on the bed and stared out the window, very thoughtful. "It is the organization that must be kept pure and free from scandal. You are a part of the organization."

"I am a part of nothing," I said.

"You owe something to the organization," she said.

"And does it not owe something to the other fellow?" I said. "What does it owe to Bub Castetter that give it 10 years and then was cut adrift? What does it owe to Ugly Jones? Does it not owe Ugly at least a visit to the hospital?"

"Ugly is being took care of," she said.

"Have you paid a visit to Ugly Jones that you screwed out of 2,000 dollars 1 fine night in Aqua Clara?"

"Who has made such a statement?" said she.

"It is common knowledge," I said.

"It ain't true," she said.

"And you would behave towards me in the same way if you thought it would keep me in line," I said. "But I have learned a lot this year. I remember what you said of Ugly 1 night in Aqua Clara. You said his brain was down below his belt. But mine ain't."

I believe I hit home with that, for I know very well that there was nothing, neither money nor her own self, that Patricia would not part with to smooth the path of the organization. It was her club that her father give her, her baby, her precious thing, and she would keep it rolling at any cost. I admired her for that, and I said so to her face, saying also that there was a time when for the touch of her flesh I would of done anything, said anything, apologized 300,000 times to the newspapers for what I said to Krazy. But living and hearing and seeing learned me that if I was to be a man—a *man* like the kind of a man Holly Webster wished me to be—I was best off at a far distance from Patricia.

And she seen that she could not budge me, and she said that she even admired me for it, though she hoped it would not reflect too bad on the organization, and she tore up the 2 papers and dropped them in the basket on the way out.

At 11 we pushed off for Philly, drilling a long drill that afternoon and freshening up our memory on some of the special features of the Philly park, and afterwards we sat around in the clubhouse where way back in April we pulled that crazy raping-tool business on Squarehead Flynn. I said it seemed like 1,000,000 years ago, and the boys all said the same.

Not 1 man on the club ever mentioned Krazy's article. I guess they knowed Krazy too well, and *me* too well. What do the boys care for your view on politics and such? The boys care only for what will bring them base hits and tight twirling and the melon in the end. You could be down with leppersy for all of them.

The rest is history. The Series opened on Wednesday with all the usual hoopdehoo, yours truly on the mound for New York, Coker Roguski at shortstop so nervous he could barely breathe at the start, Canada Smith in center field and hardly much better off, the Mammoths heavy favorites in despite of the fact that both Ugly and Lucky would never see action, the crowd set at capacity about 35,000 though that mark was later topped by far when we moved back to the Stadium for the third, fourth and fifth game.

Philly tried 2 corny stunts, both flops. First off they tried to rattle me by carping and harping on that old business of rooming with Perry which was tried in our own league until after once around the circuit when they seen it rolled off my back like a duck out of water, and then the other thing they tried was crowding the plate, knowing I had this fear of beaning anybody. This was also tried in our own league and come to nothing, much thanks to good handling by Red. Meanwhile the scoreboard looked like the number 2 switch went haywire, for we scored 2 in the third, 2 in the fourth, 2 in the sixth and 2 in the seventh.

The fans took up the cry, "Leave us forget it, Henry. Leave us forget it, Henry," clapping and stomping and having a gay old time, and between innings once somebody heaved down a whole armful of these little blue forget-me-nots. They did not like my views on Korea, believing them out of place, though I noticed 1 section behind first base with the seats tore out to make room for about 8 rows of soldiers in wheel chairs with blankets around them, and I heard no sound from there. We led 8-1 after the top of the seventh.

In the last half of that inning Philly loaded the bases with 1 down, and the clapping and the hollering and the stomping interfered a good deal with my concentration. So for a long time I stood on the hill with the ball in my hand, waiting for it to quieten, and when it did not I simply stepped off the rubber and kept warm by throwing down to George at third a couple minutes until the rumpus simmered down.

Then I throwed 1 pitch to Ralphie Carucci (Vincent and Pasquale's kid brother, a righthanded hitting shortstop) and he slashed it down towards second. Gene took it on 1 hop and flipped to Coker for the force, and Coker fired to Sid for the double, and I turned to the crowd, first to the first base side and then to the third base side, and I give them the old sign—1 finger up.

I probably caught more customers with that vulgar gesture then anyone ever done before or since, not only 35,000 in the park in Philly but millions more on TV because I understand it took the camera crews off balance.

It really wasn't supposed to be vulgar, though. I don't know what it *was* supposed to be. I guess all I was saying was they could go their way and I would go mine, and some folks is born to play ball and the rest is born to watch, some folks born to clap and shriek and holler and some folks born to do the doing. I was born to do the doing and know nothing of wars and politics. All I know is what I like and what I do not like. But I did not know how to say all this. So I said it the best way I could.

I guess the truth is it was probably 1 of the dullest Serieses on record. The only really good ball game was Thursday, which Sam lost 4-3, Knuckles winning 7-1 when we opened in New York on Friday, and Hams on Saturday by 6-0, the best pitched game of all.

I worked and won on Sunday, the whole thing wrapped up in the bottom of the first when we batted around. Canada and Vincent and Sid all hit, and then, after 2 was out, Gene and Coker connected and Red mopped up with a home run in the upper stands in left just before I come to the plate in time to fan for the third out. I fanned 4 times that day.

It was 10-2 when the curtain come down. Most of the afternoon the crowd took what pleasure it could from riding me about 1 thing and another, thinking they could needle me into a vulgar gesture or 2. But I give them no such bonus for their money.

And when it was all over with we sat till after dark in the clubhouse promising to write each other a letter over the winter and then never doing it though more then once I sat down with the best of intentions. Now there seems no use, it being February again and just about time to shove off south. This year the contract calls for 12,250 on the head.

I phoned home and told them wait up, for I was about to catch the 11 o'clock Albany train out of Grand Central, and I done so.

It was raining when the train slowed for Perkinsville. I jumped clear, throwing my bags out ahead, and the platform was slick and I almost fell. But I did not fall, and I went back for my bags and then down behind the depot to the parking lot where my Moors had sat since February. I opened her up and slid in behind the wheel and started her. But she would not start, for she would not turn over. That goddam Evva-life battery hands me a laugh.

I left her there, bags and all, and started on foot across the square. There was not a soul in sight. It must of been 2 or maybe after, and I walked rather brisk, down past the Embassy Theater, past Borelli's where my picture was hung before they took it down, past Fred Levine's Cigar Store, past Mugs O'Brien's gymnasium just across from the statue of Mr. Cleves, turning north at the pharmacy corner and heading up Lincoln and out of town.

It drizzled all the way. About 1 mile later I seen up ahead 2 lights coming towards me on the opposite side of the highway, and they drawed up beside me, and a voice called out, saying, "What is the matter, Henry, did Dutch make you walk home for striking out 4 times?" and the voice was the voice of Aaron, and I crossed the road and climbed in, and Pop and Holly was there, Pop driving. "We got worried," said Pop. "We heard the train go through."

"My battery is dead," I said, and we drove down to Perkinsville, and me and Holly got in the 50 Moors and Pop goosed her a few times from behind until we straightened her out and headed her downhill, and then he kept pushing until she turned over, and finally she started up with a roar.

"Henry the Navigator has come home at last," she said, "and I for 1 am glad to see him."

"He is glad to be home, too," said I. "He sure got put through the ringer these last couple months."

"He went many places and seen many things," she said.

"He done all the things he ever wished to do in life," said I, "up to and including pitching in the World Series. But if he ever had a friend in the world he has lost them."

"Oh no," she said. "I doubt that."

"Then after he done everything there was to do," said I, "all the kick was gone. You dream and you dream and you dream, and then when the dream comes true it falls flat on its face."

"Not *my* dream," said she. "According to my dream this was to be a year of great victory for you, and I believe it was."

"The statistics back you up in that," said I.

"Oh no," said she, "they show nothing of the sort. They show only games won and games lost and your E. R. A. and such as that. What they do not show is that you growed to manhood over the summer. You will throw no more spitballs for the sake of something so stupid as a ball game. You will worship the feet of no more gods name of Sad Sam Yale nor ever be a true follower of Dutch Schnell. And you will know the Krazy Kresses of this world for the liars they are. You will never be an island in the empire of Moors, Henry, and that is the great victory that hardly anybody wins any more."

"I believe it is at that," said I. "I never thought about it much. Yet I thought about it a little bit at that, noticing how even the boys theirselves buckled and lost their courage when the heat was on."

"The boys are no different then anybody else," she said. "The boys are the world, and they are ruled by their belly and their fear. You have learned to do different, and I hope you will always go on following your head and your heart and the things that they tell you about men and money and what happens to courage when the heat is on."

"I will try," said I.

Yet we was hardly 100 feet up the Observatory road when my *belly* begun to need attention. "Any chance of anybody whipping up a batch of hot chocolate?" I said.

"Maybe so," she said. "Is there anything else you wish to ask me?"

"No," said I, "for I asked you in February, and I asked you in April, and I asked you in September. After a man has struck out 3 times he begins to think maybe he just ain't much of a hitter. I struck out 4 times this afternoon and consider it an evil hex."

"Perhaps you will have better luck this time," she said. "You have sharpened your eye since February and April and September."

So I asked her then, for the fourth time, though it wasn't like I planned it a-tall. I was tired from the ball game and sweaty from the trip and the rain was half raining and half not raining, 1 of them dreariest nights in the world, and then I never even kissed her, or at least not the way I planned it, for we hardly got in the house when Pop and Aaron come chugging in in the 32 and klumping up the steps like a couple oxes.

This reminds me to say a "Thank You" to the many fans that sent cards and such both when we was married and through the winter. In the beginning the mail was enough to make a fellow sick, about 5,000 letters by actual count between the day of Krazy Kresses column and the middle of October, air mail and special delivery on a number of occasions, 19 out of 20 of the nasty sort, after which it slacked off pretty sudden, though even now a letter still comes from a chap first getting up his nerve.

It picked up again in the middle of November (we was married on the 10th by Judge Real, the Mayor of Perkinsville's brother) and carried over past Christmas and the first of the year, but this time all of them pleasant and cheerful from people that said what I said was right, and actually I begun to feel like a human being again. There was a time when I doubted that I had 5 friends in the world, when many people in Perkinsville would hardly speak to me, when the mail brought nothing but hate and the papers wrote nothing but insults. But then the drift of the mail changed, and then, as you know, the writers themselves voted me both Most Valuable Player and Player Of The Year which I believe I mentioned before in this book but see no harm in mentioning it again for the sake of those folks that might of missed it.

I could also use this space to answer the 1 thing most people most usually ask, "How do things look for this coming year?"

I do not know. I think New York will be the team to beat. Boston is cleaning house from top to bottom, as you know, and it will be a few years yet before they are back in it. I can't see Brooklyn a-tall. The youngsters at Cleveland are now 1 year smarter, so I expect it will be Cleveland give us the most trouble. 1 year can make a great difference.

But I do wish the Mammoths could come up with 1 more left-hander, for Sam Yale is on the long road down and I do not think Keith Crane can fill his shoes. It is the whole history of the Mammoths that they are short dependable southpaws.

Otherwise the book is done. There is probably a lot that ought to went in but got lost in the scuffle and probably lots more already in that needs to be scratched out. Take it or leave it. Believe it or not. I do not care too much what you believe. Holly says tell folks the truth and they will sooner or later come to believe it, and Aaron says the same. Anyhow, this is it. It sure run long.

THE END